WHAT
MIGHT HAVE
BEEN

OTHER BOOKS BY MATT DUNN

WHAT
MIGHT HAVE
BEEN

Matt Dunn

LAKE UNION
PUBLISHING

Published by Lake Union Publishing

www.apub.com

Amazon, the Amazon logo, and Lake Union Publishing are trademarks of Amazon.com, Inc., or its affiliates.

ISBN-13: 9781477825020
ISBN-10: 1477825029

Cover design by bürosüd⁰ Munich, www.buerosued.de

Library of Congress Control Number: 2014937701

Printed in the United States of America

For Tina. Forever.

PART ONE

THEN...

PART ONE

THEN...

1

I bet you'd look super wet, too.'

The man sounded a little drunk, and as he continued to stare at her chest, Sarah Bishop's first thought was to slap him, until she realised his pathetic chat-up attempt was a reference to the 'Superdry' T-shirt she was wearing. She sighed to herself and tried her best to conjure up a smile that suggested polite disinterest.

'Well, that's something you're never going to find out,' she said, raising her voice to make herself heard above the noise of the busy club.

The man elevated both eyebrows, reminding Sarah of a ventriloquist's dummy. 'You're an American!'

'Yes,' she said patiently. 'I know.'

She peered towards the stage, hoping the band were about to come on and save her from what was the fifth chat-up attempt in as many minutes, though it was impossible to tell, seeing as the man was blocking her view. He wasn't bad looking, she had to concede, but given the bright-red braces she could see peeking out from underneath his pin-striped suit jacket, he was probably a banker, and the last thing Sarah wanted was to spend what was left of the evening hearing him boast about how much money he earned. She got enough of that in the office every day.

'Where from?' asked the man, and Sarah was tempted to reply 'America,' but a response like that might have been construed as flirting, and that was the last thing she wanted.

'New York.'

'Aha!' He clicked his fingers to summon the barman, and Sarah frowned.

'What are you doing?'

'Ordering you a Manhattan. Should make you feel right at home.'

The man grinned down at her, obviously pleased with himself, so Sarah swivelled round on her stool and indicated the untouched glass of wine on the bar next to her.

'I've got a drink, thank you.'

'Well, I'm getting you a Manhattan,' he insisted. 'Unless you want something else?'

The bouncer was Sarah's first thought, glancing towards the club's entrance, where a man as wide as he was tall was guarding – or rather, blocking – the door.

'Well?' said the man, and Sarah took a deep breath.

'Listen, I just came here to listen to some jazz,' she said, and as she met his gaze defiantly, he rolled his eyes.

'Suit yourself,' he said, adding 'Bloody Yanks!' under his breath before disappearing into the crowd, and Sarah had to resist the temptation to follow him and throw her drink over his expensively tailored suit, but that wouldn't have been a good idea – not in the least because it would have left her without one. She'd been in enough clubs like this to know a single woman was seen as fair game – or on the game – and since she wanted to be able to enjoy the music, a full glass of wine was a useful prop if guys came up and offered to buy her one. Not that it seemed to be working this evening, but perhaps this part of London was simply too close to the City. The guys who worked there were different. Weren't used to being told to take a hike. And often even struggled to take a hint.

She gazed around the faded interior of the club, eyeing the peeling paint, grateful she wasn't sitting underneath what appeared to be a very precariously secured mirror-ball hanging from the ceiling. Even in the more run-down parts of Harlem, a building like this would probably be condemned, and Sarah couldn't help but wonder whether it was typical of the London jazz scene. She was used to the traditional, smoke-filled New York clubs, having spent many an evening watching her father play sax in venues with names that formed parts of album titles, and they – well, they'd been a world away from this place.

Worried she might suddenly burst into tears, Sarah reminded herself why she'd come here this evening. Her first six weeks away from New York had been pretty tough, but places like this had the potential to make things a little more bearable, so when she'd spotted the flickering neon sign alternately proclaiming 'The G-Spot' and 'Jazz Club' from her cab on the way home from a night out with a few of the women from the office, and a sudden desperate feeling of homesickness had overwhelmed her, she'd seen it as a chance to feel like a New Yorker again, at least for one evening. So she'd told the driver to pull over in front of the entrance, handed her share of the fare to Sally, the woman she'd been sharing the cab home with, and had all but run inside.

Her Blackberry buzzed, and as Sarah fumbled for it in her jeans pocket, she noticed another man trying to make eye contact from the other side of the room and hurriedly looked away. She'd become good at declining the many male advances that came her way – as a woman working in the City, you had to be – although recently, she'd run out of excuses where David, her boss at the bank, was concerned. She glanced down at her phone to see his number flashing on the screen, and quickly answered the call.

'David? Hi.'

'Just calling on the off-chance you're still awake?'

She glanced at her watch, saw it was only eleven o'clock, and smiled. 'Well, if I wasn't, I am now.'

'Are you having a good time with the girls?'

Sarah almost laughed. 'Girls' was pushing it – Sally had been the next youngest, and she was probably nudging fifty. Old enough to be her mother, she realised with a start. And while she hadn't wanted to go out with them this evening, David had suggested it might be good for her. Would even help her integrate. And she'd been too uncertain of her position – either at work, or relationship-wise with David – to refuse.

'It's been a blast,' she said, flatly.

'Pleased to hear it,' he said, failing to pick up on her tone. 'Listen, I can hardly hear you. So, you know, have fun, and I'll see you at the office tomorrow.'

'Sure. See you tomorrow,' she said, then slipped her phone back into her pocket. In truth, she was a little irked that David had called, and wondered whether it was more to check she'd actually taken his advice and not cried off. He'd been the one who'd engineered her move from the U.S. – although not strictly for professional reasons, she suspected. From almost the moment she arrived he'd begun asking her out, and she'd been flattered by his refusal to take 'no' for an answer, so eventually she'd stopped giving it. And while their first date – dinner the previous weekend at Nobu, a breathtakingly expensive sushi restaurant on Park Lane, where David had completely failed to get her 'this place is called *knob you?*' joke and instead had given her a lecture on Japanese pronunciation – hadn't quite been the beginning of the fireworks-going-off-overhead romance she'd been hoping for, Sarah had begun to suspect that the only fireworks she'd ever experience would be every Fourth of July. Assuming she ever made it back to the States, that was.

She looked up to see the man still watching her and considered just drinking her wine and leaving, but like she'd told Mr. Manhattan, she was here to hear some jazz, and Sarah was blowed if she was going to let anything – or anyone – spoil her plans. Besides, and to her relief, the lights were finally dimming, so she relaxed and focused on the stage, grateful that at least now she could enjoy the music.

The band appeared through the curtain at the back, the traditional line-up of a drummer, double bass, and – she saw the familiar golden glint – a sax player, and as he stepped into the spotlight, Sarah caught her breath. He was tall, the mid-length, dark brown hair that framed his regular features unstyled enough to be stylish, and slim – not quite athletic, but not skinny either – remarkably healthy for a Brit, she thought. While the bright stage lights perhaps emphasised his lack of a tan, Sarah didn't worry about that. She knew jazz musicians didn't get to see a lot of daylight; plus, this was England, a country not exactly known for its summers. And while she always paid special attention to sax players, given her father's influence, they rarely looked this good – or had a smile that was capable of melting her inside like the one he'd given as he'd appeared onstage.

The band launched into *I Just Want To Make Love To You* – one of her father's signature numbers. They were good, too: a little out of sync, possibly because they hadn't performed together that much, but more than competent, and Sarah enjoyed the familiar tune. Then the sax player began his solo, and she found herself suddenly transported back to Harlem, back to the club on 112th Street where her father would take her to see him play. The club she'd take him to when he'd eventually become too frail to even pick up his instrument. The club where they'd held the tribute concert the night of his funeral . . .

She reached for her glass and gulped down a mouthful of wine as she fought back the tears, willing herself to concentrate on the music, and for the minute or so the sax player held centre stage, Sarah was mesmerised. He was good, better than her father, even, and there was something magnetic about the confidence he exuded when he played – a confidence he hadn't shown until he'd put the instrument to his lips. She watched his fingers dancing over the keys and shivered with anticipation at the prospect of them dancing over her body like that, wanting the solo to never end, though once it did, Sarah had to stop herself from clapping louder than anyone else in the room. Then he smiled awkwardly at the audience – perhaps a little overwhelmed by their reaction – leaned into his microphone, and said something she couldn't quite catch, and at the rich, sexy sound of his voice, Sarah couldn't tell whether the thumping sound she could hear was her own heartbeat, or the drummer beating a steady rhythm on the stage next to him.

The sax player seemed to be searching for someone in the crowd, and – surprised to feel a flash of jealousy – Sarah looked for them herself, then felt a little foolish when she realised the woman she presumed it must be was in fact an older, bald man leaning against the other side of the bar. His manager, maybe, or more likely, the club's owner – she recognised the type. Whichever, Sarah knew he was lucky to have someone as talented as that playing here. They didn't come along that often in life.

The man caught her eye, and she smiled shyly, suddenly embarrassed. 'He's good,' she mouthed, jabbing a thumb towards the stage, and the man nodded, then picked his glass up and came over.

'I know,' he said. 'Though I'm not sure he does.'

'Really?'

'Do you think he'd be playing a dump like this if he did?'

'It's not so bad . . .'

The man broke into a grin. 'It's okay. I own it.' He held out his hand, and Sarah shook it. 'Melvin. Mel, to my friends.'

'I'm Sarah. Nice to meet you, Melvin.'

'*Mel*, please.'

She pointed to the sign behind the bar. 'I have to ask. The *G-Spot*?'

Mel shrugged. 'It should say 'J-Spot.''

'As in "J" for 'jazz'?'

'Exactly. But the guy who made it had this strong Brummie accent, and things kind of got lost in translation. Anyhow, it's a talking point, isn't it?'

'I suppose.' She glanced back at the stage. 'So what's his story?'

'Evan?' Mel puffed air out of his cheeks. 'He used to be famous. And then gave it all up.'

'Why?'

'You'd have to ask him that. But nowadays, he just . . . plays.'

'Where?'

'With a talent like that, wherever he wants. Though that does seem to be here, fortunately for me. Bums on seats, and all that.' Mel grinned again. 'And I don't mean "bums" like you Americans might.'

'You mean "arses", right?' Sarah said, in her best Dick-Van-Dyke-in-Mary-Poppins British accent, and Mel laughed.

'Yup.' He nodded. 'Arses.'

Sarah spotted the man who'd tried to chat her up earlier sizing up his next target over in the corner. 'Well, the place is certainly full of them,' she said.

She wanted to ask more, but Mel had moved to serve someone at the far end of the bar, and besides, the sax player – *Evan*, she reminded herself – had resumed playing, and as Sarah turned her attention back to the stage, her eyes met his.

And while she wasn't naïve enough to believe in thunderbolts – except for the ones the British weather kept throwing at her – at that exact moment, though it lasted almost no time at all, Sarah knew they'd sleep together.

2

Evan McCarthy finished his solo, then looked up from his saxophone and nodded to the crowd, modestly acknowledging their applause. Muddy Waters' *I Just Want To Make Love To You* was always guaranteed a warm reception, especially when you played it as well as Evan did, though in reality he had Etta James to thank, seeing as the non-jazz aficionados in the audience would probably recognise it from her version in that Diet Coke ad.

But however they knew it, as long as they knew it, Evan was happy – music was all about connecting with people, and aside from playing the themes from either *The Pink Panther* or *The Benny Hill Show*, there was no surer way for a sax player to do that than by playing a crowd-pleaser. Which, Evan realised sheepishly, given the unnecessary flourish he'd added at the end, was a description that also applied to him.

Not that it was completely one-way traffic: He loved playing here at Mel's – as the G-Spot was more affectionately known. There was just something about performing at a small, intimate venue that was hard to beat, especially one that was usually packed to the rafters, a thing Evan always found strange, particularly given the club's name and the fact that it wasn't the easiest place to find, hidden down a side road in Borough. After all, who in their right mind would stop some stranger on a dark South London street and ask, 'Excuse me, but do you know where The G-Spot is?'

Empty, the club looked exactly like what it was – a walled-in arch under the railway viaduct which served London Bridge station. The vaulted brick ceiling – in the middle of which Mel had hung an 'ironic' mirror-ball that looked like it might fall down at any moment – needed a new coat of paint. The bar that ran down one side of the room had been salvaged from the much smaller pub that had once stood across the road and therefore stopped abruptly some way short of the far wall, causing more than one drunk punter to perform the classic 'Del Boy' fall where they'd assumed it had continued. The stage Evan and the band occupied was little more than a scuffed, hastily assembled chipboard-and-wooden-pallet platform that had lasted some five years now, and probably fell foul of most health and safety laws. If you chanced upon the place in the daytime, you probably wouldn't want to come back. But call in at night, mix with the eclectic crowd that some of the best jazz in London drew, and you wouldn't leave until Mel threw you out. Which was only – but not always – when you'd run out of money for drinks.

He grinned across at Pete, the drummer, who'd just begun his own solo. It was currently being ignored by the still-applauding audience, so Evan readied his best 'jazz' voice – really just an impersonation of Mel's gravelly chain-smoker's tones – and leaned down towards the sax-level microphone in front of him.

'Thank you,' he growled, followed by, 'Pete Watson on drums,' and as the crowd obediently switched focus, Evan stepped backwards out of the spotlight and peered into the darkness. He caught Mel's eye, and the club's owner – nursing his ever-present glass of Scotch – smiled up at him from his usual spot at the end of the bar and gave him the thumbs-up, and Evan shrugged, happy not to be the centre of attention. After all, he suspected he'd already been granted more than his fair share.

He flexed his fingers as he checked his mouthpiece, the anticipation of playing the next riff bubbling up inside him. *This* was music – not the lightweight pop song that he'd once feared would be the only tune he'd ever play again, and to hordes of teenage girls screaming so loudly they couldn't even hear it. Here at Mel's, the only screaming you'd ever get was when a drunk City boy barged into the ladies' toilets and wondered aloud whether one of them might like to 'blow his bonus'.

Putting his sax to his lips, he stepped back in to the spotlight, drinking in the expectation of the audience as they moved their attention back onto him from the now-sweaty drummer. Then he began to play the familiar refrain once more; it was a simple tune, but to make it sound as smooth as Evan did was hard. Took hours of practice. Years, in fact. Not that he'd ever minded putting the time in. Especially when a reaction like *this* was the result.

He scanned the crowd again as he played, enjoying the almost hypnotic way the music could turn a room full of individuals into one cohesive group, then almost stopped mid-blow. Sitting at the bar, not far from where Mel was leaning, was a woman who took his breath away. Her long, dark hair cascaded down around a face that simply had everything in proportion, including the cutest upturned nose that was surely something any woman might tell her plastic surgeon she wanted, and perhaps it was the way she was twirling a strand of that hair distractedly between the fingers of one hand, or the way her full lips were ever-so-slightly parted, or even the rather tight 'Superdry' T-shirt she was wearing, but one thing was certain – she was the sexiest woman Evan had ever seen.

His heart began to race. She seemed to be looking at *him* – though of course, he realised almost instantly, feeling a little stupid as he did so – so was everyone else in the club. He tried not to stare back, mainly because the dazzling arc-lights were making him squint unattractively, but the way she was swaying gently to the rhythm – her movement fluidly sensuous, one of the audience yet somehow apart from the crowd – meant he couldn't take his eyes off her. And while he didn't think love at first sight existed – though possibly only because he'd never been lucky enough to experience it – his lust at first sight felt real enough.

In truth, Evan was finding her distracting, and a couple of times he had to think hard to remember what order the notes came in – not a problem with improv jazz, but tonight's audience were here to hear something traditional, tunes they could recognise. He considered closing his eyes, but though he could play most of the songs with them shut, he worried that musicians who did that were a bit pretentious, and he didn't want to look like an idiot, particularly *now*. Instead, reluctantly, and with the greatest of effort, he averted his gaze and played on, knowing he had to perform for the room, and not just one person in it.

He rushed through the rest of the set, almost turning *Summertime* into a dance tune, and by the time he got to his last number, all Evan could think about was how on earth he was going to get hers. But when he took his final bow, then stood up and looked for her in the crowd, he noticed only one thing. The woman had gone.

As the applause died down, a loud throat-clearing – more like the sound of someone trying to cough up a lung – caught his attention from the side of the stage, and he looked down to see Mel grinning up at him.

'Very nice!'

'My thoughts exactly.'

'Huh?'

'Nothing.' Evan forced a smile. 'Thanks. Assuming you were referring to our set?'

'What else?' said Mel quizzically. He clapped Pete on the shoulder, stood back as Dave, the double-bassist, hauled his instrument off the stage, and then, once they'd disappeared behind the curtain, handed Evan a piece of paper. 'Here.'

'What's this?'

'Your audition tomorrow morning, remember?'

'Oh yeah. Thanks.'

'Don't be late, now.'

'Yes sir!' Evan peered at the note. 'It's in a hotel room?'

'That's what the man said.'

Evan frowned. The last job that had come via one of Mel's contacts had turned out to be playing an 'amusing' refrain to soundtrack a film of a Labrador puppy running amok in a bathroom, and while he had to eat, he also had standards. 'I don't know, Mel. I . . .'

'Relax. It's not another toilet roll ad.'

'You're sure?'

'No shit.' Mel grinned. 'You staying for a quick one?'

Evan glanced around the club, trying to locate the woman he'd seen earlier, but there was still no sign of her. 'I suppose,' he said, unclipping his sax from the cord around his neck. 'With you in a minute.'

'You OK?'

Evan nodded. 'Yeah. Just thinking about missed chances.'

'Well, don't let that be the case tomorrow.' Mel gave him a look, then turned on his heel. 'I'll be at the bar.'

Evan smiled wryly as he retrieved his saxophone case from the back of the stage and began to put the instrument carefully away, trying to stop himself wondering what might have been, though he knew he was fighting a losing battle. Like most musicians, he was a romantic – after all, how could you play anything with feeling if you weren't capable *of* feeling?

Though while he'd always believed that love, like drunkenness and old age, was something that slowly crept up on you, this evening was about to prove him wrong.

3

Sarah had waited until the applause started, then she'd downed the remainder of her now-warm glass of Chardonnay and rushed to the ladies' to fix her make-up, a task made difficult by the fact that – to her surprise – her hands seemed to be shaking.

She exited the toilets, squeezed past the queue of cross-legged women that had quickly formed outside, then made her way towards the stage, watching silently while Evan pulled the mouthpiece from the end of his sax, examined it carefully, then dried it thoroughly with the cloth he kept in its case. As he gently slotted the instrument into the velvet-lined recess and softly clicked the lock shut, almost as if he were putting a newborn to bed, Sarah felt something catch in her chest – her father had treated his sax with the same care, and she loved the routine, the attention these musicians lavished on the tools of their trade. When, finally, he was done, she took a few breaths to calm herself, sidled up behind him, and tapped him on the shoulder.

'Hi.'

She smiled as he nearly dropped his sax in shock. Close up, a little sweaty from his on-stage efforts, he seemed even sexier. A bit dishevelled, maybe, but that only added to his allure.

'Hello,' he said, placing the case carefully on the edge of the stage. 'I'm . . .'

'Evan McCarthy?' she said, then wondered why his face had fallen.

He regarded her suspiciously. 'And you know who I am because . . . ?'

'Lucky guess,' she said, then she pointed at the poster on the wall behind him advertising tonight's gig. 'Well, that and the fact that I can read.'

'Ah. Right. Of course. Sorry.'

'I'm Sarah,' she said, pleased his expression seemed to have brightened.

'Sarah,' he repeated, and at once she loved the way his accent softened the vowels.

'You play well.'

'Thank you.'

'For a Brit,' she added. 'Your solo gave me goose bumps.'

'Are you sure that wasn't the air conditioning? Sometimes it's on a bit high . . .'

'Hey, don't put yourself down. You're good. And I loved that first song.'

'I Just Want To Make Love To You?'

She reached across and poked him in the ribs. 'At least offer to buy me a drink first!'

'That's not what . . .'

'Are you always this easy?'

Evan smiled back at her. 'Buy *me* a drink and you might find out.'

'Touché.' Sarah laughed. 'Seriously, though, Muddy Waters is one of my favourite musicians.'

Evan's eyes widened. 'You know your stuff.'

'I'm a New Yorker – jazz is virtually on the school curriculum. Plus my father played sax.'

'Played?'

'He died. Last year.'

'I'm sorry.'

'Don't apologise. You weren't the one who gave him cancer,' Sarah said. All of a sudden, she couldn't meet his eyes, and even though she knew it was an automatic defence mechanism, the harshness of her own response had surprised her.

Evan hesitated for a second, then rested a hand gently on her shoulder. 'Are you okay?'

'Yeah. Sorry. It's just that hearing you play tonight kind of reminded me of . . .'

'Your dad?'

She swallowed hard, then nodded. 'So,' she said, after a moment, struggling to think of anything apart from the warmth of his touch. 'I met Melvin.'

'Melvin? Oh, you mean . . .' Evan removed his hand, and Sarah glanced over towards the bar, where an amused-looking Mel was watching them. 'I'm sorry,' he continued. 'The only people I ever hear call him Melvin are people he owes money to. Which, come to think of it, includes me.'

'He told me you used to be famous.'

'What?' spluttered Evan. 'Hardly.'

'Come on.' She nudged him in the ribs again. 'Spill.'

'There's not much to tell.'

'Yeah, right.'

'And it was a long time ago.'

'And don't tell me – you needed the money?'

Sarah had folded her arms, so Evan sighed. 'Does the word "Jazzed" mean anything to you?'

'"Jazzed" as in "being high"?'

'No, as in the band.'

'Sorry. Never heard of them.'

Evan made a face. 'You and most people. What about a television programme called "Rising Falls"?'

Sarah's eyes widened. 'You were in that?' She softly sang the first few bars from the theme tune and hoped Evan was wincing at the song, rather than her voice. 'I *loved* that show.'

'Well, the music? That was us. *Jazzed.*'

'Wow!' She thought for a moment, then frowned. 'Wait. I remember seeing the video on MTV. There were two of you, right?'

'Yup. Me, and a guy called Finn.'

Sarah nodded towards the stage. 'Was he one of those two?'

'No. We don't play with each other anymore.' Evan reddened as he realised what he'd just said. 'As Jazzed, I mean.'

'So why'd you give it up? Tired of being chased down the street by screaming girls?'

'Actually, no. Tired of that *not* happening.'

'I find that hard to believe,' said Sarah, and as Evan blushed awkwardly, she smiled. 'Still, you had your fifteen minutes. That's pretty impressive.'

'Actually, it was more like seven and a half minutes each.'

'Even so.'

'We were just lucky.'

'How come?'

'It's a long story.'

'I've got all night,' she said, surprising herself with her forwardness.

For a moment, Evan seemed lost for words, then he leaned against the side of the stage. 'Okay, condensed version coming up: Finn was seeing this girl who worked for Sony, and managed to convince her to play our demo tape to her boss. One thing led to another, then Rising Falls came calling, and we got a number three hit on both sides of the Atlantic on the back of it.'

Sarah whistled appreciatively. 'Do you still hang out?'

He smiled at the Americanism. 'Yeah. Finn owns a café on Borough High Street. Best coffee in town. I go there quite a bit.'

'And get all wistful about the old days over a cappuccino or two?'

Evan shook his head. 'Not really. Though mainly because I only drink espresso. Besides, they were only a matter of days.'

'Hey – at least you still have a musical career.'

Evan laughed. 'If you can call playing here every Tuesday, Thursday, and Friday a musical career, then yes, you're right.'

'So what was the problem?' Sarah made the quotation-marks sign in the air. '*Musical differences?*'

'No, we just . . .'

Evan's voice had tailed off, and Sarah couldn't work out the look on his face. 'You just what?'

'Stopped playing.'

'Shame.'

'Sometimes people just do. Circumstances . . .'

'Tell me about it,' said Sarah, sadly.

In the silence that followed, Evan appeared to be resisting the impulse to take her in his arms and comfort her, and Sarah found herself wishing he would. 'Listen,' he said, eventually. 'That drink you mentioned earlier? Can I buy you it? Not, you know, because of what you said about the song . . .'

Sarah thought for a moment. Right now, a drink was the last thing she needed, otherwise she'd probably burst into tears. 'Do you have a car?' she asked, suddenly desperate to be anywhere but somewhere that brought back so many memories.

Evan looked at her blankly. 'A car?'

'You know – four wheels, an engine, that sort of thing?'

'I know what a . . . Yes. It's parked out the back.'

'Can you give me a ride?'

'You mean a lift?'

'Yes, sorry, a *lift*,' Sarah said, enunciating the word in her best English accent.

'Where?'

Sarah shrugged. 'Anywhere.'

Evan looked like he didn't need to be asked twice. 'Sure,' he said picking up his sax and then leading her past the bar.

Sarah glanced self-consciously at an open-mouthed Mel as she followed Evan out through the fire exit and towards an old white Mercedes convertible parked just across from the club's entrance. 'Is this yours?' she asked, running her hand seductively along the bodywork, then surreptitiously re-attaching the piece of chrome trim she'd accidentally dislodged in the process.

'Yeah,' he said, proudly, as he locked his sax in the boot. 'It's new. Well, not *new*, of course. But new to me, if you see what I mean?'

He coughed lightly at his own tongue-tiedness, then walked round to open the passenger door for her, and as he politely stood back to let her get in, Sarah felt something somersault inside her.

'Can I drive?'

'I don't know. Can you?'

'One way to find out,' she said, clambering across to the driver's side.

Evan regarded her for a moment, then he grinned. 'Here,' he said, tossing her the keys and then hurriedly jumping into the seat she'd just vacated.

Sarah turned the key in the ignition, and after the briefest of refusals, the engine roared into life. 'Now, what is it you Brits say instead of "buckle up"?'

'Fasten your seat belt,' said Evan.

'Well in that case . . .' She revved the engine a few times for effect, adjusted the rear-view mirror, then flashed him a mischievous smile. 'Fasten your seat belt.'

4

Sarah peered through the windscreen, biting her lower lip in concentration as she piloted the big car through the dimly lit backstreets, and Evan couldn't take his eyes off her. She glanced to her left and caught him staring, and he looked away, embarrassed.

'What?'

'Nothing.' He cleared his throat loudly. 'Keep your eyes facing in the direction of travel, please.'

'What is this? Driver's ed?'

'Driver's ed?' Evan frowned. 'Oh, you mean like a driving instructor?'

'Yeah.' She flashed him a smile and turned her attention back to the road ahead. 'Just like a driving instructor. Where are we going, anyway?'

'You're the one driving.'

'And if this was NYC, I'd be taking you to all my favourite spots. But it's not. So why aren't you?'

'Point taken. What do you fancy doing?'

Sarah had to stop herself from replying *You*. 'I'm in your hands,' she said, suggestively.

'Okay.' Evan cleared his throat again and thought for a moment. 'Well, would you like to go and hear some more music? Or we could get something to drink? Or to eat? Or matching tattoos?'

'All of those things sound good.' Sarah frowned suddenly. 'Though where would we get the tattoos?'

'Sorry, I didn't realise I'd said that last thing out loud. But there is this twenty-four-hour place near Waterloo station . . .'

'No, where on our bodies?'

Evan's mouth suddenly went dry. 'Perhaps we should get a drink before we make that kind of decision,' he said pointing at an upcoming junction. 'Take a left here.'

'Left. That's your side, yeah?'

'Right. If you see what I mean?'

'I do.' Sarah gave the rear-view mirror a cursory glance before throwing the Merc round the corner. 'It drives well,' she said, and Evan tried to ignore the screeching from the tyres.

'I wish I could say the same about you.'

'Hey – no fair! I'm not used to driving on the wrong side of the road.'

'Is that why we're in the middle of it?'

'. . . or handling, you know . . .' She tapped the top of the gear lever. 'A stick.'

'It's called a . . .' Evan stopped talking.

'What?'

'Well, a "knob", actually. And besides, this car's an automatic. Don't tell me you hadn't noticed?'

'So *that's* why it's making that noise whenever I try to change gears.'

'Very funny.'

Sarah laughed. 'I'll have you know I'm driving very carefully. You have to, when you've had as much to drink as I have this evening.'

Evan looked across sharply, then saw she was joking – or at least, he hoped she was. 'Pull in here,' he said, indicating a space on the left.

'Yes, sir,' she said, bringing the Mercedes to a halt in front of a large brick wall, where the car's headlights illuminated a sturdy-looking metal door. 'What is this place?'

'Secret,' said Evan, climbing out of the car.

'I only asked!'

'No, it's called "Secret". Come on.'

Intrigued, Sarah switched off the ignition and followed him out of the Mercedes, hanging back a little as he walked up to the door and pressed the buzzer. Almost immediately, a metal spy flap slid open with a loud clang that made her jump, though not as much as the sight of the bald man with tattoos covering most of his head suddenly appearing through the gap did.

'Evan,' the man said gruffly. He slammed the flap shut, then after a rough sliding of bolts, the door was flung wide open. As the two men exchanged a complicated handshake that she was sure she'd never be able to copy, Sarah saw that the tattoos extended down his arms, and even to the backs of his hands.

Evan ushered her inside and, as the doorman secured the bolts behind them, led her down some stairs into a dimly lit cellar, its minimalist styling and smart clientele belying the understated entrance. On a small stage at the far end, just past the whitest bar she'd ever seen, a familiar-looking woman was singing a breathy jazz vocal, accompanied by a guitarist who looked suspiciously like . . .

'Is that . . . *Elvis Costello?*' whispered Sarah.

Evan glanced casually towards the stage, then nodded. 'With his missus.'

'What are they doing here?'

'Well, I'm no expert, but it looks like she's singing while he plays the . . .'

'No I meant . . . what is this place?'

'Just a bar.'

'It's hardly just a bar. And is that . . .' Sarah was staring at a booth in the corner, where someone she was sure was a famous Hollywood actor was sitting, surrounded by a gaggle of blondes dressed more for a day on Miami Beach than the chilly London night.

'Yeah,' said Evan. 'Want me to introduce you?'

'You know him?'

Evan shrugged. 'Only because he's a regular here. As are most people. It's members only. People come to Secret for a bit of privacy.'

'And how do you get to be a member?'

Evan tapped a finger on the side of his nose. 'That's the secret.'

The music finished, and as the crowd applauded politely, Evan nodded hello to the performers, who waved him up onto the stage. As he shook his head and indicated Sarah by his side, she turned to him, a look of wonderment on her face.

'You're quite the celeb.'

Evan laughed. 'That's the point of this place. No-one's a celeb.'

'Well, I'm impressed.' She gazed around the room. 'Do you play here too?'

'Sometimes. It's open mike.' He nudged her. 'You can get up and sing if you like.'

'Me?' Sarah looked at him, aghast. 'I couldn't.'

'Why not?'

She nodded towards the woman stepping down from the stage. 'Her voice is an instrument. Mine's more an instrument of torture. Fine for karaoke, maybe. But bad karaoke.'

Evan smiled encouragingly. 'There's no such thing as bad karaoke, just an unappreciative audience. And by the looks of this lot, they're drunk enough to appreciate anything.'

'Evan, I haven't sung a note since . . .' Sarah stopped talking. Saying 'since my dad died' would have brought the evening right down, almost before it had got going.

'You sang earlier. In the G-Spot.'

'A few bars of the theme tune to Rising Falls hardly counts as . . .'

'Come on. It'll be fun!'

'No, I . . .' Sarah started to protest, but Evan was already dragging her gently up onto the stage. He handed her the microphone, then picked up the acoustic guitar.

'What's it to be?'

Sarah gazed out at the expectant audience, her heart pounding as she recognised another couple of chart-topping musicians in the crowd. This was seeming a worse idea by the second, but she couldn't see a way out, and as Evan sat with his fingers poised over the strings, she had an idea.

'I only know the one song.'

'Which is?' asked Evan, innocently.

Sarah looked at him mischievously, then took a deep breath and raised the microphone hesitantly to her lips. *'Why do I know you'll hurt me?'* she breathed, and Evan blanched, then reluctantly began strumming the familiar chords to Jazzed's one and only hit.

He played on as Sarah found her voice, impressed by how she'd risen to the challenge, and also by the power and clarity of her voice – as the audience seemed to be, too, judging by the way they'd all stopped their conversations to listen – and for the first time in he couldn't remember how long, Evan found himself happy to be playing 'his' song. It was strange, too, to hear a woman sing the lyrics – *Finn's* lyrics – that Evan knew weren't simply about affairs of the heart.

'I thought we'd be forever. But forever didn't last. And now I see that you and me, we never stood a chance.'

Sarah made a face at Evan as he strummed the final few bars, then she replaced the microphone in its stand, embarrassed by the applause rippling round the room, and they stepped down from the stage.

'That was amazing,' he said, beaming proudly as they squeezed into a booth in the corner. 'Although your choice of song was a little mean.'

'And forcing me up on stage to sing wasn't?'

'You enjoyed yourself, didn't you?'

She shrugged, still a little flushed from the experience. 'I'm not sure "enjoyed" was the right word.'

'You were great.'

'Again, I'm not sure "great" really nails it.'

'Rubbish.'

'Now *that* might be a more appropriate description.'

Evan rolled his eyes, then frowned as the barman deposited two Martinis on their table. 'But I didn't . . .'

'From that table over there,' said the barman, indicating the Hollywood star and his entourage, and Evan waved his thanks.

'Here you go,' he said, sliding one across the table to Sarah. 'Whatever else happens this evening, you'll at least be able to say that a famous Hollywood actor bought you a drink.'

She smiled, and raised her glass in the direction of the star's table. 'As opposed to a famous British pop star?'

Evan made a face. 'Not any more, thank goodness,' he said, clinking his glass against hers.

'You didn't really say what happened.'

'When?'

'Earlier. When I asked you what the deal was with Jazzed.'

'Ah.' Evan wondered how best to explain it. The official reason that Jazzed had split up – the one he'd usually tell people, at least – was because they'd reached their peak, and had nowhere else to go. Their hit single had been down to luck more than anything else – record companies hadn't wanted to know them until the song had been picked up by the TV show – and so the chances of them ever doing anything better had been pretty unlikely. And while that was the party line, he found himself reluctant to admit that to someone he'd just met, and especially someone he found himself wanting to impress. But as for the real reason . . . well, that was even more of a secret than the club they were sitting in.

'So?'

'We just thought we'd retire at the top. You know the old show-biz maxim – *always leave them wanting more . . .*'

'And is that your philosophy towards everything in life?' said Sarah, retrieving the cocktail stick from her drink, then, with her eyes fixed on his, she pulled the olive delicately off it with her teeth in a way that made Evan's head spin. 'What?' she said, noticing his expression.

'Nothing.' He gulped down a mouthful of his cocktail, desperate to change the subject. 'So you're from New York?'

She nodded wistfully. 'Yeah. You been?'

'A couple of times. Always wanted to spend longer. Some people think New Orleans is the place to be where jazz is concerned, but for me, Harlem has the best . . .' He stopped talking, worried he was being insensitive, as Sarah's expression had hardened a little. 'So what are you doing here in England?'

'I got transferred.'

'Like a footballer?'

'Huh?' She frowned as she took a sip of her drink. 'Oh, you mean a *soccer player.*'

'Yup.' Evan nodded. 'Soccer,' he said, putting on a bad American accent, and Sarah kicked him lightly under the table.

'No, it was just . . . After my dad died, I just felt I needed a, you know . . .' Her voice trailed off.

'Change of scene?'

'Yeah.' She smiled again, to Evan's relief. 'A change of scene. And this opportunity came up, and so six weeks ago . . . What is it you Brits say? "Bingo!"'

'No other family? No one to keep you in America?'

Sarah's smile faded, and immediately, Evan regretted asking. He'd only meant it as a subtle enquiry to ascertain whether Sarah had someone special back in New York, but this current line of questioning didn't seem to be doing him any favours.

'Nope.' Sarah shook her head. 'Dad you already know about,' she said, counting off on her fingers, 'no brothers or sisters, and my Mom left when I was four, which kind of did it for her as far as I was concerned.' She smiled flatly. 'So no, no family to speak of. Just little old me.'

'Your mum left you?' Evan didn't quite know how to react, mainly because the matter-of-fact way that Sarah was talking didn't seem to invite any sympathy.

'People leave. What can you do?'

'Right. Nothing, I suppose.' Evan stared into his glass for a second or two. 'And have you never tried to track her down?'

'What would be the point?' said Sarah, brusquely.

'Well, to . . .' Evan wanted to kick himself at his insensitivity. 'No, I suppose there wouldn't be any.'

'Quite.' She picked up her drink and drained the rest of it, and Evan was grateful for a chance to change the subject.

'Another one?'

'I don't have to sing for it, do I?'

Evan laughed. 'Not unless you want to.'

'I think you know the answer to that,' Sarah said, then she stood up. 'And I'll get these. What would you like?'

Evan smiled up at her. 'Surprise me.'

She regarded him for the briefest of moments, then walked round to his side of the table, sat down on his lap, and kissed him full on the lips.

And Evan found himself thinking it was the best surprise he'd ever had.

5

Evan lay in the semi-darkness and watched Sarah sleeping, the duvet clutched protectively to her chest, remembering a quote he'd read in an Oscar Wilde anthology about all American women behaving as if they were beautiful and that being the secret of their charm. From what he'd seen so far, Sarah behaved as if everyone else was. He'd already decided it was one of the things he liked best about her.

Miles Davis's *Kind Of Blue* was playing softly in the background – she'd set it on 'repeat' when they'd gone to bed – and he contemplated getting up to switch it off, but she was looking so peaceful next to him that he didn't want to do anything to disturb her.

He gazed around the unfamiliar bedroom. Apart from their clothes, which were strewn across the floor (and in the case of his boxer shorts, he was embarrassed to note, hanging from one of the light fittings), it was pretty tidy – tidier than his, at least – but without the usual personal touches and adornments he'd come to expect whenever he'd spent the night at a girlfriend's house. If anything, it looked almost temporary, like some hotel room, and as if the occupant was just passing through, and Evan found himself hoping that wasn't the case.

The glow from the clock on the bedside table caught his eye – four a.m., he noted disappointedly. Not that he had anywhere to be – at least, not until his audition – Evan just didn't want what had already been the best night of his life to end. They'd left Secret straight after they'd kissed – to a round of applause, which had embarrassed Sarah a second time until he'd reminded her it was probably for her singing and not the kiss – and driven back through the still-teeming streets, Sarah wide-eyed at the late-night life in this part of London, stopping only to pick up Turkish food from a stall behind Borough Market, which they'd taken back to her flat to eat. Though it was still sitting in its container on the hallway table – the only hunger they'd felt when they'd got home had been for each other.

He was a little surprised to find that sleep wouldn't come, especially given the intensity with which they'd leapt on each other once they'd shut the front door, and Evan smiled at the memory. He'd somehow known sex with Sarah was going to be good, but couldn't have imagined it'd be *that* good, and – unless Sarah was as talented an actress as she'd turned out to be a singer – pretty incredible for her, too.

Suddenly thirsty, he reached for what had been a half-full bottle of Moët that Sarah had retrieved from the fridge on their way to the bedroom. Finding it empty, he slipped out of bed and – careful not to wake her – made his way out of the bedroom. He padded along the hallway until he located the kitchen, feeling slightly self-conscious as he walked naked through someone else's flat, and fumbled for the light switch.

'Don't mind me!'

Evan wheeled around in shock. Leaning against the worktop, eating ice-cream straight from the tub, was a blonde girl about his age, dressed – barely – in a vest-top and pyjama bottoms, and strikingly pretty which, for some reason he couldn't fathom, seemed to make his predicament worse. He quickly flicked the kitchen light off, and grabbed the tea towel from where he'd spotted it hanging on the front of the oven.

'Sorry,' he said, covering himself with it as best he could, before cautiously switching the light back on with his elbow.

'No need to apologise,' said the girl. 'Unless you're here to burgle the place?'

'Naked?'

'You never know. I've watched *C.S.I.* You might simply be trying not to leave any fibres. People have been caught and convicted on less.'

'I'm not here to steal anything, honest,' he said, his heartbeat slowly returning to normal. 'After all, where would I put it?'

'Now there's a question.' The girl grinned. 'Sarah didn't tell me she was entertaining this evening.'

'She didn't tell *me* she had a flatmate.'

'Ah. And you're naked in the kitchen because . . .?'

Holding the tea towel like a matador whose cape had shrunk in the wash, Evan indicated the fridge with his elbow. 'I was after something to drink.'

'Well, you've come to the right place.' The girl reached over and retrieved a carton of orange juice from the refrigerator door, then found a glass on the draining board and looked around for something to wipe it with, though when her eyes alighted on Evan's groin area she evidently changed her mind. 'I'm Grace, by the way.'

'You'll excuse me if I don't shake your hand?'

'Of course.' Grace smiled. 'So, you work with Sarah?'

'Me? No. I'm a musician. My name's Evan.'

'Oh. Right. Sorry.' She sounded a little surprised, though Evan realised that could of course simply be a reaction to her seeing him like this. 'Juice do you?'

'Sure.'

Grace filled the glass. 'Please. Sit,' she said, placing it on the table in front of him and nodding towards the nearest chair, but Evan shook his head.

'Better not,' he said. 'The towel doesn't quite go, you know, right round.'

'Suit yourself.'

He stared at the glass, and Grace frowned.

'Bits a problem?'

'Pardon?'

'The orange juice.' She pointed to the wording on the side of the carton. 'It's got "bits" in. And not everyone likes . . .'

'No. That's fine. It's just . . .' Evan glanced down at the tea towel. 'Only one pair of hands.'

'Ah.' Grace snapped the lid back onto her tub of ice cream. 'In that case I'll leave you to it,' she said, slotting it back into the freezer compartment. 'It was nice to meet you, Evan.'

'And you, Grace.'

She made her way out of the kitchen, and Evan stood and listened until he heard what he assumed must be her bedroom door shutting, then downed the glass of juice in one and hurried back along the hallway. As he closed Sarah's bedroom door behind him, he saw she was watching him from the bed.

'Dare I ask?'

'I just met your flatmate.'

'And she asked you to help with the dishes?'

'No.' He slipped back under the duvet. 'But I was naked. And this was the only cover to hand,' he said, waving the tea towel in the air.

'Which she'll never want to use again, probably.' Sarah smiled as she snuggled up against him. 'Sorry. I thought she was on nights this week.'

'Nights?'

'She's a doctor. Here at Guy's Hospital. Psychiatric department, in fact.'

'Really? She doesn't look . . .'

'Not all blondes are dizzy, Evan.'

'I was going to say "old enough".'

'She's thirty-three.'

Evan lay there for a moment, and realised he knew more about Sarah's flatmate after that short briefing than he did about Sarah herself. 'So,' he said, as casually as he could. 'Tell me about yourself.'

'Jeez. What kind of a question is that?'

Sarah had propped herself up on one elbow, and as she adjusted the duvet, Evan tried not to stare at her exposed breast. 'Well, I just thought, now that we'd, you know . . .'

'Fucked?' said Sarah mischievously, and Evan's eyes widened, but he supposed she was right. After all, you could hardly call what they'd just done 'making love', and 'had sex' hardly did it justice.

'Yeah. I was hoping we could share something else. Apart from bodily fluids.'

She curled a leg suggestively around his thighs. 'What did you want to know?'

'Well, your surname would be a start.'

'It's Bishop.'

'And?'

'Just Bishop,' she said, plumping up the pillow beneath her head and lying down next to him. 'I know most of you English all have these posh double-barrelled names, but we Yanks like to keep things simple.'

'No, I meant *and* what do you do, how old are you?' He stared up at the ceiling. 'What's your favourite colour?'

'Of what?'

'Huh?'

'*What's your favourite colour?* What am I – five years old?'

'I hope not, otherwise I'm in serious trouble.'

She turned her head and looked at him. 'Okay. Well . . . colour? I'd have to say "red", if we're talking wine. Otherwise black.'

'Black's not really a colour.'

'Pardon?'

'It's an absence of colour.'

'It'll be the colour of one of your eyes in a minute, if you continue being a wise ass.' Sarah grinned at him. 'I've just turned thirty-four. And I work in the City. That's "City" with a capital "C".'

'The City's a big place.'

'For a bank called MC&P.' She rolled over and reached for her handbag, retrieved a business card from an inside pocket, and handed it to him. 'Strictly speaking, we're what's called a hedge fund. And no, that's nothing to do with gardening, before you ask.'

'I wasn't going to.'

'What we do is . . .'

Evan held his hand up. 'Make a lot of rich people richer. Isn't that what everyone in the City does?'

She laughed. 'Most of them. Especially themselves.'

'And do you enjoy it? The work, I mean.'

Sarah paused. 'Not much.'

'Why not?'

'Sometimes it can get a little . . . complicated.'

'What is it you do, exactly?'

'I'm in Risk Management.'

'Oh. Right.'

Sarah raised one eyebrow. 'Do you know what that is?'

'Will I understand if you tell me?'

'Probably not. Some days I don't get it myself. And they're the days I don't enjoy.'

'So leave.'

'Yeah, right. Great strategy.'

'What's wrong with it?'

'Because I've worked too hard to get where I am to give up on it. And where would I go, for one thing?'

'There's always somewhere.'

'Really? Try suggesting that to the Palestinians.'

'That's hardly the same thing.'

'Evan, not everyone's as lucky as you. We can't all do the thing we love.'

'You mean "do" in the English sense, right, and not the American?'

'Very funny.'

'Okay, okay. Forget I said anything.'

Sarah rolled over and rested her chin on his chest, then noticed the faint, semi-circular scar on his navel. 'What's this from? Knife fight? Jealous girlfriend?' She traced the outline with her index finger. 'Alien emergence?'

'Car crash.' Evan took her hand and gently moved it away from the injury. 'When I was a kid. Drunk driver.'

'Were you hurt badly?'

'Nothing that couldn't be fixed,' he said, though in truth, it had been touch and go, and even now, on cold days, Evan's insides ached where they'd stitched him back together.

'What happened to the drunk?'

'He died. Along with my mother, unfortunately.'

Sarah sat up suddenly. 'Evan, I'm so sorry.'

'It was a long time ago.'

She shook her head. 'Serves him right, though. How did your father cope?'

'My father was the drunk, Sarah.'

She stared at him, wide-eyed, then half-smiled. 'Aren't we just the happy family pair?'

He puffed air out of his cheeks. 'It's not so bad. Mel's been looking out for me as if he's my dad, and Finn . . . well, he's like the brother I never had. Besides, like you said earlier – what can you do?'

Sarah squeezed his hand. 'Still, least we won't have to endure any of those dull Christmases at the in-laws'.'

'Quite.' Evan flipped over onto his stomach. 'So, where were we?'

'You were pumping me. For information.'

'I was, wasn't I? Right. Important question coming up . . .' He looked directly at her. 'What's your favourite food?'

'Sushi.'

Evan made a face. 'And there was I thinking we had all this stuff in common.'

'Huh?'

'It's just . . . they treat it like some amazing delicacy, charge you loads of money for it, and . . .'

'And what?'

'It isn't even *cooked*.'

Sarah burst out laughing, and Evan picked his pillow up and hit her playfully with it. 'Okay, okay,' he said. 'Favourite food: Sushi. Duly noted.'

'What are you doing, anyway?' She wrestled the pillow from him. 'Writing my résumé?'

'No. Just trying to work out where I can take you to dinner some time. Assuming you're not just . . .'

'What?'

Evan rolled back over and did his best to look vulnerable. 'Using me for sex.'

Sarah's eyes searched his face, then she threw the duvet to one side and climbed on top of him. 'Would that be such a bad thing?'

Evan tried to ignore the stirring in his loins. 'I suppose not,' he said, thinking the exact opposite.

6

Sarah reached over and hit 'snooze' on her alarm, then propped herself up on one elbow and gazed at the indentation in the pillow where Evan's head had been. They'd eventually drifted off to sleep, but woken early and had sex a third time, then he'd left rather suddenly, though he'd explained that it had been more to do with not wanting to get a parking ticket than any morning-after awkwardness. Perhaps he'd also wanted to avoid a repeat of the previous evening's embarrassing encounter with Grace, and Sarah couldn't blame him – she felt embarrassed enough herself. And while she was relieved Grace evidently hadn't mistakenly called him David, she still wasn't sure how she was going to explain last night away.

Slipping reluctantly out from under the duvet, she pulled her robe on, stuck the scrap of paper Evan had hurriedly scribbled his number on into her pocket, and checked her phone for messages, though she was sure David was unlikely to have called again. Even though the two of them hadn't made any promises of exclusivity to each other, something about what she'd done last night seemed wrong. Though perhaps because it had felt so right.

At the club, she'd never wanted a performance to be over so quickly, whereas once they'd tumbled into bed, the opposite had been true. And while it had been relatively straightforward to get him there – let's face it, it was for most women – their first time had been different to any other first time she'd had. There had been none of the usual unfamiliar fumbling, no awkward re-positioning, or any stop-starting. Just good sex. Great sex, in fact. And she'd been shocked at the level of her passion. Even before they'd done it for the first time, Sarah had known they'd be doing it again – and not, she now suspected, just that evening.

She glanced back towards the bed, wondered whether she'd ever see Evan again, and felt a twinge of sadness at the thought. Though perhaps it was good he'd left like he had – why ruin the fabulous memories of what might have been just a one-off with embarrassed small-talk over breakfast until such time as it was polite to leave? Evan was a musician, after all. He probably had women throwing themselves at him every night. Perhaps he even had a girlfriend . . . Sarah shuddered at the possibility, and felt a little foolish. She'd given in to her baser instincts – been unable to stop herself – and while it had felt good at the time, she hoped she hadn't done something she'd regret. She checked the date on her phone, then did a quick calculation in her head and relaxed a little, pretty sure she was nowhere near her 'fertile' time, though shamefully she realised it hadn't occurred to her to ask Evan to use some protection. Not that she'd given him the time, such had been her eagerness to jump him almost as soon as they'd arrived home.

She glanced at her clock again – she still had an hour before she had to leave for the office, but she didn't want to hurry for another reason. Being at work would mean seeing David, and right now, that was a complication she could do without. With a sigh, she put her phone on to charge, then made her way into the kitchen, grinning guiltily as Grace raised one eyebrow from behind a mug of tea.

'Sorry. I thought you were on nights.'

41

'I swapped. As it would appear you have.' Grace pushed a chair out from underneath the table with her foot, and Sarah sat down obediently. 'Not seeing David any more, then?'

Sarah felt herself start to redden. 'Not necessarily.'

'Well, it looked like you were giving . . .' Grace took a sip of tea, then put her mug down. 'What was his name again?'

'Evan.'

'. . . *Evan* a pretty good stamp of approval last night, seeing as how he was naked in the kitchen, and you and David haven't even . . .' She frowned. 'What is it in American – *got to third base?*'

Sarah stretched one leg out under the table and prodded Grace affectionately on the shin. She'd responded to her ad for a roommate while she was still in New York, and had known they'd become best friends the moment Grace – still in her pyjamas on a Sunday afternoon – had begun giving her a guided tour of the flat via Skype. 'It's not that simple. Besides, I have no idea whether we're compatible.'

'You sounded pretty compatible to me last night. Twice.'

'Sorry.' Sarah blushed again as she recalled the events of the previous evening. 'Like I said, I thought you were at work. But last night was, well . . . I only *met* Evan last night.'

Grace raised both eyebrows this time. 'I'm confused.'

'*You're* confused?' Sarah got up and walked over to the coffee machine, chose the strongest pod from the rack, and slotted it into the front – having had so little sleep last night she could do with the caffeine hit. 'I'd just about decided to make a go of things with David, and then I chanced upon this little jazz club . . . Maybe I was feeling emotional, maybe a little drunk, but I tell you, the moment Evan appeared on stage . . .' She shuddered with pleasure at the memory. 'There was just something about him.'

'So what's the problem?'

Sarah retrieved a mug from the cupboard and placed it on the drip tray, then stabbed at the button on the front of the machine, and the aroma of fresh coffee filled the kitchen. 'Well, for one thing, he's a musician.'

'So?'

'The life. The hours. The uncertainty. The lack of money. I went through it all as a kid, Grace, and I'm not sure I want to again. I know I don't want my kids to.'

'Kids? You've only just met him!'

'Yeah, but you've got to think about those things, haven't you?' Sarah waited until the machine had finished, then picked up her cup, blew across the top of her coffee, and took a sip.

'After one night?'

'Of course. Especially at, you know . . .'

Grace widened her eyes. 'Our age?'

'Exactly. You can't tell me that you don't?'

'Maybe. Which is probably why I'm still single.' Grace stared wistfully into her mug. 'Still, you can always just write it off as a one-night stand.'

'I could. If . . .'

'What?'

Sarah made a face. 'If I wasn't desperate to see him again.' She helped herself to a muffin from the packet on top of the bread bin. 'So, what should I do?'

As Sarah sat back down, Grace reached over and broke herself off a piece of muffin. 'I don't know – maybe have a bit of fun with him?' she said, popping it into her mouth. 'See how it goes. You can always talk about kids once . . .'

'About *David*.'

'Oh.' Grace chewed thoughtfully. 'Do you want to keep seeing him?'

Sarah stuck her bottom lip out. 'I don't know. He kind of wore me down into going out to dinner with him, but once I was there . . . I mean, I am attracted to him. He's got this charm about him, and self-confidence, and we had, well, not fun, exactly, but there's something about David that's . . . reassuring.'

'Reassuring?'

'Yeah. And in a strange country . . .'

'You mean "strange" as in "unfamiliar", right?'

'If you say so. But reassurance is attractive.'

'But not as attractive as the guy you've just spent the night with?'

'Maybe not. And I can't see them both.'

'Is that even an option?'

Sarah shook her head. She'd 'dated' before in the U.S., where it was common practice to see different men at the same time until you decided to go steady with one. It was how all her girlfriends back in New York behaved before they'd got married, and what American men expected, but she had a feeling that any English – what was the word, *suitors*? – might not quite understand the concept. Sarah wasn't sure she quite bought into it herself, which was another reason she'd felt a little awkward around Evan this morning as he'd left, telling her in a terrible American accent to *have a nice day*, then immediately apologising in case he'd offended her.

'I mean, it's what I'd do in the States, but over here . . . it wouldn't be fair.'

'It'd be fun, though.' Grace laughed. 'And you'd only have to do it until you feel you can make a choice.'

'Maybe.' Sarah allowed herself a smile. 'But what if either of them found out?'

'How would they?'

'That's not the point.' She took another sip of coffee. 'But equally, I don't want to mess it up with David. Because he's . . .'

'Loaded?'

'No . . .'

'*Reassuring?*'

'No – reliable. I haven't had a lot of that in my life.' She broke what was left of the muffin in half and passed a piece to Grace. 'And besides, he's my boss.'

'So?'

'So I might lose my job.'

'He can't fire you for breaking up with him after, what, one date?' said Grace, indignantly. 'There are rules about that kind of thing.'

'You don't know the City, Grace. It's all about winning. People don't like to lose – especially people like David. And besides, if he did fire me – and believe me, I've seen it happen – it wouldn't be for that, but everyone would know what the real reason was. And even if he didn't fire me, I'd probably have to leave. The atmosphere . . .' She shook her head and realised she was getting a little ahead of herself. After all, she had no idea whether Evan *wanted* anything more.

'You could always get another job somewhere else.'

'It's not that easy. The company sponsors my being over here, so I'd probably have to go back to the U.S. – unless I can find some nice English man to marry me, and I hardly want to spring *that* on Evan on our second date.'

'Ah.'

'Yes, "ah".' Sarah popped the remainder of her muffin into her mouth, washing it down with the rest of her coffee. Like a lot of English versions of American things it didn't quite measure up to the ones she was used to back home, but it was better than nothing – a feeling she hoped hadn't been behind her decision to date David in the first place. 'What would you do?'

'Don't ask me!'

'Come on. You're a doctor, aren't you?'

'What's that got to do with anything?'

'I need a second opinion.'

'You know I specialise in psychiatry, not the heart?'

'Even so. What do you think?'

'Well . . .' Grace drained the last of her tea, then stood up and placed her mug in the sink. 'Judging by what I saw in the kitchen last night – not to mention what I heard through the bedroom wall – if you want my professional opinion . . .'

'I do.'

She grinned. 'You'd be crazy to give up on it.'

7

Sarah stepped onto the pavement and froze. She hadn't thought anything of handing Evan her business card in bed the previous evening but now, at the sight of him leaning against his car just across the street from her office, she could see that might have been a mistake.

Not that she wasn't pleased to see him – it was more that she hadn't had time to say anything to David, although that was as much because she hadn't known how to. Dumping anyone – even after one date – was difficult enough, let alone when the ramifications could be more than a simple cold shoulder in the corridor, and particularly when things had hardly started between them. And what could she say – that she didn't think dating her boss was a good idea? Either way, he might see sacking her as a solution to that particular problem, and besides, she reminded herself, she hadn't yet made her mind up. Sure, Evan seemed like he'd be fun to be with, and the sex had been great, but it wasn't all about that – *mostly*, maybe, but not all – and while she hadn't even kissed David, had no idea what he was like in bed, there was nothing wrong with keeping her options open.

She fixed a smile on her face and crossed the road. 'What are you doing here?' she asked, glancing nervously back towards the revolving doors. She'd passed David's office on her way out to lunch and seen him firmly ensconced on a conference call, but even so, she knew she had to get rid of Evan fast, and without raising his suspicions – or any of her co-workers' – either.

'I thought we could have some lunch.'

'That's a lovely idea,' she said, hoping he'd realise the reason she hadn't kissed him hello was purely proximity to her office. 'But I don't really have a lot of time . . .'

'Long enough for a sandwich, surely?' Evan held up a carrier bag. 'Egg mayonnaise, chicken – though it could be turkey – cheese, some kind of meat, and something else that I can't quite identify.' He shrugged. 'I didn't know what you'd like, so I got a selection.'

'Of random fillings?'

'Yeah. I find it adds a certain excitement to lunchtime. Like playing Russian Roulette. But with sandwiches. Kind of like . . .'

'Sandwich Roulette?' Sarah stared at the bag, then at Evan's loopy grin, then she smiled. 'Okay. But I hope we're not just going to eat them here in the car?'

'Oh no.' Evan walked round and opened the passenger door for her, and she quickly got in. 'I know just the place.' He ran back round and jumped into the driver's seat, and as Sarah peered at him quizzically, started the engine.

'So . . .' she said.

'So?'

'How was your morning?'

'Good.' Evan flipped the indicator and carefully edged the Mercedes out of the parking space. 'As was last night.'

'Yeah, I'm sorry about that.'

'Sorry? For what?'

'Well, I kind of jumped you.'

'Oh, don't worry about it.'

'I expect that happens to you all the time.'

He smiled distractedly, concentrating on finding a gap in the traffic. 'Not nearly often enough.'

Sarah tried to meet his eyes as he accelerated out in front of a bus and along the road towards St. Paul's, but failed, so instead she just sat there silently as he drove quickly along Aldersgate Street, enjoying being ferried around this new part of town in this lovely old car, though after little more than a minute, they'd stopped outside some gardens she'd never seen before.

'Where are you taking me?' she asked, climbing cautiously out of the car. 'Is this your back yard?'

'I wish.' Evan grinned as he slotted a handful of coins into the parking meter. 'But sadly, no. This . . .' – he made an extravagant sweeping gesture with his arm – '. . . is Postman's Park.'

'Postman's Park?'

'That's right. Come on.'

They walked in through the entrance, and Sarah looked around at the various benches, where numerous suited city-workers were sitting, staring into their phones, or eating lunch, or most usually, doing both at the same time.

'Well, where are they?'

'Who?'

'All the . . .' She stopped herself. She'd been about to say 'mailmen'. 'Postal workers.'

'You mean "postmen"?'

'Postmen, mailmen, what's the difference?' She smiled at him. 'I don't buy all this "two countries separated by a common language" crap.'

'No?'

'Give me an example, then.'

'Well . . .' Evan thought for a moment. 'For you, the Mall is where you go shopping. Here in London, it's the street the Queen drives along to get to Buckingham Palace.'

'Enough already with the Queen's English. I meant a *real* example.'

He gave her a light slap on her behind. 'Where have I just hit you?'

'My fanny.'

'Well, here in England, it's impossible for you to do the same to me.'

She frowned at him for a second, then tutted loudly as realisation dawned. 'Okay. Point taken. So, what's the deal with this place?'

'Its "deal" is only that it's the most special, memorable, magical place in London,' he said, leading her towards a series of decorated, inscribed plaques set into the wall at the park's farthest corner. 'See those?'

Sarah squinted as she tried to make out the writing, and hoped she wouldn't soon be needing glasses. 'Pretty posh graffiti you have here.'

'It's not graffiti. They're a hundred years old. More, in some cases. And they all commemorate acts of bravery.'

'Bravery?'

'Yeah. Ordinary people being brave, saving children from runaway horses, plucking drowning people out of the Thames, that sort of thing.'

'Really?' Sarah walked up to the wall, stood under the protective canopy, and peered closely at the nearest plaque, shocked to find out just how brave. In every case, in doing what they'd been doing, whether preventing suicides on the railway or rescuing old ladies from burning buildings – whatever selfless deed had earned them a spot there – all the people mentioned on the plaques had died in the act. She read on, enchanted by names that had long ceased to be popular, or professions that hadn't existed for decades, and while it occurred to her to point out that there wasn't a mailman among them, she didn't want to appear disrespectful. All these ordinary people had turned out to be, well, extraordinary. And in doing so, they'd be remembered forever.

'What do you think?'

'What do I think?' Sarah was still trying to take it in. 'I think you've taken me to a cemetery for lunch.'

Evan laughed as he sat down on a nearby bench and patted the space next to him. 'It's not a cemetery. It's a . . . well, I suppose it's a garden of remembrance. Don't you like it?'

Sarah examined the plaques again, though this time with a new-found respect. 'No, I . . . I love it,' she said, captivated by the astonishing stories, amazed no-one had ever told her about this jewel that lay hidden less than five minutes from the building she went to every day.

And, she realised, feeling the warmth of Evan's gaze, she was becoming captivated by the astonishing person who'd taken her there.

8

Evan stared at Sarah until he feared it might be perceived as creepy, then cleared his throat. 'So, have you made your choice yet?'

She looked round in shock. 'Pardon?'

He held up the carrier bag. 'Egg mayo? Cheese? Some sort of white meat that we'll identify afterwards?'

'Oh. Right. Which do you prefer?'

'I don't mind.'

Sarah peered into the bag in disbelief. 'They're tiny – and there's so many of them. What is this – the *menu degustation*?' she said, adopting a French accent.

'The disgusting what?'

'No, the . . . Never mind. Did you make them yourself?'

Evan tried not to blush. 'Take' would have been a better word, but he didn't want to admit he'd swiped them from an abandoned buffet at the hotel where his audition had been earlier. 'Not exactly.'

'Well, whatever, it's very thoughtful of you.' She helped herself to a sandwich and took a bite, and Evan followed suit, fighting the urge to sniff the suspicious-looking filling. 'So tell me about you,' she continued, 'seeing as you got the full run-down on me last night.'

'Not much to tell, really. As you know, I play the sax.'

'For a living. Which makes you pretty lucky. And special.'

'I don't know about that.'

'I do,' she said, earnestly.

Evan stared off into the distance, surprised to find himself daydreaming that, one day, Sarah might even say those two words while standing next to him, and almost laughed at the idea.

'What?'

Evan felt himself redden. 'Nothing.'

'So, you were saying, Mr. Lucky . . .' She nudged him with her elbow. 'Though it can't *all* be down to luck.'

Evan thought for a moment. He *was* lucky to make a living from something he loved. 'Actually, it was. If Finn hadn't been sleeping with that record exec . . .'

'Come on, Evan. I'm a musician's daughter, remember. What made you want to play? To put in the hours and hours of practice in the first place? I'm guessing it wasn't the money.'

Evan laughed. 'Hardly. No, it was my granddad.'

'Your granddad? Did he play?'

'Only records.'

'Records?' Sarah scratched her head. 'Oh, hang on. I think I remember my father telling me about them. Round flat black plastic things with grooves in them, right?'

Evan glared at her good-naturedly. 'Yeah. He had a bunch of old 78s – all the jazz classics. Basie, Coltrane, Monk . . . He let me play them to death on what I called his "grandadphone" . . .'

'Aww. Cute.'

'Do you want to hear this or not?'

'Sorry,' said Sarah, contritely. 'You were saying?'

'Well, it was then I decided I wanted to be a sax player. Then one day, he came home with a surprise for me.'

'A double bass?'

Evan reached into the carrier bag, removed a sandwich, and handed it to Sarah. 'Eat this. It might keep you quiet.'

'Sorry. Again.'

'So anyway, he bought me my first sax.'

'Tenor?'

'I don't know how much he paid for it.'

'No, I meant . . . Right. You got me. Very good.'

Evan grinned. 'But yeah, actually, it was a tenor sax. And a nice one too. Must have cost him most of his pension money – much to the disgust of my parents, who thought I'd play with it for five minutes then abandon it in some cupboard, much like the expensive Scalextrix set they'd bought me the previous Christmas. But I loved it, you know? Even got blisters from trying to master the thing. And then, just after my twelfth birthday, when my parents died, and I eventually got out of hospital, I moved in with my grandparents and kind of shut myself away in my bedroom to practice.' Evan stopped talking. Sarah was holding her hand up, like a child in a classroom. 'Yes?'

She put her hand down. 'Did it help?'

Evan nodded. 'Funnily enough, yeah. The sax is a very expressive instrument. Sometimes it can . . .'

'What?'

He swallowed hard. 'Express the emotions you find impossible to voice.'

'That sounds like something a shrink would say.'

'And they'd be right.' He forced a smile. 'So anyway, I got good enough to earn a bit of money busking on the South Bank and picked up the occasional gig on the South London jazz circuit, where I met Finn, and from there . . . well, Jazzed you know about.'

'And now the G-Spot?'

'Yeah. Which I love. And while perhaps it isn't where I see myself playing out the rest of my career, there's always some session work to look forward to, and the occasional tour . . .' He took a deep breath, then his nerve failed him, and he couldn't meet Sarah's eyes. 'But it certainly isn't a bad way to pay the mortgage – ignoring the fact that, given that it's the only thing I'm any good at . . .'

'I wouldn't say that.'

'. . . it's my *only* way to pay the mortgage.' Evan did a double take, realising what Sarah must have just been referring to, and for the second time in as many minutes, fought to control the blush he could feel starting. He fished inside the carrier bag, removed a sandwich, and stuffed it into his mouth, wondering how on earth to tell Sarah that – given this morning's developments – soon he might not have a mortgage, then looked up to find her smirking at him.

'What?'

'Your mouth. You've got . . . Hang on.' She leaned across, took his face in her hands, and brushed his lips suggestively with the tip of her tongue. 'Mayonnaise,' she said, her mouth millimetres from his. 'At least, I hope it was mayonnaise.' Then she kissed him.

And at that precise moment, Evan felt his legs go so weak he was glad he was sitting down.

9

Sarah sat at her desk and stared out of the window, replaying her and Evan's lunchtime encounter in her mind. They'd kissed for what had seemed like hours before she'd realised where they were and had breathlessly broken away to finish her lunch in an awkward silence. Then she'd raised her eyebrows at what she'd assumed was Evan's rude suggestion that she might fancy a quick '99', but when he'd pointed to the nearby ice cream van and explained it was actually the name of some sort of ice cream cornet with a chocolate flake stuck into it – which had still sounded rude to her – she'd laughed, pointed to the rain clouds that were gathering overhead, and suggested they go back to his flat for a proper dessert instead. Though they hadn't gotten much farther than the garage in Bermondsey where he parked his car – where they'd been interrupted by the grinning garage owner knocking on the windscreen – before she'd remembered that she in fact had a job to return to.

As she was re-applying her lipstick in the cab she'd insisted on flagging down to take her back to the office, Sarah hadn't been able to get the park's incredible stories of self-sacrifice out of her mind. Would David ever be brave enough to do something like that? Sarah hoped so – though somehow she *knew* that Evan would. And it was then she knew she needed to have a little courage herself, and make a decision – and soon. She knew she owed them both that in return, at the very least.

'Penny for your thoughts?'

She looked up with a start. David was standing in her office doorway, and immediately she felt guilty.

'Is that your best offer?'

He smiled down at her, absent-mindedly fiddling with one of his cuff-links. 'Well, how about dinner this evening?'

Sarah regarded him for a moment. He was tall, his swept-back hair probably the same style he'd had since public school, impeccably dressed, and with strong, confident features, but handsome in more of a well-groomed way, rather than naturally good-looking – completely the opposite of Evan, she realised. 'I can't,' she said, realising she had to play for time. 'Tonight, I mean. I'm going out,' she added, quickly.

'Anywhere nice?'

For a moment, Sarah worried he was angling for an invitation. 'A jazz club,' she said, and when David made a face, she knew she'd said the right thing. 'Near London Bridge. There's a friend of mine playing there.'

'A friend?'

Sarah hesitated, then thought *what the hell?* 'Yes. His name's Evan. He's a musician.'

'I guessed that from your use of the word "playing".' David smiled, then pulled his Blackberry out of his pocket and consulted the calendar. 'How about tomorrow?'

'Tomorrow?' Sarah looked up at him, and realised Grace was right. If she *was* going to cool things with David, better to do that before things went any further, no matter how difficult that made things for her at work, and over dinner tomorrow might well be the perfect opportunity. Besides, David was a nice guy. Surely he wouldn't do anything, well, *nasty*. She'd go to see Evan tonight, just to make sure, and then . . . well, if she did choose him, it would be much better to tell David over the weekend, and give him a day or so to get used to the idea.

David was looking at her expectantly, his thumbs poised over his phone's keyboard ready to type her name into the appropriate time slot on his schedule, so Sarah fixed a smile on her face. 'That'd be lovely,' she said.

10

Evan cursed his lack of nerve as he drove out of the car park. He'd been desperate to tell Sarah his news, but he didn't want to seem like he was bragging, and besides, how did you tell someone you'd just met – someone who'd moved here *from* the States – that you were about to move there for the next twelve months?

He'd been still buzzing from their night together when he'd arrived at the hotel earlier, and was sure that had carried itself into the way he'd played at the audition – though 'audition' was stretching it – it had been more like an audience. He'd recognised the man himself at once, of course, even though he'd been sporting a beard, but Evan had assumed Sting had just wanted someone to do some session work on one of his jazz albums. Little could he have guessed that the Police were reforming for one last farewell – and that it would mean he might have to make a few farewells of his own.

He felt sorry for the guy he'd be replacing – after scarcely a week's rehearsals, the band had been having their doubts about him, and had wanted to see who else was out there – but even though the offer had been last-minute, he knew the tour was too good an opportunity to turn down – a year, travelling the world with one of its biggest ever bands, starting and finishing in the States – and the *money* . . . But then again, for Evan, it was never about the money. Though he cursed his bad timing. Finally, he'd met someone he might have a chance of some sort of future with – though he'd be hard pressed to explain why he thought that already – and his music, the thing that had brought them together, was likely to keep them apart. And as much as he wanted to go on the tour, Evan found himself almost wishing he hadn't been asked.

Gunning the Mercedes through an amber light, he drove quickly towards Borough, then circled the block in search of a parking space, eventually squeezing the car into a bay at the top of Long Lane. It was still too early to phone Mel – the hours he kept were somewhat nocturnal – so, keen to share his news with someone who'd understand, he headed towards the familiar café and peered through the window. As usual, Finn was busying himself behind the counter, his hands whizzing expertly around the front of a huge chrome-plated coffee machine, just like they used to do over the keyboards he once played in Jazzed.

Evan paused to hold the door open for a young black woman struggling with an enormous pushchair, then made his way towards the counter and cleared his throat noisily. 'Can you tell me where the nearest Starbucks is, please?'

Finn, still with his back to him, stopped what he was doing. 'You not a coffee lover, then?'

'Would I be here if I was?'

'That's a bit of a deep question for a Friday.'

As Finn turned round and grinned at him, Evan leaned heavily against the counter. 'You ain't heard nothing yet.'

'What's up?'

'I've got some good news.'

'Doesn't look that good, given the expression on your face.'

'No, it is, it's just . . .'

Finn turned back towards the coffee machine, placed an espresso cup under the spout, and punched a button. 'Do I need to tell the missus to buy a hat?'

'Nothing like that. Though . . .' He waited until the machine had finished its noisy spluttering. 'I have kind of met someone.'

'Kind of?'

'Yeah, but . . . it's complicated.'

'Aren't all of yours?' Finn gave Evan a look over his shoulder. 'Does she have a name?'

'Sarah.'

'And what's the complication?'

'I've been offered a gig. A big one.'

Finn removed the cup from the machine and placed it on the counter. 'The Police thing?' he said, waving away Evan's attempt to pay.

'How did you . . .?'

'Well, they asked me first, obviously, but I've got the café to think about, and . . .'

'And you can't play the sax.'

'That too. Though to be quite honest, even if I could, they wouldn't have offered it to me. Too worried I'd draw the attention away from the main men.' Finn ran a hand through his thinning hair. 'Mel told me you were up for it.'

'When?'

'You're not my only customer, you know?'

Evan looked around the near-empty café, hoping his friend was right. He often wondered whether Finn ever dwelt upon the old days, although he supposed he didn't have the time, what with a business, a wife, and two kids. His life made Evan's schedule look positively lightweight, but then Finn had always thrown himself into everything he was involved in – something Evan knew to his cost.

'Mel knew it was for a tour?'

Finn nodded. 'Yup.'

'I wish he'd told me.'

'He didn't want to make you nervous. And wanted to make sure you showed up for it.'

'Why wouldn't I have?'

Finn shot him a look. 'What was the name of that Whitney Houston song? *Didn't we almost have it all?*'

'You almost did, if you remember. More than was good for you.'

'Yes, well, that was a long time ago. And it wasn't all bad.'

'Come on. All that stuff – the limos, the way we had to dress, that stupid interview for *Smash Hits* where we had to pretend we hated each other – it wasn't really *us*, was it? And then . . .' Evan's eyes searched his friend's face. 'You can't tell me you miss it?'

Finn forced a smile. 'Of course not. No, for me, MTV was always just a stepping stone to where I am now, serving coffee to ungrateful punters in a café in South London. Anyway,' he continued, clapping Evan on the shoulder. 'Congratulations.'

'Thanks. I think.'

'You are doing it, right?'

'Yeah, it's just . . .' Evan picked up his coffee and took a sip.

'Sarah?'

'I think I like her, Finn.'

'How long have you been together?'

'That's not the point.'

Finn raised both eyebrows. 'What did she say when you told her?'

'That I like her? Or about the gig?'

'Either.'

'Well, there's the thing . . .'

Finn helped himself to a bottle of water from the fridge underneath the counter. 'You've got to tell her. Both of those things.'

'It's a little . . . early.'

'How early?'

'We, um . . .' Evan coloured slightly. 'Met last night.'

'*Last night?*'

'But I really think we had some kind of connection, you know? And I don't want to spoil things.'

'Don't you think buggering off to America without telling her might do that?' He unscrewed the top from the bottle and took a swig. 'Do you think she likes you?'

Evan shrugged. 'Maybe. Yeah. I think so. Though I met her today for lunch, and she initially seemed a bit . . . distant.'

'So will you be, when you're in the States.'

'That's not funny, Finn. Though what *is* funny is that she's American.'

'Well, there you go. Ask her to come with you.'

Evan almost dropped his cup. 'I couldn't!'

'Why not?'

'Well . . . Because she wouldn't, for one thing.'

'You don't know that.'

Evan made a face. 'People don't just up and leave the country just like that,' he said, clicking his fingers. 'Especially with people they hardly know.'

'You're about to. And besides, that's not the point.'

'It isn't?'

Finn folded his arms and rested on the counter. 'The point is that you've asked her. Whether she can go or not is neither here nor there. Unlike where the two of you'll be, of course.'

'She won't think it's too . . .' Evan tried to find a better word than 'inappropriate'. 'Forward?'

'Nah. But better she does than you say nothing and lose her, surely?'

'I suppose. And you're sure it'll work?'

Finn grinned. 'Just think of it like eBay.'

'Like eBay?'

'Yeah. You see something you really want, you don't just stick in a bid and hope. You've got to go in with your best offer. *Buy it now*, and all that.'

'You think?'

'Only one way to find out,' said Finn, walking round from behind the counter to collect some empty cups from a nearby table.

Distracted by shouting from outside, Evan looked out of the window, where a minor shunt between two cars had escalated into a fist-fight between the drivers, though currently, neither of the two participants was standing close enough for their flailing arms to actually connect. He watched for a moment, then downed the last of his espresso and decided that maybe Finn was right – he *could* ask Sarah to come with him. She had admitted she missed the U.S., and that there were times she hated her job . . . At the very least he could ask her to wait for him – he'd even fly back home regularly to see her, or she could come out and see the show, maybe take some holiday, and . . . He turned his attention back to his friend, conscious that Finn had reappeared behind the counter and started speaking again.

'But if you do ask her, just be prepared for one thing,' he was saying.

'What?'

Finn smiled, then laid a hand on Evan's shoulder. 'She might actually say "yes".'

11

'Looking for someone?'

At the voice from the far side of the bar, Sarah looked up sharply, then recognised the short, balding man from the previous evening. What had he said his name was? Mal? No – *Mel*.

'Evan, actually.'

'He's not coming.'

'The poster said he played here on Fridays.'

Mel nodded at the empty stool in front of her, and after a moment's hesitation, Sarah sat down. 'He did.'

'Did?'

'Not anymore.'

Sarah felt suddenly disappointed. She'd come to the club early with the hope of catching Evan before he played, but at the moment, the place was almost empty, and she was feeling a little like a groupie. 'Why not?'

'Well, Beyoncé wants her old spot back, so . . .' He held his hands up and shrugged in a 'what-can-you-do?' way, and Sarah laughed, though mainly because Mel had pronounced the singer's name as if it was a quaint English seaside resort.

'Seriously, Mel.'

'Well, for one thing, it'll be a long way to travel for a sixty-minute set.'

'Huh?'

'He did tell you, I take it?'

'Tell me?'

'His news.'

'News?'

'About his audition.' Mel had begun to look worried. 'This morning?'

Just in time, Sarah caught her frown. 'Yeah,' she said, playing along.

'I mean, touring with The Police.' Mel shook his head in admiration. 'And for a year . . .'

Sarah gripped the edge of the bar for support. 'A *year*?'

'I thought you said he'd told you?'

Mel was peering intently at her, but Sarah couldn't meet his gaze. 'He did. Just not how long for. You know Evan.'

'I didn't know that you did.'

Sarah blushed. 'How on earth are you going to replace him?'

'I could ask you the same question.'

'Evan and I . . .' She swallowed hard. 'It's just a bit of fun, that's all.'

Mel arched one eyebrow. 'Does Evan know that?'

'Oh, for sure.' Sarah forced a smile, willing herself to appear relaxed, but she suddenly felt desperate to get out of the club. 'Still, it's good news for him, I guess.'

'It is. If he goes.'

'Why wouldn't he?'

'Why do you think?'

She stared at him for a moment. 'That's hardly up to me.'

'I didn't say it was. Although I suspect you could help him make his mind up.'

'Evan's a grown man. I'm sure he can make his own decisions.'

'Maybe. But how much do you know about him?' Mel grinned as Sarah started to redden again. 'Sorry. Silly question if you and he *are* just a bit of fun. He told you about Jazzed, right?'

'Yeah. Though I had to practically force that out of him.'

'Evan's finest hour.'

'He didn't tell me what happened, though. Why they stopped.'

'Well, that's Evan for you.'

'So what's your point? That once he's got what he wants, he gives up on it?'

'My point, young lady, is that he needs this tour for his career. He's far too good to do session work, or advertising jingles, or porn soundtracks, and especially to play at the likes of this place for the rest of his life. America was good to him once. It might be again. They don't call it the land of opportunity for nothing. And this tour? It's a hell of an opportunity.'

Sarah marvelled at Mel's generosity, even though she'd begun to feel a little sick. She wouldn't be the only one who'd be giving up their main attraction, she realised. And she also knew Mel was right.

'What do you want me to do?'

Mel shrugged. 'Convince him to go.'

'I'm not sure he'll listen to me.'

Mel made the 'yeah, right' face. 'Well, find some other way, then – or at least, don't give him a reason to stay. Not everyone gets two chances, Sarah. And if you haven't taken the first one that life dealt you, then you sure as hell have to make sure you grab the second with both hands and hang on tight.'

'I don't need a lecture, Mel. My father was in the business. I know what it's like.'

'All the more reason for you to let him go.'

She looked at him incredulously. '*Let* him?'

'You're not in love with him, are you?'

'Don't be . . .' Sarah was shocked that she actually found herself wondering if she might be. 'What business is that of yours? Jeez, what are you going to ask me next – what are my *intentions* towards him? Who are you? The father of the fucking bride?'

The club had started to fill up, and their argument was beginning to attract attention, so Mel held both hands up. 'Relax. And trust me, Evan's like a son – I mean, a younger brother – to me.' He grinned again. 'If I thought he'd found the love of his life, then the last thing I'd be doing would be getting him to walk away from it. So unless you think that *is* you . . .'

'How do you expect anyone to know that?' Sarah hissed.

Mel regarded her for a moment, then he sighed. 'Sorry. Sermon over.' He reached down behind the bar and produced a couple of glasses, closely followed by a bottle of bourbon. 'All I'm saying is . . . I dunno what I'm saying. Except, perhaps, just do what your conscience tells you.'

Sarah stared at him as he splashed a healthy measure into each glass, feeling more than a little stunned. She already suspected her father had missed out on what could have been a decent musical career because of her, and she knew she'd never forgive herself if the same thing happened to Evan.

She waved away the drink Mel was offering her, then jumped down off her stool and hurried towards the exit. If she'd listened to her conscience, she knew, perhaps she wouldn't be in this situation in the first place.

12

Evan gazed out of the window as he waited for Sarah to arrive. He loved this view, from the seventh floor café at the Tate Modern, with the London skyline stretched out in front of him, its mix of old and new architecture reminding him of the way different jazz instruments combined to produce one beautiful melody.

He'd been pleasantly surprised to get her reply – they'd parted after lunch on Friday with no plans to meet up, and Evan had momentarily feared he might have overstepped the mark by turning up unannounced at her office, so he'd spent a nail-biting night, then texted this morning and asked her to meet him for a coffee, and when she'd responded almost straight away her tone had seemed . . . Insistent was the best description he could think of. And while he knew better than to read anything into a text message, he'd taken it as a positive sign.

As he sipped his coffee anxiously, he noticed his hands were trembling, and wondered whether he should have ordered decaf – or perhaps even a brandy instead. Up on stage he'd always felt comfortable, whatever the size of the audience – perhaps because he had confidence in his ability – but for as long as he could remember, he'd been nervous whenever simply asking a woman out. Asking one if she wanted to come away with him, and for a year . . .

Of course, it was a little far-fetched to think she could just drop everything and go, but after his conversation with Finn, he'd been feeling he had to make some sort of gesture. Offer Sarah something, at least to show her that Thursday night hadn't just been a one-off. And while, back in the café, he'd almost laughed at how preposterous Finn's suggestion had sounded, he'd been rehearsing it all morning, and unlike when you repeated a word so many times it lost its meaning, he'd been surprised at how much more sense the idea had made the more he'd said it.

While in his heart of hearts he suspected a long-distance relationship was the best he could hope for, his request might at least soften the blow when he told Sarah about the tour, though to be honest, even the prospect of trying to keep something going made him nervous. A year or so ago, he'd struggled to maintain seeing someone who'd lived in Bethnal Green, and that had been just across the Thames. The Atlantic? That was a whole new – and much scarier – prospect.

He looked down at the crowds on the South Bank, scurrying around as if grateful to be freed from their day jobs, and allowed himself a smile. Evan had never had a day job – and while he had to work what were known as 'unsociable' hours, he didn't see them like that at all. His job was about as sociable as you could get – playing for people when they were out having a good time, a few drinks, perhaps even joining them for one afterwards. Plus, he'd always loved having his days to himself. The freedom of being able to get up whenever he wanted – particularly if he'd had a late night – and not having to be woken up by the alarm, iron a shirt, or jump on the underground with the millions of commuters that swelled London's population by so much every weekday was, he knew, a blessing. Being tied to the nine-to-five that most of his school friends – and a good many of his music-school friends – had ended up doing just wasn't for him.

Though while the free time was one of the joys of his occupation, recently Evan had begun to feel his days weren't quite as much fun as they could be. The lack of urgency had begun to seem more like no sense of direction. The solitude he used to enjoy was starting to feel like loneliness. On one or two occasions, he'd found himself desperate to go and sit in a café and drink a coffee just to be surrounded by people: he'd found that a little worrying. And then two days ago, he'd met Sarah, and already he'd begun to wish he could spend all that free time with her.

He checked his watch for what seemed like the thousandth time. She was late – although given his upcoming absence, he could hardly complain about her timekeeping – and he swivelled round on his stool to get an unobstructed view of the lift doors. The last thing he wanted was for her to miss him – assuming she turned up. Even though he was bound to miss her if she turned him down.

He chuckled at his own joke and wondered whether he should use it to break the ice when she arrived, although given Sarah's expression when he spotted her, Evan suddenly feared he'd need a much better one than that. As she hurried over to where he was sitting, he stood up to greet her.

'Hi.'

'Evan, I . . .'

Sarah hesitated before sitting down, and he began to feel uneasy. 'What's wrong?'

'Nothing,' she said, though Evan wondered why she hadn't kissed him hello – and seemed to be having trouble meeting his eyes. 'It's a stunning view.'

'Yes,' he said, staring at her. 'From where I'm sitting, it is. Quite possibly my favourite one.'

She turned to face him, colouring slightly when she realised he was looking at her as he spoke, then her expression hardened. 'How are preparations going?'

'Preparations?'

'For the tour,' she said, flatly.

The colour drained from Evan's face. 'How did you . . .?'

'Mel.'

'Mel?'

'Don't be pissed at him. He thought you'd told me.'

'How could he possibly think that?'

Sarah shrugged exaggeratedly. 'I don't know. Maybe because it's the kind of thing you should tell someone before you . . .' She stopped mid-sentence, perhaps remembering the events of the night before last were at her instigation.

'I'm sorry. I only found out yesterday morning. And I wanted to say something when we were having lunch, but I just couldn't find the right moment.'

'And when was the right moment going to be – when you were just about to get on the plane? Which is when, exactly?'

Evan looked at his watch, shocked to realise he'd be leaving in less than twenty-four hours. 'Tomorrow,' he said, softly.

'*Tomorrow?*'

'Yeah.' Evan swallowed hard. 'I know we don't have a lot of time. Which is what I wanted to talk to you about.'

She held up a hand to stop him. 'I understand. You must have a lot to sort out.'

Evan frowned, sure from the tone of her voice that Sarah *didn't* understand. And besides, apart from finding his passport, packing his suitcase, and dropping his car off at the garage, he didn't actually seem to have that much *to* sort out. Except this, of course. 'Well, there is one thing.'

'Evan, before you say anything, there's something I need to . . .'

'Whoa.' He reached up to wipe away the solitary tear that was running down her cheek, but Sarah had already turned away from him. 'What's the matter?'

'Don't.' She stared out of the window, though Evan suspected it wasn't to marvel at the view. 'Please.'

'Right. Sorry.' He glanced over towards the bar. 'Would you like something to drink?'

'Bourbon.'

'Are you serious?'

'Do I look like I'm joking?'

'No,' he said. 'You don't.' He took her by the hand, and when she didn't pull away, felt a glimmer of hope.

'I'm sorry,' she said, her lower lip trembling. 'It's just . . .'

Evan stroked the back of her hand with his thumb, readying himself to ask her. After all, if it was him leaving that she was upset about, then what better way to try and put that right? But just as he was preparing his announcement, Sarah turned to face him.

'I'm seeing someone.'

'Seeing someone?' He pulled his hand away and stared at her, open-mouthed, feeling like he'd been punched in the stomach. 'Who?'

'Someone else.'

'What?' he whispered, though more for something to say than because he hadn't heard properly. 'Where . . .'

'Someone from work.'

'From *work*? What's his name?'

'His name's David.'

'But . . .' He narrowed his eyes, unable to make sense of things. 'The other night . . .'

'Was lovely. But a mistake. Especially now that you're leaving.'

Evan ignored her attempt to turn the conversation back to the tour. 'How long have you been seeing him?'

'Does it really matter?'

Yes, he wanted to shout. 'I suppose not. And when were you going to tell *me*?'

'I just did,' said Sarah, quietly.

'Are you in . . .? I mean, do you . . .?' Evan couldn't bring himself to use the word. 'I don't understand. At the club. And then yesterday. Why did you . . .?'

'I'm sorry. It's . . . well, it's kind of how dating works in the U.S.'

'We're not *in* the U.S.' Evan stared at her in disbelief. 'But what about *us*?'

'Is there an "us", Evan? Would there ever have been?'

'Well, I thought . . .'

'With you away for a *year*?' She rolled her eyes, then sighed. 'Come on. You can't be that surprised. What did you think would happen?'

'I'm sorry, Sarah. I'm just . . .' He stopped talking, and instead, simply shook his head, and as Sarah looked at him, Evan recognised the pain in her eyes. Because he was feeling it too.

'Disappointed?' she said, and he felt that might just qualify for the most obvious statement of the year award.

'Of course I am. Because this – *us* – has to end.'

Sarah turned back to the view, and took another deep breath. 'Yes,' she said, eventually. 'It does.'

And at that point, if he hadn't before, Evan understood that saying anything else, asking her what he'd been planning to, was pointless. More importantly, more painfully, he realised something else.

That he and Sarah were over. Before they'd had a chance to begin.

PART TWO

NOW...

13

'van?' Sarah breathed his name as if it was the answer to a question she wasn't sure she'd got right. 'Fuck me!'

'I was going to suggest a coffee, but if that's what you'd . . .' Evan stopped talking abruptly. Judging by her expression, Sarah evidently hadn't found his attempt at humour funny. His heart was pounding so loudly he was sure she'd be able to hear it, and not knowing what else to do, he leaned in to plant a kiss on her cheek, revelling in the soft feel of her skin, her scent provoking a euphoric crackling through his senses like the first hit of a relapsed addict.

'What are you doing here?'

'Well, I needed some milk, and . . .'

'Not here in Waitrose, Evan. In *London*.'

Sarah hadn't returned the kiss, though he took some comfort from the fact that she hadn't pulled away or, as he'd originally feared, slapped him, but as she reached up to touch the place where his lips had just been, as if unable to believe what had just happened, Evan couldn't help notice the huge diamond on her engagement ring.

'I'm, you know, *back*,' he said, smiling broadly. The moment he'd seen her, he'd known with an absolute clarity that coming home was the right thing to do, and that Sarah was the woman he wanted to spend the rest of his life with. Although given how the look on her face had changed so quickly from astonishment to what he hoped wasn't anger, and the way she was gripping a bottle of

Chardonnay rather menacingly by the neck, he wondered whether the rest of his life might not actually last that long.

'But you didn't think to let me know you were coming? And now, of all the times . . .'

There it was. The first reference to next Saturday's wedding. 'Well . . .'

'Then again, why should I have expected you to?' she interrupted. 'After all, I had to find out from someone else that you were going.'

Immediately, Evan felt guilty, even though arguably he was the injured party, although he could appreciate why Sarah might not see things in the same way. 'I thought you understood?' he said, wincing as she almost threw the bottle of wine into her shopping trolley. 'Opportunities like that don't come round very often. And so when they do, you've just got to go with them . . .' He stopped talking again, realising he could just as easily be referring to David's proposal, and in his defence, she hadn't told him before accepting that.

He shifted the shopping basket containing the bottle of Moët he'd been planning to doorstep her with later into his other hand, its cargo suddenly seeming a little inappropriate, and reached out to touch her arm, but before he could launch into the speech he'd rehearsed on the plane and say that, actually, he'd come back for *her*, Sarah's eyes darted to somewhere over his shoulder.

'Don't,' she warned, taking a half-step away from him. 'I'm . . . David and I, we're . . .'

As the words died in Sarah's throat, Evan pulled his hand back hurriedly and wheeled round to see David striding along the aisle towards them, barking into his mobile phone. At least, he assumed it was David; Evan had only seen his photograph, yet he knew it had to be him. He'd met City boys before, and this one seemed like a prime example, his brisk manner matching his weekend attire –

the impeccably laundered chinos and tucked-in, erect-collared rugby-shirt combination that seemed to be the City's standard off-duty uniform. Though given the animated way he was gesticulating as he talked, David didn't look at all off-duty.

As Evan wondered whether it was too late to duck behind the stacked boxes of special-offer German lager piled high in the middle of the aisle, David caught sight of the two of them. Ending his call abruptly, he marched over to where they were standing and snaked a protective arm around Sarah's shoulders.

'Sweetheart?'

Evan smiled, despite himself. The endearment was phrased like a question, and while clearly directed at Sarah, David was looking him up and down, perhaps trying to work out what someone who so obviously *didn't* own an iron was doing talking to his fiancée.

'David,' said Sarah, a little unnecessarily, and Evan wondered whether it was perhaps for his benefit. 'You remember me mentioning my friend Evan?'

'Evan? Of course,' announced David, although not altogether convincingly. He removed his arm from Sarah's shoulders and peered at Evan closely, as if studying his face for clues. 'You're the musician, aren't you?'

Evan tried hard not to look surprised. 'That's right.'

David's palm came suddenly towards his face, and Evan's first thought was to duck, but it was only after David grabbed and shook the hand he'd raised to protect himself that he understood David was attempting some hip 'down-with-the-kids' handshake – though the gesture came across more like he'd just scored a goal at polo.

'Lovely to meet you,' said David, with what sounded like genuine warmth in his voice – at least compared to Sarah's earlier frostiness.

'And you.'

'Sarah mentioned you'd been . . .' David thought for a second, then gave a little shake of his head, as if it was too full of important banking-related stuff to have bothered storing any more than Evan's basic details. 'Overseas?'

'That's right.' Evan smiled at David's quaint turn of phrase, interested to hear he'd been a topic of conversation between the two of them – not that Sarah was saying much about anything at the moment. 'I've just got back. From the U.S.'

'The U.S.?' David let out a short laugh. 'No-one calls it "America" any more. Not even this one, and she's from there.' He put his arm back around Sarah and gave her a squeeze. 'Why is that, do you suppose?'

Evan scratched his head thoughtfully. 'It saves a syllable, I guess.'

'It's like "the U.K." No-one says "Great Britain" any more either.'

'Maybe because it's not that great,' suggested Sarah.

'Was that why you left?' David asked him.

'Something like that,' said Evan, then he corrected himself. 'Actually, I've been away on tour.'

'On tour?'

'With The Police.'

'The Police?'

'For a year.'

'For a *year*?'

As Evan wondered whether he was repeating everything on purpose, David nodded slowly, sticking his bottom lip out at the same time to indicate he was impressed. Then suddenly, he frowned. 'I thought they'd split up?'

'They had.' Evan tried to make eye contact with Sarah, but failed. 'They decided to get back together.'

'Oh yes?' David smirked. 'For the money, I'll bet. One last chance to top up the old pension funds.'

'I'm sure they had lots of reasons.'

'Several million of them, probably.' David shook his head slowly. 'When it comes down to it, people *always* do things for the money. What other reason is there?'

'The love of something, perhaps?' Evan suggested, conscious he was still staring at Sarah.

'Really?' said David, incredulously. 'So, a year, eh? And are you back for good now?'

Evan shrugged. He didn't know the answer to that yet. 'That depends,' he said, hoping David wouldn't ask him on what, but fortunately Sarah chose that moment to finally stop studying whatever it was in her trolley that had been fascinating her.

'When did you get back?' she said.

'What's today?'

David consulted the expensive-looking chunk of metal on his wrist. 'The twenty-third.'

'No – what *day* is it?'

David checked his watch again. 'Saturday.'

'In that case, last night. Possibly. I'm still a bit jet-lagged, to tell the truth.'

David reached into Evan's basket and tapped the bottle of Moët: Sarah's favourite – or at least, Evan thought, it used to be. 'Well, this should sort you out. Though I thought that Cristal stuff was what you musician-types drank.'

'You're talking rap.'

David's eyes widened. 'No need to be rude. I was only . . .'

'No, rap music. I'm a jazz musician.' He glanced at Sarah, who looked ready to make a run for it, as if worried his presence here might provoke some sort of showdown. And while that was actually what Evan was hoping for, he didn't want it quite so soon. Not until he'd had a chance to explain, and to tell her what he hadn't realised when he'd left – that he loved her. Then all he had to do was to convince her to dump David and marry him instead – and given that today *was* Saturday, he needed to achieve all that in less than a week.

'So,' said David, clapping Evan so heavily on the shoulder it nearly made him drop his basket. 'You'll be here for the wedding?'

'The wedding?' Evan thought for a moment, then nodded. He supposed he was. Though, of course, to stop it. 'I guess.'

'Excellent!' David grinned. 'In that case, what are you doing this evening?'

'Well, nothing. I mean, um . . .' He coughed awkwardly, suddenly worried David was going to invite him round for dinner, and unable to think of anything worse. While he'd wanted to see the two of them together to check whether Sarah was happy – after all, David was bound to be; look what he was getting – he hadn't planned to head straight into the lion's den. And even though he'd promised himself on the flight over that he'd back off if she was, he'd known the moment he'd seen her it was a promise he wouldn't be able to keep. 'Why?'

'It's my stag night. Soho House for cocktails and dinner, and then . . .' He nudged Sarah, then winked at Evan. 'Who knows? But you should come.'

Evan suddenly realised there *was* something worse than a cosy tête-à-tête with the two of them. But while it was an offer he hadn't been prepared for, judging by the way the colour had drained so quickly from Sarah's face, she certainly wasn't.

'Thanks, David, but I'll pass. I won't really know anyone, and . . .'

'You'll know me.' David folded his arms and regarded Evan levelly, almost challenging him to accept. 'And you know the girl

WHAT MIGHT HAVE BEEN

I'm marrying, of course. Not that she's coming. No women allowed. Apart from the ones that charge by the hour, if you see what I mean?'

Evan stared at him, the idea of the kind of evening David and his City-boy friends were evidently planning repellent to him, but before he could come up with a better excuse, Sarah found her voice again.

'David, Evan's just got back. I'm sure he doesn't want . . .'

David held up a finger to cut her off, and the gesture clearly annoyed her. 'Eight o'clock?' he said, more of a statement than a question. 'Dress . . .' He glanced at Evan's worn leather jacket, no doubt seeing second-hand instead of vintage. 'Well, it's supposed to be formal dress, but like I said, as long as you're not *wearing* a dress, you'll be okay.'

Evan smiled politely at David's joke. 'I'm not sure it's my kind of thing.'

'Oh? Don't worry. It's on me.'

Evan felt himself start to bristle, but managed to bite his tongue – after all, he reasoned, David probably reckoned he was doing him a favour. Besides, why should he feel too proud to take advantage of David's hospitality? He was planning to take an awful lot more if he could. And even though it occurred to him that David out on his stag night meant the coast would be clear for him and Sarah to talk, maybe going tonight might provide some inside track on the wedding, or even help him understand David a little more, show him what he was up against. Besides, judging by Sarah's reaction so far, he wasn't sure she *wanted* to talk.

'In that case, how can I refuse?' he said, before tipping an imaginary cap. 'Gawd bless yer, guv'nor.'

As Sarah stifled a smile – something Evan noted with more than a little relief – David looked at him strangely, either not getting the reference, or perhaps beginning to doubt the wisdom of his invitation. 'Eight o'clock *sharp*, then,' he said, emphasising the time by tapping the face of his watch. 'You know where Soho House is, I take it?'

Evan swallowed the obvious answer – and a little bit more of his pride – and nodded. 'I think I'll be able to find it.'

'Super.'

The three of them stood there awkwardly until, as if on some inaudible signal, David grabbed hold of Sarah with one hand, the trolley with the other, and began to steer them both towards the checkouts.

'Well,' he said. 'See you later.'

'Yeah. See you later,' said Evan, and as Sarah mumbled her farewell, he hoped she'd realise his statement was directed at her too.

He watched them walk away, willing Sarah to turn round, telling himself that if she maybe just gave him the slightest of smiles, then there was some hope for them, a chance that his journey back across the Atlantic would have been worth it. But when they reached the end of the aisle, it was David who quickly glanced back at him.

And Evan couldn't help wondering if that meant the exact opposite.

14

Evan spent the next five minutes in the magazine aisle, pretending to flick through the latest issue of *NME* while actually peering through the supermarket's huge glass window and watching David load his shopping into the boot of a large black BMW.

He ducked down behind the magazine as Sarah glanced briefly back towards the store before climbing into the driver's side, and wondered for a moment whether it was perhaps her car, but quickly dismissed the thought. She wasn't a 'large black BMW' kind of girl – or at least, she hadn't been a year ago. And besides, the way that David had casually tossed her the keys and how she was having to adjust the driver's seat and mirror, suggested otherwise, as did the car's personalised number plate – B4NKR.

As Sarah reversed out of the parking space and drove past the other side of the window, he ducked down again, an uneasy feeling in the pit of his stomach, and while that was partly due to the dread of what tonight might have in store, he knew it was more down to Sarah's reaction – or perhaps lack of it – upon seeing him.

'Are you going to pay for that?'

'Probably,' said Evan, before realising the scowling shop assistant who'd just materialised at his elbow was referring to the now-crumpled magazine he was holding, and not the evening he'd just committed to with David and his no-doubt-identical friends. 'I mean, yeah. Sorry.'

He waited till the assistant had gone, then hid the magazine behind a copy of *What Car?*, put the Moet back on the shelf, and made his way towards the exit, trying unsuccessfully to stifle a yawn. Dealing with the jet lag was already proving difficult enough without the prospect of a late night, and Evan wondered whether he should perhaps go home to bed, but time wasn't a luxury he had, so instead, he headed out of the store and down towards the river, striding purposefully across Tower Bridge and towards Bermondsey, drinking in the vibrant atmosphere, happy to be back. He loved this part of London, the vitality of the people, the new-found energy of the streets – in the year or so before he'd left, almost every time he'd walked out of his front door it had seemed some new, exotic restaurant had opened up, or a shop selling the kind of thing that you suddenly wanted despite not quite understanding what it was had taken over from some failing former business. Now Bermondsey Street was almost completely transformed: a Vietnamese sandwich bar sat next to yet another new estate agent's; the Garrison pub on the corner of Tanner Street now sported a sign advertising 'film nights' every weekend, whereas until recently 'fight nights' would have been more appropriate. He was pleased to see Al's – the greasy spoon café and a Bermondsey institution, where he'd occasionally go to see off his hangovers with a full English – was still there, although if he were a betting man, he wouldn't give it long.

Turning right up Long Lane, he began the five-minute walk towards Borough, hoping a stroll in the late-spring sunshine might kick-start his sluggish system. As was usual for a Saturday morning, the streets around the market were throbbing with a mix of wide-eyed tourists, trendy South-Londoners and well-heeled City boys, the latter desperate for the over-priced Foccacia and expensive selection of obscure cheeses that they bought every

weekend, no doubt feeling that this marked them out as sophisti-
cates, whereas Evan knew the stallholders, unable to believe their
luck that people would pay these exorbitant prices, saw them
simply as marks.

He walked past a stall which sold fancy French bread by the
kilo and winced at the cost, wondering whether it might not be
cheaper to actually hop on the Eurostar train to France to buy a
loaf, yet the ridiculously high price hadn't stopped a queue forming. But Evan wasn't surprised; enough people lived around here
now with the kind of money to afford this sort of thing. People like
David, for example. And he couldn't resent it. He'd never have met
Sarah if they didn't.

Besides, David and his ilk all lived in Shad Thames, the
hyper-desirable area just east of Tower Bridge, or in one of the
expensive warehouse conversions that dotted the South Bank
between there and the Tate Modern and gave them easy access
into the City by day and across the river to Covent Garden at
night. Evan, on the other hand, lived at the Bermondsey end
of SE1. Just far enough from the river that he could afford the
mortgage on his one-bedroom flat on his musician's wages, yet
not so close to Elephant and Castle that he felt he was going to
get mugged on his way home every night. He'd bought it ten
years ago, back when his career had been on a high and prop-
erty prices had been low, as nobody had wanted to live south
of the river – nobody pretentious, at least – and certainly no-
one had been brave enough to live *south of* south of the river.
But Bermondsey was trendy now, at least according to a piece
in *The Evening Standard* he'd read on the tube coming in from
Heathrow the previous day. Whether he still belonged here if
that was true, Evan hadn't quite made his mind up, but as he
looked up at the new Shard development towering above him,

he felt strangely proud of how much it had grown in a year, and realised he was pleased he was home. Even though Sarah hadn't seemed to share the sentiment.

He wondered whether he was crazy to come back for her, and an idea occurred to him – the memory of a distant conversation – so Evan quickened his pace and, two minutes later, found himself in Guy's Hospital's waiting room. He peered around the brightly lit interior, hoping that Grace was on duty, careful not to stand too close to anyone – he could never afford to get ill, literally, given his no-play, no-pay occupation, but fortunately, it didn't take him long to spot her. She looked different at work, her long blonde hair scraped back into a pony-tail, the petite but curvy figure he'd had to stop himself from gawping at when he'd met her in Sarah's kitchen hidden by the shapeless green scrubs she was wearing. He found it strange to see her in her junior doctor's garb. It almost didn't suit her, as if she were wearing it for a fancy dress party.

'Grace,' he called, and she looked up distractedly from the clipboard she'd been studying.

'Yes?'

'Hello again.'

She blinked at him uncomprehendingly. 'Do we know each other?'

'Would it help if I was holding a tea towel over my, you know . . .' He pointed both index fingers towards his groin, then watched in horror as Grace's eyes flicked towards the security guard in the corner. 'Don't you remember? You asked me if I had a problem with my bits, and . . . No, hang on, that's worse. Um . . .'

To his relief, Grace's eyes widened in recognition, though they quickly narrowed. 'Evan, right?'

'Sorry – I shouldn't have expected you to recognise me.'

'Don't tell me – with your clothes on?'

'No, I meant since we'd only met the once, but now you mention it . . .'

'What are you doing here?'

'Well, I owed you a tea towel, and I wanted to check what design you wanted before I went to John Lewis and . . .'

'Seriously, Evan.'

For a moment, he considered launching straight into his explanation, then thought better about it, so instead, just repeated the answer he'd given Sarah earlier.

'I'm back.'

'Back?'

Evan frowned at her. Surely Sarah had at least told Grace where he'd been, and why he'd left so suddenly. Though perhaps not, if she *had* just regarded him as a one-night stand. 'I've been away. In the U.S.'

'So I heard.' Grace regarded him suspiciously. 'Does Sarah know?'

'That I'm back? Yes. *Why* I'm back, no. At least, not yet. I just bumped into her, funnily enough. In Waitrose. But she was with, you know . . .'

'Her fiancé?'

Evan swallowed hard. 'Well, David, yeah. Which, if you've got a moment, is kind of what I wanted to talk to you about.'

'David?'

'Yeah. Well, no. More about me and Sarah, in fact.'

'Is there a "you and Sarah"?'

Evan stared at the floor, as if hoping to see his next line written on that, although all he seemed to find there was an instruction to blush furiously. 'Okay. About Sarah, then. And whether she's happy. With him, I mean.'

Grace shrugged. 'I'll ask her for you tonight when she gets home from spending the day with him like she does most Saturdays, shall I? Or perhaps it might be better if I quiz her for you later at her hen night? Although seeing *as* it's her hen night, which unless I'm very much mistaken is an event that typically happens before someone's wedding, and a wedding isn't something you usually have unless you're happy with the person you're marrying, I'd think it was safe to assume so. Wouldn't you?'

'Well, not necessarily.'

'Didn't you hear what I said? She's . . .'

'Getting married?' Evan forced the words out. It wasn't getting any less painful to admit, perhaps because it was becoming more of a reality by the day. 'Yeah. Which, like I said, is what I, you know, wanted to . . .' His voice began to crack, and he had to clear his throat. 'Discuss.'

Grace's face went through a series of complicated expressions, finally settling on indignation. 'Don't tell me *that's* why you came back?'

'Well, yeah. That, and the fact that I, um . . .' He swallowed even harder. 'Love her.'

'Christ, Evan. Of all the . . .' Grace folded her arms, opened her mouth as if to say something else, then shut it again, and Evan couldn't help wondering why she seemed so hostile.

'Please, Grace. Just give me five minutes?'

'Why should I?'

'Well, because . . .' It was a good question, and he was stumped as to how to finish the sentence.

'I'm sorry, Evan, but this is a hospital, and I've got an afternoon of back-to-back psychiatric appraisals.' She indicated the waiting room full of patients, some of whom were watching their exchange with interest. 'You don't just march in here and . . .'

'Can't you just pretend I'm, you know . . .' He lowered his voice. 'Nuts?'

Grace stared at him for a moment, then shook her head slowly, before heading off down the corridor towards a set of doors marked 'Staff Only'. Though as she glanced back at him over her shoulder, her expression implied she'd already decided that was the case.

15

Sarah piloted the BMW along Tower Bridge Road, her eyes firmly fixed on the car in front. She hadn't dared look back down the aisle at Evan, not just because David had been there, but more because she'd had such a hard time putting him out of her mind this past year. Mel had suggested the Police tour might lead to other things, that he'd maybe even stay in the U.S., and she'd fully expected never to see him again, but just when she thought she might be beginning to forget him, here he was again, *and* right before she was due to get married, for Christ's sake.

Sure it couldn't be a coincidence, she glanced across at David, wondering how it was possible to fall in love with two such different people, then she corrected herself. It couldn't have been love with Evan – not when they'd known each other for so little time. No, it had been more of an infatuation, whereas with David, perhaps to her surprise, she'd grown to love him. She shook her head to try and clear her thoughts, causing David to look up momentarily from the message he was composing on his phone, and her heart started racing again at the fear she might be found out. *Pull yourself together*, she told herself. In just one week, she'd be Mrs. Sarah Cook, then she could relax.

Sarah repeated the name under her breath as she drove towards Shad Thames. *Cook.* A good, solid, dependable name, much like the person who was giving it to her. Whereas Sarah *McCarthy* . . . She smiled ruefully as she turned into David's road – as if *that* had ever been an option.

The interior of the car suddenly felt stifling, so she cracked the window open a little, reaching over to switch the climate control off before David could do it. She hated driving his car, or rather, hated the way he liked to 'help' whenever she did, but she'd insisted, as she did most Saturday mornings. The alternative was to grip the edge of her seat tightly as David steered the 5-Series with one hand and thumbed through last night's emails on his ever-present Blackberry with the other, and she didn't need the stress today – especially after what had just happened.

She pressed the button on the remote that opened the imposing metal gates guarding the enclave where David's riverside flat was and carefully steered the huge car through, then squeezed the BMW into the parking space underneath his building and waited for him to notice they'd arrived. Eventually, he glanced up from his phone and did a double-take at the view through the windscreen, seemingly surprised by their location, as if he'd somehow been magically transported from the supermarket.

'We here, then?'

Sarah switched the engine off. 'That'll be a tenner, mate.'

'Pardon? Oh, right. Like in a taxi. Very good.'

'Thanks,' said Sarah, sarcastically. David didn't always get her jokes, and even when he recognised she was making one, his dissection of it afterwards tended to ruin the moment.

'Seems like a nice chap,' said David, distractedly.

Sarah cleared her throat awkwardly. 'Who?' she said, immediately fearing she'd given the whole game away with that one word.

'Your friend Evan.' David was still focussed on his Blackberry, and for once, Sarah was grateful for the intrusive little device.

'He is. Was. I mean, I haven't seen him for ages, obviously.'

'Where do you know him from again?'

She stared straight ahead through the windscreen. 'He plays – well, played – at that club under the arches near London Bridge Station. The G-Spot. It's a jazz club,' she added, quickly.

'Ah yes.' David reached down and unbuckled his seatbelt. 'Jazz.' Sarah hated the way he pronounced the word: It sounded facetious, as if he was reciting the name of a particular food he had an aversion to. He knew about her father, of course, but despite this, David had never quite accepted her musical tastes, and while he knew the music was important to her, it remained something he just didn't get, preferring to play the kind of middle-of-the-road, middle-aged music on his state-of-the-art hi-fi that quite frankly turned her stomach. Then again, Sarah knew she couldn't expect them to be compatible on every level.

'Still,' he continued. 'It must be nice to see him again?'

'Yes,' she said, although part of her felt the complete opposite. 'You didn't have to invite him to your stag night, though,' she added, harshly.

'Well, it's done now.'

David sounded a little hurt, and Sarah immediately felt awful. He'd probably thought he was doing her a favour. Looking to the future. Trying to turn one of her friends into one of theirs. Though while she could understand why David had extended the invitation, she was clueless as to why Evan had accepted – unless he was planning to spill the beans about the two of them. Maybe he'd get drunk, and . . . She took a deep breath and told herself Evan wasn't like that. Not vindictive. And certainly not indiscreet; she'd learned that about him even in the short time they'd spent together.

'I'm sorry,' she said. 'I didn't mean it like that. It was very nice of you.'

David shrugged. 'I'm a nice guy,' he said, as he got stiffly out of the car. 'And anyway, he might not turn up.'

'No,' said Sarah, hoping that was the case.

'He didn't seem all that keen, for some reason.'

She pushed her door open and stepped out of the BMW, wishing she could leave the conversation as easily. 'Maybe he was just a bit jet-lagged,' she said, desperate to provide David with an answer, even though she wasn't sure he'd asked a question.

'Maybe. It's a tiring flight. Especially if you don't do it in business.'

Sarah bit off her reply as she headed round to the back of the car and popped the boot open. David made these assumptions about everyone – even her, sometimes – though it was just the world he was used to, and besides, she knew she shouldn't feel offended on Evan's behalf. She hefted the shopping out and handed David a couple of the bags, and together they made their way towards the elevator, accompanied as they walked by the clinking of his usual purchase of half a dozen bottles of wine – a week's supply.

'So . . .' David pressed the 'call' button, then smiled at her. 'You coming up?'

She shook her head as she lowered the carrier bags carefully to the floor. Despite David's repeated requests, they still didn't live together, Sarah preferring to keep their arrangements separate until the last possible moment. 'I ought to get home,' she said, passing him the car keys. 'I've still got a bit to do to get the apartment ready for this evening.'

'Of course. Your big hen night.' He glanced at his watch. 'You'd better get going. Those crisps won't jump into bowls on their own.'

Sarah poked him firmly in the stomach. 'No need to be sarcastic.'

He grinned, then prodded the button again, as if the action would hasten the lift's arrival. 'I don't know why you didn't want to go out somewhere nice instead. I'd have paid.'

'David, for the millionth time, I've got my own money. I just wanted something a bit more sophisticated than the rowdy evening of debauchery you've probably got planned.'

'Sophisticated? The girls coming round to get roaring drunk on Cosmopolitans?'

'It's the American way.'

'Sounds riveting.'

'Fuck off.'

David couldn't prevent his jaw dropping open. Even after a year together he wasn't used to her occasional profanities, and the shock on his face every time she cursed still made her smile.

'I'm only teasing you,' he said, handing her back the car keys. 'Here.'

'What's this – an early wedding present? You shouldn't have.'

David laughed. 'I'm not going to need the Beamer again today. Plus, the amount I'm planning to drink tonight, it's probably best I don't drive tomorrow either. You keep it round at your place.'

'Sure,' said Sarah, grateful she wouldn't have to walk home. This thing that the English called 'springtime' could be as cold as some of the worst Manhattan winters, and she still wasn't used to what seemed to be the ever-present grey skies overhead. The seasons were something she missed; in New York, there were four distinct ones, but here, it seemed to be permanently cold and rainy, punctuated by the occasional sunny day in July – and she meant 'occasional'. Though, she reminded herself, she hadn't come here for the weather.

A *ping* announced the elevator's arrival, and David half stepped inside, jamming one foot against the door to stop it closing. 'Well, have fun tonight,' he said. 'And don't do anything I wouldn't do.'

Sarah fought the urge to raise one eyebrow. 'You too,' she said, standing up on tiptoe to peck him on the cheek. 'I'll call you in the morning.'

David looked horrified. 'Better make that the afternoon. Late afternoon, in fact. We might go on somewhere after dinner. You know how the guys are.'

Sarah rolled her eyes – she knew exactly how the guys were. She smiled, stopped herself from saying something inappropriate like 'Look after Evan' and instead saluted smartly. 'Duly noted.'

She walked back over to the BMW, then turned and watched David struggle into the elevator with all his shopping. He was a member of a gym; they all were, at work – one of the perks of the job. But David had visited it the once, decided exercising was something that would only cut into his valuable after-work drinking time, and so had resolved never to go there again. Since then, walking to the pub was about the only exercise she'd managed to get him to take, and even that was generally accompanied by his insistence they flag down what he called the 'black buses' that cruised round the city for the five-minute journey back. As a consequence, he was starting to look a little paunchy, but Sarah told herself she could work on that once they were married. Although she'd decided not to tell David that just yet.

Clambering into the driving seat, she waved at her fiancé through the closing elevator doors, trying – and failing – not to compare him to Evan. In the few moments she'd allowed herself to steal a glance at him earlier, she'd noticed how good he looked; a little fitter, if anything, and ashamedly, she still felt the twinges of lust that had attracted her to him in the first place.

She waited until the numbers on the digital display above the elevator door had begun to climb upwards, then fished her mobile out of her handbag, wondering whether she should call him and ask him not to go this evening. She still hadn't deleted his number from her speed-dial, where it had been secretly stored under 'gynaecologist' – somewhere she was sure David would never look – but as she stared at her contacts list, she stopped herself. He might not have the same mobile number – a lot of things could change over the course of a year – and besides, what would she say?

Perhaps she should warn him about what he was letting himself in for. Sarah worked with most of the other invitees, and didn't think they'd be Evan's 'cup of tea', to use that quaint English expression. And while she didn't really think Evan would let on about the two of them, she wondered what would happen if David *did* find out. Surely he wouldn't call the wedding off at this late stage. He'd be too wary of what other people would think.

Her thumb hovered over the 'dial' button, but she couldn't bring herself to press it. Just thinking about Evan made her feel, well, 'giddy' was the best that she could come up with, and Sarah almost laughed at how she couldn't quite describe the sensation without sounding like a character from a Mills & Boon novel – and that wasn't a position to make rational decisions from.

But something other than the fact he was back was worrying her. Evan had seemed as if he'd been preparing to make some announcement. Maybe he'd been about to say that he'd come back for *her*, Sarah realised with a start, and she wasn't sure how she'd feel if that were the case.

The more she thought about it, the more she realised she was going to have to confront him – and soon. She needed to tell him in no uncertain terms that whatever they had was in the past, and if he *had* come back for her, well, he was too late. She *was* getting married next Saturday. To David.

Grace's number was just above 'gynaecologist' on her phone's contact list, but she'd be at work, and while she'd know what to do, Sarah didn't like to interrupt her on duty. Besides, they'd have a chance to talk at her hen night later.

With a sigh, Sarah slipped her phone reluctantly back into her bag, started the car, and headed slowly home.

16

Evan turned his collar up against the chill wind that seemed to have started the moment he left the hospital, and began the short walk back towards Bermondsey Street, trying desperately to analyse his brief conversation with Grace. He couldn't work out why she'd seemed so angry with him, almost as if she assumed he'd given Sarah the old slept-with-once, never-called-again routine – but surely she'd have told Grace that hadn't been the case? Though while Sarah hadn't seemed that happy to see him either, she also hadn't seemed that happy, *full stop*. Admittedly, Saturday morning supermarket shopping was never the most fun of activities, but surely doing anything with your fiancé a week before your wedding should at least put a smile on your face?

He realised he might be clutching at straws. Trying to see problems where there weren't any. But straws were all he had at the moment, and as he hurried along Tanner Street, he realised he'd grab frantically onto as many as he could if it gave him the slightest chance of getting Sarah back.

Passing the funky new warehouse conversions that overlooked the viaduct, he rounded the corner into Riley Road and walked into the old factory building. As usual, he unleashed a quick Rocky-like one-two combination as he passed the punch-bag that Mick, the car park's owner, had hung up next to the toilets, then rubbed his knuckles as he weaved his way through the selection of Ferraris and

Aston Martins that the City boys didn't dare park on Bermondsey's streets. Even before he'd gone to the States, Evan had begun parking here overnight too, after some scary-looking teenagers had removed the badge from the Mercedes' bonnet one evening outside his flat, then tried to sell it back to him with menaces the next day.

He reached the white-painted six-by-four shed that served as an office and spied Mick sitting inside, reading the paper, so he rapped loudly on the door-frame.

'Afternoon.'

'Bleedin' Nora!' Mick threw his copy of *The Sun* on his desk and stood up. 'Look who it isn't!'

Evan smiled. Mick always spoke like he was auditioning for a Guy Ritchie movie – which made him a rarity nowadays in this part of London. 'Nice to see you too,' he said.

'Released you early, did they?'

Mick was looking him up and down, and Evan nodded. 'Time off for good behaviour,' he said, playing along with the joke.

'Christ on a bike!' Mick clapped him on the shoulder. 'How was it?'

'Fine. Good, actually.'

'Good? But it must have been tough, yeah? Being, you know, *away* for so long?'

Evan shrugged. In truth, the only tough part had been being away from Sarah. 'A bit.'

'A bit?' Mick widened his eyes. 'I ain't sure I could have done it.'

Evan frowned. He couldn't remember telling Mick what it was he'd been doing for the past year, partly because he hadn't wanted to sound like he was bragging, but particularly because he didn't want him to charge through the nose for looking after the car, though maybe word had gotten around.

'It had its moments.'

'I geddit.' Mick tapped the side of his nose with his index finger. 'You don't want to talk about it.'

'I don't mind. It's not as glamorous as you might think, though.'

'Glamorous?'

Mick looked confused, and Evan laughed. 'Yeah. Basically all you're doing is staring at the guys' backsides every evening, thankful that they let you play with them. Then, as long as you remember to blow when you're supposed to . . .' He stopped talking, as Mick had taken a half-step backwards.

'What was it you did?' he asked, eventually.

'I played the sax.'

'And they gave you a year for that?'

Evan stared at him. Maybe it was the jet lag, but they seemed to be talking at cross-purposes. 'Where do you think I've been, exactly?'

Mick shrugged. 'That bloke you used to 'ang around with mentioned something about the police, and that you'd be gone for a year. He seemed pretty pissed off about you being, like I said, *away*, so I didn't want to ask.'

'What bloke?'

'The bald geezer. Owns that jazz club under the arches.'

'Mel?'

'That's the fellah.'

'And you assumed I was in *prison*?'

Mick stuffed his hands into his pockets. 'Nuffink to be ashamed of. We've all done a bit of time in our, you know, *time*.'

Evan shook his head in disbelief. 'I was away on tour, Mick. In the U.S. I'm a musician.'

'Oh. Right.' Mick nodded slowly. 'The *Police*. Not the, er . . .' He cleared his throat, obviously keen to change the subject. 'So, you'll be wanting 'er back, then?'

Evan did a double take, before realising Mick must be referring to the Merc. He'd never known why cars like his were always referred to in the feminine. *Maybe it was because they were high maintenance*, Mel had suggested once.

'Yeah. Have you been taking good care of it? I mean, *her*?'

Mick looked mortally offended. 'Of course.'

'And taking her for a spin?'

He nodded. 'Once a week, like clockwork. Just, you know, round the block, an' that.'

From the shifty look on Mick's face, Evan supposed that the odd trip might have been a little more than round the block, but he didn't want to ask what 'and that' had actually involved. Mick had been doing him a favour, and as long as a blurred picture of the car speeding away from a bank robbery hadn't appeared on *Crimewatch* in his absence, he knew he ought to be grateful.

'Great. Thanks.'

'Don't mention it.' Mick picked up a clipboard, selected a bunch of keys from a hook inside the shed, then led Evan over to a space in the far corner occupied by a Mercedes-shaped tarpaulin. 'Ta-da!' he said, grabbing the corner and whipping the cover off like a game-show hostess.

Evan gazed at the gleaming chrome, the immaculate bodywork. The car still looked as good, even after a year. Just as Sarah had, he found himself thinking.

'Thanks, Mick. So, what's the damage?'

'Ain't no damage. Whaddaya take me for?'

'Sorry. No, I meant how much . . .' Evan saw Mick was joking and stopped talking.

'Well, how long you been . . .' Mick winked. '*Away* for?'

'A year, give or take.'

'A year. Right.' Mick peered at the clipboard, leafing through the attached A4 sheets, then frowned when he couldn't find any reference to Evan's car. 'What did we say again?'

'You said that if I let you take it for a drive once a week, you'd keep it here for free.'

For a moment, Mick seemed to be trying to remember whether that was actually the arrangement, then he let out a short laugh. 'Good one,' he said, pulling a pencil from behind his ear and licking the point. 'Well, normal rate's twelve quid a day.'

'Oh-kay . . .' Evan did a quick calculation in his head, and his stomach lurched – the car wasn't worth much more than the figure he came up with. 'So . . .'

Mick jotted some figures down on his clipboard. 'A monkey all right with you?'

'Mick, I'm sorry, I don't have my Cockney Rhyming Slang dictionary with me.'

'A monkey.' Mick rolled his eyes. 'Five hundred nicker.'

'And "nicker" would be "pounds", right?'

'Want me to check them figures again? Maybe I underestimated . . .'

'No. Sorry. That's great.' Evan grinned as he reached into his pocket and removed his wallet. 'Credit card OK?'

Mick laughed, even harder than before, then doubled over in a coughing fit. 'Pay me when you can,' he wheezed, his face a deep shade of purple.

He tossed Evan the keys, then started back towards his shed, but as Evan unlocked the car door and climbed into the driver's seat, Mick reappeared at the window.

'Oh yeah, I almost forgot. I saw that bird the other day.'

Evan looked up sharply. 'What, er, bird?'

'You know. The one I caught you playing tonsil tennis with in 'ere a while back. The Yank.'

'And?'

Mick shrugged. 'I've seen 'er a couple of times. Out with some ponce. Never looks that happy. And always seems disappointed when she clocks me behind the wheel and not you.' Mick sucked in his belly and puffed out his chest, then coughed violently as a result. 'Can't imagine why.'

Evan grinned, heartened slightly by Mick's observation. 'Neither can I.'

'You off to pick her up?'

Evan nodded as he turned the key and the engine rumbled into life. That was exactly what he was off to do.

He waved goodbye to Mick, then gunned the car out of the garage and into Tanner Street, enjoying being back behind the wheel. He'd bought the Mercedes on a whim when some session work he'd done for what he'd found out afterwards had been a porn soundtrack had unexpectedly paid him some royalties – not that he'd needed a car, and in truth, it was a bit of a liability in this part of London, but he'd seen it parked on Morocco Road one day, a handwritten 'For Sale' sign taped to the inside of the windscreen, and had fallen in love straight away. It was older than he was, but seemingly in better condition, its flawless white bodywork lovingly restored at great expense by one of the previous owners. The four-and-a-half-litre engine produced an almost musical note through its stainless-steel exhaust but drank petrol at an alarming rate, although to tell the truth, Evan hadn't given any of the technical specifications much thought. He'd simply liked what he'd seen, and for most of the major decisions he'd made in his life, that had always been enough.

And Evan had loved it – it was a cool car to cruise around London in, especially when he put the roof down, although he didn't dare do the same with his foot – he couldn't afford the fuel or the fines. What's more, he loved the reaction he got from other motorists; the appreciative glances, other drivers stopping to let him out into the traffic – everyone except BMW drivers, funnily enough – but then again, his car was a classic, and people appreciated something classic, whether it was a car, a piece of music, or a beautiful woman. Most importantly, Sarah had seemed to like it, and that fact alone had been enough of an incentive for Evan to keep it while he'd been away.

He hadn't driven for the best part of a year, and even though the London traffic was too stop-start for him to get out of second gear, as his confidence returned, he began throwing the car from lane to lane, and accelerating into gaps that were barely there. He toyed with the idea of putting the roof down, but in a car of this age that was a two-man job. Besides, it wasn't the warmest of days, and Evan always thought it was only ever posers who drove around in convertibles when the sun wasn't out.

By chance, he found himself at the end of Sarah's road and, on a whim, drove along it, wondering whether he should call in. He could tell her he'd been passing and had thought he'd drop by to 'shoot the breeze', as she might say, but he quickly decided against it: two instances in as many hours might be seen as stalking, plus he suspected she might need a little time to get used to the idea of him being back.

He spotted a parking space outside her flat and almost changed his mind, even slowing down to measure the Mercedes' length against it, until he noticed David's BMW parked in the adjacent bay. Suddenly panicked, he hunkered down behind the wheel and pressed his right foot flat to the floor, and as the car leapt forward, a red warning light flickered briefly on the dashboard.

And Evan couldn't help feeling that was strangely appropriate.

17

Sarah held her breath as she watched the Mercedes through her window, wondering whether Evan was stalking her. The roof was up, so she couldn't tell if it was him or the guy from the quaint old parking lot who spoke like some east-end mobster and who she'd seen driving it a couple of times this past year, but given what had happened earlier, it was surely too much of a coincidence that it should be driving down her road. She could only suspect that someone had been looking after it for him while he was away. Maybe he'd been assuming the same thing about her.

She half-hid behind a curtain as the car cruised slowly along her street, admiring the way the sun glinted off the polished chrome bumpers, and felt a surge of affection that surprised her. The first time she'd seen it after Evan had left, her heart had leapt and she'd found herself hoping he'd given up on the tour and come back home. In her excitement she'd nearly stepped out in front of it, almost forgetting David was with her, then the driver had noticed her staring, and she'd had to look away before he'd had a chance to pull over and talk to her. *That* would have been awkward.

She peered at the number plate, positive it was him. After all, there couldn't be that many white convertible Mercedes in this part of London – not old ones, at least. There weren't that many old vehicles, full stop, given the generous car allowances the banks tended to give their employees, and no-one she worked with would ever want to own the *oldest* car on the block.

Sarah had found Evan's obsession with his car charming, particularly in a country where the miserable climate meant you could hardly ever use a convertible anyway, though she could see why he loved it. Unlike David's BMW, which was like piloting a rocket-propelled armchair through the streets, the Merc had real character. She'd loved driving it that night, plus it looked cool, and most importantly, so had Evan when she'd seen him waiting outside her office before their lunch in Postman's Park, leaning against the fender like some fifties movie star.

But there had been something else too: For some reason, it had reminded her of home. Maybe the shape, maybe the size, but there was just something American about this German classic car – though it had taken her a while before she'd remembered what it was: Sue Ellen had driven one in *Dallas*, one of the rare happy memories she had about her mother from childhood, watching re-runs with her before she'd done a runner herself. When she'd remarked on this to Evan driving back that afternoon, he hadn't had a clue what she'd been talking about – or so he'd said. But he'd loved the car with a passion. And that was one of the things she'd really liked about him.

The Mercedes slowed outside her apartment building, and Sarah was surprised to find herself willing it to pull into the empty parking space behind David's BMW. Then she heard the engine rev loudly and it shot off down the road and out of sight, leaving a patch of oil on the road, and it was then that Sarah had known for sure it had been him. She stared out into the street for a few more moments, then moved away from the window. Had he lost the nerve to come in, perhaps worried that David might have been there? She couldn't be sure. But one thing she knew: she wasn't ready to face him yet. Not until she'd had a chance to think what his return meant. Or rather, what it meant to her.

The sound of the doorbell made her jump, and she rushed nervously back to the window, but there was no sign of the Mercedes in the street, so she made her way over to the video entry-phone, relaxing when she realised Grace had simply forgotten her keys. Was it going to be like this for the next few days, Sarah wondered, every time the buzzer went, or whenever her mobile rang? Was her heartbeat going to quicken at the possibility it might be Evan?

Cursing to herself, she let her flatmate in, wondering whether the disappointment she'd felt when she realised it *wasn't* him was significant.

'What's going on?' said Grace, unbuttoning her coat and throwing it onto the sofa.

'What do you mean?'

Grace rolled her eyes. 'You know what I mean. *Evan.*'

'What about him?'

'He came to see me at work. Said he wanted to talk.'

'What about?'

'You and David, of course.' Grace marched into the kitchen, though Sarah was close behind her. 'Though I'm guessing he really meant you and him.'

'What did he say?'

'I got the feeling he wanted me to help him.'

'Help him?'

'Get you back.'

Sarah caught her breath. So that *was* the reason he'd returned. 'He never really had me, Grace.'

Grace let out a short laugh. 'You and I both know that's not true,' she said, filling the kettle with one hand while simultaneously removing a couple of mugs from the cupboard with the other, and

Sarah leaned against the refrigerator and silently watched her friend make tea. It still struck her as odd that the British thought this drink was a necessary accompaniment to any serious conversation or stressful situation – back where she came from, it was more likely to be a Jack Daniels, and boy, could she do with one of those now.

'What am I going to do?' she said, as Grace placed a steaming mug on the table in front of her.

'Do?' Grace sat in the chair opposite, blowing on the top of her tea until it was cool enough to risk a sip, as if she couldn't contemplate the question until she'd had some. 'Were you in love with him?'

'How could I have been? We weren't together long enough to . . .'

'But you were considering leaving David for him?'

'That's not fair. David and I had only just started seeing each other.'

'Even so. You seemed pretty into Evan.'

'I . . . well, okay, I could see how I might have started to, you know, *develop* feelings for him, obviously.' Sarah stared into her mug, wondering when she should remove the fast-stewing teabag. The two of them had shared a flat for fourteen months, and Sarah hadn't ever had the heart to tell Grace she was more of a coffee girl. 'But I haven't seen him for a year. Besides, how can you love someone who you hardly know?'

Grace shrugged. 'He does.'

'What do you mean?'

'Evan loves someone he hardly knows.'

'How could you possibly think that?'

'He said.'

Sarah caught her breath. 'People say a lot of things,' she said, after a moment.

'I saw his face, Sarah. He meant it.'

'How could he possibly?' said Sarah, indignantly.

Grace held both hands up, as if at gunpoint. 'That's hardly for me to say, is it? But ask yourself something – what would you have done if Evan had stayed?'

Sarah warmed her hands on her mug as she thought about this. The truth was, she didn't know – couldn't imagine, even – what a normal relationship with Evan would have been like. The sex had been, well, *mind-blowing*, but even after such a brief time together, she suspected they had more than just a physical connection – they'd seemed to have a similar sense of humour; their shared love of jazz would have been something to explore . . .

'I don't know, Grace,' she said, unwilling to dwell upon what might have been. 'It never seemed like an option.'

'It is now.'

'Are you asking me or telling me?'

'I think you know the answer to that.'

Sarah slid her mug out of the way, then rested her elbows on the table and put her head in her hands. 'It's not as simple as that.'

'Well, maybe it should be.'

'It *can't*. Not with, you know, *Saturday*.'

Grace gave her a tight-lipped smile. 'What about David?'

'What about him?'

'I'm assuming you love him?'

'I guess so.'

'You *guess so*?' Grace raised one eyebrow. 'Have you told him about you and Evan?'

'Of course not.'

'Don't you think you'd better?'

'Why?'

'Why do you think, Sarah?'

'That's . . .' Sarah swallowed hard. She hadn't told Grace the whole story, and now perhaps wasn't the time. 'Well, it's not important anymore. And what is there to tell, really? The facts are that Evan and I had a . . . well, a brief fling, just when David and I had started dating. So what?'

'How do you think he'd feel if he ever found out?'

'How's that going to happen if I don't tell him?'

'Because Evan could.'

'He wouldn't.'

'Why not? I might, in his situation.' Grace sipped her tea. 'And how do you feel about him being back? Especially if he's come back for you.'

'I don't know.' Sarah stared helplessly up at the kitchen ceiling. 'Flattered. Confused . . .'

'Which one is it?'

'It's . . .' Sarah thought for a moment. 'Both.'

'And why are you confused?'

'Why do you think?'

Grace shrugged. 'Well, if I was playing devil's advocate, I'd say it's because you had doubts about getting married.'

'Yeah, well, it's a big step, isn't it?'

'And are these doubts about getting married, or marrying David?'

'Are you trying to psychoanalyze me?'

Grace grinned. 'Maybe.'

Sarah sighed. 'Grace, what woman doesn't have doubts about the man she's marrying? That's just the way it works, isn't it? None of them are perfect, and so eventually you've just got to make a decision. Go for it. Decide whether you can live with them. At work, we'd call it a cost/benefit analysis . . .' Sarah stopped talking, because Grace's expression was turning into one of horror.

'Is that how you really feel about him?' she asked. 'David, I mean.'

'I don't know. Not really. Well, perhaps a little.' Sarah made a face. 'I mean, they've all got their faults, haven't they?'

Grace took another sip from her mug, then she smiled. 'I suppose so.'

'Especially Evan,' continued Sarah.

Though long after her tea had gone cold, she still couldn't think what they might be.

18

Evan cursed his stupidity as he drove up Bermondsey Street. Of course Sarah and David were going to be spending the day together, probably off to some pretentious restaurant to eat food served in portions that cost four times as much despite being one quarter of the size, then trailing round Harrods afterwards, or Harvey Nicholls, or wherever it was these City boys went to fritter away their outrageous salaries.

Though with Saturday fast approaching, maybe their last few weekends had been an endless procession of wedding duties or household chores instead, and if that was the case, Evan hoped it might count in his favour – as far as he could tell from the one time he'd been in her flat, Sarah hadn't seemed like one for domesticity. He took some comfort that she still lived in the same place, which meant – probably – she and David didn't live together, which was a good thing. Prising her out of a situation like that would be even more difficult.

He eased the Mercedes into the traffic inching its way along Jamaica Road, smiling when he spotted the familiar railway viaduct up ahead, then gunned the car towards the arches just before the station. The dashboard clock told him it was nearly midday – nine hours until the club opened – though given Mel's questionable living arrangements, that didn't necessarily mean he wouldn't be there. Parking the car underneath a notice warning him he'd be clamped if he left it there – although seeing as he'd helped Mel paint and hang the sign, Evan wasn't worried – he walked purposefully up to the dilapidated building and banged loudly on the door. After a few moments he heard the heavy bolts sliding open, and Mel's face appeared through the gap.

'Fuck me!' said Mel, blinking in the sunlight, before pushing the door wide open and giving Evan a hug that squeezed the breath out of him.

'I'll pass, thanks.'

'You never wrote, you never called . . .'

Evan grinned at his friend. He looked like he'd just woken up, which was a distinct possibility. Mel wasn't exactly someone you'd describe as a morning person – or an afternoon one, come to think of it – which was just as well, given that the club stayed open till five a.m. most nights.

'That's not strictly true, is it?'

'Well, you didn't say you were coming home.' Mel shook his head slowly, as if unable to believe who he was seeing. 'When did you get back?'

'Last night.'

'You're looking good, man,' said Mel, giving him the once-over. 'Mister Sumner been kind to you, I see?'

'Can't complain.' Evan folded his arms. 'So are you going to invite me in, or just make me stand here?'

For a moment, Mel pretended that that was exactly what he was going to do, then he held the door open and ushered Evan inside. 'So,' he said, walking round to the other side of the bar and jabbing a thumb at the row of bottles behind him. 'What would you like to drink?'

'Mel, it's not even lunchtime yet.'

'And your point is?'

Evan hopped up onto the nearest stool and patted the bar affectionately, happy to see the club hadn't changed in the year he'd been away. Mel had given him the closest thing to a residency he'd ever had, every Tuesday, Thursday, and Friday night for the best part of two years, and while the money hadn't been great – and some nights, had been non-existent – and his fellow band members had come and gone, Evan had loved it, so he'd stayed. Up until Mr. Sumner – as Mel liked to call him – had come calling, and Evan had gone too.

He caught sight of the spot a few stools along where Sarah been sitting when he'd first noticed her, almost as if he expected to see a blue plaque commemorating the location, and he smiled to himself. It was the kind of thing a lovesick teenager might do, and he and Sarah weren't teenagers. Though during their brief time together, it had almost felt like they were.

Mel coughed noisily, breaking Evan's train of thought. 'Well?'

'Sorry.' Evan thought for a moment. 'Whiskey, please.'

Mel indicated the row of bottles on the shelf behind him. Maker's Mark, Knob Creek, Jim Beam, and of course, Jack Daniels. All classic jazz drinks. 'Bourbon or rye?'

Evan pointed at the Jim Beam. 'I'm more of a rye man.'

Mel winked. 'Like the stationers,' he said, then he roared with laughter at his own joke, and as Evan couldn't help but join in, he realised it was the first time he'd laughed in a while.

'So,' Mel splashed healthy measures of whiskey into a couple of glasses, then slid one Wild-West-Saloon-style across the bar towards him. 'When are you going to play for us?'

'I don't know. I'm not sure I'm in the mood.'

'Too high and mighty now after your brush with rock royalty? Which you owe me for, don't forget.'

'Not at all. It's just . . .'

'Come on,' Mel insisted. 'There's some good guys here now. You might even learn a thing or two.'

Evan picked his glass up and clinked it against Mel's. 'Okay.'

'Tonight?'

'I can't. I'm . . . busy.'

'Well, when?'

Evan thought for a moment. 'Tuesday night,' he said.

'Great. Just like old times. And make sure you play that song I like.'

'Which one?'

'The Nat King Cole one.'

'That doesn't narrow it down a lot.'

'You know – the one I can never remember the name of.'

'*Unforgettable*?'

Mel grinned. 'That's the one!' He downed his whiskey in one, then grimaced, as did Evan when he realised that was probably Mel's breakfast. 'So the tour was good?'

Evan nodded, then took a mouthful of Jim Beam. The whiskey burned his stomach, and he remembered he hadn't eaten anything yet either. 'Yeah.'

'I sense a "but" in there somewhere.'

Evan stared into his glass. 'I missed her, Mel. Really missed her. And couldn't help thinking that I'd made a mistake.'

'By going on tour?'

'By going, full stop.'

Mel leaned over the bar and punched him lightly on the shoulder. 'Well, now you're back. Sorted.'

'Not quite. She's getting married.'

'Not to the wanker?'

'He's a *banker*, Mel.'

'Same thing.' Mel frowned as he refilled their drinks. 'When?'

'Saturday.'

Mel stared at him. '*This* Saturday? As in a week's time?'

'Yup.'

'Well, what are you doing sitting here with me then? Go get her.'

'It's not as simple as that.'

'Why the hell not? If you love her, go and tell her. If she loves you back, you're sorted.'

'She's hardly going to "love me back". Not after one night, and especially a year down the line.'

'Depends how good a night it was.'

'Be serious, Mel.'

'I am being serious. You never know. Besides, if she doesn't, then there's nothing you can do about it anyway.' He put his glass back down on the bar. 'But love at first sight does exist, you know.'

'Says the man who's been married how many times now?'

'Three. Which proves my point.' He grinned again. 'Seriously, go and see her. Now.'

A flake of paint had fallen from the ceiling and into Evan's glass, and he fished it out with the tip of his finger. 'I've already seen her.'

'And?'

'And nothing. The, er, *banker,* was there.'

Mel made a face. 'And he has no idea about you and her?'

'Well, he didn't punch me in the face, so I'm guessing not.'

'So what's your next step?'

'Well, it's his stag night tonight.'

'Excellent.'

'Why is that excellent?'

'Because it leaves the coast clear for you to go and see her.'

'Well, it would, if it wasn't her hen night tonight as well. And besides . . .'

'Besides?'

'I'm kind of going. To the stag.'

Mel stared at him, his glass halfway to his mouth. 'I was going to ask why, but that'd be a bit bleedin' obvious of me, wouldn't it?'

'It seemed like a good idea at the time.' Evan leant back against the bar. 'And I can't really not turn up now that I've said "yes".'

Mel rolled his eyes, and reached for the whiskey bottle. 'Let's hope that's not how Sarah feels next Saturday, eh?' he said.

19

Evan adjusted his bow tie self-consciously using the reflection in the tube window, and wondered whether he'd be the only guest this evening wearing a pre-tied one. He'd flirted with 'proper' bow ties before, but had quickly decided that unless you had someone else to tie it for you, or were James Bond – who could probably tie his one-handed and in the dark – life was too short to waste on trying to get the damn things to look half-respectable.

He tutted under his breath as he fiddled with his collar. The evening hadn't even started and he already felt at a disadvantage, sure the rest of this evening's guests had probably been taught bow-tie tying on their first day at Eton, along with clay pigeon shooting, how to talk down to the help, and how to be an arse.

David's words still irked him slightly. *Of course* he owned a dinner suit. Most professional musicians had one, in case they were called upon to play at some upmarket hotel gig or private party, and his hadn't been cheap when he'd bought it some five years back. He'd been worried whether it would still fit; his most recent engagement – he bristled a little at the word – that had required formal dress had been at the Hilton on Park Lane three Christmases ago, but after he'd nervously discarded the plastic dry-cleaning sleeve that had kept the suit dust-free in the back of his wardrobe since then, he'd been relieved to find that he could still get into the trousers.

Evan let out a short laugh at the phrase, remembering his discussion with Sarah in Postman's Park about the way Americans spoke English, and realised he could have used the difference between 'trousers' and 'pants' in that sentence to make his point, though he knew he should forget getting into her pants, seeing as he suspected he had some way to go before he could even get into her good books.

He sighed loudly, and a distinguished-looking old lady sitting in the next seat looked at him strangely.

'Are you all right, dear?'

'Yes. Sorry. It's just these damn . . . I mean, these ties. Even the Velcro ones don't make it easy for you.'

'Hold on.' The woman reached across and untwisted the fastening. 'There.'

'Thank you.'

'You're looking very smart. Going somewhere nice?'

'No . . .' said Evan, before he could stop himself, then he quickly added '. . . where special. It's a fr . . . someone's stag do.'

'Oh. Are you the Best Man?'

'I hope so. I mean, no. I don't really know the groom. I'm more a . . .' He cleared his throat. 'Friend of the bride.'

'Oh yes?' The old lady stood up unsteadily as the train pulled in to Charing Cross. 'So you're going to check he's good enough for her, are you?'

Evan nodded as he got up to help her off the train. 'That's right,' he said, though he suspected he already knew the answer to that.

He smiled to himself as he sat back down. That was about the size of it – though whether Sarah would take any notice of his opinion was another thing entirely. She hadn't seemed too shocked when he'd agreed to go this evening, although he had to hope that was because she was a little stunned at seeing him rather than pleased that he seemed to be accepting the fact of her forthcoming wedding. And she must have known he was bound to see their wedding announcement – it had been in all the U.S. papers, after all – so maybe she just wanted him and David to be friends. Perhaps that was all she might ever want of him and her too, though trouble was, that wasn't what Evan wanted at all.

He pulled the crumpled newspaper clipping out of his wallet and stared uncomfortably at the photo of the two of them, wondering where it had been taken. David was smiling from ear to ear, and Sarah . . . Well, Evan didn't like to admit it, but she looked happy too.

For a second, he felt like getting off the train and going back home, but he reminded himself this was something he had to do, knowing he couldn't go the rest of his life wondering what might have been, just like he'd known he couldn't turn down the Police tour. Okay, so it wasn't quite on the same scale as the man who turned down the Beatles, but you just knew some things in life had the potential to eat you up forever, and besides, it was important he went this evening to find out what he was up against. He couldn't present his case to Sarah without at least some knowledge of his rival, and if it wasn't strong enough, well, he'd just have to live with that. And at least he'd always know he'd tried – though Evan doubted that would be much of a consolation.

Not that he was scared of a little competition. Musicians faced it all the time. But this was different to his music, where Evan was confident in his ability; whenever he was auditioning, people usually judged him on merit against other sax players. He rarely found himself in competition with a completely different sound, or someone who played another instrument entirely. And that, unfortunately, was how he saw things between him and David.

He took a last look at his reflection in the window, then stepped off the train at Leicester Square and fought his way through the usual Saturday evening Soho crowds. It was nearly eight o'clock, so he reluctantly quickened his pace, mindful of David's earlier emphasis on punctuality – while he'd prefer not to spend more time than was necessary with David's friends, Evan didn't want to start the evening off on the wrong foot by being late and upsetting what he was sure were his carefully laid plans for the night.

Pausing at the corner of Greek Street and Old Compton Street, he looked up at the grey-green building, checked the discreet silver plate next to the door, then headed up the stairs towards the reception desk, before stopping suddenly at the top. What the hell was David's surname? Had he even told the club that the booking was for a stag party? Establishments could be funny about things like that.

As he stood there, the girl behind the desk flicked her eyes up at him. She was pretty, in a slightly emaciated way, as if she believed that those size zero women she was reading about in the magazine half-hidden under her desk weren't simply models, but role models.

'I'm looking for a private party,' he said, realising too late how sleazy that sounded.

'Cook?' said the girl, consulting her clipboard.

'No, I'm one of the guests,' he replied automatically, before remembering he did, in fact, know that was David's surname. It was on the wedding announcement, after all. 'I mean, yes. The, er, Cook party.'

The girl half-smiled before directing him up a further flight of stairs. 'They're in the top-floor bar,' she said. 'Would you like someone to show you the way?'

Evan shook his head. By the looks of the various people milling around the club's reception, dressed in that geeky-yet-trendy way the London media world liked to style themselves, his party would be easy to spot. 'I'm sure I'll find them.'

He made his way up to the third floor and walked into the bar, where a group of maybe half a dozen men dressed like just like him – though a variety of shapes and ages – were standing in a corner, identifiable as much by the braying noise they were making as by the outfits they wore. David had his back to him, and Evan took the opportunity to size him up: He was tall, sure, but all those business lunches hadn't done him any favours, and he looked like he'd be out of breath running for a bus – though Evan had to wonder whether David had ever been on a bus in his whole life. Plus, he was a drinker – that was obvious from the slight paunch that had been straining against his rugby shirt earlier, not to mention the contents of his shopping trolley. Couple that with the soft features, and what looked like the beginnings of a bald patch . . . While David had a confidence about him, and could probably be charming company once you got past all that public-school bluster, physically, at least, Evan was confident he had the edge. The year on the road had been refreshingly different in that it hadn't subjected him to the usual excesses of touring life. There had been very few drugs, hardly any alcohol, and thanks to the well-documented healthy lifestyle of his employer, the hotels they'd stayed in had been picked for the quality of their gyms rather than the quantities in their mini-bars, and for the first time in his professional life, Evan wondered whether he hadn't actually put on a little muscle and lost a little weight. He even feared he'd lost the taste for beer, although that may have been down to that American 'lite' stuff that had been the only backstage option.

Trouble was, this wasn't a beauty contest. Evan knew from past experience how pragmatic women could be – he could name at least two former girlfriends who'd taken up with him because he was a musician, and then left him a few months later for precisely the same reason – and when it came to making a long-term bet, he knew he'd find it harder to compete. There was no way he could match David financially, but the Sarah he'd known back then hadn't seemed that fickle, couldn't possibly be that mercenary. He hoped that was still the case.

With a last anxious tweak of his bow tie, he strode purposefully over towards the group and tapped his rival on the shoulder.

'Evening.'

David wheeled round, then smiled in recognition. 'Evan! Pleased you could make it,' he said, though Evan suspected he was resisting the temptation to look at his watch. 'Come and say hello to the chaps.'

He found himself being steered into the centre of the group, and readied himself for the usual pissing-competition round of handshakes. Sure enough, as David's friends were introduced to him, each one tried to crush his fingers in turn, though years of handling a saxophone meant Evan could give as good as he got.

'Evan's a friend of Sarah's,' announced David, which produced a round of raised eyebrows and 'aye-aye's from the group.

'And what do you do?' asked one of them, whose name Evan had already forgotten.

'I'm a musician,' he said, smiling through the customary five seconds of silence that answer always invoked, as if he'd just admitted to being a pornographer or a serial killer.

'And are you . . . I mean, do you make a living at it?' someone else said incredulously, as if any kind of occupation that didn't involve moving other people's money around for vast profits couldn't possibly put food on the table.

'I get by,' Evan said, pleasantly.

'Don't be modest,' said David. 'Evan's quite famous. He's just been on tour. With The Police.'

Evan glanced at the sea of blank faces that surrounded him. Judging by the lack of reaction, it was clear that the only Police record any of this lot might have would be for insider trading, and he worried he was in for a long evening.

'In fact,' continued David, 'he and that Sting fellow are on first-name terms. Isn't that right, Evan?'

Evan shrugged, then took a gulp from the glass of Champagne that someone had handed him. 'Well, technically, Sting's only got a first name, so I suppose so,' he said, reluctantly playing along, though the truth was, even after touring with the band for so long, he wasn't sure Sting even knew his name wasn't 'sax'.

'So, how do you know Sarah?' someone else was asking him, and Evan had a sudden, crazy impulse to tell him the truth, but the waitress had arrived to tell them their table was ready. Downing the rest of his Champagne, he stifled a burp and followed the group through into a side room, where a table was set for the seven of them.

'Come on,' said David, draping an arm round his shoulder. 'You sit here next to me.'

And to his surprise, Evan found himself feeling more than a little grateful.

20

South of the river, Sarah fixed her make-up, then practised fixing a smile on her face as she waited for the first of her guests to arrive. Despite the fact that they didn't broadcast their relationship in the office, everyone at the bank knew she was the boss's girlfriend, and treated her with a mixture of respect – especially since she and David had become engaged – and friendliness, although Sarah was sure the women were probably bitchy behind her back. She didn't get that many invites for girly lunches – though she didn't get that many lunch offers from David either – but that was fine. She had Grace, and Sarah had long ago decided she couldn't afford to let that many people in – especially since those she'd let in the past seemed to make a habit of leaving her.

And while she'd got to know some of her female co-workers quite well over the past year, tonight was more out of duty than because she'd wanted a party. David had insisted on a small wedding with just family and a handful of close friends, possibly to avoid the minefield of who to invite/not to invite at work, and that had been fine by Sarah – her mother's disappearing act had pretty much destroyed any childhood dreams she'd had of a big, fancy wedding. But her fiancé's well-broadcast desire to drink London dry on his stag night had prompted a few of the women to ask what she was planning in response, and so Sarah had felt obliged to invite them for drinks this evening. She hadn't expected them to pay, and certainly didn't want David to, hence the reason they were having it at her flat - and besides, she mixed a mean Cosmopolitan, better than most of the bartenders in London, anyway. Though as the evening had approached, for some reason, she didn't feel at all like celebrating.

Sarah hoped it was just a case of cold feet, rather than anything to do with Evan's sudden reappearance, though she couldn't help thinking that maybe the two were related. A part of her had always hoped he might come back, even though she'd known that once she'd accepted David's proposal, the Evan chapter of her life would finally come to an end. She'd had a while to get used to the idea, so she'd been a little surprised to find herself still so angry at him. Maybe she resented him for making her do the ending; certainly she'd been sure Mel was right, and she'd had to do what she did, but even so, Sarah hadn't wanted things between them to end like they had. And yet here he was, not even back for five minutes, and she was questioning, well, *everything*.

She stared at her reflection in the bathroom mirror, wondering what Evan – no doubt looking sexy in his dinner suit – was going through this evening. Maybe the strangest thing would happen, and he and David would actually bond, or find out they had something in common – something other than her, at least. But she doubted it. You could hardly find two people more different than David and Evan. Which was what had made her situation all the more difficult.

Just before she'd learned of Evan's imminent departure, Grace had suggested making a list on a piece of paper – Evan's name at the top of one column, David's above the other – of all their good points, everything she liked about them, and all their bad points, too, but she'd rejected the idea almost immediately. Because while she'd known that was a useful exercise if you had to make a choice between, say, two similar apartments you were interested in buying, this had been like trying to decide between a bohemian house in the West Village and a Park Avenue condo. Both were so different, both would have offered her such opposite lifestyles, and she could see the merits in either of them, but as for picking one logically – *and for the rest of her life* – she may as well have tossed a coin.

In the end, of course, she hadn't had to choose between them. Fate had done that, and then circumstances had taken over, and David had proposed, and she'd said yes, partly *because* of circumstances, but perhaps also, as she now suspected, because she hadn't thought there was any alternative. Plus Sarah understood there was a problem with getting what you thought you wanted in life – you were too frightened to find out it wasn't perfect, or certainly not all it was cracked up to be. She was sure this would be the case with David, just like she knew it was bound to be with Evan, because experience told her that ultimately, reality let you down. Her mother leaving when she was a little girl, and then her selfless father's long, painful, but ultimately losing battle with cancer had taught her life just wasn't fair.

She sighed, then checked her lipstick and walked out of the bathroom and into the kitchen, where Grace was arranging sushi on a tray, and a thought suddenly occurred to her. Had she agreed to marry David only because she was grateful that he'd proposed?

'Ready?' asked Grace, pouring her a large glass of Chardonnay.

Sarah shrugged, then hugged her friend. 'As I'll ever be,' she said.

And she had to concede that that, at least, might well be true.

21

Evan had flirted with the idea of just getting drunk in order to get through the evening, but he didn't want to risk losing it completely and blurt something inappropriate out to David, so in the end, he'd decided to nurse his drinks. As the night wore on, he'd been glad he was pacing himself, because the alcohol had kept on coming, and despite his relative abstinence, he was already fearful of the following morning's hangover.

He was amazed at these City boys' capacity to put it away, and – despite his earlier resentment – glad he wasn't paying, given the number of Champagne bottles that had kept materialising, not to mention the wine, the port, and then the bottle of Napoleon brandy that had made its way round the table which, given its price tag, Evan feared had actually *been* Napoleon's brandy.

They'd finished their dinner, then moved back into the bar until eleven-thirty, when their increasingly noisy party had been politely but forcibly asked to leave. Evan had thought of calling it a night, but he hadn't wanted to be the first, and no-one else had looked like they were going, which was why he now found himself in some 'gentlemen's club' – though ironically, the place was full of barely dressed ladies – just off the Strand that one of the party knew. As soon as they'd arrived, the whole group had become women-magnets, though Evan suspected that had more to do with the contents of their wallets than any laws of attraction. As he looked for somewhere to sit that wouldn't come with a compulsory overpriced bottle of cheap Champagne, a heavy arm draped itself around his neck, and Evan looked up to see a glassy-eyed David grinning at him.

'Having a good time?'

Evan decided to dodge the question. 'Thanks for inviting me.'

'You're welcome.' He seemed to be forming his words with a bit of effort, though Evan was amazed he could talk at all. 'Any friend of Sarah's, and all that.'

Evan knew it was his turn to speak, but so far, and apart from the obvious, he'd struggled to find much common ground between the two of them this evening. 'So . . . looking forward to the big day?' was the best he could manage.

David stared at him for a moment, then raised both eyebrows. 'You mean next Saturday?'

'Yeah.'

'Oh yes. Though it's a bigger day for Sarah, of course.'

'How so?'

David removed his arm from Evan's shoulders. 'You not married, Evan?'

Evan shook his head. 'Nope. Never . . .' He'd been about to say 'met the right girl' but that wasn't exactly true, so he left it at that.

'Well, it's what they're all after, isn't it?' said David, addressing Evan as if he were delivering a lecture. 'Huge diamond on the finger, two-point-four kids, the full housewife experience. Or rather "home-maker", as the Yanks prefer to call it.'

'And you're . . .' – Evan was aware he needed to choose his words carefully – '. . . sure that's what Sarah wants?'

'Like I said, they all do.' He grinned, though it was more of a leer. 'And in any case, it's what I want.'

'But she's got her, you know . . .' Evan swallowed hard. 'Career.'

David let out a short laugh. 'This is the City, Evan. Women don't really have careers here. Besides, there's only one kind of working girl I'm interested in, and speaking of which . . .' He rubbed his hands together theatrically. 'Time to get stuck in.'

With a lopsided smile, David headed over to the stage in the middle of the room where two girls were demonstrating the kind of flexibility normally only seen in Olympic gymnasts, and lured one of them down with a wave of a twenty-pound note. Evan watched in disbelief; the picture he was beginning to form of Sarah's fiancé was hardly a flattering one, at least where his attitude to women was concerned. Surely David was different when he was with Sarah, he thought, though a part of him hoped he wasn't. It would certainly make his job easier.

Suddenly desperate for the toilet, he peered around the club's dingy interior, taking in the heavy purple curtains and red velour booths. He'd been to a couple of places like this in the U.S., dragged along for the occasional after-party by the other boys in the backing band, yet the only thing they'd ever done for him was kill the post-show buzz. He found them depressing and always felt sorry for the girls, even though they probably earned more than he did. Sure, some of them were just paying their way through college, but he knew a few had either a drug problem, or – even though they seemed to be little more than teenagers themselves – a family to support, and were happy to supplement their incomes by going way beyond the 'no touching' rule.

One of David's friends paid for a private room, and as the party went in, it became clear that a number of girls came with it, one of whom was doing her best to interest Evan in – well, he didn't like to imagine what – by showing him just how easily she could touch her toes. She couldn't have been more than eighteen, and even at such a young age she was sporting such an over-the-top breast enlargement that Evan was impressed when she managed to stand back upright.

'Fancy a dance, love?' she said, swaying suggestively to the thumping background music. 'Or something else?'

Evan lowered himself into the nearest chair and tried his best to maintain eye contact, though her side-to-side movement coupled with her out-of-proportion physical attributes meant her chest kept obscuring her face. 'Can you tango?' he said, trying to make a joke, but the girl just frowned.

'I don't think we sell 'em.'

'Sell what?'

'Cans of Tango.'

Before he could reply, the girl jumped onto his lap and rubbed herself against him, her backside pressed into his groin, which only served to remind Evan of his painfully full bladder. As she climbed slowly off, he admired the series of floral tattoos that spread across her back and disappeared into her barely-there underwear, wondering what drove someone to do this to themselves. *A lack of self-esteem* was the textbook answer, though at times like this he found that hard to believe, given how the girl was gyrating in front of him in next-to-nothing.

He glanced around the room. The rest of his group seemed to be mesmerised by the girls, encouraging them into more and more daring acts by dispensing twenty-pound notes at an alarming rate, and while David was nowhere to be seen, Evan wasn't surprised. Given the amount of alcohol he'd been mainlining all evening, by now he was probably asleep in a corner somewhere.

'So,' the girl said, licking her lips, revealing a tongue piercing that made Evan wince. 'That dance?'

'Maybe later,' he said. 'Can you tell me where the gents are?'

'Ain't no gents dancing here, sweetheart. If that's your bag then you should be at a different club.'

'No, the gents' *toilets*.'

The girl glanced across at the huge bouncer, then leaned in close. 'I'll show you if you like?' she whispered, a mischievous glint in her eye.

'No. That's fine.' Evan reached into his pocket for his wallet. 'Here,' he said, handing her a twenty-pound note. 'Keep my seat warm for me.'

'Ooh,' said the girl. 'Kinky.'

In the far corner, two other girls had begun to kiss, causing David's friends to cheer as if they were watching a fist-fight, so Evan slipped out to find the gents'. Under the watchful eye of the bouncer, he headed back along the corridor, aiming for where he thought the toilets must be, but instead, found himself faced with three unmarked doors. Assuming they'd *all* be gents' – after all, he doubted any of the club's customers were likely to be female – he cautiously pushed the middle one open, and for a moment, his eyes wouldn't adjust to the gloom, but once they had, he found himself transfixed by the sight of David lying face-up on the sofa in front of him. From what Evan could tell, he seemed ill, or was maybe having some kind of heart attack, given the moaning sounds coming from his mouth and the semi-naked girl bouncing up and down on top of him, as if trying to perform some over-vigorous cardiac massage. Then Evan noticed the girl was facing in the wrong direction compared to any first-aid instructional videos he'd ever seen, and that David's trousers were round his ankles, and realised exactly what was going on.

David hadn't noticed him come in. His eyes were shut, and at once, Evan felt angry: at David for taking advantage of the girl, partly, but more importantly, at his betrayal of Sarah. He felt like going over and pulling them apart, but what good would that have done? Besides, there were some sights you didn't want to see, and he already knew this one would stay with him for a long time. And while the girl seemed not to be phased by what was going on – in fact, and out of David's line of vision, she seemed to be using her free hand to compose a text on her phone while randomly shouting an enthusiastic 'oh baby!' every few seconds – somehow that made it worse.

He backed swiftly out of the room, careful not to make any noise, and as he shut the door behind him, Evan suddenly realised something. He'd *won*. All he had to do was tell Sarah what he'd seen, that this was the kind of thing David got up to, and he'd be home and dry.

It occurred to him she might demand some sort of evidence – and a picture snapped on his phone would do – but somehow, taking a photo seemed a little too sordid. Sarah would just have to take his word for it – and surely David wouldn't be able to deny *this*. He marched back down the corridor, a spring in his step, and found the toilets, but as he relieved himself, something else became clear to him. He didn't want to win by default. No, Evan thought, he needed to make Sarah realise she should be with him because he was what she wanted, not because some bad deed by David had pissed her off. But at the same time, he was smart enough to know this was a piece of information that he'd keep filed away, close to his chest, and only use in an emergency. Though what constituted an emergency, Evan wasn't sure yet.

He headed back to the private room. Only a couple of the group were left in there now, the others probably having been enticed somewhere *more* private, just like David had, and Evan wondered how many of them had girlfriends, or were even married, and whether this was just par for the course. Sarah had told him how sexist, how chauvinistic the City was, and he imagined visits to these kinds of places were all part of doing business. Given how David had seemed to be on first-name terms with the barman, Evan could believe it.

Just then, the girl who'd been 'dancing' for him earlier came over from where she'd been enjoying a sit-down at his expense.

'Anywhere else you'd like me to sit, love?' she said suggestively, but all Evan felt was a sudden need to be anywhere but here. He retrieved his wallet from his pocket, slipped the girl a couple of notes, and made his way quickly towards the exit.

22

The girls had brought presents, which explained why Sarah was wearing a pair of what she understood from Grace were called 'Deely-boppers' on her head, a flashing plastic model of a bride on the end of one of the springs and the equivalent groom on the other. Mary from accounts had brought her a pair of thermal socks 'in case she got cold feet', a statement which had sent the room into hysterics, and Sarah had laughed too, of course, though somewhere at the back of her mind, she'd wondered whether Mary knew something she didn't.

Her least-favourite gift – the square plastic learner-driver's L-plate strung around her neck – kept digging in to her cleavage, but she felt duty bound to keep it on, despite the fact that most of the girls were snapping photos with their phones every chance they got. And while Sarah worried the pictures would surely end up on the notice board at work, she let them have their fun. Though she was having fun too, she had to concede, mainly due to the five or six Cosmopolitans she'd already consumed, and while Grace was worried they'd never get the cranberry juice stains out of the rug, Sarah had to admit it was actually nice to get some girl time. The women were different out of the office, as if they all felt they could let their hair down – literally, in some cases, given how prim some of them were at work.

Grace looked over and winked from where she was having what appeared to be a serious conversation with an extremely drunk Sally,

David's PA, who, despite being almost twenty years older than Sarah, wore her skirts at least ten inches shorter, and guarded his diary with the ferocity of a Doberman. She'd had the job for years, and while Sarah wasn't exactly sure about her relationship with David, she was pretty sure they'd never slept together – normally, those kinds of things didn't result in such long-term employment – though while their relationship appeared to be purely professional, Sarah suspected a much deeper feeling on Sally's part. Several times she'd guessed the gifts David occasionally presented her with had actually been chosen by Sally, mainly because they'd been even less tasteful than usual, and Sarah was sure that had been on purpose. She hadn't really wanted to invite her, but had felt it politically correct to do so, especially since David had dropped a number of not-so-subtle hints about how she'd been particularly put out by not receiving a wedding invitation, and – mindful of the expecta-tions her new role might well carry, and suspecting it wouldn't be the last time – Sarah had reluctantly stepped up to the plate.

She raised her glass and smiled back. Throughout the evening, Grace had been checking up on her. Several times Sarah had caught her watching whenever she'd gone and helped herself to another drink. It had become so bad that at one point she'd had to take Grace to one side to reassure her she was okay, though she was sure she hadn't managed to convince her. As fond as she was of her flat-mate, Sarah still missed her New York girlfriends, most of whom were too busy having babies to come over for her wedding – not that David had wanted her to invite them given his low-key plans for the day. But these women would do; she saw them every day, and apart from Grace, they were the closest thing she had to a circle of friends here. Given the sexism rife in the office, they'd all kind of bonded as if in some sort of blitz spirit, and if there was resent-ment that Sarah was marrying the boss, so far none of them had shown any – or at least, not to her face. Besides, that kind of rivalry only existed between the PAs, whose sole purpose in life seemed to be to nab one of the partners for themselves, even though the office operated on a strict *Upstairs, Downstairs* policy – a reference to some obscure British television programme that David had tried to explain to her once – and the moment anyone tried to overstep the boundary, there was always trouble. Some of the partners spent more time with their PAs than they did with their wives, but they all knew that anything more was strictly out of bounds – and in any case, there were plenty of other ways to have a bit of fun on the side. And although Sarah wasn't completely sure whose target she'd 'nabbed', she'd had her suspicions about Sally for a while. She was certainly a good-looking older woman, but the trouble was, most of the men at the firm didn't want an older woman. Mainly because they were already married to one.

She excused herself from the front room with a nod to her empty glass, and was standing in the kitchen opening another bottle of vodka when Grace came in behind her.

'Having fun?'

'Grace, for the millionth time . . .'

'Sorry.' Grace made a guilty face. 'It's just that I've never been a maid of honour before. And I've never organised a hen night, either.'

'Well, you're doing a great job – assuming what you Brits do on these kind of occasions is get drunk and set about trying to embarrass the bride-to-be?' Sarah gave her a hug, causing the L-plate to dig painfully into both her breasts. 'It's perfect. Just what I wanted.'

'You're sure?'

'Yes, I'm sure.' And in truth, while it hadn't been anything like the bridal showers she'd been to back home, Sarah had found herself enjoying playing along when they'd made her wear these silly things, and pretending to be suitably shocked when the inevitable male blow-up doll had been produced. And she'd more than kept pace with the rest of them where the cocktails were concerned.

'And you're not thinking about you-know-who?'

'I wasn't. Now I am.'

Grace made a face. 'Sorry. Forget I mentioned him.'

'I'll do my best.' Sarah adjusted the Deely-boppers, which were starting to slip off the back of her head. 'It's my hen night. Not a night to be thinking about Evan, or even David. Tonight is all about having fun – and drinking a lot.'

'Cheers to that,' said Grace, then she noticed Sarah's empty glass. 'Another Cosmo?'

'Rude not to. Though I might regret it tomorrow.'

Grace gave her a flat-lipped smile. 'Let's just hope you won't be thinking the same thing next Saturday.'

Sarah opened her mouth to answer, but the sound of the front door opening followed by a commotion in the hallway stopped her. 'What's that?' she asked.

Grace shrugged. 'Probably the pizzas we ordered. Though I did hear a rumour about a stripper . . .'

As Sarah's stomach rumbled, she knew exactly which she'd prefer it to be, and wondered just what that said about her.

23

Evan checked his watch and considered walking home. Even though it had just gone half-past midnight, he was still on U.S. time, so the night felt relatively young, but the miraculous sight of a taxi passing with its 'For Hire' sign illuminated was too strong a lure, and after a moment's hesitation, he flagged it down and climbed in.

One thing he was sure of, having spent even a short time with David, was that David absolutely didn't deserve Sarah. There had been something so disrespectful about how he and his friends had treated those women at the club – not as people, but like commodities – and it had made Evan sick to his stomach. If that was their view of womankind in general, how could he let a woman he cared about marry someone like that?

He needed to meet her, to tell her – but when? Once she'd had a little more time to get used to the idea of him being back, perhaps. Plus, as Grace had told him, it was her hen night this evening, and he didn't want to spoil that for her – especially since he was planning to spoil the wedding. He thought about texting her, but quickly dismissed the idea – a hundred and sixty characters were hardly enough to craft the heartfelt message he wanted to convey – and what if David saw it? No, he needed to resort to more primitive means.

As the taxi crossed Tower Bridge, he borrowed a scrap of paper and a pen from the cabbie and jotted Sarah a note that simply said 'call me', adding his number afterwards just in case she'd deleted all evidence of their previous liaison, then directed him up Sarah's street and asked to be dropped off in front of her building.

He waited till the cab had gone, then peered at the bank of post-boxes on the wall next to the door, trying to locate the right one, until a middle-aged woman carrying the smallest dog with the biggest, buggiest eyes that Evan had ever seen appeared in the foyer. She took one look at him in his dinner jacket, evidently decided he was unlikely to be a burglar, and opened the door a few inches.

'Can I help you?' she said, in a strong South African accent.

Evan moved to pet the dog, then jerked his hand back as it bared a needle-sharp set of teeth. 'I'm looking for Sarah Bishop's post-box. I've got to drop off a note.'

'Sarah? She's 6-E,' said the woman, and Evan frowned.

'Well, I think she's sexy too, but do you know what number flat . . .'

The woman laughed. 'No, 6-E,' she said, tapping an expensively manicured fingernail on the relevant box. 'Although I can see why you'd think that. Is it important?'

'Yeah,' said Evan, stopping short of telling the woman it was quite possibly the most important note he'd ever delivered.

'In that case, it might be better if you go up and slip it under her door. She might not check her post until Monday.'

The woman opened the door just wide enough to let him in, and – avoiding the softly growling dog – he mumbled his thanks. Slipping the note under her front door was a better plan, he told himself as he walked purposefully into the lift and pressed the button for Sarah's floor – after all, with the wedding so close, he wasn't sure he could afford the extra day. After a moment, as if giving him a chance to change his mind, the lift doors closed and it lurched upwards, though when they opened again, the music he could hear coming from the other end of the hallway almost made him wish he had.

He crept up to Sarah's front door and tentatively pressed his face against the opaque glass panel, trying to peer inside. From what he could tell, the lights were all on, and judging by the sounds emanating from within, they'd brought the party home with them. But as he stood there, wondering whether he should go back to his original plan of leaving the note in her post-box downstairs, the door was suddenly flung open and he almost fell inside.

'You're late,' said a girl he didn't recognise. She was attractive – about Sarah's age, but blonde and with a fuller figure – and very drunk.

Evan hurriedly stuffed the note into his pocket as he automatically looked at his watch. 'I'm sorry?' he said, as the girl grabbed him by the arm and pulled him through the doorway.

'I said, you're late. But worth waiting for,' she answered, giving him the once-over. 'I like it!'

'Like what?' he said, distractedly. Being back in Sarah's flat felt strange, and while he knew he should just turn around and leave, he allowed himself to be led along the hallway.

'The James Bond look,' she said, fingering his lapel. 'Now listen. Everyone knows you're coming.'

'Everyone? How . . .'

'Except for Sarah, of course, so don't be surprised if she's a little shocked. Did you bring some music?'

'Music?' They'd stopped by the living room door, and Evan couldn't work out what was going on. Not only did the party seem to be expecting him, they also seemed to be expecting him to *play*. 'Er, no.'

'Never mind – I'm sure we can find something suitable – or rather, getting-out-of-your-suit-able.' The girl giggled and placed her hand on the door knob. 'But I warn you, it's a bit raucous in there.'

Evan didn't need her to tell him that – from the sounds he could hear coming from the living room, it sounded like a full-on rave was taking place. Realising his best option was just to go with it, he followed the girl in through the door, wincing as she put her fingers in her mouth and whistled loudly. The room held perhaps a dozen women, all equally dressed-up and apparently equally as drunk, and as he tried to spot Sarah in the throng, one of them leapt up off the sofa and squeezed his backside roughly.

He stood there, too shocked to move, although not as shocked as Sarah, who'd just followed Grace in from the kitchen.

'What the fu . . .'

Evan smiled awkwardly, conscious that conversation was impossible thanks to the combination of the cranked up music coming from the stereo in the corner and the fact that the women seemed to have broken into a chorus of 'Off! Off! Off!', then his stomach lurched. *Christ*, he suddenly realised. *They think I'm a stripper.*

For a second, and drawing a complete blank on any other options, he toyed with the idea of playing along, maybe even removing his jacket, but by the look of horror on Sarah's face, that wouldn't have been a good idea. Fortunately, she'd read the situation too, and as the girls' chanting got even louder, she strode over to where he was standing, grabbed his arm, and all but frog-marched him into the kitchen.

'What are you doing here?' she said, pushing the door shut behind them, which only served to increase the volume of cat-calls from the next room.

Evan stared at her, wanting to tell her how beautiful she looked – despite the Deely-boppers and the L-plate round her neck – but he suspected that was probably inappropriate. He cleared his throat, painfully aware that the last time they'd been alone together, it had been to say goodbye.

'I wanted to leave you a note,' he said, retrieving the crumpled piece of paper from his jacket pocket and holding it out towards her, but Sarah made no move to take it.

'And you thought that crashing my hen night was the best time?'

'I'm sorry. I didn't think you'd be here.'

'*Jesus*, Evan. What if David turns up?'

Evan knew that was rather unlikely, given how when he'd left him an hour or so ago, David had had other things on his mind – or rather, his lap. 'He won't. He's still with . . . at some club.'

Sarah rolled her eyes. 'I'll bet.'

'Listen . . .' He took a deep breath, wondering how to begin. 'Sarah, I . . .'

'Don't, Evan.' She nodded towards the door, or more specifically, the noise coming from behind it. 'Not now. Not unless you want to parade naked around the flat. Mind you, it wouldn't be the first time.'

Evan tried to read her expression, pleased she seemed to be making a joke, but the baying from the lounge was getting louder, and he realised she was right – now wasn't the time, certainly with a room full of her drunken friends next door. 'Well, when? I'm not going to go away, you know?'

'That'll make a change,' said Sarah, then she caught herself. 'Tomorrow. But not here.'

He thought quickly. 'The Tate? One o'clock? In the café.' It was the first place that had sprung to mind, and the suggestion seemed to take Sarah by surprise.

'The Tate?'

'You know, where we . . .'

'I remember.' There was a strange look in her eyes, and Evan felt a sudden surge of hope. Going back there might help remind her what it was they once had – even though it was where they'd said goodbye. She swallowed hard, and he reached out to touch the side of her face.

'Don't cry.'

'It's my party,' she said defiantly, forcing a smile, and when she didn't back away, Evan wondered whether a kiss would be pushing his luck, but the answer to that was evidently 'yes', as the kitchen door suddenly burst open, and the girl who'd let him in leapt into the room.

'You're still dressed!' she moaned, then turned to Sarah. 'Don't you like him?'

Sarah smiled. 'Thanks, Em. But I think strippers are a little tacky, don't you? No offence,' she added, for Evan's benefit.

'Well,' harrumphed the girl. 'If you don't want him to strip, maybe he'll do it for us?'

The rest of the women let out a cheer behind her, and Evan started to feel uneasy. Particularly because for a second, it looked like Sarah was considering the idea.

'Sorry,' he said, quickly. 'I can't. Contractually, I mean. If the person I was originally hired for doesn't want me to, you know, *perform*, I can't.'

'Why ever not?' said the girl.

'Health and safety?' suggested Sarah.

'Yeah,' said Evan. 'It could be dangerous.'

'Dangerous?' said the girl, disbelievingly, staring at Evan's groin. 'What have you *got* down there?'

Sarah smiled, mock-regretfully. 'We'll never know, sadly.'

Evan hid his sigh of relief as the girl made a face. 'Spoilsport,' she said, then she walked over where he was standing and pecked him on the cheek, slipping something into his jacket pocket as she did so.

He allowed Sarah to escort him back through the front room and to the door, ignoring the booing from the other girls as they went.

'Tomorrow?' he whispered, as he stepped out into the hallway.

'Tomorrow,' agreed Sarah. 'Now piss off!' Then after the brief-est of smiles, she closed the door between them.

Evan stared at the glass panel for a few moments, and then, suddenly tired, he turned and walked along the hallway and into the still-waiting lift. This, he thought, was progress – of sorts. At least he'd secured a chance to talk to her properly, and she hadn't told him where to go. At least, not seriously.

Back at ground level, he removed the envelope full of ten pound notes the girl had slipped into his pocket, and supposed he ought to put it into Sarah's mailbox, but as he reached the front door, a bemused-looking body-builder wearing a poorly fitting fancy-dress policeman's outfit was peering at the door buzzers. Evan let himself out, and the man looked up at him.

'You don't know where a Sarah Bishop lives, do you, mate?' he asked desperately. 'Supposed to be here an hour ago. Couldn't get a bloody taxi.'

Evan nodded. '6-E,' he said, enunciating carefully. 'You're too late, though.'

The man cursed under his breath. 'Party over, is it?'

Evan smiled. 'It will be soon.'

The man turned away dejectedly, and Evan tapped him on the shoulder. 'Here,' he said, handing over the envelope. 'I think this was supposed to be yours.'

And as he began the walk back to his flat, he found himself hoping David would soon be saying the same thing to him.

24

Evan reached over to hit the 'snooze' button on his alarm clock, then, just as he remembered he didn't own an alarm clock, realised the annoying buzzing sound was coming from his mobile on the chair in the corner of his bedroom. He leapt out of bed and lunged for it, stubbing his big toe painfully on the bedside table, then cursed when he saw the number displayed wasn't Sarah's as he'd hoped, but Mel's.

'What time is it?'

'What am I?' said Mel, gruffly. 'The fucking speaking clock?'

'That sounds like one of those dodgy 0800 numbers.'

'Huh?'

'Never mind.' Evan located his watch on top of his chest of drawers. To his relief he hadn't overslept and missed his appointment with Sarah. 'Sorry, Mel. I'm still a bit groggy. Jet lag and a hangover aren't the best combination.'

'So how was the big stag night?'

'Confusing.'

'Don't tell me – you didn't know which knife and fork to use for each course, or what way to pass the port?'

'No, nothing like that. It's . . .' Evan sat on the edge of the bed and rubbed his throbbing toe. 'I just can't work out what she sees in him.'

'He's rich, right?'

'Yeah, but . . .'

'Good job, nice car, posh flat, expense account, probably gets his condoms tailor-made on Savile Row.' Mel laughed 'Well, there you go.'

Evan sighed. He was pretty sure it wasn't the money – Sarah didn't seem the type. When he'd taken her out to lunch by bringing her sandwiches to eat in the park, she'd seemed delighted with that. Had fun, even. And while he couldn't help wondering about the kind of restaurants she and David went to, or where they spent their free time, David simply didn't seem like a fun guy.

'Sarah's not impressed by that kind of thing.'

'Okay, okay. But it's probably the circles she moves in, yeah? So maybe impressed is the wrong word. "Accustomed to" might be a better way of describing it.'

'She's not like that, Mel.'

'You positive, are you?'

'Pretty much. I mean, I've known women in the past who were all about money or status, their goal in life to land the rich guy, or the one up on stage in front of them . . .'

'Like she did with you?'

Evan opened his mouth to answer, then shut it again. He knew well enough that there was something about musicians that women seemed to find attractive – simply being part of 'the band' would increase even the most average-looking person's sex appeal ten-fold. Ask most teenage boys who played an instrument why they took it up in the first place, they'd tell you it was to meet girls, and if they didn't, they were probably lying.

'It wasn't the same.'

'No?'

'No!'

'How can you be sure?'

'Hello? Jazzed? I've been there, remember. And even on the Police tour we had a few hanging around, trying to get noticed by the main men . . .'

'Old men, you mean? They're closer to drawing their pensions than I am!' Mel laughed down the phone. 'Which just proves that fame and money are aphrodisiacs. It's just a shame you don't have either anymore. And that your new bestie has the latter.'

'Mel, he's not my new bestie.'

'Well, he seems to be Sarah's, so there has to be something about him. But what will you do if it *is* the money?'

'Borrow some from you?'

'I'd have to get it back from my ex-wives first,' said Mel, bitterly. 'But seriously . . .'

'Then Sarah's not the girl I thought she was. And so she's not for me.'

'Well, let's hope that's not the case, eh?' There was a pause as Evan heard Mel light a cigarette, followed by a loud series of coughs. 'Anyway, what are you up to?'

'Sleeping.'

'Lazy sod.'

'Mel, I had a late night, more alcohol than even *you* could put away, and I'm still on American time. So unless the club's on fire, or you're trapped under something heavy . . .'

'I should be so lucky.' Mel laughed again. 'Fancy continuing this conversation over lunch?'

'I can't.'

Mel sighed loudly. 'Don't tell me – you're meeting up with David for Pimms on the lawn, followed by a game of croquet.'

'I'm meeting Sarah, actually.'

'Great,' said Mel. 'You can stop wasting my time and ask her yourself, then.'

'Yeah, right.'

'Oh, and go and see Johnny. He's got some news for you.'

'Johnny? My agent Johnny?'

'No – Johnny Cash.' Evan could almost hear Mel roll his eyes. 'Of course Johnny your agent. Though funnily enough, you might start calling him Johnny Cash after . . .'

'Bye, Mel.'

Evan ended the call and flopped miserably back down on the bed. Mel was right – there had to be something. And aside from asking Grace, which he hadn't been able to do, or even quizzing Sarah directly, which he didn't *dare* do, Evan couldn't think how to find out what it was, and if he couldn't, then how on earth could he compete with it?

He stared blankly up at the ceiling until the room stopped spinning, then hauled himself up and headed for the shower. *One thing at a time*, he told himself, and at the moment, the most important thing was to actually leave Sarah in no doubt as to how he felt about her. Next, he'd need to make her see that David wasn't right for her, and after that . . . well, that *he* was. And then? He'd deal with that if things ever got that far, because right now, the prospect of achieving those first two objectives was looming above him like the North face of the Eiger.

And he had to start climbing.

Fast.

25

Sarah was leaning on the sink, inspecting her face in the bathroom mirror. Under the harsh fluorescent light, make-up free, *and* with a hangover, she worried she looked older than her thirty-four years. Thank heaven for concealer, she thought, rummaging around in her make-up bag.

She was tired, too, which no doubt contributed to the dark circles underneath her eyes. The last of the girls had left at around three a.m., and she and Grace had been up for a further half an hour dabbing at the rug with 1001. Cosmopolitans were all well and good except when they spilt everywhere, as the third or fourth one invariably did.

She rubbed gingerly at the faint scratches on her breasts, courtesy of the sharp corners of last night's L-plates. It had been a fun evening, up until Evan's unscheduled appearance, and while she didn't know what had happened to the *actual* stripper, Evan had been a shocking enough interlude. And according to Grace, the look on her face had been priceless.

The smell of bacon drifting in under the bathroom door was making her stomach do somersaults, so she made her way into the kitchen, where Grace was standing in front of the grill.

'How can you?'

Grace turned and smiled at her. 'Best hangover cure ever. Well, second best. But seeing as I'm currently single, it'll have to do.' She pulled the grill pan out and inspected the charred rashers, then nodded towards the kitchen table, where several slices of thickly-buttered-and-ketchupped white bread had been piled on a plate. 'Want one?'

'How many people are you making breakfast for?'

'Just you and me.' She peered over Sarah's shoulder. 'Unless a certain someone stayed over?'

Sarah turned red, feeling guilty for not telling Grace last night that she'd agreed to see Evan today, but she could hardly believe she'd agreed to it herself. Besides, Grace might not approve, and the last thing Sarah needed at the moment was her friend's disapproval, especially since she suspected she might need her support over the next few days.

'Don't start.'

'Sorry.' Grace grinned mischievously. 'How are you feeling?'

Sarah flopped down into the nearest chair. 'I don't know. Him turning up like that . . .'

'I meant your hangover.'

'Huh? Oh. A bit rough, actually. I think it might have been the fish.'

'As in you drinking like one?'

'Ha ha,' said Sarah. At least the splitting headache she'd woken up with was fading, thanks to the Advil she'd taken at breakfast. None of that lightweight English paracetamol for her – Americans knew how to medicate. Though Sarah knew it could have been worse, but Evan's surprise appearance had sobered her up pretty quickly, and as soon as she'd known she was seeing him today, she'd stopped drinking altogether. 'You feeling bad?'

'Nothing one or two of these won't fix.' Grace turned the grill off and switched into bacon sandwich assembly-line mode. 'Here,' she said, handing Sarah a plate, along with a glass of orange juice. 'Get that down you.'

Sarah hesitated for a moment, then picked the sandwich up and took a bite, causing ketchup to drip onto the front of her dressing gown.

'I didn't actually mean "down you".' Grace handed her a piece of kitchen towel. 'It's lucky we *don't* have guests . . .'

'*Grace.*'

'Sorry.'

They ate in silence for a few moments, until Grace couldn't help herself.

'So . . .'

'So what?'

'Any thoughts?'

'About?'

Grace just stared at her, so Sarah sighed resignedly and put her half-eaten sandwich down on her plate. 'He asked me to meet him. To talk.'

'When?'

'Today. Lunchtime.'

'You're not going?'

'Well . . .'

Grace paused, mid-chew. '*Sarah* . . .'

'I just thought, well, he's flown all the way back over, and it might be the last time I ever see him, so . . .'

'What about David?'

'What about him? I'm not planning to *do* anything.'

'You weren't planning to do anything a year ago, and look what happened then.'

'This is different.'

'How?'

'Because I'm engaged.'

156

'Which is exactly why you shouldn't be meeting your old boyfriend. And especially one who's unfinished business.'

'He's not an old boyfriend.'

'I notice you didn't correct my second observation.' Grace picked up her sandwich and took another bite. 'Is he coming here?' she mumbled, covering her mouth with her hand as she spoke.

'No. We're meeting at the Tate. In the café.'

'Isn't that a bit public?'

'Which is exactly why it's okay.'

Grace looked horrified. 'What if David sees you? Don't you think you should phone him to see where he is? Or at least find out how his evening was, and maybe buy yourself a few hours?'

Sarah glanced at the clock on the front of the cooker. It wasn't yet midday, and knowing David's capacity for lie-ins (not to mention his capacity for alcohol) she decided to leave him be. 'It's the Tate. The only time he goes anywhere with art on the walls is if it's for sale, so I think I'll be safe, especially in the café. David wouldn't be seen dead in a venue with a laminated wine list.'

Grace raised both eyebrows. 'Isn't everything for sale at the right price?'

Sarah laughed. 'I think the Tate collection's beyond even him. Besides, the only thing he hates more than jazz is modern art.'

'I think he might change those two things around if he knows what you're up to.'

'I'm not "up to" anything, Grace.'

'No?'

'No.' Sarah put the rest of her sandwich down on her plate. 'Maybe this'll be our big clear-the-air session. So we can deal with all those unsaid things that have been left hanging for the last year, and part as friends.'

'I didn't think you could have a friend whose clothes you wanted to rip off every time you saw them. *Especially* if you're married.' Grace smiled wryly. 'You are going to finish it, aren't you?'

'There's nothing to finish, Grace.'

'I meant your sandwich,' said Grace, eyeing Sarah's plate hungrily. 'What time are you meeting him?'

'One.'

'Well, don't you think you ought to get dressed? You don't want to be late. For your hot date. At the Tate. 'Coz he might not wait . . .' She'd adopted a sing-song voice, and Sarah glared at her good-naturedly.

'Grace, please.'

'Then again, he's waited a year . . .'

Sarah shook her head as she slid her plate over towards her flatmate. 'Here. Hopefully this'll shut you up.'

As Grace wolfed down the rest of her sandwich, Sarah sipped her orange juice, then she got up and made her way to the bathroom to a chorus of 'Can't be late for your date at the Tate,' from a full-mouthed Grace. She found Evan's choice of meeting venue interesting – of course, he couldn't come here to the flat, and she wouldn't have trusted herself at his, and to name a random coffee bar for their rendezvous might have been risky, but there? She'd been back many a time since that fateful day. It was her favourite view of London. His favourite view *in* London, he'd told her once – and he'd been gazing at her at the time, so maybe he was trying to be clever. Remind her of the old times. But then again, old times were exactly that. Things were different now.

She brushed her teeth, shaved her legs, then faced the clothing dilemma. If she and Evan were together, she wouldn't care what she wore to meet him, as it'd only end up in a pile on the bedroom floor within minutes of their kiss hello. But they weren't, so she needed to convey an image that said that she was off the market – though how on earth did you do that if a flash of your engagement ring and the imminence of your wedding hadn't worked?

Pulling on a pair of jeans, she checked her rear view in the full-length mirror, then selected a simple white blouse, doing up the buttons until they just hid her bra, then undoing one again. While today was show-and-tell, she couldn't resist a little show-and-tempt too – she'd always found Evan's lustful gaze so flattering. David never looked at her like that, his expression generally more grateful than excited, like a faithful old Labrador about to be fed.

She finished applying her make-up, then stood back from the mirror, deciding she'd hit upon the right combination of casual and sexy. Just what a girl wanted to look like if she was meeting a former lover. *That was it*, she told herself. He'd been a fling, nothing more. Whereas David had been her boyfriend, now he was her fiancé. On Saturday he'd be her husband – and that made a big difference.

She caught sight of the time and felt the butterflies in her stomach increasing, although they were nothing new. She'd been feeling like this ever since the wedding had loomed up out of the distance, and now it seemed to be marching inexorably towards her. And while so far she'd managed to keep it in her peripheral vision, Evan's sudden reappearance had brought next Saturday front and centre.

With a sigh, Sarah picked up her keys, shouted goodbye to Grace, and walked out of her front door. *Yes*, she thought, fingering her engagement ring as she walked past David's BMW, *things were definitely different now.*

Although she was a little worried that she had to keep repeating that fact to herself.

26

Evan gazed out through the café's window, marvelling at the view across the Thames as he sipped his third espresso, though as yet, the coffee didn't seem to be having any effect on the jet lag he was still struggling to shake off.

He checked his watch, noticing both that Sarah was late and that his hands were shaking, and while that may have been down to the caffeine fighting for dominance with the alcohol still in his system from the previous evening, he still felt as jumpy as a teenager on a first date.

Not that he could recall his first date, though he remembered the first girl who'd rejected him – Julie Cowan – back when he was an awkward eleven-year-old, and before he'd discovered the musical ability that had made him suddenly visible to the opposite sex. He'd worshipped her from afar at school – though she probably hadn't had the faintest idea who he was – and when he'd eventually plucked up the courage to call her from the phone box at the end of his street and ask her out, all she'd done was laugh down the line at him, so Evan had put the phone down and begun the walk home in shame. It was only when he'd got halfway down the road that it had occurred to him he might have accepted her 'no' prematurely, so he'd turned and sprinted back to the phone box, where – with a sudden burst of misplaced confidence and his last ten pence piece – he'd rung her back and told her that if she changed her mind, she should give him a call. Then – as now – he'd sat waiting for something that, as time had dragged on, had seemed more and more unlikely to come.

He still felt embarrassed at the memory. Even now, he could remember the sniggering as he'd walked, shame-faced, into school the next day, past where Julie had been standing, pointing at him while whispering to her friends. Though while this time he didn't mind embarrassing himself, he worried he might not even get the chance to – Sarah could simply be planning to turn up, tell him to leave her alone, then go. But Evan hoped he'd read her better than that, and that she'd at least be interested in hearing what he had to say. Surely he could stretch that out over a drink – especially since it might be the last drink they ever had together.

For the hundredth time, he glanced down towards where the Millennium Bridge – or the wobbly bridge, as everyone still referred to it, given how its lack of stability when first built had made crossing it feel like, well, like Evan had felt the first time he'd seen Sarah – met the South Bank, to see whether he could see her among the lunchtime crowds, and spotted her hurrying towards the gallery's entrance. His heart began to hammer, so he pulled the adjacent vacant chair he'd been guarding for the last twenty minutes closer, took a moment to calm himself, then subtly checked his breath in his cupped hand. Not that he thought there'd be any kissing, but you never knew – he'd even tidied his flat and put clean sheets on the bed, although he reckoned the likelihood of anything like *that* happening was pretty small. Still, be prepared, and all that. Sarah could surprise you. Evan knew that to his cost.

A *ping* announced the lift's arrival, and as the doors opened, she fought her way through a group of Japanese tourists. As she slipped off her coat, he fixed a smile and stood up, enjoying the sight of her walking towards him.

'Thanks for coming.'

Sarah looked at him levelly. 'Did I have any choice?'

'I suppose not,' he said, noticing her blouse was undone an extra button, trying – and failing – not to stare at her cleavage. He didn't feel confident enough to chance his luck with any physical contact, so instead, just nodded towards the chair. 'Sit. Please. Can I get you anything?'

Sarah hesitated, as if considering whether accepting either a seat or a drink would be starting out offering too many concessions, then she draped her coat over the back of the chair and sat down.

'Just a sparkling water, please. Ice, no lemon.'

'Heavy night last night?' he said, almost unthinkingly, and Sarah scowled at him.

'Heavier than I wanted, yes.'

Evan winced, then walked across to the bar and ordered Sarah's water, repeating the order twice to the girl behind the counter, then checking again once she'd poured it, as if everything hinged on getting her drink right. He carried it carefully back over to their seats, and sat down nervously.

'Here.'

'Thanks.' Sarah stared at her glass for a moment, then pushed it away. 'What did you think you were doing?'

'What do you mean?'

'Last night.'

'Oh. That.'

'Yes, Evan. *That*.'

'Like I said, I was only planning to drop off a note.'

'Yes, but . . .' Sarah shook her head. '*David*.'

'What about him?'

'You went on his *stag night*,' she said, incredulously.

Evan held his hands up. 'I was caught off guard when I bumped into you. And I certainly didn't think he'd invite me to his, well . . .' He almost laughed. The situation had been pretty ridiculous.

'You didn't have to go, you know?'

Evan wondered whether Sarah meant a year ago, then understood she was referring to David's stag. 'Yes, I did,' he said, before realising, ironically, that the same answer was true a year ago too.

'You could have just said no.'

Evan bit his tongue, then decided *What the hell.* 'So could you, Sarah.'

'How, Evan? How exactly could I have said no? And more importantly, why should I have? Especially since you'd decided you weren't going to hang around.'

He stared at her, open-mouthed. Had she forgotten the actual sequence of events? 'How the hell could you have got engaged to someone you . . .'

'Cheated on?'

'Yes.'

'Because he asked me, Evan. He had the balls to step up to the plate and ask me. Whereas you were quite happy to sleep with me and then never call . . .' She stopped talking, suddenly conscious of how loud she was being.

'I didn't even think I was in the frame.'

'In the frame?' said Sarah indignantly. 'What did you think? That I slept with every man I knew?'

'Of course not.' He shifted round on his stool and stared out of the window. 'I thought we were having a good time. Had potential, even. And then you announced that you were seeing someone else. What was I supposed to have done?'

'I don't know.' Sarah threw her hands in the air theatrically. 'Not leave? Or at least keep in touch? Or . . .'

'Or?'

'Fight for me?'

Evan turned back to face her. 'That's what I'm doing now,' he said, softly.

'With my wedding a week away?' She was staring at him in disbelief. 'Did you not think it might be a little bit late?'

'You tell me.' Evan met her gaze. 'Is it?'

And there it was. The hesitation Evan had been hoping for. A sign that perhaps all wasn't well between her and David.

'I've made him a promise.'

'And you hadn't before? When we . . .' He hunted for the right word, but couldn't find it.

'Christ, Evan,' she said, the steeliness back. 'I'd only just met him. It wasn't like we were having some major romance.'

'But you are now?'

She held up her left hand, and for a moment Evan wondered why she seemed to be giving him the finger, until he realised she was showing him her engagement ring. 'What do you think?'

'I'm not sure.'

'What's that supposed to mean?'

'David. He's . . .' He puffed air out of his cheeks, trying to compose his thoughts, remembering he didn't want to make this about David. 'Nothing.'

Sarah sighed loudly. 'What am I doing here, Evan? Or rather, what are *we* doing here?'

'Okay.' He took a deep breath. 'Here it comes.' He sat up straight, then fiddled with his coffee cup. 'Right.'

'Evan . . .'

'Sorry.' He cleared his throat awkwardly. 'Say you'd made a mistake, or made the wrong choice, and you had the slimmest of chances, the smallest window of opportunity, to go back and try and correct that, what would you do? Just go "Oh well" and ignore it, and let it fester for the rest of your life, always wondering what might have been? Or at least investigate the possibility that there might be a chance that you could, you know . . .' He cleared his throat again. 'Put it right.'

'Evan, I'm . . .'

'Don't say "flattered", please.'

'No – "sorry". Really I am. But I'm getting married to David. On Saturday.'

Evan felt something shrivel up inside. 'Are you?'

'Of course. What did you think – that you could just ride in here like some knight in shining armour and whisk me away? I don't need rescuing.'

'Will you at least think about it?'

'Think about what?' Sarah was getting angry again. 'Calling off something I've been planning for the best part of nine months and disappointing someone who loves me simply because you've suddenly decided you might have made a mistake a year ago and so you've popped back over the pond to see if there's any chance that we could hook up again?'

'It's not like that,' he said, realising it was, actually, like that.

'What *is* it like, then? What are you offering me, exactly?'

'Offering?'

'Yes. Are *we* going to get married? Elope? Or did you just want us to pick up where we let off, but this time with David out of the picture?'

'Well . . .' Evan stopped talking. He hadn't expected such a direct question. What *did* he want? Just Sarah, really. Beyond that, he hadn't really thought. Although he was beginning to wish he had.

'You see, that's your problem,' Sarah said, exasperatedly, as if she'd read his mind. 'You don't know what it is you want.' She moved to get off her stool, but Evan put a hand on her arm.

'Don't go,' he said. 'Not like this.'

'Evan, you're . . .' She looked upset, and Evan worried she might start crying. 'You're confusing things. And I can't afford to be confused. Not now.'

'Tell me there's not a part of you that doesn't feel something for me.'

She shrugged his hand off. 'Of course there is. But that doesn't mean there's not another part of me that feels more for David.'

'Maybe you wouldn't, if you knew . . .'

'Knew what?'

Evan was aware that this was his chance to land what could well be the killer blow, but for some reason, he couldn't bring himself to tell her about David's indiscretion. Instead, he took her hand. 'That I love you.'

'What?'

'I love you,' he repeated, surprised how easily the words came out, how natural they sounded. 'That's why I came back. To tell you that.'

Sarah pulled her hand away, almost in tears now. 'How can you? We just . . .' She shook her head. 'It was only one night.'

'The best night of my life.'

'Christ, Evan. Your timing . . .'

'Next week would have been worse,' he said, attempting to lighten the mood, but judging by her expression, Sarah didn't find it in the least bit funny.

'I have to go,' she said, standing up abruptly.

'Don't. Please.'

'Give me one good reason not to.'

'Haven't I already?'

'Evan . . .'

'Okay. Well, you haven't finished your drink,' he said, desperately.

'My drink?' Sarah picked her glass up, then to his surprise, emptied it over his head. 'Happy now?'

'What was that for?'

'For running out on me.' She grabbed her coat from the back of her chair and started towards the lift. 'And then, for coming back.'

Evan slicked his wet hair back off his face, causing an ice cube to slip down the inside of his shirt collar. 'But don't you understand?' he said, leaping off his chair to follow her. 'I came back for you.'

'No you didn't.' Sarah strode angrily into the waiting lift and wheeled round to face him, her expression warning him not to follow. 'You came back for *you*.'

'Sarah, wait,' he pleaded, as she stabbed the 'down' button repeatedly. 'Both those things are related.'

'How can they be?'

'Because I came back for *us*,' he shouted, as the lift doors closed.

Though if Sarah had heard him – or even cared – it was impossible to tell.

27

Sarah dug her nails into her palm as the elevator descended, struggling to hold herself together. She didn't want to cry in front of the group of French students who'd got on at the next level and were now crammed in around her, jabbering excitedly to each other, but something about Evan's out-of-the-blue declaration had unsettled her.

She fished in her coat pocket for a Kleenex to stifle the tears she knew were coming, though she feared the couple left in the packet might not be enough. With Evan out of the picture, she'd managed to convince herself that accepting David's proposal made sense, but now, with him back . . . well, she couldn't help wondering whether she was doing the right thing.

She wasn't surprised to find she still had feelings for him – that kind of thing didn't just switch off – but after a year of no contact, she was shocked how strong the physical attraction still was. The one night they'd spent together had been so exciting – they'd almost instinctively known what would turn the other on – whereas sometimes, sex with David . . . She'd joked to Grace once that at times it was like a transatlantic flight: you prayed for sleep in the middle, and that you'd wake up and it'd be over. Once or twice, on the less-frequent occasions she and David made love nowadays – he was often too tired from work, or too drunk after yet another late-night client-entertaining session at those bars and clubs he and the other male partners loved to visit – she'd found herself fantasising about Evan. The way he'd touched her. How he'd made her feel. And the response that that never failed to provoke had, ironically, always put a smile on David's face.

The elevator doors opened, and she hurried out through the gallery's foyer and into the fresh air, hoping Evan hadn't followed her, determined to put some distance between them, although she realised that was perhaps a little futile – the Atlantic ocean evidently hadn't been enough. The impulse to kiss him had been strong – almost stronger than the anger she felt towards him for loving and leaving her like he did – and she wasn't sure she could resist it again. Maybe she should have poured the glass of cold water over herself.

She strode along the South Bank, her head still reeling, wondering what she would have done if Evan *had* decided not to go. It would have been a difficult call – from the off, she'd known David could offer her security, marriage, kids, the whole nine yards, whereas a life with Evan would have meant what, exactly – living from gig to gig? Though that was unfair. Evan made a decent living from what he did – a lot more than most musicians – plus his recent tour must have paid him well, and besides, the money had never been a factor. But David had asked her first, and sometimes, asking first *did* make a difference.

She glanced tentatively back over her shoulder as she turned into her street, but Evan was nowhere to be seen, so she slowed her pace as she neared her building, replaying what had just happened in her head. It was almost comical, what she'd just done. Melodramatic. Not like her at all. But then again, Evan's announcement hadn't been like anything she'd ever experienced either.

With a sigh, she rode the elevator up to her floor and unlocked her front door, then stopped dead in her tracks at the sight of David dozing on her couch. Grace must have let him in before leaving for work, and even though he'd have no way of knowing where she'd been, Sarah was sure it was written all over her face. Her first thought was to sneak back out without disturbing him to give her time to concoct an alibi, but as she reached for the door handle, he jolted awake. Fortunately, by the look of things, he didn't seem particularly with it.

'Afternoon,' she said, as cheerily as she could.

'Is it?'

She walked over to where he lay, his loafer-clad feet protruding over the armrest, and kissed him tenderly on the forehead. 'How are you feeling?'

David attempted to sit up, then evidently thought better of it. 'Like someone's used my head as a rugger ball. You?'

'Fine. You know me – a couple of Advil, and I'm okay. Just thought I'd go for a walk along the Thames. Get some fresh air.'

'So Grace said.'

Sarah made a mental note to thank her. 'You should try it.'

He groaned. 'Fresh air's the last thing I need. A Bloody Mary and a full English, however . . .'

Sarah grimaced at the thought of both of those things. 'Did you walk round here?' she asked, remembering his car was parked outside, although on reflection, she knew the answer to that already.

'Yah, right.' He smirked. 'So how did it go?'

'It?'

'Last night.'

Sarah nodded. 'Good. Fun, in fact.'

'Were you surprised when he turned up?'

Sarah froze in the middle of shrugging her coat off, as if playing a game of musical statues and the music had just stopped. 'When who turned up?' she said, glad she had her back to him.

'The stripper. Emma let slip she was getting you one. Asked my permission first, of course.'

Sarah gave him a look. 'I didn't know your permission was required.'

'So were you? Surprised?'

'A little,' said Sarah, sitting down in the armchair opposite. 'But I didn't let him, you know . . .' She flushed slightly at the thought of Evan taking his clothes off. 'Strip.'

David widened his eyes, the effort obviously causing him some distress. 'Why ever not? I thought you'd be desperate to see another man naked. After all, it's only been me for the last year. Though I suppose when you've been used to steak at home . . .'

He grinned, and for a moment Sarah toyed with the idea of reminding him the rest of that quote was something about everyone fancying a hamburger once in a while.

'And how was your evening?'

'Expensive.'

'Where did you end up?'

David reached up to massage his temples. 'Some place that Hans knew.'

'I bet.' Sarah knew better than to ask what kind of place, particularly given the nickname of 'Wandering Hans' that the younger PAs in the office had given him. Trouble was, she did want to ask about Evan, but aside from mentioning him by name, she couldn't think of a way to bring the subject up. 'So,' she said, eventually. 'Did everyone have a good time?'

David shrugged, wincing with the effort. 'I'd say so, judging by the size of the bar bill. Although I'm not sure about your friend.'

'My friend?'

'Evan.' He peered at her. 'Tell me something.'

Sarah braced herself. 'Uh-huh?'

'Does he bat for the other side?'

'I beg your pardon?'

'Is he, you know, *gay*?'

Sarah had to concentrate hard to stop herself from laughing. 'I don't think so, no. Why ever would you think that?'

'At the club. All the chaps were enjoying themselves with the girls, but he seemed . . .' David shrugged again. 'Offended by the whole thing. In fact, I think he might have left. Certainly didn't say goodbye.'

Sarah stared at him, strangely pleased to hear that. 'Maybe he was just tired,' she said, after a moment. 'He said he was jet lagged.'

'Ah. Of course.'

'And what about you, David?' she tried to ask levelly, but couldn't keep the suspicion out of her voice. 'Did you "enjoy yourself" at the club?'

'Sorry, sweetheart.' He yawned, then rolled onto his side and buried his face in a cushion. 'But you know how it is. What goes on tour stays on tour, and all that.'

If only, Sarah thought, half-wishing Evan had stayed on his. 'Fine. I won't ask,' she said, making her way into the kitchen.

She carried the kettle over to the sink and turned on the tap, then had to lean heavily against the counter. She'd realised what it had been, why she'd never allowed herself to consider a future with Evan, and it had almost knocked the wind out of her. It was obvious, now she thought about it: the one thing he hadn't done, the only thing she'd wanted him to, was simply to ask her.

Exactly like he appeared to be doing now.

28

Evan watched the numbers count down on the display, not knowing what to do next. The other lifts were all on different floors, so he sprinted for the stairs, taking them two at a time as he fought his way through the hordes of dawdling visitors. As fit as he was, he knew seven flights of stairs was a big ask against the gallery's modern lift system, and as he'd feared, by the time he reached the ground floor, Sarah was nowhere to be seen.

He ran through the turbine hall, up the ramp, then round towards the South Bank, scanning the crowds anxiously, not knowing which way she'd gone, before collapsing helplessly onto the nearest bench and putting his head in his hands. His hair was still wet from the soaking Sarah had given him, and water dripped from it onto the pavement in front of him; with his chest heaving from the effort of the run, any casual observer could be forgiven for thinking he was crying.

Cursing softly, he caught his breath, then leaned back and stared up at the cloudless sky. He'd seen some dramatic exits in his time, and he had to hand it to her – that had been by far the best one. And while he hadn't expected Sarah to pay him back for crashing her bridal shower by giving *him* a drenching, at least he'd had a chance to state his case. To say what he'd come back to say. And if she still didn't want to see him after that, well, he'd just have to find a way to live with it. After he'd exhausted every opportunity to change her mind, of course.

He replayed their conversation in his head, still a little troubled by Sarah's 'what are you offering?' remark. Had she meant *financially*? Thanks to the tour he was a little more secure, although nowhere near what he imagined David's league was, but while he knew he couldn't compete with David on paper, that didn't worry him; real life was never played out on paper.

He shook the water from his hair, then hauled himself up off the bench and headed west along the South Bank, not really sure where he was going. The cinema at the NFT was showing Capra's *It's a Wonderful Life*, but that was the last thing Evan wanted to see, particularly since he didn't actually believe that it was. Not after what had just happened.

As he reached the top of the steps by Waterloo Bridge, a jogger heading in the opposite direction almost knocked him back down them. She was pretty, and about Sarah's age, and as she smiled her apology at him, her expression changed to one of surprise.

'You're him, aren't you?' she said, pulling her headphones out of her ears and jogging back over to where he was standing.

Evan made a face. 'No I'm not,' he said, continuing on his way.

'Yes you are,' she said, running backwards in front of him as she studied his face, but as Evan tried to go around her, she blocked his way, then put both hands on his shoulders.

'Yes?'

'You're . . .' She stared at him, then let out a frustrated yelp. 'No, you're going to have to tell me.'

'Tell you what?'

'Who you are.'

Evan frowned. 'So hang on. You stop me and tell me I'm someone, then you have to ask me who it is that you think I am?'

The woman was still jogging on the spot in front of him, dodging from side to side, preventing him from passing. 'Yeah. Come on.'

Evan shrugged. 'The Pope? Nelson Mandela?'

'No, silly!' The woman grinned. 'That guy from that band. You know who I mean.'

Evan felt the familiar sinking feeling in the pit of his stomach. 'What band?'

'You were on TV the other day.' The woman was hopping from one foot to another now, as if she needed the toilet. 'Some programme about one-hit wonders. "Where Are They Now", it was called. Or something like that.'

Evan sighed resignedly, realising there was only one way out of this. 'Jazzed?'

The woman shook her head. 'No. I'm just out of breath from my run.'

'No, the band. It . . . We were called Jazzed.'

'I don't think that was it.'

'Yes it was. I should know. I came up with the name.'

'Jazzed?' The woman narrowed her eyes and thought for a moment. 'What was your biggest hit?'

'Do you remember the theme to Rising Falls?'

'Never heard of it. Name another one.'

Evan looked at her. 'What was that programme about again?'

'One-hit wonders. Why?' The woman stared back at him, then realisation dawned. 'Ah. Right. Sorry. So how did the theme from . . . What was it?'

'Rising Falls.'

'*Rising Falls* go?'

'Forgetting for one moment the fact that I don't have my sax with me, you surely don't expect me to play it, here on the street?'

The woman looked as if that was exactly what she expected him to do. 'You could hum it?' she suggested.

Evan raised his eyes to the heavens and mentally counted to five. 'Listen, it's always a pleasure to meet a fan, but you're quite clearly not one, so if you don't mind . . .'

As he resumed his journey, the woman's face fell. 'Okay,' she called after him, disappointedly. 'Sorry. But it was nice meeting you.'

Whoever you are? said Evan, under his breath. He kept on walking, then heard footsteps running up behind him, so he swivelled around, hoping it might be Sarah.

'Me again,' said the woman, then she reached into the pocket of her running top and removed a sweat-moistened business card. 'Here.'

'What's this for?'

The woman blushed, which, given how her face was already red from her run, made her look as if she was suffering from sunstroke. 'In case you fancied a coffee some time,' she said, giving him the briefest of smiles before jogging off in the opposite direction.

Evan shook his head as he watched her go, and realised he *did* fancy a coffee – along with the side order of advice Finn usually served up with it, so he changed direction and headed towards Borough High Street. As he walked, he examined the card the woman had just given him, then tossed it into the nearest bin. Under different circumstances he might have taken her up on her offer, but given his current obsession with Sarah, he'd barely registered it. This had been a common occurrence on tour, and one of the reasons he'd known the thing with Sarah was unfinished business – despite all the women he'd met in the U.S., he just hadn't found himself interested in anyone else. Hadn't even slept with anyone for the best part of six months, and even when he had, it had been down to loneliness rather than anything else – once, Evan had been plucking at a guitar during rehearsals, and a girl had come over to tell him the song he'd been playing was nice. He hadn't had the heart to tell her he'd just been tuning the instrument, and then later that evening, hadn't had the heart to tell her he didn't want to sleep with her either.

Strangely, if anything, it had only made him more sure of how he felt about Sarah. He'd woken up in shame the following morning, almost as if he'd been unfaithful, and had tried to justify what he'd done by telling himself that everyone had one-night stands. Maybe, he sometimes feared, that was what Sarah had been. But you didn't fall in love with someone you had a one-night stand with – and he had to hope that Sarah saw things the same way. What he'd do if she didn't, he didn't dare think about.

He reached the café and peered in through the window, pleased for his friend that the place was pretty busy, then spotted a poster advertising some upcoming nineties revival night on the wall next to their framed gold disc, the thought of which made Evan shudder. While Finn still played at the odd nostalgia gig, he'd never been tempted to join him, always of the mind that you should never try to relive past glories – although he found it ironic that he was ignoring his own advice where Sarah was concerned. He pushed the heavy glass door open, loosened his coat at the blast of heat that hit him, and made his way towards the counter, where Finn was noisily frothing a jug of milk. Smiling at the woman waiting by the till, he cleared his throat loudly.

'I've got a complaint!' he shouted.

Finn stopped what he was doing. 'Well, the doctor's surgery is two doors down,' he said, then he looked up, a huge smile on his face. 'Look what the cat dragged in.'

'Nice to see you too.'

Finn poured the milk into a large paper cup and clicked a plastic lid onto the top. 'Give me just one second,' he said, handing it to the woman, then he leaned over the counter, grabbed Evan's face by the cheeks, and gave him a loud kiss on the forehead.

'What did you do that for?' Evan wiped his forehead with his sleeve. 'It's embarrassing.'

'That's why I did it!' Finn winked at him as he took the woman's money and rang it through the till. 'When did you get back?'

'Couple of days ago.' Evan looked him up and down carefully. 'How are you? Been looking after yourself?'

'I'm good. And yes, thanks, Mum.' Finn squeezed him affectionately on the upper arm, doing a double-take at the muscle he could feel. 'Touring life suits you, I see?'

Evan shrugged. 'Oh, you know.'

'I wish I did, mate.' He made a face. 'Does Johnny know you're back?'

Evan shook his head. 'Not yet. Why?'

'No reason.' Finn grinned. 'So what brings you here?'

'Couldn't resist one of your coffees.'

'After a year of drinking that American sludge I'm not surprised. What can I get you? Your usual?'

'Great. Thanks.'

'Anything with it?'

Evan peered up at the chalk board on the back wall for inspiration, but couldn't find any. 'Some advice, maybe.'

'Advice?' Finn retrieved a couple of tiny espresso cups and placed them on the machine's drip tray. 'What about?'

'Marriage.'

Finn raised both eyebrows. 'Marriage?'

'It's, um, for a song I'm writing.'

Finn shook his head as he loaded the machine with coffee. 'Pull the other one, Evan.'

'Okay. Well, I'm just trying to make sure a friend of mine is making the right decision, that's all.'

'A "friend"?'

'Sarah.'

Finn smiled knowingly. Evan had told him about Sarah's newspaper announcement in a drunken late-night phone call a few weeks earlier. 'In that case,' he said, exchanging the cups for larger ones, 'I'd better make them doubles.'

'So, I was wondering,' said Evan, struggling to make himself heard over the noise from the coffee machine. 'When you ask someone to marry you . . .'

'What about it?'

'Well, how do you know it's the right thing to do?'

Finn regarded him curiously. 'Shouldn't you be asking David that?'

'Will you just answer the question, rather than giving me grief?'

'Sorry.' Finn carried their coffees over to a window table, and Evan followed him obediently. 'Well, I'm afraid you'll only really know afterwards.'

Evan's jaw dropped open. 'After you've got married?'

'No. After you've proposed. It's one of those questions. It never feels quite right in the lead-up to it. You almost always stumble over the words, and in fact, it's not until you've actually given them life – like when you play a piece of music for the first time – that you know whether it sounds right.'

'Yeah, but . . .' Evan sipped his espresso as he stared out into the street. 'How can you tell?'

'Because if it does, it's the best thing in the world. Better than sex, even.' Finn laughed at Evan's expression. 'But it can be the shortest-lived feeling ever too. Depending . . .'

'On?'

179

Finn reached over and rested a hand on Evan's shoulder. 'Her answer. Remember, she'll probably have put as much thought into that as you have into the proposal.'

'Great.' Evan put his coffee cup back down miserably. 'So what you're saying is, because she's said yes to *him*, that she's already made her choice, and so I shouldn't bother?'

'Not necessarily.' Finn smiled at him across the table. 'Did it ever occur to you to wonder why Sarah started seeing you, when she was already going out with him?'

'Well, she must have, you know . . .'

'What?'

Evan felt himself colour. 'Liked what she saw.'

Finn smirked. 'More likely she was trying to make her mind up.'

'About what?'

'David. Because that's normally what people do when they're trying to select something. Look at you and the Police gig. It all came down to you and that one other bloke, didn't it?'

'I guess,' said Evan. 'Although I didn't know that at the time.'

'Not unlike the Sarah situation.' Finn laughed. 'But there you go. Whatever you want, if it's a car, or a house, you draw up a short-list, right? Except you can't do that when you're dating, can you? Can't normally see two people at the same time, then decide which one you like.'

'Americans do.'

Finn folded his arms. 'Proves my point.'

'How?'

'Think about it. Most people – most *English* people, anyway – go out with a series of partners. Learn something from each one. Apply that to the next relationship they look for, then eventually end up with something, or some*one*, approaching the finished

180

product. That way, they've manoeuvred themselves into a position where the one they're with is the one they're meant to be with. But only after a lot of trial and error.'

'I'm sorry, Finn – this point you're trying to prove . . .'

Finn grinned. 'Is that she obviously didn't want to put herself through all that time and effort. She wasn't able to make her mind up about him, so she started seeing you, just to give her something to compare him to.'

'Is that supposed to make me feel better?'

'Doesn't it?'

'Not really, no.'

'Well, it should.'

'How?' said Evan, exasperatedly. 'She chose him. I obviously didn't measure up.'

'Doesn't sound like that to me.'

Evan sighed, then drained the rest of his coffee. 'Well, it's what she did, Finn. So it must have been.'

'Maybe not.'

'What do you mean, maybe not?'

'She picks you as her yardstick. You bugger off before she can make up her mind. And either she sticks with him because the clock is ticking, or she feels guilty about what she's done, or because he senses he might be losing her and redoubles his efforts.'

'Which might have been all she was after in the first place.' Evan shook his head slowly. 'I'm sorry, Finn. I just don't buy that.'

'Okay. Look at it this way. Say you'd ordered a latte, then the minute you did it, you realised you'd made the wrong decision.'

'This is hardly comparable to ordering a coffee.'

'That's not important. What *is* is the uncanny way you know you've made the wrong decision the instant after you've made what you thought was going to be the right one. Right?'

'I suppose so.'

'Right.' Finn leaned in closer and lowered his voice, as if explaining plans for a bank heist. 'So say Sarah was trying to engineer a proposal out of David. Then one day, bingo. She gets it. Says yes almost automatically, because that's what she's been after all along. And then, the second she's said it, she realises there's a chance she might be making a mistake.'

'Well then, you'd just back out of it, wouldn't you?'

'Would you? Like you just said, it's hardly ordering a coffee. And what if by that time you've only got the one option, unless you can bluff someone else into making you the same offer, so at least you're making your decision on a level playing field?'

'Why?'

'Perhaps because there's a part of you thinking that this might be your last chance. And so you don't want to blow it.'

'So you're saying that she's got an offer – an acceptable offer – but she's decided to use that fact to see if she can leverage a counter-offer, just to make sure in her own mind she's doing the right thing?'

Finn nodded. 'Oldest trick in the book. Why else would she have placed the announcement?'

'Because she wants to be rescued?'

'Rescued? This isn't the Middle Ages, and she's certainly not some damsel in distress. If she wanted out of there, she'd be out of there, don't you worry.'

'So what, then?'

Finn glanced towards the till, checking for customers. 'You don't jump from a sinking ship unless you know the one you're jumping to can float, do you? So maybe it's her last shot at getting you to lay it on the line for her, so she can convince herself that her last-minute jitters are just that. Or not.'

'Yeah, but this is pretty extreme. I mean, she can't be thinking about, you know, spending the rest of her life with someone after just one night.'

'Why not? You are.' Finn smiled. 'Of course, it could simply be the "kids" thing.'

'*Kids thing*? What kids thing?'

'As in her wanting them. Did you two ever have that discussion?'

Evan sighed loudly. 'Finn, Sarah and I didn't really have time to discuss our views on anything.'

'Well, just remember that most women are driven by this need at some point in their lives. Sarah's that age, and if that's the case . . . she might just see David as the better bet.'

'That's ridiculous.'

'Is it?'

'Yeah. If Sarah did have such a biological urge, why would she have wasted her time having an affair with me?'

'Affair? I'd check your dictionary definitions, if I were you. One night . . .'

'And one lunch,' protested Evan, weakly.

'Whatever. But perhaps some sort of switch has flipped inside her while you've been away. Maybe she's suddenly decided that that *is* what she wants, and that this guy's in the best position to provide her with them – or rather, provide *for* her and them. And if that's the case, then you can't really argue with that.'

'*Thanks*, Finn.'

'Don't mention it.'

A young Asian girl coughed politely from where she'd been waiting patiently by the till, so Finn got up to serve her, and as his friend headed back behind the counter, Evan wondered how he'd feel if that *was* the deal-breaker. Finn's observation had thrown him a little, and while he liked kids – well, he liked Finn's kids – children were a little off his radar at the moment. He didn't know many musicians – multimillionaires aside – who were good at playing happy families, perhaps given the piecemeal nature of their work. The only ones he knew with children were those who'd had them accidentally, and either lugged them around on tour like an extra over-heavy piece of luggage, or relied on a parenting technique that involved little more than posting a cheque once a month. If the pram in the hall was rumoured to be an issue for women in the arts, it certainly was for men. You couldn't play until the small hours *and* come home to a small baby.

Could he see himself as a dad? He supposed so. After all, wasn't it one of those things that you just *did*, like learning to drive, or playing an instrument – seemingly impossible at first, with too much going on all at once, but eventually it just became second nature? But then again, he only had a one-bedroom flat. He didn't want to have to move, and yet surely they couldn't start a family living like that . . .

Start a family. Evan fought to stem the panic he could feel rising in his chest. He'd had a goldfish a few years ago but had forgotten to feed it, and he'd come back from a series of gigs in Germany to find it floating upside-down in its bowl. Once, he'd even thought about getting a dog, but deemed the responsibility, the commitment, too much. He knew he was perhaps jumping the gun a bit, but for the first time, wondered what he might be taking on. Marriage? And *kids*? The idea was making him break out in a cold sweat.

He looked over at Finn, the former blue-eyed boy of Jazzed now with a couple of blue-eyed boys of his own, noting the lines around his eyes, the flecks of grey in his hair, and what looked sus-piciously like the beginnings of a paunch. And no matter how hard he swallowed, Evan couldn't dislodge the lump that had formed in his throat.

29

Sarah cursed the men doing roadwork outside at such an early hour, then realised the loud rumbling that had woken her was in fact David's snoring, and wondered where she was before working out that the total absence of light meant they'd gone back to his apartment yesterday evening. He could only sleep in complete blackness, and while she'd joked with him that this wasn't the kind of fumbling in the dark she wanted, Sarah still hadn't managed to change his habits. She preferred to sleep with the curtains open, and the black eye-mask David insisted on wearing whenever they spent the night at her place always made her feel like she was sharing a bed with Zorro.

She held her pillow over her head to try and block out the noise, wondering whether it was too late to add 'earplugs' to the wedding gift list, then retrieved her mobile phone from the bedside table and checked the time. It was just gone six, and although she didn't have to be in the office for another two hours, Sarah decided she'd get up and go home first.

Careful not to wake him, she slipped quietly out from under the small corner of duvet she'd managed to prevent David wrestling from her as they slept, and – using the light from her mobile as a torch – gathered her clothes from the chair in the corner, crept into the hallway, and pulled her skirt on. She was anxious to get home and shower – at her initiation they'd had sex last night – and while from memory it hadn't quite been up to her and Evan's standard from their one night together, she'd made sure she put in a good performance. Even if David hadn't.

Sarah caught herself, wondering why she'd suddenly become so critical of him. Was it simply pre-wedding nerves, or just that Evan being back on the scene meant she couldn't help comparing every aspect of her and David's relationship to how things with Evan might have been? She thought back to Grace's idea of drawing a line down the centre of a piece of A4 and listing their respective good – and bad – points, wondering whether it'd be useful, but dismissed it again. With less than a week to go, that would be a little desperate.

She finished dressing to the accompaniment of David's rasping, which to her amazement even penetrated the bedroom door, and wondered whether Evan snored. *Would it make a difference?* she asked herself. And did it really matter that David did?

If it had been Evan lying next to her this morning, she'd have woken him up so they could have sex once more, then she'd have gone to work with a spring in her step, the taste of him on her lips, and a buzz coursing through her body for the rest of the morning – just like they'd done a year ago. With David, she'd done everything she could not to wake him. And she found that even more disturbing than his snoring.

But this was marriage, she reminded herself, not an affair, and not even dating. Things were *supposed* to be different. Marriage was, well . . . How did she know what it was? Her mother's disappearance meant she'd not been old enough to see how her parents' marriage had worked – though it evidently hadn't. Her father had done his best to bring her up on his own at the expense of his own love life – and Sarah had always felt guilty about that. And while she knew it was illogical, that was one of the things she wanted from David. Someone who'd always be there. Unless, perhaps, he found out what she'd been up to back then with Evan.

But even that was in the past. History. Besides, if it ever came out, Sarah was sure she'd be able to explain it away as simply keeping her options open. After all, since then, she'd been completely faithful – and in any case, she still didn't see what she and Evan had done as being unfaithful. Though she knew hers might be the minority view.

She took her coat down from the rack, tiptoed along the hallway, and quietly let herself out through the front door, hoping David wouldn't be annoyed to wake up and find her gone, although that would presume he remembered they'd spent the night together in the first place – his hangover cure, following the couple of Bloody Marys he'd had with their late lunch, had been the best part of two bottles of wine. Besides, why shouldn't she be free to come and go as she pleased? He might as well get used to it; her independence was one of the things she was determined to maintain after they were married. And as silly as that might sound, given the amount of time that David spent in the office, she was pretty sure that life for her could pretty much go on as it always had. She was planning to keep her room in Grace's flat – she suspected it might come in handy when she fancied the odd night away – and while David would surely think it an extravagance, they hardly needed the money, particularly with both of their incomes. No, Sarah assured herself, theirs would be a modern marriage. A partnership. Not quite an arrangement, but not far off, and she could be – *would* be – happy with that.

But as she walked home, her coat fastened tightly against the morning chill, she tried not to think of the one major downside to marrying David – that she couldn't ever allow herself have anything more to do with Evan. How big a downside that was, she couldn't really tell, but one thing she knew: It wasn't one she wanted to dwell upon.

30

Evan walked down Carnaby Street, side-stepping the usual charity canvassers hanging around outside the Liberty department store, then turned left towards Soho. Just opposite a large neon art installation of a plug and socket that always seemed to have one or other of its tubes flickering, he stopped by his agent's black-painted door and rang the buzzer.

'Fuller Benson.'

Evan smiled to himself as the crackly female voice emerged from the speaker. Having a double-barrelled name gave the agency more gravitas, Johnny had told him once. And he supposed it did. Right up until you found out that Benson was Johnny's dog.

'Evan McCarthy. To see Johnny Fuller.'

There was a pause, possibly while the receptionist consulted with Johnny to see if Evan was actually a client, and then the door buzzed noisily open. He made his way inside and headed up the narrow stairwell, but before he reached the top, he was assailed by a familiar voice.

'I thought you were dead!'

Evan looked up to see Johnny grinning down at him. He hauled himself up the last few stairs by the banister and held his hand out, but instead, found himself enveloped in a bear hug.

'Not quite,' he wheezed. 'Sorry I'm late, though. It's like Piccadilly Circus out there.'

Johnny rolled his eyes at what had become their standard greeting. 'It *is* Piccadilly Circus out there. When did you get back?' he said, holding Evan at arm's length and looking him up and down, as if to check it was really him, and that he still had all his limbs.

'Friday.'

'And you only come and see me now?'

'I'm sorry. Jet lag.'

'Well, it's good to see you. Finally.'

'You too. How have you been?'

'Worried.' Johnny led him through into the reception area, where a stunningly pretty girl was staring in bewilderment at a computer screen. 'Jocasta,' he said. 'This is Evan. Evan's our star client. He's just been on tour with The Police.'

Jocasta smiled up at him. She couldn't have been more than twenty-one, twenty-two at the most, probably there on internship from University like most of the agency's previous staff – a strategy Johnny justified by insisting it gave them an opportunity to get a foot in the door and gain some hands-on experience, though Evan suspected it was more so he could get out of paying them, and – given that they were usually picked more for their looks than their brains – get some hands-on experience of his own.

'Wow. The Police. Cool,' she said, wide-eyed, although Evan was pretty sure she hadn't even been born when they were famous. Possibly hadn't even heard of them until Johnny had mentioned them just now.

'Impressive, eh?' said Johnny, proudly, and Evan couldn't help feeling flattered. Sometimes Johnny had the ability to make him feel like he was his only client. Maybe he was. Certainly Evan had never seen anyone else whenever he'd visited the agency. 'Anyway. Enough being star struck,' Johnny continued, taking Evan's arm and escorting him past Jocasta and into his office, where a scruffy black dog of indeterminate breed lay in front of the radiator. As they walked into the room, Benson briefly twitched his tail, and then, as if the effort had been too much for him, yawned and went back to sleep.

Johnny leaned over his desk and pressed the intercom button. 'Two coffees, please, Jocasta,' he said, though he could have just as easily voiced the order through the open doorway. He raised his eyes to Evan. 'Black, right?'

Evan nodded, and Johnny beamed back at him, pleased he'd got it right. At times, he was as eager to please as a puppy, though thankfully not as toothless when it came to negotiating on his clients' behalves.

'And see if you can find some biscuits,' continued Johnny, causing Benson's ears to twitch at the word.

'Not for me, thanks,' said Evan.

'What makes you think they were?' Johnny grinned, then walked round behind his desk and flopped dramatically down into an expensively upholstered leather chair. Evan hadn't seen this particular piece of furniture before, and wondered whether he'd paid for it; the tour had been lucrative, and Johnny had taken his agent's cut gladly. 'So . . .' There was a luxuriant squeak of leather as Johnny leaned back and linked his fingers behind his head. 'How are things?'

For a moment, Evan was of a mind to tell him, but his agent had never really been much of a confidante. 'Fine. You?'

Johnny shrugged. 'Can't complain. Could do with some of our clients getting out to work a bit more often, though. You up for a few gigs now you're back?'

Evan shook his head. He'd only reluctantly agreed to a night at Mel's, and playing was the last thing he felt like doing, especially since for the last few weeks of the tour, it had taken the greatest of efforts just to walk out on stage. 'I need a break.'

WHAT MIGHT HAVE BEEN

'Fine. But just remember, a break's one thing, career suicide's another. And why on earth did you come straight back here? Why not head down to Hawaii for some R&R?'

'I had some things to take care of.'

'Have you seen Finn?'

'I might have done,' said Evan, suspiciously.

'Did he say anything?'

'No – apart from asking me whether I'd spoken to you yet. As did Mel, come to mention it.'

'Good.'

'Why?'

'Well . . .' Johnny leant further back in his chair and hefted his feet up onto the desk, then caught himself as he nearly overbalanced. 'There's a possibility of a thing. In America. For you and Finn.'

'Johnny, I've just got back, and I've told you, reforming Jazzed isn't . . .'

Johnny held a hand up. 'It's hardly reforming. You just have to play together the once. These reunion gigs are big business all of a sudden. And people like you are in demand.'

'People like me? In that case, find someone like me and get them to do it instead.'

'It's good money. National television. Finn's up for it.'

'He didn't mention it.'

'That's because I told him not to. Didn't want you getting the wrong end of the stick.'

Evan sighed, pretty sure that particular stick had two wrong ends. 'I'm not sure.'

'Will you at least think about it? Please?'

'Okay, okay.' Evan nodded reluctantly. 'I'll think about it.'

'Fab.' Johnny beamed at him again as Jocasta made her way into the room with two mugs of coffee and a plate of biscuits and placed them on the desk, the sound of which made Benson haul himself up from his prone position. 'And there have been other enquiries too. Another American tour. There's not that many people who can just drop everything and go like you can. No ties.'

Evan winced at the comment. 'Really?' he said, flatly.

'Yes, really. Makes you a valuable commodity.'

Evan raised both eyebrows, tempted to ask how valuable, but instead reached for his coffee. It looked like it had been made with some instant powder, remnants of which were dotted around the mug's rim, so he left it where it was.

'And what if I decided to stay in London for a while? What would my prospects be then?'

The colour drained from Johnny's face. 'What would you want to do something like that for?'

'Just say I did.'

Johnny picked up a biscuit and broke it in half. 'You really want to go back into session work with something like this on offer? And after what you've just done?'

'It pays the mortgage.'

'Do another tour and you won't *have* a mortgage.'

'I just want to know what my options are.'

'Your options?' He tossed a piece of biscuit to where Benson was sitting, and the dog caught it expertly. 'Strike while the iron's hot. While you're flavour of the month. The minute you drop off the radar, they forget about you.'

Evan swallowed hard, hoping that hadn't been the case where Sarah was concerned. 'Isn't your job to keep me on the radar?'

'Which I can't do if you go back to playing those little clubs and venues in the middle of god-knows-where . . .' Johnny gazed theatrically up at the ceiling. 'Christ, Evan. What is it with you?

The minute you're on the verge of getting what you've worked for, you turn and run in the opposite direction.'

Evan opened his mouth to argue, but thought better of it. Johnny didn't know the whole story, and had been the only agent keen to take him on when Jazzed had come to an end, and Evan valued his advice. Besides, given how he'd done exactly that with Sarah, he feared he didn't have a leg to stand on.

'Tell me something. What is it exactly that I've worked for?'

'What do you mean?'

'What have I really got?'

Johnny dunked the other half of the biscuit into his coffee, causing Benson to emit a low whine. 'A career, Evan. Doing something you love. And how many musicians do you know who have that? How many *people* can you say that about?'

'Yes, but what's it all for? I go on stage every night, playing someone else's songs about how much they love someone else. It's time to write my own songs, for a change.'

'You've tried that before, remember, and you weren't exactly Lennon and McCartney. Or even just McCartney. Even when he was writing that ridiculous one with the singing frogs.'

'I don't mean *actually* write them.' Evan sighed. 'I was speaking metaphorically. I just want some material. That's all. Someone to write *about*.'

Johnny leaned forward and rested his elbows on the desk. 'Is this all about some woman?'

'Not just some woman, Johnny. The woman I want to spend the rest of my life with.'

'And does she feel the same way?'

Evan picked his coffee up and blew across the top of the mug. 'I'm not sure,' he said, taking a sip, then trying not to grimace. 'But

I need to know that if she wants me to be here for her, then I can actually be *here* for her.'

'Of course you can. After you've done the America thing, obviously. Though that's where the money is. And one thing often leads to another, in my experience.'

'I don't want to sell out.'

'There's nothing wrong with selling out – especially if you're selling out stadiums.' Johnny paused to let his point sink in. 'It's how the world works. You want to live, you have to pay for it. So the more someone pays you for what you do, the better.' He smiled sympathetically. 'At the end of the day, it doesn't matter who you play for. Just that you play. So you might as well play for the person who pays the most.'

'It's not all about the money, you know?'

'No?' Johnny raised one eyebrow. For him, it obviously was.

'Fine.' Evan reached for a biscuit, and Benson ambled over and rested a paw on his lap. 'Like I said, I'll think about it.'

'Great.' Johnny beamed across the desk at him, then his expression changed. 'You haven't gone and got this girl into trouble, have you?'

Evan let out a short laugh. 'Not yet,' he said, holding the biscuit a few inches above Benson's nose, but as the dog angled his head, Johnny tutted.

'He won't beg, you know.'

'Why not?'

Johnny shrugged. 'It's just not in his nature.'

And as Benson stared patiently at the biscuit, Evan found himself wondering whether it was in his.

arah was having trouble concentrating on work. She'd spent a pleasant enough first hour as her guests from Saturday night had variously popped their heads round her office door to tell her how bad their hangovers had been, opened several emails containing embarrassing photos of her in her Deely-boppers and L-plates, and been bought two separate bags of Krispy Kreme donuts, having apparently blurted out how these were the one thing she really missed from back home and then expressed disbelief when informed you could get them here in London. And while she felt guilty about how unproductive her morning had been, in truth the distractions had been welcome, given how Evan was playing on her mind.

The irony of the situation wasn't lost on her: She'd kind of thrown herself into the relationship with David when Evan had gone, and now she worried that maybe that had backfired a little – he was attentive, sure, but perhaps took her a little for granted, though that was possibly because he assumed the hard work had been done in getting her to say 'yes' and so now had taken his foot off the gas. And while that was perhaps understandable, Sarah certainly didn't find it ideal.

She'd been used to male attention all her life. Her father had started it off by always making her feel she was the centre of his world, a strategy to minimise the loss of her mother, she now realised. Then at school, as a teenager, the boys had flocked round her – even then she could sense their teasing and insults were a way of disguising their true feelings towards her. Maybe that hadn't been a positive thing. But at least it had been good training for working in the City.

She was lucky, she knew, that she'd been blessed with looks. They'd opened so many doors for her, and helped her here, too. The braces she'd hated wearing as an eleven-year-old had given her a smile to be proud of – particularly compared to the 'English teeth' a few of her co-workers had – a smile which disarmed her male bosses, who'd expected her to be some air-head when in fact she was sharper than many of them. It was just a shame she didn't have much to smile about at the moment.

Rubbing her eyes, she tried to focus on her computer screen. The columns of figures were giving her a headache, and she thought about going home sick, but that might look suspicious with the wedding so close by – already she was expected to work longer hours than her male counterparts and, she suspected, for a lower salary. Plus, she was worried she'd have to explain to David why she'd left. And worried it would mean opening the floodgates.

She gazed around her office, the four walls suddenly seeming more than a little oppressive, though she knew she was lucky to have them – well, not lucky, exactly; the fight out of her cubicle and into here had been a tough one, and had meant leaving everything she knew behind. Okay, so it wasn't a corner office like David's, and her view was the back of the office block next door as opposed to the breathtaking Thames vista that he enjoyed, but she was proud of what she'd achieved. And while she didn't necessarily enjoy her work, or more accurately, the industry she worked in, Sarah didn't want to have to give it all up – which is what she was sure would happen if she didn't go through with the wedding.

She wondered how she'd found herself so out of control. She'd left New York determined to be the master – sorry, *mistress* – of her own destiny, and yet here she was, marrying a man who was used to getting his own way, and who had such clear ideas of what his – their – future would be. Whereas Evan? One of the things she'd liked about him most was his relaxed attitude. Sure, he'd seemed passionate about his music. Cared about his career. But life was all about the living for him, and the music, while part of that, hadn't seemed to be the driving force. He'd told her over lunch – their one lunch – that his philosophy, if you could call it that, was to just go through life looking at opportunities as they came up, choosing whether or not they were worth pursuing at the time; a simple strategy, maybe, but one that had worked for him so far. And that was one of the reasons why meeting Evan had been so refreshing. So different to her 'dates' with David, a man who already had his routines – the Saturday morning trip to Waitrose, the Sunday brunch at the pub – or his favourite restaurants, which they'd visit without fail once or twice a week. As for her suggesting the two of them go somewhere different to eat, well, Sarah had come to learn what his raised eyebrow meant, so eventually she'd just caved in. Let him choose. And that, Sarah now realised, had been her mistake. Because soon it wasn't just the restaurants he was choosing, but what she ate in them too. What she wore to visit them, more recently. What had surprised her most was how she seemed to have lost the will to resist. But sometimes it had just been easier.

It wasn't that David was nasty or domineering. She could just tell he didn't approve, and Sarah hated knowing that disapproval was simmering beneath the surface. So they ended up doing the same thing, what she knew would please him – in bed, as well, although that never required much of an effort – whereas everything she'd done in her short time with Evan had been new. *Everything*.

Her father had told her once that jazz was about making your own sound. Being different to everyone else. Never playing the same thing the same way two nights running – and she'd suspected Evan subscribed to that view too, particularly when it came to relationships. In just a couple of days, he'd opened her eyes to so many of the delights of this part of London: Postman's Park, Borough Market, Secret, and even the café at the Tate – not that that last venue held the fondest memories for her.

She shook her head in an attempt to clear her thoughts, and tried again to concentrate on the report she'd been attempting to evaluate all morning. The complicated financial jargon she'd usually been able to breeze through just wasn't making any sense, and what one minute looked like – on paper, at least – a good deal, was looking like a bad one the next. Of course, Sarah was experienced enough to know you could dress up any set of figures any way you liked, and she suspected the author had done this masterfully.

Exasperated, she got up from her desk and began to pace around the room. Sometimes she longed for more of a simple life. Less money-obsessed. Fewer people treating their bonus figures like a badge of honour to be worn around the office. She'd thought New York was bad, full of status-obsessed people, but at times London made it look positively Utopian. Maybe it was the environment she worked in; the kill-or-be-killed attitude everyone had. Certainly David seemed to be in constant competition with everyone he came up against, both in and out of the office, in terms of status, power, and money . . . No, actually, it seemed to be all about the money. Those who didn't have it wanted to take it from those who did, and those who did wanted to rub how much they had in the faces of those who didn't. Thus David would never think of taking her for a sandwich in the park at lunchtime, because that was what poor people did, and his years of expensive public school education, his degree from a good university, and the over-long hours he put in at the bank all went towards making sure he wasn't a poor person. It was only natural that the things he did outside of work all were geared towards impressing that fact upon everyone else.

She reminded herself that Evan was a self-made man too. He'd taught himself to play, and now, just as David did, made a living out of his talent, his hard work – it just happened to be in a different industry, with a different pay structure. Certainly Evan was brighter than many of the people she worked with – people who earned ten times as much as he probably did. And the funny, *admirable* thing was, he hadn't seemed to care. Although Sarah was beginning to wonder whether *she* did.

She enjoyed the trappings, she had to admit, although who wouldn't? She'd had rich boyfriends in New York too, and understood from an early age that her looks were a currency that could be exchanged for the finer things in life. The Cartier watch she wore, the Tiffany earrings, the huge diamond engagement ring – all presents from David. Meant to impress her – and they had – but really, she knew, also given to her to impress other people.

The problem was, these things were becoming tiresome. The gated development where David lived, the BMW with its smoked-glass windows, taxis, not the tube – these were all things designed to isolate you from the real life of the city, not let you experience it. Over the course of two short days, Evan had let her experience it. And Sarah wanted more of that.

There was no doubt that London was a great city if you were rich – but Evan had opened her eyes to the possibility that it could be a fantastic one even if you weren't. She couldn't imagine him flying into a rage if he couldn't get a table at Nobu on a Friday night, and he'd probably take more pleasure from a sandwich in Postman's

Park than a plate of some outlandishly expensive fish that – how had he put it? – *hadn't even been cooked*!

She smiled again at the memory, remembering how he'd made her laugh with his nervous observation, and wondered when was the last time she'd laughed with David like that, though the truth was, for all his other qualities, David didn't make her laugh. And right now, a laugh was the one thing she could do with.

32

'I've missed this,' said Evan, handing Mel a beer, and Mel clapped him affectionately on the back.

'I missed this too, pal. You and me, down the pub . . . It's just like old times.'

'I was talking about my *pint*, Mel.' Evan grinned, then drained a third of it in one go. Despite the early hour, it tasted good, and in any case, as far as his body clock was concerned it was still the previous evening. 'American beer just doesn't have the same appeal.'

'Unlike their women?'

'Don't start.'

'I take it things aren't going so well?'

Evan opened his mouth, then shut it again. He still hadn't made sense of what had happened at the Tate, and he wasn't really ready to share it. 'You could say that,' he said, miserably.

'Which is why you look like a wreck.'

'You're no oil painting yourself.'

'Well, that's just charming!' said Mel. 'Unless you mean a Picasso, in which case I'll take it as a compliment.'

'Sorry.' Evan sighed. 'Like I said on the phone, this jet lag's a bummer. And this "being in love" stuff doesn't help.'

'You sure, are you?'

'Yeah. I'm definitely jet lagged.'

'I meant being in love. Wanting her back.'

'As sure as I can be.' Evan put his beer down and folded his arms. 'I mean, when we were together, we weren't really *together*. We only actually saw each other, for what, two days? And even then it was only from around midnight on the Thursday to seven o'clock the next morning, plus two hours at lunch, and then a matter of minutes when she dumped me, which makes a total of . . .' The maths was getting beyond him, so he took his phone out and, as Mel waited patiently, punched the numbers into the calculator. 'Ten hours.' He stared disbelievingly at the result. 'Less than half a day.'

Mel nodded thoughtfully. 'That's hardly enough time on which to base a decision about the rest of your life.'

Wary of the table's sticky surface, Evan put his mobile down on a beer mat. 'I dunno,' he said, glumly. He'd bought his flat after a viewing of less than ten minutes, the Mercedes after a cursory five-minute inspection – and two of those minutes had been spent staring blankly into the engine bay hoping in vain that some instinctive mechanical knowledge might suddenly kick in. But he'd been happy with both of those things for years, and compared to that, the time he'd spent with Sarah was positively long-term research. 'I have to believe it is, Mel. We were obviously . . .' He searched for another word for 'fond', but couldn't find one that didn't sound as pathetic. 'I mean, even so, we became pretty close. Had fun. Got on well. Even in such a short space of time, I could tell we had potential. But then it all came to an end. Because of her . . .'

'Boyfriend?'

'Circumstances.'

'Shame you didn't you try and change those "circumstances", eh?'

Evan could almost hear the quotation marks around that last word. 'I didn't have time, Mel. Or rather, she didn't give me the opportunity.'

'Okay – tell me something. Back then, if you hadn't been going away, and you'd have asked her, do you think she'd have dumped him and taken up with you?'

'I think so.' Evan stared into his glass. 'I don't know. But that was then. This is now. All I know is that I've got to ask her.'

'Why?'

'Because there's no-one else who's ever made me feel like she does,' Evan said, in a stage whisper he realised with embarrassment was louder than his normal voice.

'And you don't think part of that is *because* of the circumstances?' Mel leant in close. 'That the only reason you feel like this is because it's unfinished business. You still resent her for choosing what's-his-name . . .'

'David.'

'. . . over you. And so you want to prove to her she's making a mistake. And most of all, you want to beat mister posh boy banker by taking back the thing he pinched from under your nose.'

'What?'

Mel held both hands up. 'Just playing Devil's advocate.'

'I'd hardly have flown halfway around the world just to get one over on some City boy. Though it's true I can't stand the thought of her with him.'

'I wonder why she's doing it. Marrying him, instead of you.'

'Apart from the fact that I haven't asked her to marry me?'

'Maybe she loves him.'

The idea made Evan uncomfortable. 'Doubtful, given the fact that she cheated on him with me.'

'Yeah, but wasn't that in the early days?' Mel gulped down another mouthful of beer. 'She obviously loved him enough to say yes when he proposed.'

'Not necessarily. What was the alternative? I was maybe her last chance to get out of that relationship. Then I left, so he was her only option.'

Mel regarded Evan sceptically over the top of his glass. 'Have you been talking to Finn, by any chance?'

'What makes you think that?'

'It's the kind of bollocks he'd come up with.'

'And he's happily married, right? Whereas you . . .'

Mel glared at him for a second, then he smiled. 'So basically, you're saying the only reason Sarah agreed to marry this David bloke is because you didn't hang around and give her an escape route.'

'Well, yeah. Maybe. I don't know. But he's her boss. So things would have been pretty uncomfortable for her at work if she'd said no.'

'Surely there are laws about things like that?'

'The City's a pretty sexist place, Mel.'

'Even so, she's a bright girl. Despite her choices in men.'

'Ha ha. So?'

'So that doesn't sound like the kind of thing she'd do.'

'Yes, well . . .' Evan sighed loudly. 'It's complicated.'

'Maybe she only agreed to marry him to try and shock you into coming back. Did you think about that?'

'I did. Then dismissed it as pretty ridiculous.'

Mel laughed. 'So is what you've just said to me.'

'Well, okay. Maybe it's not quite as black and white as that. But even if he is her second choice, her runner-up prize, it doesn't mean that she feels she's lost. Just had to compromise a little bit. And like you said on the phone yesterday, there are certain things about him that maybe make up for that.'

'I wonder why she was interested in the likes of you, then? Someone so different.'

Evan shot a glance at his friend, wondering whether he was taking the mickey, but Mel seemed genuinely interested.

'You'd have to ask her that.'

Mel grabbed Evan's mobile. 'Give me her number and I will.'

'Don't you *dare*,' said Evan, snatching the phone back.

'Well, why do *you* think it was?'

'Excitement? Something different? Maybe even because I . . .'

'What?'

Evan couldn't help remembering their initial musical connection. 'Reminded her of her dad.'

'Ignoring how creepy that sounds, that only gets you so far. Something was obviously not right about that David bloke, otherwise she wouldn't have felt the need to spend time with you, and so if I were you, I'd start by finding out what it was. Then, you need to play to your strengths – which you can't do if you don't have a clue what your strengths are.'

'I don't know . . .'

'Come on, Evan. You wouldn't get up on stage without being sure what your audience had come to hear, would you?'

Evan held his glass against his temple, relishing the coolness. He knew Mel was right – he needed to play to his strengths. Trouble was, aside from actually asking Sarah directly, he couldn't think how on earth he could find out what they were.

'Christ, mate,' continued Mel. 'You haven't left yourself a lot of time.'

'Tell me about it.'

Mel leaned back in his chair and linked his fingers behind his head. 'Do you want my advice?'

'Again, you're on your third wife, right?'

Mel nodded. 'Doesn't mean I don't know how they tick, though. Even though I always seem to manage to tick them off.'

Evan laughed, despite himself. 'Just tell me one thing, Mel. Do you think I'm wasting my time?'

Mel smiled. 'Well, that would depend on whether you had something more valuable to be doing with it, which – from where I'm sitting – you don't. But bear in mind she might simply want to be Sarah the banker's wife more than she wants to be with a musician, and if that's what she's really after, then you can't compete – no matter how much you blow your own trumpet.' He took a large gulp of lager. 'And yes, I know, you're a sax player.'

Evan smiled sarcastically at his friend's joke. 'That's not what she wants,' he insisted, although he was beginning to wonder whether he wasn't trying to convince himself.

'You sure? Because in my experience, a lot of them do. Women are more practical than men. More pragmatic. They value security. Comfort. Reliability. Make decisions based on what's best for their futures, rather than what they want right now. Which is pretty much the opposite of what us blokes do.'

'What about excitement?'

'Hello!' Mel leaned across and rapped him on the forehead with his knuckles. 'People don't get married for excitement. They get married because they want to settle down. Start a family. She might have just kept seeing you on the side.'

'You're wrong, Mel,' said Evan, crossly. 'She started seeing me because there was something not quite right about David. My being out of the picture doesn't mean that all of a sudden, everything's okay with the two of them.'

'Suit yourself.' Mel drained the last of his beer. 'But tell me something. What'll you do if you don't get her back? If things *are* . . .' – this time, he made the speech-marks sign with his fingers – '. . . *okay* with the two of them. How are you going to feel?'

Evan shrugged. Coming back to London had felt like coming home, with everything almost as he'd left it, especially since Sarah wasn't quite married. But if the wedding went ahead, and she was still living here, but married to someone else . . . He didn't want to contemplate what that might be like.

'I haven't really thought that far ahead,' he said, following Mel's lead and downing the rest of his pint.

'Well, maybe you ought to. I mean, it's going to be tough, isn't it? You've already bumped into her once. What if it keeps happening? I don't know about you, but that'd really do my head in. Get under my skin. In fact, I'm not sure I could stand it, seeing the woman I love with someone else, day in, day out . . .'

'Thank you, Mel.'

'I'm just saying these things usually end in tears.' Mel nudged him, then stood up. 'Anyway. Let's hope it doesn't come to that, eh?'

As Mel picked up their glasses and headed off to the bar, Evan sat there miserably. Mel was right – it *would* eat him up, seeing the two of them together. Despite what he'd said to Johnny, maybe his best option *would* be to go back to the States. His work visa was certainly good for a while, and even if this reunion turned out to not be the great opportunity Johnny was making it out to be, with the Police tour on his CV he was sure there'd be plenty of other job offers along with the one Johnny was talking about. But that would be running away – and he'd already done that once, and besides, why should Sarah force him to leave his beloved London? He'd just have to deal with it. Move on. Build his life back up. Without her. He shut his eyes and rested his head heavily on the table, grimacing as his hair stuck to it, then opened them to find another pint had appeared in front of him.

'There are lots of other women around, you know?' Mel said, squeezing back into his seat. 'Plenty more fish in the sea, and all that. And most of them without the same complications.'

Evan sat back upright. 'For the millionth time, Mel, I didn't know there were any complications when I met her.'

'You knew she was American, so there's one, for a start. Then again, they're all women. Which is about the biggest complication you can get.'

'That's not very fair on . . .' Evan stopped talking. Despite knowing Mel for the longest time, he couldn't remember the name of his current wife. 'Mrs. Mel.'

'Why do you think I spend so much time at the club? Seriously, Evan, you should start thinking about alternatives. Just in case.'

Evan shook his head. 'I can't, Mel. I can't even let myself believe that I'm not going to get her back. Otherwise I might not be able to go through with any of this.'

'Maybe some distance might help?'

Evan wiped the condensation from the side of his glass distract-edly. 'I've had some distance, Mel, both geographically and time-wise. And that's why I've come back for her. Because there's never been anyone like Sarah. Ever. And I think there's a pretty good chance that there never will be. I've realised that. And she will, in time.'

'Yeah, but like you said, that's the one thing you don't exactly have a lot of. Unless you'd be just as happy dating a divorcee?'

'Huh?'

'Play the waiting game. So what if she gets married on Saturday? If you're right about her and David, then it won't take her that long to realise that she's made a mistake, and if you're still hanging around, and ready to take her back . . .'

Evan took another mouthful of lager. It wasn't his preferred alternative, but it was *an* alternative. A way to get what he wanted, albeit not the most direct route. 'Maybe that's what'll happen. After all, it took me leaving to realise I'd made a mistake. So maybe it'll take her getting married to realise that she has.'

'Well, there you go. Sorted.' Mel clinked his glass against Evan's. 'Though how long will you give it?'

'Pardon?'

'How long will you hang around, not moving on with your life, waiting until she has this epiphany that she's made a dreadful mistake and realises you were the one for her all along? A month? A year? Five years? Or are you just going to hang around for the seven-year itch?'

Evan put his glass back down. 'Hang on, this is your idea we're talking about.'

'Although, maybe you won't have to. Maybe you can just be her bit on the side again. After all, that's how the two of you met, so . . .'

'That's not how it was.'

'Isn't it?'

'No. She . . . she was looking for something David wasn't giving her. And I was it. Then I left. And so . . .'

'So it wasn't that important to her anymore, so she decided to get married to him, and didn't give you and her a second thought.'

'That's not exactly what happened.'

'But it is one interpretation.'

'Your interpretation, you mean,' said Evan, angrily.

Mel sighed. 'Evan, I like Sarah. You know I do. But that doesn't mean I have to like the way she behaved.'

'The way she behaved?'

'Shagging you behind her boyfriend's back.'

'Well, that's because . . .' Evan sighed. 'You know her history, Mel. You can understand that, perhaps. Besides, she was confused.'

'But she isn't now.'

'Well, that's what I'm trying to help her with.'

'By making her even more confused?'

'No.' Evan shook his head slowly. 'By helping her to see sense.'

'And that's your problem, Evan,' said Mel, grabbing a couple of menus from the next table and handing him one. 'Love isn't about seeing sense, but for some reason, it looks like Sarah's decided to go down the sensible route by marrying David. And until you understand exactly why she's doing that – unless you've got some dirt on him – you haven't got a hope in hell of convincing her not to.'

As Mel turned his attention to the menu, Evan realised his morals were being tested. Aside from the 'should he/shouldn't he tell' issue regarding David and that lap-dancer, he had to wonder whether he was the kind of man who'd steal someone else's girlfriend – fiancée, even?

Given that he'd flown halfway around the world to do exactly that, he decided there and then that obviously, he was. And if that was the case, then what on earth was he waiting for?

33

Evan was feeling like a criminal. He'd been hanging around the entrance to the Robert Dyas store opposite Sarah's office building for an hour, and the bank's security guards were beginning to give him funny looks, although he didn't care. He'd wait here all day if necessary.

He'd thought about simply marching into her office and pretending he had an appointment. He could risk David seeing him – after all, he and Sarah were supposed to be old friends, and what was wrong with an old friend dropping by to say hello? But Evan had suspected she might not want to see him, and if that was the case, he didn't think he could trick – or even fight – his way in past reception. This wasn't the movies – if it was, he'd have gotten the girl by now. So in the end, he'd bottled it, which was why he'd decided to wait in the street and try and catch her on her way to lunch.

He stood in the doorway, wishing he smoked, or at least did something that would give him a reason to be hovering here like this. Every now and then, groups of office workers would appear on the pavement opposite, puffing away on their cigarettes, one or two of them already on their second or third smoke break, and when from time to time they glanced across at Evan, perhaps surprised to see him still there, all he could do was pretend to be fascinated by the garden furniture display in the window.

Though that struck him as strange. He wondered how many cheap plastic folding chair-and-table sets got sold to a clientele who lived in flats which probably didn't even have gardens. What on earth was a hardware store doing here anyway, in the middle of all this high finance? Surely the last thing you wanted when you finished your job selling bonds was to go home and put up a shelf, or re-grout your bathroom?

Just when he was beginning to fear he must have missed her – and regretting the two pints he'd consumed earlier and the lack of a nearby toilet – Sarah appeared through the revolving doors. Evan steeled himself to cross the road to intercept her, but stopped on the kerb when he noticed she wasn't alone; not accompanied by David, fortunately, but by some girl he didn't recognise. This changed his plans a little – he could hardly confront her with someone else there.

After a moment's deliberation, he followed the two of them from his side of the street, relieved when they ducked into a Moroccan deli on the next corner, although now Evan didn't know what to do: wait for Sarah to emerge – and perhaps be faced with the same problem – or give up and go home. Too cold to wait any longer, too desperate for the toilet, and with no intention of giving up on her, he crossed the road and followed them inside.

The deli was one of those wooden-floorboards-and-distressed-furniture affairs, cheaply decorated, but – judging by the menu on the chalkboard on the back wall – with prices at the other end of the scale. It was busy, full of City workers picking up lunch and coffee-to-go, and two queues had formed in front of the tills at either end of the counter. As Evan glanced over to where Sarah was standing, her back to him, chatting animatedly with her friend, he was pleased to see she hadn't noticed him come in, so he joined the adjacent line, grateful for a few moments to work out what he was going to do.

As he watched her, enjoying his view of her backside in her snugly fitting business suit, he weighed up whether the old 'accidental meet' might work. But even if it did, how would he get rid of the friend? Maybe he wouldn't be able to. Perhaps this was Sarah's tactic: to come out with a chaperone, as if she was expecting him to surprise her.

His queue was moving faster than Sarah's, and before he knew what was happening, he found himself at the counter. Never mind his dilemma as to what to do with Sarah, he had more immediate problems to deal with.

'What can I get you?' said the man behind the till.

Evan looked blankly back at him. He wasn't hungry, but what the hell was he doing here if that was the case? 'Er, just some water.'

'You need to get that before you join the queue,' said the man, pointing over to a large, unmissable fridge in front of the far wall, which was packed with bottles of mineral water, and sporting a sign which read 'Please collect before paying'.

'Ah. Right. Sorry.' Evan realised he'd have to push past Sarah and her friend to get one. 'How about a coffee instead?'

'Coffee?'

'That's right.'

The man looked at Evan, perhaps wondering if he'd ever been in a deli before, then his eyes flicked to the growing queue behind him. 'What sort?'

Evan shrugged. 'Surprise me.'

'I can't.'

'What?'

'I can't surprise you. You have to order something. Then I make it. That's how it works.'

Evan frowned, conscious he was holding the queue up, and therefore in danger of making a scene. He hadn't realised there were

213

so many rules for buying lunch nowadays – things certainly had changed since he'd been away.

'Do you have espresso?'

'Espresso, espresso . . .' The man stroked his chin and pretended to think for a moment, then he nodded. 'I think I can rustle one of those up for you. Single, right?'

'Well, yes, I am, but . . .'

'Your *espresso*. Single? Or double?'

'Ah. Sorry. Single. Thanks. Oh, and make that "to go",' he added, just in case Sarah made a run for it and he had to give chase.

The man turned away, and Evan suddenly felt a tap on his shoulder. Assuming it must be Sarah, he fixed his best 'surprised' face, and spun round.

'Well, hello again.'

Evan went white. It wasn't Sarah, but the girl she'd come in with. And she seemed to know him.

'You don't remember me, do you?' she said.

He peered at her face. His first thought that was she was yesterday's jogger, but that would have been way too weird. Close up, she was pretty, and though not quite Sarah's level, still the kind of girl you'd notice on the street, and for a second, he thought about maybe flirting with her in front of Sarah, but quickly dismissed that as being immature.

'I'm sorry, I . . .'

'The other night.' The girl smiled. 'You wouldn't take your clothes off in front of me.'

Evan frowned down at her, acutely aware she'd said that rather loudly, then had a sudden revelation. She must have been at the hen night, and – assuming Sarah hadn't set everyone straight – would still think he was a stripper.

'Yes, well, like I said, health and safety . . .'

'Here's your coffee, *sir*.'

Evan looked round. The man behind the till was sliding an espresso across the counter towards him, an amused expression on his face, and Evan did his best to ignore the sarcastic tone. 'Excuse me,' he said to the girl, then he reached into his pocket for some change, and realised with a start he'd fed the last of his money into the parking meter. 'I, er . . .'

The girl removed her purse from the bag over her shoulder. 'That's okay,' she said, finding a couple of pound coins and placing them down on the counter. 'Have it on me.'

'Thanks. And I'm sorry. I don't usually . . . I mean, this has never happened before.'

'I hope you don't make a habit of saying that to women?'

'No. No, I don't.' Evan picked up the tiny paper cup and moved out of the queue, a little disorientated. He didn't even want a coffee, and certainly didn't want someone who thought he was a stripper to be buying it for him, particularly when the woman he loved was . . . He glanced back over to where Sarah had been standing. Where *was* she?

'Evan.'

'Sarah?' He wheeled round, relieved to hear her voice, and tried to sound surprised, but only succeeded in squeaking pre-pubescently, something he feared was probably appropriate given the way he was acting. As they regarded each other silently, Sarah's friend cleared her throat.

'You two know each other? Apart from the other night.'

'Well . . .' Evan was unsure how to answer, but Sarah evidently wasn't.

'Oh yes,' she said, quickly. 'In fact, we're old friends.'

As Evan wondered whether that was in fact the way Sarah saw things, the girl let out a short laugh.

'Really?' she said. 'What a coincidence.'

Sarah nodded. 'Which is why I didn't want him to, you know . . .'

'Strip,' said Evan, miming a little dance, doing his best to play along.

'Shame.' The girl smiled. 'Aren't you going to introduce us?'

Sarah shot Evan a glance. 'Of course. Amanda, this is Evan. Evan,' she added unnecessarily, 'Amanda.'

'And is he single?' Amanda asked, shaking the hand Evan had offered her.

Evan raised one eyebrow at Sarah, but she just stared evenly back at him. 'No,' he said, after a pause. 'I'm taken.'

Amanda let his hand go. 'Another shame. Well, I've got something important to get on with back at the office,' she said, indicating the coffee and pastry she'd bought, before handing Evan her business card.

'What's this for?'

'Just in case.'

'In case of what?'

She leant in close to him. 'In case you'd like someone to take their clothes off for you for a change.'

As Evan's mouth dropped open, Amanda waved goodbye, winking at Sarah as she left. Sarah was smiling, and he supposed this was a good thing, although he also suspected she'd guessed straight away his being here was no accident.

'A bit forward, isn't she?' he said.

Sarah shrugged. 'You don't ask, you don't get,' she said, then she reddened slightly. 'Bit off your usual patch, aren't you?'

'Not at all. This place is one of my favourites.'

'Really?' She folded her arms. 'What's good here?'

'Er . . .' Evan glanced back up at the chalkboard behind the counter, unable to recognise – or even pronounce – half of the Moroccan dishes listed there. 'Everything.'

Sarah's smile disappeared, as if a switch had been flipped. 'Seriously, Evan, what are you doing here?'

'I needed something to eat.'

She nodded down at his espresso. 'Are you going to eat that?'

He thought about trying to make a joke, then sighed exaggeratedly. 'Guilty as charged.'

'So you're following me now?'

'Well . . .' He took her arm gently and steered her towards a nearby table, relieved when she didn't resist. 'Maybe.'

'Why?' she said, as she sat down. 'Or is that a dumb question?'

'I had to see you. Especially after the last time.' He slid into the chair opposite, put his coffee on the table, then made a play out of moving it out of her reach, and she half-smiled at the gesture. 'I couldn't leave things like that.'

'Things?'

'Us.'

Sarah went to move his coffee back into the middle of the table, and instinctively he grabbed for it, their fingers brushing, her touch sending a shock through his body.

'Evan, I'm sorry. Maybe it was out of order . . .'

'Don't worry about it. It was only water.'

'Not that. Like you said – us. I mean, what you and I have. *Had* . . .' – she corrected herself quickly – '. . . was something special. Something I'll always treasure, even though it was just the one night. But . . .'

'Don't give me "but", Sarah. Why won't you even think about what I said?'

'Because it *was* just the one night. And I can't,' she said. 'I just . . . can't.'

'Okay.' Evan sat on his hands to stop them from shaking. 'But just tell me something, and I'll leave you alone.'

'What?'

'Tell me that David makes you feel the same way I do.' He swallowed hard. 'Or, you know, *did*.'

She met his gaze defiantly, and for perhaps the first time since he'd been back, Evan thought he caught a glimpse of the old Sarah. 'I can't, Evan. You know that. But David makes me feel . . . cherished. Loved in a different way.'

'And is that what you want?'

'Maybe it's what I need.'

'But he's not right for you.'

'What makes you say that?'

'Because I . . .' He wanted to say 'am', but couldn't get the word out. 'Know you.'

'How? How can you possibly?' She looked away. 'Don't try and sow these seeds of doubt. It's not very nice.'

'What else am I supposed to do?'

'You're not supposed to do anything, Evan, apart from stay away from me. Leave me alone. Not come back here and try to . . .'

'Win you back?'

'I'm not some sort of prize' she said, angrily.

'That's not how David sees it, I'll bet.'

'What do you mean by that?'

'Nothing. Sorry. I'm just . . .' He held his hands up, and Sarah's expression softened slightly.

'Why can't you just accept that I'm with him now? You had your chance.'

'When? When exactly did I "have my chance"?'

'Back when we, you know . . .'

'Slept together behind your boyfriend's back?'

'Well, yes.' Sarah's gaze faltered. 'But then you left.'

'Only because you never gave me any indication that things might be different if I stayed. Or asked you.'

'Asked me what?'

'To leave him. And . . .' Evan frowned. The words 'go out with me' seemed so inappropriate. So childish. He shook his head – he didn't have time for dictionary definitions now. 'To be with me. And not him.'

'But you didn't, did you? And did it even occur to you to try?'

'Of course it did. But if you remember, you'd pretty much told me to get lost.'

'Yes,' she said, quietly. 'I remember.'

They stared at the table, his coffee, anything except for each other, until Evan broke the uneasy silence. 'Answer me one more question, Sarah. And be honest. You owe me that.'

She coughed nervously. 'I can't promise . . .'

'Why did you and I . . . you know? Even though you were already with David.'

'I . . .' She looked directly at him, and Evan could see what he thought was pain in her eyes. 'I don't know.'

'Yes you do. What did you think I could give you that he couldn't? And why did it suddenly stop being important?'

Sarah reached across the table and rested a hand on his arm, and Evan had to fight the impulse to grab hold of it and never let go. 'It didn't stop being important. It just became less important. And I didn't have much choice but to get used to it. Seeing as you weren't around anymore.'

'And do you understand why I left? Why I had to go?'

'Yes,' said Sarah. 'I think so.'

'So, what was it?'

Sarah removed her hand, and sat back in her chair. 'It's complicated, Evan.'

'I'm sure you can explain.'

'He and I . . . David, well . . .' Sarah paused. 'If I tell you why I'm marrying David, you'll laugh. If I tell you why I . . . felt what I felt for you, why I . . .'

'Picked me up that night, and mercilessly used me for sex?' He smiled, trying to lessen the viciousness of the remark, but Sarah's expression showed him he'd made his point.

'You might not understand.'

'Try me.'

'Okay.' She took a deep breath. 'It's going to sound like a cliché, but David's safe. Solid. Reliable. Trustworthy. And if I'm going to stay in a country that doesn't seem to want to make me feel welcome, doing a job that some days I don't really understand, then he's the kind of person I need to make it bearable. You? Well, what we had – sorry, *did* – was exciting. Spontaneous. Different. And I'd never had that before. Not someone who made me feel . . .'

'Alive?'

She stared at him for what felt like the longest time. 'It's just . . . easy with David.'

'Easy? Or easier?'

Sarah ignored him. 'But you and me . . . It was just one night, Evan. *One night.*'

'And lunch the next day,' he reminded her.

'Even so. It wasn't *real.*'

'It was for me, Sarah. And I think it was for you too.'

'But David's . . .'

'Boring?'

Evan was smiling, and to his relief, Sarah followed suit. 'No, not boring, exactly. Just, well, steady.'

He looked at her across the table, trying to ignore the sinking feeling that was building up inside him. 'And you really think he's going to be happy for you to work, you know, after . . . wards?' he asked, still not wanting to use the words 'the wedding'.

'Why wouldn't he be?'

'Well, for one thing, I'm sure it hardly fits in with his idea of married life. Who's going to stay at home and make sure the butler doesn't sell off the family jewels?'

Sarah laughed. 'We haven't discussed it. But I think David's aware . . .' Evan's raised eyebrow stopped her mid-sentence. They both knew 'David's aware' wasn't a phrase that you could be sure of.

'And you'd be happy to be one of those corporate wives?'

'David doesn't expect me to be.'

'Doesn't he?' He smiled sympathetically. 'All I'm saying is this. Think long and hard about what it is that you're doing. Because I might not be here when you realise you've made a mistake.'

Evan knew he'd made one himself almost as soon as the words had left his lips, but before he could begin to apologise, Sarah was on her feet.

'How dare you lecture me.'

'I'm sorry.' Evan tried to keep his voice calm, aware other people were watching them. 'I didn't mean it like that. I'm just trying to make sure you've thought about . . .'

'I've done nothing but think for the past year, Evan. And I've made my mind up. I'm marrying David,' she said, her voice raised. 'Can't you understand that?'

'No,' said Evan, firmly. 'I've met him, and no, I can't.'

Sarah opened her mouth to reply, then her eyes flicked to somewhere over his shoulder. She suddenly turned pale, and before he could stop her, she'd wheeled around and headed straight for the door.

And although Evan didn't know it, sitting in the seat behind him – and the reason for Sarah's panicked exit – was Sally, David's PA, sipping her coffee smugly.

34

Sarah hurried along the corridor, nodding a curt hello to a couple of the other women on the way, her body language indicating she didn't have time to stop and chat. What Evan had been saying had troubled her – and there was only one way to deal with it.

She threw her coat and bag onto her desk, then headed back out and along the corridor to David's corner office and peered through the blinds that obscured the glass. As usual, he was sitting at his desk with his back to the window, oblivious to the stunning London panorama behind him. She'd asked him once why he didn't turn his desk round to face the other way, and he'd mumbled something about not being here to look at the view. It hadn't taken Sarah long to realise that was his philosophy for most things in life. Sally wasn't back yet – she'd have to deal with that later too, she knew – but David's door was ajar, so with a cursory knock, she walked inside. At the sound of her approach, David looked up from one of the three screens that bordered his desk, a momentary look of annoyance on his face.

'Darling?' he said, but not before he checked she'd closed the door securely behind her. Since the beginning he'd insisted they keep their romance secret, as he hadn't wanted to be seen 'banging the help' – his little joke, although she'd almost dumped him there and then for making it. But he'd apologised with an expensive dinner at The Ivy, and – although it had taken until she'd finished her sticky toffee pudding – Sarah had forgiven him.

'Got a minute?'

David glanced at his watch. Sarah was sure it was an automatic reaction, but it still bugged her.

'If it is just a minute.'

'Great.' She hopped up onto the corner of his desk. 'I was just wondering. After we're . . . after Saturday. How did you see things going? With me.'

'Going?'

'Here, I mean.'

David leant back in his chair, and folded his arms behind his head. 'You mean your career?'

Sarah listened for a trace of sarcasm, but couldn't detect one. 'Yes.'

'Ah. Tricky one.'

'Why tricky?'

'Well, it might be a little awkward, don't you think?'

'Awkward?' She tried to keep her voice level. 'Why awkward?'

David let out a short laugh. 'You'll be the boss's wife, won't you? And that might make things uncomfortable.'

'Who for?'

'Well, you.'

'Why?'

'Okay. For me as well. I'll hardly be able to order you about like I will at home, will I?'

He'd obviously meant it as a joke, but Sarah didn't find it particularly amusing. 'You don't now.'

'But you're in my department, aren't you? So, technically, I do.'

'So what are you suggesting? That I should ask for a transfer to another department?'

'Ah. You could, I suppose. Although you've already had one, don't forget. From the U.S.'

'Which was your idea.'

'And besides, there aren't a great number of opportunities else-where in the bank for someone with your . . .' He cleared his throat. 'Skills.'

'Fine. I'll just stay here, then. No sense rocking the boat.'

'Ah.'

'What does *that* mean?'

'Like I say. It might make things a little tricky.'

'Why? Does the bank have a policy that says employees can't be married to each other?'

'I wasn't talking about bank policy, sweetheart.' David leaned forward and rested his elbows on his desk – a pose that she'd seen him use with colleagues whenever he didn't want to be argued with. 'I mean, you can't really expect to just carry on as before once you're my wife.'

'Do you mean generally, or just here in the office?'

'Here, of course.'

Sarah was beginning to suspect the other might be true as well. 'Why not?'

'Well, how many of the other partners' wives work here?'

Sarah shrugged. Hardly any of the other partners' wives worked *full stop*. 'So?'

'So it just wouldn't be the done thing.'

Sarah laughed, but bitterly. 'And just what is the "done thing", David? I spend my days shopping in Harvey Nicks, then get home in time to make sure your dinner's on the table like the good little wife?'

'Well, what did you think would happen?' David had raised his voice a little. He caught himself, and smiled. 'Besides, what would be the point of you working? I earn more than enough money for the two of us.'

Sarah fought a rising tide of unease as she began to see that life with David might not be exactly perfect. 'But what if I *want* to?'

The *ping* of an email arriving on his Blackberry surprised them both, and Sarah glared at him, daring him to read it. She suddenly felt foolish – what had she been expecting? David was used to getting his own way – it happened here every day at work, and she had her suspicions that being an only child had certainly taught him that sharing was something other people did. At the same time, she knew he didn't *mean* to be selfish – it was more that it never occurred to him to look out for other people. But why would you, if everything you did was based on the assumption that everyone would see things your way – including your fiancée?

'Sweetheart?' He was peering at her strangely. 'What's brought this on?'

Sarah suddenly felt an irrational desire to tell him, but before she could get a word out, his desk phone bleeped; Sally, back from her lunch break, to tell him he had a conference call waiting.

'I have to take this,' he said, patting her knee. 'But we'll talk about this later, I promise.'

Sarah jumped down off the corner of the desk and made for the door. 'Good,' she said, though whether it would do any, she wasn't so sure.

She waited until she heard David connect to his call, then shut the door behind her and walked purposefully over to Sally's desk, hovering at her side while Sally took her time finishing whatever it was she was typing, then cleared her throat.

'It wasn't what you thought,' she said.

'What wasn't?' Sally said, sweetly enough, although she still hadn't looked up from her computer screen.

'What you saw earlier. In the deli.'

'And what do you assume I thought?' Sally leant back in her chair and regarded Sarah over the rim of her tortoiseshell-frame glasses. 'That it was some kind of tryst? Surely not, with your wedding this Saturday.'

Sarah stared back at her, trying to keep her anger in check. 'Evan's a friend,' she said. 'He wanted to make sure I was doing the right thing. That's all.'

'Evan, you say?'

Sarah tried to ignore Sally's arched eyebrow, and hoped she wouldn't come to regret letting his name slip. At least she hadn't seemed to recognise him from the other evening.

'That's right.'

'And has he? Made sure?'

Sarah felt herself start to blush, but didn't want to show any sign of weakness in front of Sally. On occasion, the PAs acted like a pack of hyenas, and she'd seen women who dropped their guard be slowly and systematically picked off. She suddenly felt awkward, as if she'd made some rookie mistake – her intention had been to try and dismiss the incident as something trivial, but now she feared Sally would suspect it *was* something important, simply because she'd come over and made a point of mentioning it.

'Anyway,' she said, ignoring Sally's question. 'I just wanted to let you know.'

'I won't give it a second thought,' said Sally, turning back to her computer screen, but Sarah didn't believe her. It wouldn't take long before the news would spread like wildfire through the circle of PAs, and then, possibly, even to David. Unless . . .

'Oh. One more thing. You are coming to the reception on Saturday, I take it?'

'The reception?' Sally looked up sharply. 'Really?'

'Of course. David was just telling me the other day how important you were to him, and that he – well, *we* – would love you to be there.'

'Well, I . . .' For a moment, Sally seemed genuinely shocked. 'I mean, I'd love to.'

'Great,' said Sarah. 'That's settled, then.' She forced a smile, then turned on her heel and headed back to her office, sure Sally was probably already emailing the other PAs *en masse* with news of her invite. David would be livid, but there was no other way she could see to guarantee Sally's silence – she'd be more interested in boasting to the other girls that she'd been invited, and therefore would want the wedding to go ahead so she could report back any gossip, and so certainly wouldn't want to do anything to jeopardize it actually happening. *Yes*, Sarah thought to herself, *that was masterful*. Of course, what Sally did with the information afterwards was anyone's guess – assuming there *was* an 'afterwards' . . .

Sarah knew she had more immediate problems – not in the least how to tell David she'd invited Sally. Though given a choice between that and explaining what she'd been doing with Evan, she knew which one she'd prefer.

35

Evan sat in the café, alternating between sipping his coffee and looking at his watch. Grace was late, and although he felt ashamed of the call he'd made to her at the hospital earlier begging her to meet him, quite frankly, he hadn't known what else to do.

Even a run along the Thames path hadn't helped him figure things out; instead, he'd struggled even to put one foot in front of the other, mainly due to the wind and driving rain that had been in his face for most of the way, and had eventually forced him to stop. As he'd turned back towards his flat, he'd thought about his last few encounters with Sarah, and decided that the weather and his lack of progress had been somewhat apt.

While Grace's initial unfriendly 'Why should I?' hadn't been particularly encouraging, his 'Because there's something you need to know' seemed to have done the trick. And even though he suspected he might be in for a hard time, as far as he was concerned, anything that might give him a little more insight would be worth it.

The café, Al's, on Bermondsey Street, was one of his favourites. It had been here for longer than he could remember, possibly since before he'd been born. Anyone discovering it for the first time might think they'd wandered into some trendy retro establishment given the Formica tables and wood-chip wallpaper, but they'd probably been part of the original décor back in the sixties. And while the cuisine – full English breakfasts with sausages Evan was beginning to wish he was as thick-skinned as, mugs of tea so strong you could stand your spoon up in them, or even today's 'special' of pork chop and chips for four-ninety-nine – wasn't quite in keeping with the other establishments that lined the now-funky street, he would have hated to see it go, leaving the area with nothing the older residents might recognise. That was partly why he continued to support it, he told himself, as if he was doing a service to the community, although in truth, there were times you just needed a good old-fashioned fry-up.

Distracted by a movement in the doorway, he glanced up to see Grace standing there awkwardly, as if she'd taken a wrong turn down a dodgy street – not that there were many of those in Bermondsey nowadays. He caught her eye with a wave of the menu, and she came and sat down, her relief at seeing a familiar face quickly replaced with the kind of expression he used to see on the faces of his teachers at school whenever he'd been in trouble.

'Thanks for coming.'

'I'm here for Sarah, not you, Evan.'

'Still . . .' He slid the menu across to her. 'At least let me buy you a coffee.'

Grace gave the laminated sheet a cursory glance, wrinkling her nose at the spatterings of fossilized food clinging to it. 'I suppose a decaf latte would be out of the question?'

Evan smiled. 'Depends on your definition of latte. Or decaf,' he said, nodding at his own chipped mug, where a tar-like residue coated the bottom.

Grace studied the menu again. 'Maybe a cup of tea, then,' she said, as if expecting to see her choice of drink preceded by the word 'builder's'.

Evan waved Al over and gave him the order, ignoring the mumbled 'last of the big spenders' he heard in reply. 'So, how is she?' he asked, once Al had shuffled back behind the counter.

Grace shrugged. 'How do you think? Confused, angry, upset.'

'I'm sorry. I didn't mean to upset her. I just . . .'

'What did you think would happen?' interrupted Grace. 'That she'd welcome you back with open arms a week before her wedding?'

'I don't know what I thought, Grace. I just knew I had to do this.'

'Did you not consider that it might be a little selfish?'

'Maybe.' He sighed. 'But I'm not the only one.'

'What?'

'I'm not the only selfish one. Sarah was the one who picked me up without telling me she was already seeing someone else. So, you tell me – how does that make me the bad guy in all of this?'

'Because . . .' Grace was still glaring at him, but he sensed that a little of her hostility had evaporated. 'Because that was then. Now? She's made her choice.'

Evan looked anxiously round the café, conscious that some of the other occupants were watching what they probably assumed was a lover's tiff, though given the average age in the place, they probably couldn't hear what was going on without turning up their hearing aids. 'She didn't *have* a choice, Grace. I didn't give her one.' He paused as Al – evidently sniggering at his last sentence – placed a steaming mug of tea in front of Grace, although by the dismissive look she gave it, drinking it wasn't even a remote possibility. 'And in fact, I did the decent thing by both her and David by leaving them to get on with it.'

'So why did you do the indecent thing by coming back? And now, of all the times.'

'Because I realised something while I was away.'

'Which was?'

'Like I told you. That I love her.' Each time, the admission seemed to drain him a little more, and Evan leaned heavily back in his chair.

In the silence that followed, he toyed with the idea of ordering another coffee, but he was starting to feel like he'd done nothing but drink coffee these past few days, and worried for his ability to sleep for the rest of the week if he did. Though that might not be a bad thing, he realised, given how the clock was ticking.

Grace picked her tea up wordlessly, took a tentative sip, then put it straight back down again, so Evan thought he'd try a different tactic. 'And you think she's doing the right thing, do you?'

Grace frowned. 'In what way.'

'Marrying *him*.'

'As opposed to marrying you, you mean?'

'That's not what I meant. Is David really the kind of person you can see Sarah being happy with?'

'Well, that's Sarah's choice, isn't it? Not mine.'

'If it was a choice, yes.'

'What is this really about, Evan?'

'It's about . . .' Evan swallowed hard. 'About her marrying someone who doesn't deserve her. And who certainly doesn't respect her.'

'I hardly think you meeting David for five minutes in Waitrose qualifies you to make a character judgement.'

'I went on his stag night, Grace. I think I know him a little better than . . .'

'Whoa.' Grace sat bolt upright. 'You went on his *stag night*?'

'He invited me. In Waitrose. Sarah didn't say?'

'No, she didn't, Evan. Probably because she couldn't believe you'd do something so stupid, so *selfish*. But that still doesn't mean you can decide whether or not he's good enough for her, unless . . .' Grace peered at him accusingly. 'Did something happen? On the stag?'

Evan shifted uncomfortably in his chair. 'Grace, I can't . . .'

'Oh god.' She closed her eyes for a second, then looked at him levelly. 'Does Sarah know?'

'I'm not saying anything. And I'll bet he hasn't.'

'And you want *me* to,' she said, staring at him in disbelief. 'Is that why you asked me here?'

Evan shook his head, already worried he'd let too much slip. 'No. I'm just trying to show you that he's not right for her. What kind of person he is. Sarah's your best friend, Grace. Do you really want to see her end up with someone like that?'

Grace smiled, although there wasn't a lot of humour behind it. 'I'm sorry, Evan. Even if that were true, just because David might have done something meaningless with – what, some stripper? – on some drunken night out, which the vast majority of men have probably done . . .'

'I haven't.'

'. . . it doesn't mean he's not fit to marry her.'

'Grace, I'm not saying he did – or didn't do – anything, and if he did, he has to be the one to tell her. But something like that isn't meaningless. It shows a lack of respect.'

'Whereas sleeping with you behind his back was her showing him respect?'

'That's not the point. They'd only just met, and it was only the once.' He hated saying that, as if it diminished what he and Sarah had.

Grace regarded him for a moment, as if weighing something up. 'Evan, if you had any idea how headstrong Sarah was, you'd know you were wasting your time. And even if I were to talk to her, what good would it do? Besides, what's her alternative?'

'Well, she could, you know . . .' Evan stared into his empty mug. 'Marry me instead. Eventually.'

Grace let out a short laugh. 'And have you asked her?'

'How? She won't take my calls, and whenever I do manage to see her, she storms off before we can finish a conversation.'

'And doesn't that tell you something?'

'It tells me that she still has feelings for me. Strong ones. And that's not good if you're getting married to someone else.'

'That depends what those feelings are, doesn't it?'

'Why are you giving me such a hard time?' Evan asked exasperatedly. 'What would you have done?'

'We're not talking about me here, Evan, are we? We're talking about you.'

'Even so. Tell me, Grace. Please. You're the psychiatrist. What's your professional advice in all of this?'

'Are you serious?'

'Deadly.' Evan retrieved his wallet from his jacket pocket and pulled out a handful of notes. 'What do you charge for a private consultation?'

Grace placed both hands on the table. 'Tell you what, Evan. I'll do you for free. You're delusional, and irrational, and suffering from a severe case of . . .'

'I'm in love, Grace. That's all.'

'Well, I'm afraid there's no cure for that.'

'Yes there is. It's giving the person who loves you the opportunity to love you back.' Evan regarded her across the table. 'I'll be playing at the club tonight, Grace. Just tell her that . . .' He sighed. 'Just tell her that. Please.'

'If you really loved her, you'd leave her alone.'

'I can't.'

'Christ, Evan,' said Grace, standing up angrily. 'It's taken Sarah the best part of a year to get over losing the baby, and now you're putting her through this . . .' She shook her head vigorously, then without another word, made for the door.

And as Evan watched her go, it didn't even cross his mind to follow her. He was too busy thinking 'what baby?'

36

Sarah stared nervously at her mobile as it buzzed on her desk, relaxing when she saw Grace's name on the screen. She'd known she was meeting Evan, though when Grace had asked what she should say to him, Sarah hadn't known exactly how to answer that. She picked her phone up, walked over to close her office door, and answered the call.

'How was he?' she said, surprising herself, when 'How did it go?' was perhaps what she should have opened with.

'Well . . .' Grace sighed. 'He said that he loves you. Again.'

'And did you . . .' She swallowed hard. 'Tell him to leave me alone?'

'I did my best. I'm not your enforcer, Sarah. And I think it would take a lot more than me telling him where to go to get him to, well, *go*.'

'Thank you. So what now?'

'I'd say you've got a choice to make.'

'Do I really?'

'Of course you do.'

Sarah walked over to the window and stared out at the darkening sky. 'Tell me what the alternatives are, Grace. I go ahead and marry David, which is what I've been planning for the past nine months, or I lose him, risk losing my job, and all for what? The promise of what might have been?'

Grace sighed loudly down the line. 'Well, that depends.'

'On what?'

'On whether you want to have any regrets.'

Sarah smiled, wistfully. She already had regrets, where both Evan and David were concerned: That she'd accepted David's proposal so quickly, that she hadn't even thought about how Evan might have felt when she'd picked him up – and then sent him away. But she'd been confused. It had been a tricky enough situation as it was, and then there was the pregnancy, and the miscarriage . . . She shuddered at the memory. The miscarriage was the key to all of this, and the reason she and David were getting married, even though the baby possibly hadn't been his. She'd never told Grace what had actually happened. Maybe now was the time.

'I already do, Grace,' she said.

'About Evan? Or David.'

'Both.' Sarah took a deep breath. 'You don't know the full story . . .' Her voice trailed off, and she felt guilty for not having been honest.

'Whatever the circumstances were, David was the one who did the decent thing. That counts for a lot.'

'Even if it wasn't his baby?'

'You don't know that. You'll never know that. So there's no point beating yourself up about it. At least he didn't ignore it, unlike . . .'

'Evan didn't know!' Sarah almost shouted.

'What?'

'I didn't tell him I was pregnant.'

There was a pause, and then, 'Tell me you're joking.'

'No,' said Sarah, meekly.

'Why ever not?'

'Because I didn't want to guilt him into coming back and messing up the biggest break of his career because of something that might have been nothing to do with him.'

'But it probably was his, right? You said that you and Evan didn't take any precautions.'

'No.' This was true. She'd wanted to feel him inside her, with no barriers, nothing between them. When she and David had sex – in the early days at least – David would always break off from her and head into the en-suite to get a condom from the bathroom cabinet, coming back a minute or two later 'suited and booted', as he'd always describe it, and there had always been something so mechanical, so *impersonal*, about that. Whereas with Evan, she'd wanted sex to be personal. 'We sort of got carried away.'

'But you only did it the once?'

Sarah started to colour. 'Three times, actually.'

'In one night? Tell me why you're not marrying Evan again?'

'*Grace!*'

There was a pause on the other end of the phone, before Grace spoke again. 'Tell me something,' she said, sternly. 'Is there, sorry, *was* there any chance that the baby could have been David's. Any chance at all?'

'Of course there was,' said Sarah, indignantly. 'Accidents happen. Condoms break. You never know.'

'But there's more chance it was Evan's?'

Sarah nodded, then realised it was a pretty pointless gesture on the phone. 'I guess.'

'And you didn't think you *ought* to have told him?'

'I didn't know how to get in touch with him.'

'That's not really true, is it?'

'Okay. Maybe not. But I wasn't thinking straight. Finding out I was pregnant kind of sent me into a spin, and before I could get my head around what had happened, David spotted my discarded pregnancy testing kit in his bathroom waste-bin – I don't know how I could have been so stupid to have left it on show – and put two and two together. I thought he'd be angry, but to my surprise he was the exact opposite, so when he so selflessly got down on one knee in front of me, I was confused. Didn't know how to react.'

'So you said yes?'

'Yeah. But mainly because saying no would have been too difficult, too *complicated,* to justify. And then, instead of wondering whether to tell Evan that he might be a father, I had a bigger problem to contend with – telling him not only that, but that I'd got engaged too – and that had kind of made the first part irrelevant. Besides, he'd only just gone. It wouldn't have been fair to make him feel he had to come back – or at least, that's how I justified my actions to myself. And then a few weeks later, when I lost the baby, I was fully expecting David to say the engagement was off. But if anything, it made him keener to marry me. And that really threw me.'

'And you haven't thought to tell Evan since?'

'What would have been the point? I'd lost him, and the baby had . . . I'd lost it too. I couldn't cope with losing David as well. He'd been so good about it all, and yet I knew that inside he was devastated. So how could I take *us* away from him as well?'

'How does David feel about it all now?'

'He's . . .' Sarah thought for a moment. 'Very matter of fact about it. You know, we'd got pregnant once, we can do it again, that sort of thing.'

'Have you been trying?'

'Well, we haven't been trying not to, if you see what I mean?'

'But nothing's happened.'

'No.'

'And how do you feel about that?'

Sarah stared out of the window, grateful she didn't have to look Grace in the eye while she thought about her answer. There were dozens of people milling about on the pavement below, and she suddenly longed to be among them, anonymous. 'I don't know,' she said, eventually.

'How did you feel when you thought the baby might be Evan's?'

'Scared. But like I couldn't wait to tell him. Though didn't dare.'

'Because you thought he'd be pleased? Or because you were worried about what his reaction would be?'

Sarah began to pace around the office, the four walls she'd fought so hard to earn suddenly making her feel claustrophobic. 'A bit of both, perhaps. But maybe . . . maybe losing the baby was a bit of a blessing. Because how would we ever have told whose it was? And what would I have done if I'd had it and it wasn't David's?'

Sarah was surprised at how clinical she sounded. In truth, back then it had surprised her how much the whole episode had hurt. With Evan not around, she'd kind of resigned herself to the fact that she was marrying David, and having his child – well, having *a* child, and David would be the father – just perhaps not the biological one, and if there were potential problems down the line as a result of that, she'd convinced herself she'd deal with those if and when she had to. Then, when she'd lost it a few short weeks later, Sarah had cried for days, and while she knew that was probably hormonal, maybe it had also been because she'd lost a part of Evan, the last bit of him that she'd been desperately clinging on to. Once or twice, she'd even thought about writing to him to tell him, but tell him what – that he might have made her pregnant, and then she'd lost the baby anyway? She hadn't seen any upside in that.

'Anyway,' she continued. 'Why all the questions about the baby? I thought that subject was pretty much . . .' She stopped herself – she'd been about to say 'dead and buried', but the phrase seemed overly harsh. 'Forgotten about.'

'Maybe not,' said Grace, awkwardly. 'In fact, I think Evan might suspect something.'

'About what?'

'You having been pregnant.'

'What? How on earth . . .?'

'I was mad at him. I let it slip out, okay? And besides – I wasn't aware he didn't know.'

Sarah forgave her friend instantly. After all, mistakes happened. As she well knew. 'And how did he react?'

'I didn't give him a chance to.'

Sarah slumped down into her chair, stared wistfully up at the ceiling, and suddenly realised what her biggest regret was.

Neither had she.

37

Sarah twirled her engagement ring anxiously round on her finger as she sat at her desk. She was surprised Evan hadn't called after Grace's slip, but that was just as well. She didn't have a clue what to say to him.

She played with the diamond that probably cost more than Evan's car, and did her best to look forward to the weekend. She couldn't ignore the fact that, with David as a partner here, she certainly wasn't making a bad decision, even if it was partly a practical one, though she reminded herself that that wasn't necessarily a bad thing. After all, her father had married for love, and had ended up with heartbreak – though perhaps that hadn't been his fault – and she did love David, although that love was perhaps a combination of comfort, familiarity, and . . . what? Gratitude? It was hard to say. But Sarah wasn't sure she knew what real love felt like anyway, and if that was the case . . . well, you couldn't miss what you'd never had, could you?

The two of them were compatible – she was pretty sure of that. And while compatibility hardly smacked of excitement – and her brief time with Evan had been exciting – marriage was different, wasn't it? The Mercedes was fun around town but probably a nightmare on a long run, whereas the BMW? It was easy to drive. Reliable. Felt like it could keep on going forever. And wasn't that the way to look at marriage?

Yes, Sarah decided, she was doing the sensible thing. As to whether she was doing the *right* thing, well, that depended on your definition of the word. Trouble was, all this speculation about what Evan might have done had he known he might have gotten her pregnant had thrown up a more important question: Had David only proposed because he thought *he* had?

She fetched herself a coffee from the machine in the hallway – her third of the day, she noted, worryingly – and set it down on her desk, then noticed the bag of donuts sitting in her in-tray. They still looked relatively fresh, and for a moment, she was tempted to eat them both, until she remembered she was still on her pre-wedding diet. The dress she'd ordered months ago from a designer in Hay's Galleria just about fitted her, and she was already going to spend most of her wedding day breathing in as it was.

She checked the time. David was bound to have finished his conference call by now, so she picked the donuts up and headed off down the corridor. Forcing herself to give Sally a friendly smile on the way past, she walked into his office and placed the bag on his desk.

'What's this?'

She smiled, sheepishly. 'Peace offering.'

David looked at the bag, and then up at her, a surprised expression on his face. 'There was no need.'

'There was. Besides, the girls bought them for me, and I've got to watch my figure.'

David peered inside the bag, his face lighting up at the contents. 'Excellent,' he said, extracting a chocolate-covered donut and devouring half of it in one bite.

'I hope you had a decent lunch?' she said, a little worried the donuts might be off, but David had a cast-iron constitution. Or at least, she hoped he did. 'And by "decent", I mean "healthy".'

'This *is* my lunch.' He crammed the rest of the donut into his mouth. 'Calls all morning, and now a bloody board meeting starting in ten minutes,' he said, as he chewed. 'No doubt it'll go on till the evening. Then we'll probably go for dinner . . .'

'Right. Well, in that case . . .' She walked over and shut the door. 'Can I ask you something?'

'Sure.' David glanced nervously at his watch, no doubt fearing a resumption of their earlier discussion. 'If it's quick. Like I said, board meeting.'

'It is. At least, it should be.' Sarah perched on the corner of his desk again and took a deep breath. 'Why are you marrying me?'

'Pardon?'

'Why are you marrying me?'

David leaned back in his chair and folded his arms behind his head. 'Because I love you and you're a good shag. That do you?'

'I'm serious, David.'

'Ah. Right. Sorry.' He sat up quickly, like a schoolboy told to take his feet off a train seat. 'What's brought this on?'

'It's just . . . it's silly, really, but I was wondering . . .'

'Wondering what?'

She shrugged, attempting to trivialise what she was about to ask. 'If I hadn't been pregnant, would you still have proposed to me?'

David frowned. 'Of course.'

'Honestly?'

He nodded, then patted her reassuringly on the knee. 'I was just waiting for an excuse to ask.'

'That was just what I needed to hear.' She reached down to brush some crumbs from his tie. 'Thanks.'

'Don't mention it.'

David made a relieved face, pleased he seemed to have navigated this particular emotional minefield successfully, and while

Sarah wanted a moment to bask in this rare flash of sincerity from him, she could tell he was conscious of the time. She jumped off the desk, then leaned down and kissed him on the top of his head.

'See ya,' she said cheerfully, making for the door.

'Sure,' said David distractedly, his attention already back on work.

Sarah walked back along the corridor and into her office, carefully closed the door behind her, and sat back down at her desk, determined to stop obsessing about Saturday and get on with her day job. She knew she should have been reassured by David's response, but the trouble was, while he might not have asked her to marry him because she was pregnant, something else was worrying her: She might only have said yes because she was.

And that was even worse.

38

Evan could tell Sarah had spotted him – why else would she have suddenly begun walking in the other direction? He three-point-turned the Mercedes quickly, causing a taxi driver to give him the finger, and caught her up.

'Haven't you heard of the word "stalking"?' she asked, as he drove slowly alongside her.

'Haven't you heard of the word "honesty"?' he called back through the car's open window.

Sarah stopped abruptly and wheeled round to face him, her expression a mixture of anger and vulnerability, and Evan stamped on the brakes, fearing he'd overstepped the mark. Then again, he reminded himself, she didn't really have a leg to stand on.

'Evan, you shouldn't be here.'

'Give me one good reason why not.'

Her eyes flicked to behind his car, where a large Routemaster was bearing down on him. 'Well, for starters, you've stopped in the bus lane.'

Evan cursed under his breath, and glared at her. 'Wait there.'

He gunned the car back out into the traffic, offering a silent prayer of thanks when he spotted a parking space a few yards further on, then kept an eye on Sarah in his rear-view mirror as he reversed the Merc into it. As he fed a couple of pound coins into the meter, she stared at him for a moment, then disappeared into a Starbucks on the corner. This certainly wasn't a conversation she wanted to have on the pavement, especially not so close to her office, and she was grateful when Evan followed her inside.

'Well?'

'Grace shouldn't have said anything,' was all she could manage.

'No,' said Evan. 'But *you* should have.'

'What do you want?' she said, as they walked up to the counter.

'The truth.'

'I meant *to drink*.'

'What? Oh . . .' Evan shrugged, wondering whether they sold alcohol in Starbucks. 'Nothing. Thank you.'

Sarah ordered herself a cappuccino, deciding it'd take the longest time to prepare, conscious she was stalling for much-needed time. She stood there silently as the barista made it, grateful for the few precious seconds it gave her to formulate an answer to the question she was sure was coming, and she didn't have long to wait.

'So come on – why didn't you tell me?' Evan asked impatiently.

She glanced around for a place to sit, but there were no free tables, so she changed her order to 'to go' and led Evan back outside. 'How?' she said, blowing through the hole in her cup's plastic lid as they walked along the pavement. 'You were off having a fine old time in the U.S.'

'Stop throwing this back at me, Sarah.' He shook his head exasperatedly. 'When did you find out?'

'About two months after you left.'

'And you didn't think I might have wanted to know?'

'No. I'm sorry.' She took the next right turn, anxious to put as much distance in between the two of them and her office as possible. 'Besides, what difference would it have made?'

'What difference?' Evan stared at her incredulously. 'All the difference in the world.'

'Why?'

'Why do you think? You were carrying my baby. *Our* baby.'

'You can't be sure of that.'

'Can you be sure it wasn't?'

Sarah couldn't look at him. 'Would you have come back? If it had been?'

'Of course I would have.'

'That's easy to say now. Now there isn't a baby.'

'Well, what did you expect?'

Sarah took a sip of her coffee, wincing as the still too-hot liquid burnt her tongue. 'It doesn't really matter what you say now, Evan, does it?'

'Christ, Sarah, You seem to be judging me as if I've failed some sort of test, when I didn't even know I was being tested in the first place,' he said, following her as she suddenly crossed the road, sprinting to avoid a white van that seemed determined to run him over. He peered at the driver, checking to see it wasn't David, then fell into step beside her. 'Was it mine?' he asked, his voice faltering, and at once, she felt sorry for him.

'How should I know? They don't exactly test for that sort of thing after you've, you know . . .' Sarah swallowed hard. She'd already had too much loss in her life, and the word always troubled her. 'Afterwards. Especially when it's so early.'

'But there was a chance it could have been?'

'Of course. Just like there was a chance it could have been David's. But we'll never know, will we?'

As he trailed her along the pavement, Evan thought back to that night. They'd had sex twice, then once the following morning, each time without any protection, and while he was no expert, surely that tripled the chances? But without knowing the intimate details of Sarah's relationship with David, he couldn't say the same

WHAT MIGHT HAVE BEEN

wasn't true for them, and that was one line of questioning he really didn't want to go down.

'I still think you should have told me.'

He looked crushed, and Sarah fought the urge to take his hand. 'You were off on this big tour of yours. I knew how important that was to you. *For* you.'

Evan stared at her. The insinuation that Sarah hadn't told him because she hadn't wanted him to interrupt the tour had taken him by surprise – but had she done that for him, or for her? 'So, you kept the fact that you might have been carrying my child from me . . .' – he was struggling to keep his voice level – '. . . for the benefit of my *career*?'

Sarah nodded, a little guilty that her admission was provoking this kind of reaction. 'Well . . .'

'And what would you have done if it *had* turned out to have been mine?' he said, angry now. 'Turned up at one of the concerts pushing a pram and wearing a t-shirt with "surprise" and a large downwards-facing arrow printed on the front? Or just married David, and brought *my baby* up as his?'

Sarah had never seen him like this, and wondered whether she'd overstepped the mark. But she had anger she could tap into, too. 'Well, that turned out not to be an issue, didn't it?'

'Conveniently.'

As soon as he'd said it, and seen the pain the word had provoked, Evan had known it was a mistake, but it had just slipped out as these things often did in arguments, and not for the first time, he wondered how on earth they'd got to this. If he could have taken it back, he would have, and he braced himself for Sarah's response, but instead, the remark seemed to have deflated her. He didn't want to push, but he felt he had a right to the truth, so he took her arm and steered her through the gateway in front of them, and into Postman's Park.

'Did David know?'

'David?' She gazed around the once-familiar setting, her impassive expression hiding a complicated churn of emotions, then met his eyes defiantly. 'Of course he knew.'

'When?'

'What's that got to do with anything?'

'Before the two of you got engaged? Or after?'

Sarah knew it was a tricky question to answer. Say 'before', and Evan would assume – like she had – that David's proposal had been instigated by the pregnancy, and what on earth would he make of that? More ammunition for this ridiculous crusade of his, probably. But to say 'after' would assume that she'd already made her decision about marrying him, and for some reason, she didn't want Evan to think that. She sat down heavily on the nearest bench, and Evan followed suit.

'David found out. By accident.' She shook her head as she placed her coffee down on the floor. 'I didn't mean for it to happen like that. And he was so overjoyed . . . What was I supposed to say?' She put on a faux-English voice. 'Hold your horses, mate, I'm not sure the little blighter's yours'?'

Under different circumstances Evan would have laughed at her accent, but right now he didn't find it the slightest bit amusing. Instead, he just stared at her, unable to compute what was going on.

'That still doesn't answer why you didn't tell *me*.'

'Like I said. I didn't want to mess up your tour, your *life*. Not until I was sure.' She shook her head. 'Maybe that was my bad.'

'*My bad*? Christ, Sarah, what does that actually mean, apart from claiming ownership of a Michael Jackson album? And when exactly were you going to be sure? When the kid was born and turned out to have my eyes?'

'Evan.' She rested a hand on his arm, but he shook it off angrily. 'Don't you think it was difficult for me too?'

'I had a right to know.'

'Know what? That there was a fifty percent chance that you might have gotten me pregnant?'

'Yes. Or ten percent. Or even just one . . .' He sighed, all the fight suddenly going out of him. 'Don't you think I'd have come back, even if there was the slightest possibility?'

Sarah looked up sharply. *That* was the thing. The crux of the matter. 'I didn't want you to come back because you thought you had to. I needed you to come back because you *wanted* to. Wanted *me*. What kind of woman would I be if I'd have used something like, you know . . .'

'Being pregnant?'

'Yes, being pregnant. To trap you.'

'It seems to have worked with David. Though I'm not sure who's trapped who.'

'Evan, I . . .' Sarah saw how upset he was, and decided that perhaps getting everything in the open was the best thing – for both of them. 'What was I supposed to do? You weren't here. I didn't know for sure who the father was . . .' She caught herself – uttering those words didn't perhaps portray her in the best light. 'I mean, would you have preferred for me to have ruined the biggest break of your career by telling you there was a chance of something that, actually, turned out not to matter?'

'Of course it matters.'

'Let me finish. And then, like I said, when David found out, he was so happy that he literally got down on one knee there and then. Then what was I going to do?'

'You could have said no,' said Evan, petulantly.

'And possibly alienate someone who, let's not forget, might actually have been the father of my child? That wouldn't have been smart. Especially since there wasn't anyone else around.'

Evan shook his head slowly. Even though it was Sarah, and not him, who worked in Risk Management, even he could see the sense in that approach – but that didn't mean he had to like it.

'Did you have to say "yes" so quickly? At least, without talking to me first?'

She looked pleadingly at him. 'I was confused. Not thinking straight. Jesus, I'd just found out I was pregnant. It had all come as a bit of a shock – especially the part where David proposed. Plus, what possible reason could I have given him for saying no?'

'What about me?' Evan said, realising how selfish that sounded the moment the words left his lips.

'What about you? Things were great for you. You got to screw me without any real commitment . . .'

'Or not, as it might have turned out.'

'That's not what I meant. You didn't tell me you were leaving before you slept with me, and that didn't stop you.'

'But I didn't know! And besides, you didn't tell me you had a boyfriend before you slept with me!' Evan put his head in his hands. 'What chance did I have?'

'You could have fought for me,' said Sarah, softly.

'Seems to me you'd already made your decision – particularly since you were quite happy to get engaged to someone else when you might have been carrying my baby. *Our* baby.'

'That's not true.'

'No? American girls seem to be allowed to date as many people as they like, so are they allowed to get engaged to lots of people at the same time too? Or is that just the Mormons?'

'That's not fair, Evan.'

'Because while we're at it, you had it pretty good too. David and me, making fools of ourselves over you.'

'Is that how you really see it?'

'How else am I supposed to see it? You played me, Sarah. Even if I'd stayed, and we'd been seeing each other, would you ever have told me about David, or would you just have kept going out with both of us?'

'Of course not.'

'Really? I wouldn't have been surprised if you'd even gone and got engaged to him just to see what my reaction would be. Whether I'd feel I had to ask you the same question. If I'd buy you a bigger ring. Would that have made the difference?'

'Don't be ridiculous.'

'Well excuse me, but I don't know what other interpretation I could possibly put on it. You had your fun with me, and then when push came to shove, you decided that David was the better bet – and especially as a father – even if it wasn't his kid.' Evan held his hands up in surrender. 'So there you have it. I'm obviously wasting my time. Because if you didn't even think it was important to let me know I was maybe going to be a dad, then that just proves how little you thought of me.'

Sarah glanced around the park. Their raised voices were starting to attract a bit of interest from the half-dozen or so people sitting on the other benches, and she deeply hoped there was no-one from her office listening this time.

'It wasn't like that.'

'Does he know?'

'Know what?'

'The whole story.'

'No.'

'Don't you think he deserves to?'

Sarah risked another sip of coffee. 'Maybe.'

'Would you like me to tell him?'

She blanched. 'You wouldn't.'

'Why not? We're mates now, David and me.'

'Evan, please.'

'Oh, don't worry. Your secret's safe with me.' He folded his arms and stared up at the sky. 'I used to think I knew you, and yes, I know that sounds funny after how little time we actually spent together. For the last year, I've thought of you as my perfect woman, but now? I'm not so sure. You've changed, Sarah. And maybe you and David *are* perfectly suited.'

'What do you mean by that?'

'Nothing,' said Evan, quickly. 'I'm sorry. I just feel like such a mug.'

'You're not a mug, Evan. Maybe I am, for not . . .' She stopped talking. To say any more would be unfair.

Evan's heart began to hammer. He wanted to ask outright if he was too late, but didn't think he'd like the answer, and the trouble was, given these recent revelations he suspected he'd been too late a year ago, and if that was the case, then what hope was there for him now? And while he was angry at Sarah for not being honest with him, given her lack of honesty – or perhaps openness – about so much else, what had he really expected?

Abruptly, he stood up. He needed a bit of distance, or he feared he might say something he'd regret – if he hadn't already.

'I have to go,' he said, starting towards the gate.

'Evan,' she called after him, not caring who was listening. 'Now you know everything. I promise.'

Evan stopped in his tracks, wheeled round, and strode back over to the bench. 'I wish I could be sure of that,' he said, then he leaned in close to make sure she'd hear him. 'But there's one important thing that *you* don't know.'

'What?'

'Back then. When I asked you to meet me in the Tate. It was so I could tell you about the tour . . .'

'So? That's old news.'

'. . . and to ask you to come with me.'

Sarah's mouth dropped open. 'Why didn't you say something?'

Evan gave her a look, then wheeled round and marched straight out of the park, glad he'd let her question hang. Even though he knew most Americans didn't really get irony, on this particular occasion, he was pretty sure this one would.

39

Evan headed miserably back to where he'd left the car, muttering under his breath as he strode along the busy pavement. Their walk in the park hadn't exactly been, as Sarah might say, a walk in the park – he certainly hadn't foreseen the conversation going like that – and although deep down he knew he still loved her, he wasn't sure he liked her very much at the moment.

He shook his head as he climbed into the Mercedes and started the engine. While he could just about accept her reasons for not telling him about being pregnant at the time – even though she'd tried to disguise them as her doing him a favour – surely he'd deserved to know afterwards? Though he knew he was being just as selfish – not once had he asked Sarah how she'd felt. How she'd dealt with the trauma of losing the baby. Whether she was okay – *inside* – as well as emotionally. As he knew all too well, some wounds never quite healed.

As he drove back towards Bermondsey, replaying their conversation in his head, he briefly considered turning round and going to find her again, maybe even apologising, but suspected that might not be such a good idea. Besides, Evan had a feeling that throwing his toys out of the pram – although that struck him as a particularly bad metaphor – might actually have done him some good in the long run. He'd actually been able to get his point across, explain how he felt, *and* leave with both a killer line and the moral high ground, and he could count on the fingers – in fact, on the thumb – of one hand the number of times he'd walked away from an argument with a woman feeling like that. *No*, he told himself, *just keep going*. At the very least, Sarah would need some time to absorb everything he'd said. To let the fact that he'd been going to ask her to come away with him sink in. And at least that might make the playing field a little more level.

He drove slowly across London Bridge, wondering what his reaction would have been if she *had* told him. Would he have been able to avoid the knee-jerk 'is it mine' response? Probably not – but surely that would have been a fair question, given the circumstances? And what would he have done if it had been? He wouldn't have stayed in the U.S., that was for sure. He'd have come back for her. For the baby. To care for them both. And then, well, maybe she wouldn't have lost it.

His insides were hurting, and he wound down the window to let some air into the car. Both Sarah and David had believed they'd lost something real. Something amazing. Something that had been a part of them, or at least, part of their lives for a while. They were allowed to feel bad, to mourn, even, but him? There were no rules for the way he was supposed to feel, so long after the event, especially given the lack of certainty. But maybe he was mourning lost chances: The *idea* that he might have been a dad; the loss of a future with Sarah – one that would surely have been cemented by the child she'd been carrying. *Their* child.

Given what had happened, he supposed he could understand Sarah's behaviour. He was no psychologist, but he imagined the loss must have been incredibly difficult, and that maybe the combination of relief – after all, there was no denying how awkward things might have been if she'd had it – and sadness had churned her up inside. The more he thought about it, the more Evan realised he had no way of imagining what she'd gone through; he'd known about it for five minutes, and already he felt hollow, even though he couldn't be sure the child had been his.

He checked the clock on the dashboard, remembering he'd promised Mel he'd perform a set this evening, and while playing was the last thing he felt like doing, at least it meant he didn't have to sit at home with his thoughts on overdrive. There was too much to mull over, too many details he wasn't sure about, though deep down, Evan knew this baby 'business' was just one of those things he'd never find the answer to. He'd be better off just forgetting about it. However hard he suspected that might be.

Besides, he had more pressing things to deal with, namely the silver-embossed invite he'd found in the jacket pocket of his dinner suit earlier – David must have slipped it in there on Saturday night – which was currently sitting on his mantelpiece at home. If push came to shove, would he really go to the wedding? Did he think his presence there might be a last trigger for Sarah, and that she might run away from the altar and into his arms? He'd been to a screening of *The Graduate* at the BFI on the South Bank once, and had been unable to believe how most of the women in the audience had cheered and cried at the ending. But stuff like that didn't happen in real life. Or rather, in his life.

He drove along Riley Road and pulled into the garage, nearly running over a dreadlocked young girl carrying a tray of food in the process. As his eyes adjusted to the darkness, he noticed a long trestle table set up in the corner, and a huge van with 'Film Catering' written on the side. Carefully, he steered the Merc towards its usual spot, and as he climbed out, he noticed Mick sitting in the corner, a half-empty plate balanced precariously on the bonnet of the Porsche parked next to him, and – for some reason Evan couldn't fathom – sporting a pair of sunglasses.

'Had enough of 'er already?' Mick said, pulling his Ray-Bans off.
'Pardon?'

'The Merc.'

'Oh. No. Just didn't want to leave it where I couldn't see it.'

'Probly best,' said Mick. 'Need to keep an eye on sumfink that beautiful. Otherwise who knows what might 'appen to it.'

'Exactly,' said Evan, glumly, then he nodded towards the catering truck. 'What's all this?'

Mick shrugged. 'Film catering. Five hundred quid for the day. And all the food I can eat.'

Evan looked at Mick's distended stomach. By the look of things, that was turning out to be quite an amount, and he wondered whether the film company was beginning to regret the arrangement. 'What are they filming?'

'Me,' said Mick, polishing his sunglasses on his shirt.

'What?'

'Fly on the wall documentary. "The Car Park".' He pointed to a dark recess behind one of the metal girders that supported the roof. 'If you look up there and wave, you'll be in it.'

'Really?' Evan couldn't stop himself from looking, then tried hard to ignore the gloating expression on Mick's face.

'Nah. Some advert round the corner. Ain't seen nobody famous, though. 'Cept for you, of course.' Mick picked his plate up off the Porsche's bonnet and held it out. 'Want some?'

'What is it?'

Mick shrugged. 'Some sort of cold porridge. Tasty though. You're supposed to eat it with these Peter breads.'

'Pita breads, Mick. And it's hummus.'

'Hummus?' Mick made a face. 'Christ on a bike. I 'ope I don't wake up dead tomorrow.'

'Huh?'

'You know. Post-hummus.' He nudged Evan in the ribs, then made his way back towards the catering truck. 'Geddit?'

Evan smiled, then made his way out of the car park and past the camera crew outside. Bermondsey was often being used for filming – people couldn't get enough of the old warehouses and the 'real' London streets. He'd even extra-ed in one himself once, at Mel's club, an advert for some new 'designer' beer which had paid him a couple of hundred quid for a morning's work and given him the worst hangover he'd had in ages. Afterwards, he'd made the mistake of mentioning it to Finn, and then had to put up with his teasing for the two months it had been on television. 'You don't have a clue how to act,' Finn had told him.

And as he walked back to his flat, Evan didn't find it at all funny that now, as then, exactly the same thing was true.

40

arah was waiting for Grace by the entrance to Borough Market. She loved this place – another one of London's delights that Evan had alerted her to – and as she watched people mill around the stalls, she wondered whether he was somewhere here too, perhaps meeting a friend to pick up some dinner like she was. She doubted it, though. Given the expression on his face when he'd stormed off earlier, he'd looked like he needed to be alone. Or at least, nowhere near her.

A year ago, after he'd left, she'd occasionally walk nervously around here with David – at least on one of the rare times she could convince him to 'slum it', in his words, and buy something to eat from somewhere he held in the same regard as the burger vans you found at sports events – wondering if Evan had perhaps come back to visit, and whether they'd bump into him, and what would happen if they did. She'd even gone as far as working out a strategy: Chat like they were old friends. Not linger. Certainly not suggest going for a coffee, or a drink. That was one threesome she'd been keen to avoid.

A tap on the shoulder made her jump – Grace, breathless from another over-running day dealing with the sick and the depressed. Sarah, worried that she was turning into the latter, kissed her friend hello, and they made their way in through the iron gates.

'How was work?'

'Crazy!' Grace rolled her eyes. 'Which is also a pretty good description of most of the people who come and see me. Including your ex.'

'Evan's *not* my ex.'

'No? Are the two of you back together, then?'

Sarah smiled, despite herself. 'Grace . . .'

'What did you say?' Grace cupped a hand over her ear as she surveyed the bustling market. 'I can't hear you for that rumbling sound.'

Sarah frowned. 'What rumbling sound?'

'My stomach.' Grace laughed, then gave Sarah a hug. 'What's it to be? I'm starving.'

Sarah shrugged. 'I don't know. Maybe just a coffee. I'm not that hungry.'

'Have you eaten anything today?'

'Just breakfast.'

'Which was?'

Sarah had to think. 'Coffee.'

'Tell me this is just some last-minute get-into-your-dress diet?'

'No, it's just . . .' For some reason, Sarah couldn't start the conversation she'd been desperate to have since Evan had stormed off.

'Don't tell me. Evan?'

'He came to find me.'

'Oh. And?'

'And what?'

Grace smiled. 'I'm a doctor, Sarah. Not a dentist. And sometimes, asking you about Evan can be like pulling teeth.'

'Sorry. Well, we talked.'

'And how did that go?'

'Pretty good. If you can call *him* stomping off this time pretty good, that is.'

'Well, that makes it quits, doesn't it?' Grace linked arms with Sarah, and led her through the stalls. 'Although I assume he didn't throw a drink over you, so maybe not.'

'He might as well have done.'

'How do you mean?'

'He said he was going to ask me to go with him. Back then.'

'Go with him? To America?'

Sarah nodded. 'Yup.'

'That was a bit of a low blow.'

'He said it because he loves me, Grace. Not because he's trying to be mean.'

'You're sure it's not just because he's selfish? Because he can't stand to see you happy?'

'I was the selfish one, Grace. It was me that expected him to be happy about being picked up and then being dumped. I hardly thought about his feelings.' Sarah stood back as a man pushing a trolley laden with fish came round the corner. 'Besides, Evan's not like that.'

Grace looked at her for a moment, then stopped in front of a busy stall. 'Jesus Christ Souperstar?' she said, pointing to the sign in front of them, and Sarah was glad for a reason to change the subject.

'Whatever do you think it sells?'

'You'd think it'd be loaves and fishes, but it appears to be soup.'

'Is it any good?'

'I read about it in *Time Out* as the latest place to eat, so probably not.' Grace laughed. 'Still, only one way to find out. Come on.'

They joined the queue, and Grace continued her inquisition. 'Forgetting Evan for a moment, how are things otherwise?'

'Otherwise?'

'Well, you're obviously not yourself. Does David suspect anything?

'No. How could he? I mean, he didn't back then, when there was something going on, and now . . .'

'There's still something going on between you and Evan. In your head, at least.'

Sarah half-smiled, then sighed. 'You're right. And it's not helping seeing him. Stirring up all these old feelings. It's the last thing I need right now.'

'Maybe it isn't. Maybe it's exactly what you need. To make sure you're doing the right thing.'

'I should know that already.'

'Yes,' said Grace, as the queue inched forward. 'You should. But you quite plainly don't.'

'I thought I did. Or rather, I thought I'd convinced myself that I did. But seeing him again . . .'

Grace looked at her, and Sarah couldn't tell whether her expression was concern or frustration. 'You told me you'd managed to forget about Evan.'

'I had. Almost. But he's just gone and reminded me, hasn't he?'

Grace sighed. 'Reminded you of what? How he fucked you, then fucked off?'

'I didn't exactly give him a lot of choice in the matter.'

'Interesting.'

'What is?'

'How you're defending him now.'

They were at the front of the queue, and Sarah was grateful they'd have to break off their conversation to order. Grace made her selection, and, finding the prospect of decision-making exhausting, Sarah just held up a couple of fingers to indicate she'd have the same.

They paid for their soup, then wordlessly pushed through the crowds until they found a bench opposite Southwark Cathedral.

'So . . .' Sarah drummed her fingers on the plastic lid of her soup carton, but made no move to start eating. 'What would you do?'

'You're asking someone who doesn't have a boyfriend to help you choose between both of yours?'

'Grace, for the last time, Evan's not my boyfriend.'

'He thought he was once. And he'd like to be again.'

Sarah put her carton down on the bench and stared at the Thames through the gap in the buildings in front of her. 'It was just a fling. A bit of fun. Now it all seems so . . . serious.'

'Welcome to real life.'

'Yes, but . . .' Sarah looked uneasily across at Grace. 'What if I'm not ready? I mean, marriage, that's such a huge commitment, right? And you've got to be sure.'

'And you're so obviously not.' Grace patted her hand sympathetically, and when Sarah didn't respond, she exhaled loudly. 'Well, the way I see it, you've got two options.'

'Don't tell me: Go through with it, or don't go through with it.'

'Actually, you could ask for a postponement. So there are three.'

'If that's supposed to make me feel better, it doesn't. And I can't ask for a postponement. That'd be the same as telling David I don't want to marry him. How can I not be sure after all this time?'

'Is that a rhetorical question?'

Sarah leaned forward and put her head in her hands. 'I suppose that depends on whether you've got an answer or not.'

'Tell me something.' Grace rubbed her back comfortingly. 'Would you still be feeling like this if Evan hadn't come back?'

'I don't know. Maybe. Maybe not.'

'Is that why you resent him? For making you face the truth?'

Sarah spun round, almost knocking her soup over. 'What is the truth, Grace? That I'm making a mistake by marrying David? How can I resent someone for making me face up to that? After all, it would still be a mistake even if Evan hadn't arrived back on the scene.'

Grace pulled the lid off her soup carton, releasing a cloud of steam into the cool early evening air. 'Hey – don't shoot the messenger. And that refers to me *and* Evan.'

'Sorry. It's this whole thing. It's just not very . . . straightforward.'

'It is from where I'm sitting. If you think you might be making a mistake, don't go through with it.'

Sarah turned her attention back to the river, watching the passenger ferries thrum up and down past the massive bulk of HMS Belfast. 'I've always loved boats,' she said, after a moment. 'My dad was in the navy. And he told me once that some ships were so big that if you wanted to stop them, you had to start the process way in advance. And that's the deal with this wedding, Grace. I can't possibly stop it now. Not so close to the day. And certainly not without consequences.'

'Surely you could ask for a postponement. If David loves you, he'll understand.'

'He won't, Grace. I'm not sure I do. And what do I tell him? "The guy I had a fling with just after you and I met – the guy I might have dumped you for had he stayed around – has come back on the scene, and it's made me question what I'm doing getting married to you"? I can really see that going down a storm.'

'Don't tell him anything. We're women. We're allowed to change our minds.' Grace waited for a group of menacing-looking teenagers to shuffle past, then swivelled round on the bench to face her friend. 'What's worse? Pissing David off a little, or making a calamitous mistake that you might not be able to live with?'

'Don't you understand? If I call it off, it's the end of everything. David, my job, maybe even being here . . .'

'Surely not.'

'Grace, I'm American, not British. I can't just stay in England indefinitely. And it's unlikely I'd find someone else to offer me the same arrangement.'

'You mean work-wise, right?'

'Yes, work-wise!' Sarah shook her head. 'No – the easiest thing is to go through with it.'

'Since when have you been someone who's always taken the easy option?'

'Well, maybe now's the time.'

Grace put her soup down and grabbed her friend by the shoulders. 'Christ, Sarah. How can you expect me to stand there on Saturday and fix a smile on my face if I know this is how you're feeling? It's hypocritical. It's unfair. And above all else, it's wrong.'

'Maybe not. Maybe the only thing to do *is* to marry David. See how it feels. Give it a while. I mean, I can always get, you know, divorced, if . . .'

'Just listen to yourself, will you?'

They sat in silence for a while, Grace sipping her soup, Sarah just holding hers for warmth, then with a mumbled 'Sorry,' Sarah hauled herself up, dropped her cup into a nearby bin, and headed for the river.

With a sigh, Grace followed her, and they made their way along the Thames path towards Tower Bridge. Eventually, Sarah stopped, and leaned heavily against the railing.

'Help me Grace,' she said, the tears visible in her eyes. 'What would you do if you were me?'

'I'd marry the person I loved. Or rather, I certainly wouldn't marry someone I didn't.'

'That's the thing. It's not that I don't love David, but my feelings for Evan were . . . different. Intense. Even after knowing him for such a short period of time.'

267

'And do you still feel like that about him?'

Sarah stared up at the bridge. 'I don't know. I assumed when he left that that was it. And while of course I've thought about him, you kind of file the feelings away, don't you?'

'Do you?'

'Whereas David . . . It's different. I'm very fond of him. And . . .'

'Grateful?'

Sarah shot her a glance. 'In a way.'

'You can't marry someone out of gratitude.'

'It's not just that, Grace. And besides, all this love and marriage stuff . . .' She sighed. 'It's not about that any more. It's . . . well, like you said, it's an arrangement.'

Grace laughed. 'Only if it's an arranged marriage.'

'You don't think this isn't? David set his sights on me when he first saw me in New York. Everything he's done since then has been with the one aim of making me his. And that's flattering . . .'

'If not a bit scary.' Grace produced an apple from her bag. 'But tell me something,' she said, peeling the sticker off, balling it up, and flicking it expertly into a nearby bin. 'If it's an arrangement, what do you get out of it?'

Sarah thought for a moment. 'Security. I get to stay here. To give up work if I want to.'

'And become a kept woman? That's not really you, is it?'

'Who knows? Maybe I'll get to like it.'

Grace puffed air out of her cheeks. 'And once David's got you, what do you think he'll do?'

'Huh?'

'How do you think he'll change, once he's won the prize he's been after for so long?'

Sarah's brow wrinkled. 'What do you mean?'

'Men like David – it's all about the chase, isn't it, right up until they clinch the deal? Whereas someone like Evan? It sounds to me like it's all about the moment. And life is made up of millions of moments.'

'I don't expect things to change. And so what if they do? No offence, but you know how hard it is to find someone.'

'Really?' Grace laughed, and nodded ironically towards the crowds milling around the South Bank. 'You managed to find two.'

Sarah smiled, despite herself. That, she knew, was her dilemma.

'If you really want my opinion, Evan's the problem,' continued Grace, as if reading her thoughts. 'You've got to get him out of your system. Once and for all.'

'What if I can't?'

'Then you can't marry David.'

'It's not as simple as that.'

'It is, Sarah. You've got to be sure.'

'And how do I do that, exactly?'

'See him. Talk to him *properly*. Find out exactly what he wants before either one of you storms off. Work out what he's offering. If, like you said, it wasn't a fair contest before, then make sure it is one now.'

'What's the alternative?'

'Well, just ask yourself one question. Can you live with David for the rest of your life?'

'I guess.'

'Could you live without Evan?'

Sarah looked up sharply, still finding it ridiculous that someone she'd spent so little time with could be worthy of such a question. 'I have done, haven't I?'

'Interesting.' Grace regarded her levelly. 'Okay, well, what are your doubts about David?'

Sarah let out a short laugh. 'You've met him, right?'

'Seriously, Sarah.'

'Well, he can be a bit, you know, controlling.'

'So you can't be yourself with him?'

'That's the thing,' said Sarah. 'I'm not sure who I am anymore.'

Grace took her hand. 'That doesn't sound that good to me.'

'Why not? What's wrong with having my decisions made for me – my life mapped out? Christ knows, I'm tired of all these twists and turns. My mum, my dad, coming here, Evan and David, getting pregnant, then losing it, and now Evan coming back . . .' She gazed at the river and blinked away a tear. 'Maybe David's the easy option. I can just relax. Let someone else dictate to me for a while.'

'And how is that you, exactly?'

'Maybe *this* isn't me,' said Sarah, desperately. 'I mean, look at me. My father dies, and how do I deal with it? By leaving everything I've ever known and coming over here to a country that keeps reminding me I don't belong every time I open my mouth. Then, right when I start seeing a good, decent, kind man, I meet someone else who knocks my socks off, but before things can even start to get serious I virtually frogmarch him onto a plane back to where I've just come from. Then the first one has the decency to propose to me and I accept, despite maybe having fallen in love at first sight with the other one, not to mention the fact that I'm quite possibly pregnant with his child. Now the other one's come back, and it's making me question what I'm doing getting married to the person who's stood by me through all of this. How can you possibly say that's a good life?' She looked at Grace, her eyes brimming with tears. 'I always thought if I made a decision, I'd stick to it. Coming here. Focusing on my career. Marrying David. Now I'm questioning all three. What's happening to me?'

Grace put an arm around her and held her until her shoulders stopped heaving. 'Listen,' she said, eventually. 'What are you doing this evening?'

'Sitting at home and slitting my wrists, probably.'

'Don't even joke about that kind of thing.'

'Sorry.' She sniffed, then forced a smile. 'Well, nothing, now you ask. David's got some work thing, and . . .'

'Excellent. Because you need a night out.'

'Grace, thanks, but I'm hardly in the mood.'

'No buts. You and me. Out on the town. I might even get you drunk. And we'll sort this out once and for all.'

'How on earth are we going to . . .?'

Sarah stopped mid-sentence. Grace had stuffed the apple into her mouth.

'Just hurry up and eat that,' she said, pointing to the clock on the side of the cathedral's tower. 'The clock is ticking.'

Sarah didn't say anything, but just chewed as instructed. That, she knew, was part of her problem.

41

Is that what you're wearing?'

Sarah scrutinised her reflection in the hallway mirror. It was the third time she'd changed, and the black knee-length dress she was wearing was maybe a little conservative for a night out, but in her defence, Grace hadn't told her where they were going.

'What's wrong with it?'

'Nothing,' said Grace, handing Sarah her coat. 'I just wanted to check you were good to go.'

'Good to go where, exactly?'

'Out on our big night out.'

'I guess.' Sarah felt a little light-headed. It was nearly eight-thirty, and they'd already worked their way through a bottle of wine while getting ready, so staying at home and getting drunk seemed as good an option as any. But staying at home and getting drunk was what David liked to do, and she had a lifetime of that to look forward to. 'So, what's the plan?' she said, as Grace steered her out through their front door and into the lift.

'Plan?' Grace pressed the 'down' button. 'We go and get a couple of cocktails down us. Maybe even find a couple of good-looking men to buy us those couple of cocktails . . .'

'Grace, I'm not really in the mood for socialising.'

'Well, they can buy me a couple of cocktails, and you can sit in the corner like an old maid.'

Sarah sighed. 'Okay. Any clues as to a venue?'

'That information's on a need-to-know basis.'

'And I need to know, Grace.'

'Well . . .' Grace glanced at her watch. 'I thought we'd go to a club.'

'A little early, aren't we?'

'Not for where I have in mind.'

They made their way outside, where Grace flagged down a taxi, then leant in through the window and whispered something to the driver. 'Get in,' she ordered, holding the door wide open, and Sarah did as she was told. The traffic was light, and after a few minutes, the cab deposited them at the top end of Tanner Street. Grace paid the driver, then led Sarah towards the railway arches, or more specifically, Sarah suddenly realised, The G-Spot.

When she caught sight of the familiar building, she stopped abruptly. 'I hope we're not going where I *think* we're going.'

'Depends where you think we're going,' said Grace, obliquely.

'Grace!'

'Relax.'

Sarah was hanging back like a child off to visit the dentist, so Grace grabbed her arm and hauled her along the pavement, but when they reached the entrance, she dug her heels in.

'Grace, I can't. Evan . . .'

'What makes you think he's going to be here this evening?'

'Why are you bringing me here if he isn't?'

Grace made a face. 'Okay. There's a chance he might be playing. But think of it as kill or cure. You need to see him here, where it all started, to realise whether you're doing the right thing, or . . .' She paused. 'The wrong thing.'

'But . . .'

'No buts, Sarah. You owe it to yourself, remember. And maybe . . .'

'What?'

'Maybe you owe it to someone else as well.'

Sarah stared up at the flickering neon sign above the entrance, wondering whether Grace meant Evan or David, and by the time she looked back down again, Grace had disappeared into the club. For a second, she considered turning round and finding a taxi to take her back home, but the annoying thing was, Grace was probably right. She took one last look up and down the street, and with a resigned shake of her head, followed her friend though the door.

The G-Spot was packed, and she peered anxiously round the club's gloomy interior, feeling strangely nostalgic despite herself. Evan could be here already, she realised, chugging back a beer before getting up on stage, and the thought sent a prickle of anticipation through her. She'd loved watching him that evening – he had a stage presence, him and that that golden saxophone, and the way he cradled it softly, effortlessly teasing almost impossible notes out of it, couldn't fail to mesmerise you. At least, it had mesmerised her.

Miraculously, Grace seemed to have commandeered a couple of stools over by the bar, so Sarah pushed her way through the crowd to join her.

'Here.'

'Beer?' Sarah regarded the bottle of Budweiser quizzically, and Grace grinned.

'America's best. You said you were feeling homesick that night, so this should help.'

'Thanks for nothing,' said Sarah. Despite the amount she'd already had to drink this evening, she felt quite sober now, which was probably just as well – the last thing she wanted was for her emotions to get the better of her, and some alcohol-fuelled mistake might well be something she'd regret in the morning.

But Grace was right – this *was* something she needed to do, if only to realise that their past encounter had been something special, but the past was where it needed to remain. She was in a different place now, surely, somewhere she wouldn't – or indeed couldn't – give in to her baser emotions. After all, there'd been no-one in the year since Evan had left who'd managed to turn her head, so this would indeed be a test. Although, she realised shamefully, one she'd taken a year ago and failed.

Her throat felt suddenly dry, so she drained half of her beer in one go. Was she really over Evan? She'd find out this evening. And as the lights suddenly went down, she realised she didn't have long to wait.

42

Evan pulled his sax out of its case, slotted the mouthpiece into place, then softly blew a few notes. Despite his reservations, it felt good to be backstage again, and while the venue wasn't quite as grand as he'd been used to over the past twelve months, there was something appealing about the intimacy of these small places and the chance to connect with the audience that allowed. Though it was connecting with the audience here that had got him into trouble in the first place.

He listened to the band warming up on stage, ready to make his entrance. He would have preferred to be out there with them, but Mel had wanted to make some sort of announcement and, as he'd reminded Evan when he'd protested, it was his club. From the buzz he could hear, the G-Spot was pretty full, and he took a few deep breaths to calm the nerves he could already feel jangling, the clear air taking him by surprise. It seemed strange without the smell of cigarettes – the ambient smoke had always been part of the atmosphere, the jazz experience, a constant presence on the classic jazz posters he'd had on his bedroom wall growing up, or the thousand-and-one album covers that featured black and white stills of the greats, grey smoke trails rising up around them as they played. It had somehow added an extra dimension to the music, but nowadays there were times he felt he could have been playing at a primary school. Then he remembered it had probably been the smoke that had given Sarah's father cancer, and his wistfulness evaporated.

Sarah. He hadn't heard from her since he'd stormed off, and he supposed he shouldn't be surprised, though it was possible she was still trying to digest his announcement – God only knew he was having enough trouble with hers. Even now, he couldn't stop thinking about her, couldn't ignore the constant reminders that seemed to appear wherever he looked – a woman in Sainsbury's earlier in a 'Superdry' T-shirt, someone else in the fruit and veg section discussing a 'big apple'. He'd even found himself staring at a mother pushing a pram earlier, and had suddenly felt he had something in his eye.

The lights went down, and as if on cue, Mel stuck his head through the gap in the curtain and winked at him. 'Ready?'

'I guess so,' said Evan, then he frowned at his sax. 'If I could only remember which bit to blow.'

Mel laughed. 'You sound like my ex-wife,' he said, before disappearing back through to the audience side. 'Ladies and gentlemen,' Evan heard him say. 'We have a very special guest this evening on tenor sax, just arrived back in London, fresh from supporting Sting and The Police on their world tour – although to hear him go on about it, you'd think it was the other way round. Mister Evan McCarthy.'

Evan blushed at the applause as he pushed his way through the curtain and waved sheepishly at the audience, suddenly remembering why he preferred to be in the backing band. Still, at least Mel hadn't mentioned Jazzed, he reminded himself, then he looked across at the drummer, nodded, and the band launched into *Take Five.*

He began playing, falling quickly into the easy rhythm set by the drummer, the notes from his sax almost flirting with the sound from the accompanying double bass, the music flowing through his fingertips, washing away the jet lag of the past few days. *This* was what he loved more than anything – though perhaps not more than Sarah: The bum note he played when he saw her, perched on a stool by the bar, seemed to go unnoticed by everyone but Mel, who raised one eyebrow from his position at the side of the stage, and for a second Evan didn't know what to do. He could hardly stop playing mid-set and go and talk to her, but what if she left before he'd finished?

As his eyes became accustomed to the lights, he made out Grace sitting next to her, a strange, almost smug expression on her face. Was it possible that she was smiling at him? He couldn't be certain – but surely their presence at the club after his earlier request was no coincidence?

He thought about trying to catch Sarah's eye, but the effort required when blowing on a saxophone wasn't always conducive to making appropriate facial expressions, so with little alternative, he played on. Unable to look at Sarah, he threw himself into the music, and – as the band segued into *So What*, followed by *After The Rain* – Evan found himself praying that he was playing so well it'd be impossible for her to leave. And while he'd planned to play only a dozen songs, by the time they'd reached their last number, *My One And Only Love* – which Evan realised couldn't have been more appropriate – he'd never been more grateful to be finishing a set.

As the band took a bow, an idea occurred to him, so he signalled 'one more' to the other guys on stage, then leant down and spoke into the microphone.

'Thank you,' he breathed. 'I'd just like to play one last number. For someone special who's here tonight.'

'I didn't know you cared!' shouted Mel, and as the audience laughed, Evan gave him a look. He took a deep breath, put his sax to his lips, then blew the familiar six notes – ba-da-bah-ba-da-BAH! – and as the rest of the band joined in, he fixed his eyes on Sarah.

It had been a long time since he'd played *I Just Want To Make Love To You* – almost a year, in fact – and through the darkness, it was hard to tell what she was thinking, but given the way her hands seemed to be gripping the edges of her seat, Evan suspected she knew he was playing for her. And play he did – hitting the high notes with a purity and accuracy that made his lungs hurt, almost rattling the club's windows with the low ones, his fingers a blur over the keys. Then, on his signal, the rest of the band stopped playing, and Evan finished with a solo, playing like he'd never played before, as if at the most important audition in his life.

He shut his eyes as he coaxed seemingly impossible sounds from his sax, sweating with the effort, toying with the melody, and then, as he reached the final few bars, bringing the volume right down, silencing the audience into hushed admiration. And then, when he finally pulled his sax from his lips and opened his eyes again, the crowd began clapping, slowly at first, their applause rising into a crescendo that seemed like it would never stop.

The lights went up and the band took their final bow, all except for an exhausted Evan. His eyes searched the area in front of the bar where Sarah had been sitting, but with the crowd on their feet it was impossible to see her, and for a moment he feared the jet lag and excesses of caffeine he'd ingested over the past few days had made him hallucinate.

As the applause finally died down, he grabbed his case from behind the curtain and quickly slotted his sax back inside, then jumped down from the stage and pushed his way through the crowd, nodding politely at the people who tried to stop him or clap him on the back, but when he reached the bar, the stool Sarah had been perched on was empty. Confused, he stared at it, reaching out a hand as if to check she hadn't simply made herself invisible. Then he felt someone standing behind him, sensed it was her, and wheeled around.

'Hi,' she said, softly, and somehow Evan knew everything had changed.

'What are you doing here?'

'It's a free country,' said Sarah defiantly. 'Besides, I didn't know you'd be.'

He smiled at her, not wanting to get his hopes up, unsure whether she'd just needed to hear some jazz, or was simply doing what he'd been attempting for the past few days – trying to replicate how things were *before*. 'That's not what I meant. I thought you'd be, you know, *busy*.'

'I am busy. Having a night out with Grace.'

'Grace?' He peered over Sarah's shoulder. 'Where is she?'

'She had to go.' Sarah smiled wryly. 'Apparently.'

'Oh. Right.' Evan nodded towards the bar, where Mel was doing a bad job of trying not to eavesdrop. 'Can I buy you a drink?'

'I didn't come here to drink, Evan.'

'Well, what did you come here for?'

Sarah folded her arms. 'I told you. Grace . . .'

'No, Sarah. What did you come *here* for?'

'Evan . . .' She stared at him for a moment, then reached out a hand and touched the side of his face. 'The way you played tonight . . . It was . . . Christ, I think every woman in the audience needed a cigarette after your solo.'

'And what about you?'

'Me?' She brushed a strand of hair behind her ear. 'I've given up.'

And then Evan leaned slowly in towards her, as if testing how close he could get without pulling away, though pulling away was never on his mind. The moment his lips touched hers, Sarah responded to his kiss with a combination of intensity and familiarity that to him seemed just so, well, *appropriate* – though maybe not for as public a venue.

Eventually, reluctantly, he broke away, his eyes searching her face for some sign that he'd overstepped the mark, but Sarah's expression seemed to suggest it was just the beginning. He leaned back in towards her, but she stopped him, placing her fingers on his lips.

'Maybe we should get a room?' she suggested, a little out of breath, and while he'd always found that particular Americanism a little crass, right now it was music to his ears.

'Are you sure?' he said, almost afraid of what her answer might be.

'That's what I'm trying to decide. Which is why we should.'

'In that case, I know just the place.'

He nodded goodbye to Mel, then took Sarah by the hand and led her outside to where he'd left the Mercedes, his heart swelling with pride as she ran a hand affectionately along the car's front wing.

'You know that's the passenger side?' he said, unlocking the door for her, and Sarah nodded as she climbed in.

'Yeah. I figured I'd let you drive tonight.'

Evan grinned as he jumped into the driver's seat, and although the kiss Sarah leant across to give him as he started the car told him he needn't be worried, he still put his foot down. They drove in silence, Evan concentrating on not hitting anything as he raced the car through Bermondsey's streets. As he screeched to a stop in front of his building, Sarah relaxed her grip on the dashboard.

'And you complained about *my* driving.'

'Yes, well.'

'Are we here?'

'Uh-huh.'

'Thank Christ.'

They got out of the car, then made their way up the steps from the street, Evan holding his front door open almost formally as he ushered her through. Once inside his flat, he flicked the light on, and Sarah glanced around the room, taking in the signed black and white jazz posters, the expensive-looking turntable on the sideboard, the huge speakers in the corners of the living room, the coffee cup and empty beer bottle sitting on the arm of the sofa.

'I like what you've done with the place.'

'Yes, well, it's hardly Grand Designs,' Evan began, though he didn't get a chance to continue, as Sarah's lips found his again.

They kissed some more, then he lifted her up and carried her to his bedroom, setting her down only so he could pull her dress off over her head. He laid her down on the bed as he began to undress, but to his surprise, she pulled him down next to her. 'Let me,' she said, slowly removing his underwear, then wriggling out of hers.

He gazed up at her as she lowered herself on top of him, made speechless by her beauty, then matched her rhythm as she moved slowly up and down, her hands on his shoulders, her eyes never leaving his. Then, just for a second, and just when Evan was in danger of reaching the point of no return, Sarah stopped.

'I don't know what I'm doing,' she said.

Evan reached up and took her face in his hands, then kissed her firmly. 'I wouldn't say that,' he replied.

She relaxed on top of him, returning his kiss with an intensity which surprised him, so he started moving underneath her, as slowly as both of them could bear, hoping it would never end, Sarah's orgasm quickly bringing him to a wrenching climax he feared might make him pass out. But instead of repeating their post-coital experience of a year ago, when they'd lain there in a tangle of limbs until their breathing returned to normal, Sarah immediately climbed off him, gathered up her clothes, and rushed out of the bedroom.

He lay there for a moment, listening to the post-slam reverberation of the bathroom door, suspecting this wasn't a good sign, and neither was the gentle sobbing he could hear. With a sigh, he hauled himself wearily out of bed, pulled on his boxer shorts, padded over to the bathroom, and knocked softly on the door.

'Sarah?'

Evan knocked again, but when there was no reply, went and sat back down on the bed to wait, his head a whirlwind of emotions. He'd thought that if he ever got this far, sleeping with Sarah would have been something to celebrate, but right now, celebrating was the last thing he felt like doing. The sex had been good – *great* – just like it had been their first time. They fitted together, him and Sarah, knew exactly how to push each other's buttons, and even after a year apart, it had felt, well, *natural*. Just like riding a bike, he thought. Not that he'd have ever dared repeat that phrase.

After a minute, though to Evan it felt like a lifetime, Sarah emerged from the bathroom, her make-up intact, a slight redness around the eyes the only sign of her distress. But when he stood up and reached for her, she couldn't look him in the eye.

'Don't say anything,' she commanded, pushing her way past him on her way to the door.

'But . . .'

'Just *don't!*'

Evan watched her go, the sinking feeling in his stomach telling him they'd been here before, then he flopped back down onto his bed and gazed up at the ceiling, unsure what to make of what had just happened. She'd initiated the evening's events, after all, even suggesting – no, *insisting* – they go back to his. In the car, he'd wanted to ask her again whether she was sure, though he hadn't dared, and then, when they'd breathlessly reached his flat, words had seemed inappropriate. They'd both known what they wanted. What to do. And instinct had taken over.

He thought back to the last time they'd slept together, when things had been so different. Sarah wasn't engaged. He hadn't known about David. This whole baby thing hadn't existed – though maybe that night had even been *when* she got pregnant. While it had been fantastic, there had been none of this kind of emotional significance – and this *had* been emotionally significant. Evan almost felt like crying himself.

How different it might have been had they suspected how things were going to change – after all, how could you sleep with someone if you knew you were never going to see them again? For Evan, the emotional connection was a major part of making love – he had to be able to let himself go, not hold himself back. That was key to his enjoyment, and in the past, he'd only really been able to let himself go with anyone when he thought they might have a future together. The concept of the 'farewell fuck'? He'd never understood that.

And then, to his horror, it hit him.

Maybe that was what this had been.

43

Sarah tried hard to maintain her composure as she walked into work, sure the events of the previous evening were etched on her face for all to see. Her tears had started again the moment she'd left Evan's flat, and she'd cried in the taxi all the way home, so much so that the driver hadn't even had a chance to begin the usual diatribe about immigration or who he'd had in the back of his cab recently, and instead had silently passed her a box of tissues through the connecting window.

She swallowed hard, and told herself this was ridiculous, but then again, her behaviour last night had been ridiculous too. She'd suspected Evan might be there as soon as they'd arrived at The G-Spot, and yet she hadn't vetoed Grace's suggestion that they go inside. Perhaps she'd just wanted to take a stroll down memory lane, but now she'd ended up going a lot further down that particular road than perhaps was advisable.

The moment she'd kissed him, she'd known they'd end up sleeping together. No – she'd suspected that before she kissed him, perhaps even *if* she kissed him, and she was the one who'd initiated the kiss, so what did that tell her? Though perhaps she *could* blame that on him – the way he'd played, the music toying with her emotions, getting under her skin, making her heart pound so loudly she'd been sure Grace had been able to hear it. And the fact he'd played *that* song – Sarah was sure she hadn't been the only woman in the club thinking about ripping his clothes off after a performance like that.

And speaking of performances, the sex had been fantastic. Incredible. Mind-blowing, even. For the past year, she'd justified her previous, albeit brief, two-timing of David by dismissing what she'd been up to with Evan as simply fucking, but now she'd reminded herself that actually it had been simply fucking amazing.

She swiped her way in past reception, reminding herself that at least halfway through she'd suddenly had a pang of conscience, as if keeping going would be going too far, but given everything else they'd done before halfway, who had she been trying to kid? And while she felt guilty about getting up and leaving like that, she'd got up and left like that because she'd felt guilty – surely Evan would understand that?

She'd been desperate to talk things over when she'd got home, but by the time the taxi had dropped her off, Grace had been in bed, and she hadn't had the heart to wake her. Then Grace had already left for work by the time Sarah had dragged herself out of bed this morning, and while she'd thought about calling her, she hadn't known what to say. She still hadn't made sense of it herself, apart from realising one thing: by fucking Evan, she might have fucked everything up.

She rode the elevator up to her floor, hurried along the corridor, then stopped abruptly in her office doorway, trying not to panic at the thought she might not have switched her PC off when she'd left yesterday. If Evan had emailed, his message might be up there on her computer screen, and given that David was sitting at her desk, idly flicking through a copy of the *Financial Times*, it would be in plain view. Dreading the prospect of an early-morning interrogation, she took a deep breath, then thankfully recalled how Evan had told her he didn't really 'do' email, unlike David, whom she'd had to ban from taking his Blackberry to bed. Hoping nothing about her body language would give her away, she fixed a smile on her face and walked over to where he was sitting.

'Morning,' she said, as brightly as she could muster.

'Morning, sweetheart.' David looked up from his paper and – once he'd checked no-one was watching – angled his face so Sarah could plant a kiss on his cheek. 'What are you doing here?'

David smiled. 'I work here. Remember?'

'No, silly.' Sarah ruffled the hair on the top of his head. 'I mean *here*. In with us common people.'

David tapped his finger on his lips. 'Keep your voice down,' he said, jovially. While that might have been how he referred to them in private, he wouldn't want Sarah to let it slip, even though she was, of course, one of them – until Saturday, at least. 'I thought I'd see if you were free for lunch.'

'Lunch?' Sarah tried – and failed – to keep the surprise out of her voice. She and David never had lunch together during the week, and in fact, apart from the donuts she'd given him the other day, she wasn't sure he ever actually ate lunch. Sure, she'd occasionally see him disappear with one of the other partners on a Friday, but food wasn't usually on the agenda, and if they made it back to the office, there'd be no more work for the day, so to actually suggest going and eating something with her, and on a *Wednesday* . . . At once, she was suspicious, but Sarah knew she couldn't let it show.

'Sure. That'd be nice.'

'Sushi do you?'

'Why not?'

'Great.' He hauled himself out of the chair and made for the door. 'I'll come by at one. Sharp.'

Sarah bristled a little at the word 'sharp', but forced a smile. 'Lovely,' she said.

'Oh, I forgot,' said David, stopping in the doorway. 'Did you have a good time last night?'

Sarah froze. 'Last night?'

'Yes. Didn't you go out?'

'With Grace,' said Sarah, quickly.

'I know. She told me.'

'When?' asked Sarah, nervously.

'I phoned when you were in the shower, or putting your face on, or whatever it is you girls do in the four or five hours it takes you to leave the house. Grace answered your mobile. Didn't she say?'

'No. No, she didn't.'

'Ah.' He raised both eyebrows. 'So, did you? Have a good time?'

She stared at him, then decided to tell the truth. 'Yes.'

'Good.' He smiled again. 'See you at one.'

'Sharp,' said Sarah, saluting to his back as he walked out into the corridor.

She hurried over and shut her door behind him, then went back to her desk, picked up David's discarded paper, and dropped it in her waste-bin. In truth, she could have done without what was sure to be an awkward lunch after last night, but she could hardly have said no. And while it occurred to her to email him later to say she was busy, work wasn't a valid excuse if your boss was the one asking you.

Her phone buzzed in her bag – she'd left the ringer set to 'vibrate' after Evan had kept calling her last night – and when she pulled it out and saw his number flashing on the display, she was glad she hadn't changed it back to 'ring'. He'd called five times this morning too, and it was easier to ignore this way.

For a moment she wondered whether she should answer it, just to check he was okay. But he'd want to talk about what had happened, and while Sarah knew they'd have to – and soon – for now, she put the phone down on her desk and stared at it until the 'voicemail' icon appeared on the screen. Though she didn't bother listening to the message. She could probably guess what it said.

She wondered what on earth she'd been thinking, though the truth was, she hadn't. She'd kind of been on autopilot, enjoying Evan's familiar touch, the feel of him – that was, until the tears had started – and they'd been the biggest surprise of this whole episode. Sarah wasn't a crier, never had been, even at her father's funeral, where she'd maintained her composure while those around her, grown men in some cases, had bawled their eyes out, and yet since Evan had appeared in her life, she'd more than made up for it. Scarcely seconds after the fireworks had finished going off inside her, she'd looked down to see him gazing up at her, the expression on his face something she'd never seen before. The look of love, she'd realised – she'd heard the song, but never actually seen it for real – though there had been something else there too: a sadness, maybe. Sadness that perhaps he was too late. Sadness at missing a year of this. And perhaps sadness because he'd suspected this might be goodbye. And that had been enough to set Sarah off.

She'd never wanted to hurt him, and at that precise moment, she'd seen just how much she had. She could tell he'd been surprised by the intensity of their love-making – she'd surprised herself. Maybe it had been because she'd realised it was what she'd been missing, though Sarah couldn't allow herself to believe that *he* was what she'd been missing. When she'd seen him up on stage, the memories – the *feelings* – had come flooding back, and she'd known that she'd go home with him if he asked her, just like she'd known she would a year ago, even though this time, like then, she'd had to ask *him*. And the funny thing was, this time, just like then, she'd hardly given David a second thought.

David. She felt a second surge of panic, and grabbed the edge of her desk for support. What if Evan had already told him? Perhaps that's what today's lunch was all about. It would be just like David not to fly off the handle when he found out about the two of them, but to schedule a 'meeting' to discuss the matter. But what excuse could she give, what reason as to why what had happened happened? Nothing that David would buy, surely, and certainly nothing that he might forgive.

She could brazen it out, of course, deny anything had happened, but David would be able to tell she was lying, and anyway, after everything he'd done for her, it was time to stop lying to David. She picked up her phone, then headed down the hallway and into the toilet, locking the door behind her, and as she stared at her reflection in the mirror, wondering how it had come to this, she realised something. She had only herself to blame.

As if on cue, her mobile buzzed again, and Sarah didn't need to look at the screen to know who was calling.

44

Evan stuffed his mobile angrily back into his pocket, then pulled it out again and hit 'redial'. Sarah hadn't answered her phone all morning, and short of marching into her office and confronting her, he didn't know how else to get in touch.

He crossed Bermondsey Street, then headed under the viaduct on his way to the G-Spot, scowling at a Lycra-clad cycle messenger barrelling down in the wrong direction. So far, he wasn't enjoying being in love, though he suspected his problem was that it was unrequited – surely no-one would want to feel like this all the time in a normal relationship?

At the sound of her voicemail, he cursed under his breath and ended the call. He'd already left a message that had simply said 'call me' – he'd been worried about rambling on like a fool – and maybe she would call, in time, but meanwhile, the waiting was something he hated. He was used to auditions, and their familiar 'we'll let you know', but nothing like this, where the outcome was so important. Besides, Sarah hadn't said she'd let him know – though whether she'd been trying to let him know something the previous evening, he still wasn't sure.

He found it hard to believe that last night had been goodbye, though maybe that *had* been her intention, and therefore why she'd left in tears. And while Evan suspected the reason she wasn't answering her phone this morning was because she was confused – which he had to see as a good thing – a part of him feared it was because she had nothing more to say to him.

He stared at his phone again, just in case he'd missed her call in the twenty or so seconds since he'd last checked it, and wondered if she was punishing him – but for what? She'd picked *him* up last night, just like she had a year ago, and he'd even – half-heartedly, admittedly – tried to stop her. He could only hope that what happened between them might kick-start some feeling in her she thought she'd buried, or some realisation that *he* was the one she wanted to be with, not David. Though as confident as he was about his prowess in bed – or rather, how good he and Sarah were together – he had to question how it fitted into her overall scheme of things, and while Evan knew he could never marry someone for whom making love seemed to be a chore you performed before going to sleep, like brushing your teeth, or checking the front door was locked, he had to cling on to the hope that that was how David approached it. After all, he'd seen David having sex, and the girl at the club hadn't seemed to be enjoying it one bit . . .

He shook his head to get rid of the memory, replacing it with a vision of Sarah from the previous evening. Surely she couldn't ignore the passion, the spark, the way they just *worked*? With a last check of his phone, he walked up to the club's front door and knocked loudly, and after a few moments, Mel cracked the door open.

'Afternoon.'

'Is it?' Mel checked his watch to make sure, then opened the door just wide enough to allow Evan inside.

'Yup.'

'Phew,' he said, lighting a cigarette and taking a drag. 'For a moment, I thought I'd overslept.'

'You stayed here last night?'

'What can I say? The missus doesn't always appreciate me rolling in at five in the morning after a night of booze and fags.'

'Maybe she should stop smoking and drinking, then.'

Mel grinned at Evan's joke, rubbing the sleep out of his eyes as he made his way round behind the bar. 'So, did it feel good to be back up there last night? I mean on stage. And not, you know . . .'

'Thank you, Mel!'

He let out a low, rumbling laugh as he retrieved a couple of mugs from underneath the bar. 'It's just that I saw her sucking the face off you, and then you didn't hang around for an encore. Mind you, neither did she, by the looks of you today.' He grinned again as he switched on the coffee machine, then caught sight of Evan's miserable expression. 'Sorry. Want to tell me about it?'

Evan shrugged. 'It's pretty much like you said. And now she won't answer her phone.'

'Poor you. Though not the having sex part, obviously, lucky bastard.' Mel positioned the mugs underneath the machine's twin spouts, then pressed a button on the front, and the machine whirred into life. 'So, what do you think it means?'

Evan felt the familiar craving as he watched the brown liquid sputter into the mugs, consoling himself that in his profession, there were worse things to be addicted to. 'God knows. For a moment, I thought I had her.'

'Was that before or after you *actually* had her?'

'Mel, *please*.'

Mel waited until the machine finished buzzing, then handed him a mug. 'Just trying to inject some humour into the situation.'

'Well, don't.'

'Sorry.' He pulled himself stiffly up onto the adjacent stool. 'So what happened?'

'I don't know what happened. One minute she was there, and the next, she was running out of the door as if the fire alarm had gone off.'

'Why do you think that was?'

'Because she's confused. I know I am.'

'Course she is. I mean, it's hardly rational behaviour, is it? Sleeping with someone else a couple of days before your wedding.'

'No,' agreed Evan. 'Unless . . .'

'Unless?'

He swallowed hard. 'She was just saying goodbye.'

'Doubtful.' Mel blew on his coffee, then took a sip. 'That's one of the fundamental differences between men and women. We'll happily shag someone even if we know we're never going to see them again, but they just can't do that. Some hormonal bollocks, apparently.'

'Really? None of your exes ever done that to you?'

'Nowhere near as many as I'd have liked.' Mel laughed, and when Evan couldn't help but smile, clapped him on the back. 'No, the way I see it, what happened last night must have re-awakened some feelings deep inside her – stuff she thought was hidden – and she doesn't want to speak to you because she hasn't been able to figure them out yet.'

'She's had a year to figure them out, Mel.' Evan shook his head. 'Maybe I am wasting my time. I mean, last year, she slept with me, then virtually told me where to go. And she's pretty much doing the same thing again.'

'Ah,' said Mel, shiftily.

'"Ah" what?'

He sucked on his cigarette, then flicked the ash into a nearby wine glass. 'There's something I haven't told you. About what happened a year ago.'

'I know you told her about the tour, Mel, before I had a chance to. It wasn't your fault.'

'Right. Well, I, er, might have also said something about how maybe she should . . .' He cleared his throat. 'Encourage you to go.'

'What?'

Mel held both hands up. 'I know, I know. But in my defence, she'd told me that you and her were just a bit of fun.'

'She said that?' Evan stared at him incredulously. 'Is that supposed to make me feel better?'

'Well, no, obviously. Except the more I think about it, the more I realise something.'

'Which is?'

'She was lying.'

'How can you be sure of that?'

Mel grinned. 'When you look like me, women lie to you all the time. *It's not you, it's me. I'm married. I can't sleep with you, it's my time of the month.* That kind of thing. Eventually, you learn to spot the signs. And more importantly, she only told me that *after* I'd told her about the tour.'

'And how does that help me, exactly?'

'I said you needed to go for the good of your career. The fact that she was prepared to give you a push . . .' He clinked his coffee cup against Evan's. 'She must have cared for you.'

'So why suddenly announce that she had a boyfriend?'

'What better way to get you to think there was no future for the two of you?'

'I don't know, Mel. Surely last night proves how little she thinks of me?'

Mel took a mouthful of coffee. 'Quite the opposite. If you were planning to marry someone in a few days' time, you'd hardly go out looking for some meaningless shag with someone else, would you?'

'David did. A lap-dancer. On his stag night.'

'Really?' Mel raised both eyebrows. 'Excellent!'

'Why is that excellent?'

'Well, because that wasn't meaningless either. It proves how little he thinks of Sarah. And more importantly, it means you've won. Just tell her that, and . . .'

'. . . and she'll think they're quits, after last night.'

'Ah.' Mel's face fell, then he brightened up again. 'Or, more likely, she'll take both of those events as a sign that neither of them should be marrying the other one. Look at the facts.' He put his coffee down, jammed his cigarette into the corner of his mouth, and started to count off on his fingers. 'One: She had enough doubts about marrying what's-his-face to come and seek you out, what, three days before her wedding, and back in the place the two of you first met. No-one puts themselves in that kind of position unless they want to give in to temptation. Two: *She* kissed *you*. And three: She went to bed with you. At any point, she could have stopped and gone home, but she didn't.'

'Until afterwards.'

'Yeah, but that's guilt kicking in, isn't it? She's hardly going to lie there and make sweet nothing small talk with you, is she? Not when she realises she's just done the worst thing possible to her ex-husband-to-be and is going to have to call her wedding off.' He nodded, evidently happy with his summing-up. 'Can you really see her going through with it now?'

Evan sipped his coffee glumly. 'I don't know. Now I've met David, I can't see why she'd have got engaged to him in the first place, but she went and did that.'

'And did you ask her why?'

'Well, er, no. Not exactly.'

Mel rolled his eyes. 'Christ, Evan. How can you expect to win if you don't know what you're up against?'

'I'm not expecting to *win*, Mel. I just want to hold my own.'

'That's the only thing you will be holding if you don't . . .'

'Mel, *please*. And it's not a competition. It's a choice.'

'From where I'm sitting, she seems to have made hers last night.'

'Well if she did, she changed her mind straight afterwards.' Evan put his mug down on the bar. 'Help me, Mel. I don't know what to do next.'

'Tell her about the lap-dancer. That might just be enough to make sure the wedding didn't go ahead. Or tell him that you slept with his fiancée. That definitely would.'

Evan shook his head. He knew he could try to sabotage the wedding by confessing all about last night to David, but would he believe him? After all, where was the proof? All Sarah had to do was deny it, and besides, he didn't want to try to 'win' back the woman he loved like that – not if he wanted Sarah to have any respect for him afterwards.

'That wouldn't be fair.'

'Fair?' Mel stared at him. 'You don't want to be fair. This is all about you convincing her you're her Mr. Right – and you won't score any points by being Mr. Righteous. It's not one of those occasions where you can look back and say *Oh well, I did my best*. You've got to do your worst too – and quickly. Otherwise it's going to eat you up until the day you die.'

Evan stared back at him. Even though he suspected Mel was right, and while the prospect of feeling this bad for the rest of his life almost made him want to pick up the phone and tell David straight away, he knew it would be wrong. As to what he'd do if she still chose David . . . well, he hadn't allowed himself to think that far ahead. He'd be devastated, of course, but life would go on. Though as for playing any more jazz, right now the blues were more his style.

He sighed, then shook his head slowly. 'I can't, Mel.'

'Why the hell not?'

'Because I want her to choose me for who I am. Not because of something bad that David's done.'

'No?'

'No!'

Mel didn't say anything, but just rolled up his sleeve and tapped his watch exaggeratedly.

45

arah picked at her bowl of edamame beans as she watched David help himself to plate after plate from the conveyor belt rotating slowly in front of them, amazed at his capacity for food, which seemed to be exceeded only by his capacity for drink. In recent months, he'd developed a liking for cigars, too, and she often wondered just when he'd have his first heart attack. Maybe on Saturday, she thought, if Evan turned up unannounced. Still, at least Evan wouldn't be surprising them *here*, she thought, given his aversion to the raw fish David was currently consuming at a rate that would make Greenpeace worry for the ocean's tuna stocks.

'So,' he said, in between mouthfuls and the regular glances at his Blackberry that Sarah was trying not to let annoy her. 'Are we all ready?'

She breathed a silent sigh of relief. David's lunch invitation seemed to be to discuss the wedding, and assuming he was talking about the arrangements, she nodded. The ceremony was going to be an intimate one: just the two of them plus a handful of close family and friends at Chelsea registry office, followed by dinner at Bluebird afterwards for the fifty or so guests. 'I guess,' she said – aside from turning up, she didn't have that much to do. 'I've got my final dress fitting later, and . . .'

'Hence the reason that's all you're eating?' David indicated the tiny pile of dishes in front of her.

'Something like that.' In truth, she'd lost enough weight these past few days to make her worry that her dress might even have to be taken in a little, though she suspected it was more to do with the stress of seeing Evan again than any change in her dietary regime. 'And you're still not telling me where we're going on honeymoon?'

'No.'

David was whisking her off somewhere – a surprise, apparently – but just for a week. End of quarter was approaching, and she knew she'd been lucky to get him to agree to even a few days' holiday when the bank's financial results were due to be announced.

'Well, how will I know what to pack?'

'You'll just have to be prepared for all eventualities.'

'That's hardly practical.'

'I'm sure you'll manage, sweetheart. Anyway . . .' David scooped up another piece of California roll and popped it into his mouth, chewing noisily while he spoke, a habit of his Sarah had always found surprising, given his upbringing. 'You won't need many clothes.'

She did a double-take, then realised he probably meant they were going somewhere hot, rather than the fact that they'd hardly be leaving their hotel room. Even so, she found herself blushing – the thought of sex reminded her of the previous evening's events. 'And you're sure you still want to do it?' she found herself saying.

'Do what?'

'Marry me. After, you know, what happened.'

David's hand hovered over his plate. 'Not this whole "losing the baby" thing again?'

Sarah nodded, trying to ignore the sudden burning in her throat. Even though David had seen how upset she'd been when she'd miscarried, he was bound to read something deeper into any tears so close to the wedding. 'It's just that I can't help feeling you kind of proposed under false pretences.' She forced a smile. 'So if you wanted to, you know, back out of it, it'd be okay.'

David put down his chopsticks, then reached over and took her hand. 'What's brought this on? You're not feeling guilty, are you?'

'What?'

'I've told you a thousand times. It wasn't your fault.'

She relaxed slightly, glad he was still referring to the baby. 'Yes, but be honest. Would you really have proposed otherwise? If I hadn't been pregnant?'

'Like I said, of course!' said David, indignantly. 'How else was I going to fight off the competition?'

Sarah couldn't meet his eyes, although surely he'd meant everyone else and not specifically Evan – after all, if he had known about the two of them, even he wouldn't have referred to it that casually. She pushed her plate away and took a sip of water.

'Okay, then. Why?'

'Why what?'

'Why do you want to marry me?'

David frowned at her, having evidently forgotten their recent conversation. 'Pardon?'

'You didn't really answer me the other day.'

He resumed chewing thoughtfully. 'Why wouldn't I? Look at you.'

Sarah knew he'd meant it as a compliment, but couldn't help feeling objectified at the same time. 'So it's just for my looks? So I can be the ornamental wife on your arm?'

'Well, no.' David shifted uneasily in his seat, aware he was getting into argument territory, but clueless as to why. 'Of course not.'

'What else, then?'

He stared back at her. 'You're serious?'

'Yes, David.'

'Well . . .' He reached for his bottle of Asahi, then, annoyed to see it was empty, clicked his fingers impatiently at the waitress for another. 'There's the *love* thing, obviously.'

'I should hope so,' said Sarah, tersely. 'What else?'

'It's not that easy to put into words.'

'Try.'

'You're being silly.'

'No I'm not. Come on, convince me you didn't just get down on one knee out of some misplaced sense of duty.'

'Bloody cheek! Of course I didn't. And in any case, what would have been misplaced about it?'

Fuck, thought Sarah. *Why did I say that?* David was getting angry now – no, she corrected herself – not angry. Haughty. Almost as if she should be grateful he'd asked her to marry him – and not just under the circumstances. 'I'm sorry, David. I . . .'

'In fact, yes, you're right. I did think I was doing the decent thing, now you come to mention it, but excuse me if it upset your precious American sensibilities. And speaking of which, if you'd have been a bit more sensible back then, maybe you wouldn't be feeling like this.'

'Fuck you, David!'

'No, Sarah,' he said, softly but firmly. He climbed down from his chair, pulled his wallet from his jacket pocket, and threw a handful of notes down onto the counter. 'Fuck you!'

'David . . .'

He opened his mouth as if to say something, then evidently changed his mind, and instead, marched briskly out of the restaurant. Sarah watched him go, angry at his reaction, but more annoyed with herself for provoking such a stupid fight so close to the wedding. What had she been expecting – that he'd take what she said as some sort of get-out-of-jail-free card, call the whole thing off, and make both their lives a hell of a lot easier *just like that*?

For a moment she considered following him, knowing she'd have to apologise and wanting to get it over with, but experience told her David would need some time to calm down, like a washing machine that had finished spinning – you still had to wait a while before it was safe to open the door. And while she was sure she'd be able to excuse her behaviour as just pre-wedding stress, it didn't help that the fundamental cause of that stress was still very much in her thoughts.

She wondered again what Evan would have done under similar circumstances. Would he have gotten down on one knee as nobly as David had? It was hard to say. From the off, she'd known David wanted to settle down, have children, the whole nine yards – he was that type – but beyond Evan's desire to have fun, she didn't know what type he was. She couldn't possibly know how he'd have reacted, and anyway, like he'd reminded her the other day, she certainly hadn't given him the chance. She knew so little about him, and she'd felt so much for him, yet she wondered whether there was anything she didn't know about David. He'd been so precise, so *specific* from the day they'd first met that she felt almost able to write an instruction manual to pass on to future girlfriends if the two of them didn't work out. Whereas Evan? She already knew that working things out as they went along would have been fun. And at that precise moment, Sarah realised just how much she missed that.

She paid the bill and headed back to work, toying with the idea that maybe she could marry David – assuming he was still speaking to her after her strop at lunch – while continuing to see Evan. Perhaps they could just pick up where they'd left off. But Sarah knew – despite recent events – that she wasn't that kind of woman; the guilt she'd felt having slept with Evan back then had been pretty hard to get past, despite her conviction that it had been acceptable under her 'dating' definition, and now, given her indiscretion last night, she feared she'd gone and messed it all up again. Though maybe she *could* still go through with Saturday after what had just happened. She'd feel guilty for a while, sure, but she could live with herself. Though after the intensity of the previous night, she wasn't sure she could live with David.

She walked into her office and closed the door behind her, wondering how it had come to this, just days before she was due to get married. Could she really cancel the wedding at this late stage, and even if she did, what would happen at work? She couldn't remain in the same department as David if she did, and he certainly wasn't going to leave. Besides, this was the City; it was tough enough for a woman as it was, let alone one who might be considered to have a 'reputation'. And in any case, David had done nothing to deserve being made a laughing-stock in the office.

At least leaving would be quick. She'd seen it happen to enough of her colleagues in recent months. They'd probably pack her off the same day, escorting her from the premises with her possessions in a cardboard box . . . She swallowed hard, wondering whether she'd be leaving David in the same way, then sat heavily back down at her desk to spend a few minutes with Google trying to work out how that would affect her being here, in England, but she soon realised her situation was hopeless. Without work sponsorship, or being married to a Brit, her visa wouldn't permit her to stay – and was she prepared to give up everything she'd worked for just because a ghost from her past had suddenly reappeared?

She put her head in her hands, trying to fight the tears that were building up inside her, and eventually just gave in to them. And Sarah was still crying when a knock on her door made her jump.

'Everything alright in there?'

At the sound of Sally's voice, Sarah quickly considered her options. The last thing she wanted was for Sally to feed the fact she was upset back to David, and no doubt spread the information like wildfire around the building. But what was the alternative – hide in her office until she left? She sniffed loudly, then dabbed at her eyes with the back of her hand.

'Come on in.'

Sally cracked the door open and poked her head tentatively through the gap. 'Are you okay?'

'I'm fine, Sally. Thank you. Just feeling a little . . .'

'Emotional?'

Sarah caught sight of her red-eyed reflection in her computer screen. 'Emotional. That's it.'

'Do you want to talk about it? David kind of stormed back in after lunch, and now . . .'

Sarah shook her head, and tried to ignore the look of disappointment on Sally's face. 'No I'm okay. Really. Just a lot going on, what with Saturday, and all that. We had a stupid little fight. That's all.'

Sally edged a little further into the room, clearly not ready to be dismissed yet. 'I understand.'

Sarah almost laughed. She wasn't sure she understood herself. 'Thank you,' she said. 'And Sally?'

'Yes?'

'Can you keep this our little secret?'

Sally beamed at her, and Sarah knew she'd said the right thing. If there was one thing that Sally loved more than a gossip with the other women, it was being taken into confidence by someone more senior.

'Of course,' she said, then she walked over to where Sarah was sitting, and after a moment's consideration, possibly wondering if she was overstepping some sort of boundary, gave Sarah's arm a squeeze. 'And if you do want to talk about anything, well, you know where I am.'

'Sure,' said Sarah, as Sally left. 'Thanks.' Though the trouble was, she didn't know where *she* was.

She double-checked her door was shut, then picked her mobile up and dialled Grace's number, but when her friend answered, Sarah cried so hard she feared she'd never stop.

46

Evan knew he could never tell David he and Sarah had slept together, and seeing as he'd failed to get through to Sarah, he'd decided he'd do the next best thing, which was why he was sitting on the wall opposite Guy's Hospital, waiting for Grace to appear. He'd already phoned reception and checked that she was on the early shift, which by his calculations should have finished half an hour ago, but as yet, there had been no sign of her. Still, he had nowhere else to be, or rather, no clue what else to do.

A flash of light reflecting off the revolving door caught his eye, and he looked up in time to see Grace emerging from the building. She looked tired, and Evan marvelled at the job she did. Hers was a worthy profession, unlike simply moving other people's money around and creaming off the profits – or, perhaps, blowing into a shiny metal tube.

He jumped off the wall and called out her name, and she paused halfway down the steps, then put her head down and started walking quickly along St. Thomas Street. With a sigh, he jogged across the street and caught her up.

'I don't have time for this, Evan.'

'Five minutes?'

'No.'

'Four, then.'

'I can't. I'm . . .'

'What?'

Grace stopped, then swivelled round to face him. 'Meeting Sarah, actually.'

'Great.' Evan tried to look cheerful. 'I'll tag along, then, if you don't mind?'

'Don't be ridiculous.'

'It was a joke, Grace.'

She glared at him, then resumed walking. 'Well, it wasn't funny. In fact, there's nothing at all funny about this whole mess. I don't know what I was thinking . . .'

He hurried after her. 'What *you* were thinking?'

'Sarah didn't know she was going to the club last night, Evan. I tricked her into coming with me.'

'What? But . . .' Evan's heart suddenly sank. It had been *Grace's* idea. But whether that changed things, he couldn't work out. 'Why?'

'I thought I owed you that, after . . . well, it doesn't matter now. But it turned out to be a mistake.'

'Why a mistake?'

'Because I don't know what you said to her, but she phoned me earlier in floods of tears, and I couldn't get a word of sense out of her. And I certainly don't appreciate being stuck in the middle of your . . .' Grace struggled for the appropriate word, and Evan didn't think he was in a position to help her. He had a hard enough time defining it himself.

'I'm sorry, Grace. Really I am,' he said, conscious he was following her along the pavement like a charity canvasser. 'But what would you do if you were in my situation?'

'I wouldn't be in your situation, Evan. I'd have too much sense for that. Too much respect. Self, and for other people.'

'So I'm supposed to just let her go? When I know she's making a mistake?'

Grace stopped abruptly, almost causing Evan to bump into her. 'How do you know, exactly?'

'Because I know Sarah.'

'Do you? You didn't seem to know she was seeing David when you had this . . . fling of yours. Factor in that you haven't seen her for a year, and then when you do come back, all you do is upset her. I wouldn't say they were the actions of someone who really knew a person, would you?'

Evan waited until he was sure Grace had finished. 'Knowing someone isn't just knowing what they're going to do. Sometimes it's not even that. It's knowing what they're like. What they like. Fundamentally. The essence of them. And Sarah . . . She's not David's wife.'

'She will be soon.'

'Come on, Grace.' Evan looked at her pleadingly. 'You're her best friend. Can you honestly tell me she's making the right decision?'

'No. But then I can't tell you that she's making the wrong one. No-one can.'

'I can,' said Evan, firmly.

'How?'

'Because I'm the only one who can love her like she deserves to be loved.'

Grace started walking again, but a little slower, and Evan noticed she'd made space for him on the pavement. He fell into step beside her, grateful for the lull in hostilities.

'That's . . .' She sighed, and shook her head. 'Very romantic, Evan. But this is the real world we're talking about.'

'Which is what makes it all the more important.' He put a hand on her arm. 'Do *you* think she's happy?'

'I think she's made a decision, a choice, which will give her a chance at happiness. And you coming back for her . . . It was a mistake.'

Evan sighed. 'The only mistake I made was leaving. Not fighting for her at the time.'

Grace stopped at the corner of the street. 'Why didn't you?'

He shrugged. 'Because she told me I'd be wasting my time. And now I know why.'

'Because of David.'

'No, Grace. Because of *me*.'

'I don't understand.'

'She thought she was doing me a favour. Giving me the OK to go on tour.'

'Whoever gave you that idea?'

'She did.'

'Evan, whatever you've chosen to read into what's happened, or what you think she's said, you need to realise one thing. Sarah knows what she wants. And it isn't you.'

'It is, Grace. Only she's too scared to admit it.'

'That's rubbish.'

'Is it? Not judging by what happened between us last night.'

'Why?' Grace was staring at him accusingly. 'What happened, exactly?'

'You'd better ask her that question. Then ask yourself whether they were the actions of someone who's doing the right thing in getting married to someone else on Saturday.'

With that, Evan spun on his heel, and headed back down the street. And as he walked, he didn't need to look round to know Grace was still staring at him.

He made his way round the corner and began the short walk home, then – checking up and down the street for muggers first – pulled his wallet out of his pocket and removed the scrap of paper he'd cut out of the *New York Times*, the scrap of paper that had been responsible for all of this. The fact that he'd stumbled across David and Sarah's wedding announcement in a discarded newspaper back-stage at – well, he couldn't remember which of the various concert venues of North America it had been – had been something of a miracle, though in truth, he was beginning to wish he hadn't.

It had been Mel who'd suggested he take the Police gig. Ini-tially, he'd been reluctant – partly because he'd felt he'd be letting his friend down by leaving the club, but mainly because Sarah had exploded into his life the night before his audition – but Mel had told him he could always find another saxophonist, and so could The Police, which was why he'd had to leap at the chance. 'Remem-ber, some things only come along once in a lifetime,' Mel had told him, and at the time, Evan had assumed he'd been referring to the tour. When he'd seen the announcement, he'd realised it applied to Sarah, too.

Initially, in an attempt to forget her, he'd thrown himself into rehearsals, both with the band, and then back in his hotel room, playing every Police number again and again until he knew it back-wards. Then the excitement of the tour had taken over – a new city every week, the buzz from being up on stage . . . To be honest, he hadn't missed Sarah that much in the early days. Until he woke up one morning and realised where he was: Her home country. With-out her.

It was then that Mel's words had come back to haunt him – as a nagging doubt at first, and then growing into something that kept Evan awake long into the small hours, no matter how many post-gig shots he did with the band, or how much partying he indulged in. And then, when he'd found himself scanning the crowd every night in the hope that he might see her face, he knew things had gone too far.

The day he'd seen the paper, he hadn't known what to make of it, though he'd suspected it had been partly aimed at him. Maybe she'd felt she needed closure, or that *he* did, and her getting married would give either – or both – of them some sense of that.

Then one morning, just as the tour was drawing to a close, he'd woken up with a start, convinced it was a cry for help, a call to rescue. Why else would she have put it in every main broadsheet newspaper in a country where she – and as far as Evan knew, David – had no relatives, except to ensure he'd see it?

He couldn't discount the possibility that she just wanted to be sure of what she was doing, and with no other way of tracking him down, luring him back to London with a series of carefully placed photographs of the 'happy' couple was the best way to achieve that. But while he wasn't expecting to play Dustin Hoffman to her Katharine Ross, he couldn't ignore the possibility that maybe she was hoping he would.

A couple of times, he'd picked up the phone in his hotel room and dialled Sarah's number, slamming it down again like a nervous teenager before the call had even connected. He'd even written her a letter, though by the time he'd filled the fourth sheet of A4, he'd realised this kind of stuff was better said in person. Besides, he knew he had to surprise her. Ambush her, even. She might be in so deep that he'd have to shock her into the realisation that she was doing the wrong thing. And he'd seen enough medical dramas on TV to know that you needed a big shock to restart someone's heart.

He'd played out the last few weeks on tour with a growing anxiety, but also an increasing sense of focus, as if he finally had a direction in life. He'd even started running in an attempt to get fit, as if he was in training for some kind of prize fight which, ironically, was how he was beginning to see it, and by the time he'd touched down at Heathrow, he felt ready. Whatever the reason she'd seen fit to announce her wedding to the world, it'd had the desired effect – he was here now, and he had to see things through.

His mind still racing, he stuffed the clipping back into his wallet, and, realising to his surprise that he was already home, unlocked his front door, walked through to his bedroom, and lay down on the bed. It still smelled of Sarah – her perfume, their sex – and he breathed in deeply, savouring the memories her scent provoked. Then, suddenly, the sound of his mobile ringing made him jump, and he sat up quickly and fumbled for it in his pocket.

'Sarah?'

'This is an important message about your PPI insurance,' said a recorded voice, so Evan stabbed the 'end' button in disgust, then – worried he might have missed her call while answering that one – checked his voicemail for what seemed like the millionth time. He considered the possibility that he might be developing OCD, then remembered the joke country and western song titled *If the phone doesn't ring, it's me* and wondered whether Sarah wasn't calling him back on purpose, trying to provoke a response, but he doubted it – despite everything, he didn't think she was into playing games. And even if she was, short of tricking his way past reception and confronting her in her office, he'd run out of ideas.

He lay back down again and closed his eyes, tired from the exertions of the previous evening – no, the last few days – knowing he needed to get some rest, and willed for sleep to come.

And for the first time in he couldn't remember how long, Evan got what he wanted.

47

'You *slept with him?*'

Sarah's cheeks pinked. 'He told you that?'

'He didn't have to.' Grace pushed past her and into the kitchen, automatically reaching for the kettle. 'I only meant for the two of you to talk. What were you thinking?'

Sarah followed her like a scolded child. 'I wasn't, to tell the truth.'

'You must have been,' said Grace, accusingly. 'I know you, Sarah. Christ, I'm supposed to be your maid of honour. How do you expect me to stand there on Saturday if . . .'

'I was just trying to make my mind up.'

'About marrying David? That's a funny way to go about it.'

'Yeah. Or, you know, about not marrying him.'

Grace froze melodramatically, a mug in one hand, her teabag in the other, and under different circumstances, Sarah might have found the spectacle comical.

'Ri-ight.'

'Am I being stupid?'

'How? By marrying David, or not marrying David, or by sleeping with Evan? Because the answer might be "yes" to all of those things.'

Sarah sat down heavily at the kitchen table. 'It's all just so confusing. I'd just about convinced myself I was doing the right thing, and now . . .'

'Whoa.' Grace finally dropped the teabag into the mug, then set it down on the kitchen surface. 'You'd "just about convinced" yourself?'

'Well, yes. Isn't that what everyone who gets married has to do?'

Grace pulled out a chair and sat down. 'Sweetie, the decision to get married should be the easiest one anyone ever has to make. Not the hardest. You shouldn't have to *convince* yourself.'

'Well, there was no-one else on the horizon . . .'

'You sound like you have to get married.'

'Don't I?'

'No, Sarah. You don't.'

'Well, why does it feel like that?'

Grace took her hand. 'Ask yourself something. If all things were equal, and you had to pick between Evan and David, who would you choose?'

'All things *aren't* equal, Grace.'

'Maybe not. But this should be a happy event. You're sounding like a condemned woman who's been asked to choose between death by firing squad or lethal injection. And if that's how you feel about marriage, then you'd better pull out now.'

Sarah almost laughed. Did she really see marriage to David as a death sentence? She didn't think so. Though maybe it was a life sentence instead.

'Listen,' continued Grace. 'Do you still have feelings for Evan?'

'I don't go around sleeping with just anyone, you know?'

'But you obviously don't have feelings for David.'

'Of course I do!'

'So why did you cheat on him and sleep with Evan, then? And twice!'

'It was just the once. I mean, I wanted to do it again, but . . . Oh, you meant a year ago.'

Grace rolled her eyes. 'Yes, Sarah.'

'Well, to . . .' Sarah had been about to say it had been to make sure of her feelings for David, but she now realised it was more about making sure of her feelings for Evan. 'Do *you* think I'm making a mistake?'

'By doing what?'

'Marrying David. Or, you know, not,' she added, helplessly.

Grace opened her mouth to respond, then paused, as if considering her words carefully. 'Well, that all depends how you feel about him, of course, but if you're asking me . . .'

'I am.'

'Well, I just think that . . . I mean, I like David, but . . .'

'No you don't.'

'I do. While he may not be my type of person, I can see that he means well, and that he cares for you.'

'Right.'

'But . . .'

'But?'

'Is he really your soul mate?'

Sarah made a face. 'Who knows? And besides, does that concept really exist outside of all those novels with pink hearts and wedding cakes on their covers? I'm not so sure.'

'Of course it does.'

'Really? Where's yours, then?'

'Where's my what?'

'Your "soul mate",' said Sarah, pronouncing the words as sarcastically as she could. 'Someone who's swept you off your feet. Who you can't bear to be without. You're a beautiful woman. You've had lots of boyfriends. I've seen men throw themselves at you. You even work somewhere called "Guy's" Hospital, yet you're still single, so where's yours? If you're playing the law of averages, he must be out there somewhere. So if he exists, why haven't *you* found him yet?'

Grace seemed a little put out at Sarah's outburst. 'Well, because I'm still looking. It's just . . .'

'. . . that no-one's matched up yet to your idea of what an ideal partner should be?'

'Something like that,' said Grace, defensively. 'And besides, my job doesn't exactly leave me much time for, you know . . .' She stopped talking while the kettle noisily came to the boil. 'Dating. Or give me much opportunity at all, come to think of it, given that the people I meet at work are mostly mad, rather than mad about me.'

'I'm sorry, Grace. I'm not attacking you. It's just . . .' She leant back and stared out of the window. 'Who do you know who's actually found theirs?'

'Evan seems to think *he* has.'

'You're missing my point.'

Grace poured boiling water into her mug. 'Which is?'

'Maybe we all set the bar too high. Let's face it: life isn't all about starry-eyed romance. You have to be practical. Find someone who doesn't piss you off too much, and work out if you can stand to be with them for the rest of your days. And do you know what? I think David stands a pretty good chance of being that person.'

Grace let out a short laugh. 'You sound like you're *still* trying to convince yourself. And it's a little close to the wedding to be doing that.'

'Okay. Maybe I am. But it's not a bad strategy, is it?'

Grace looked at her for a moment. 'What about love?'

'That's what I've been trying to tell you. It doesn't exist. Not true, full-on romantic love, anyway. You have attraction. You have lust. But they don't last.'

317

'Did you *ever* have those with David?'

'That's not . . .' Sarah shook her head. 'What I mean is, marriage isn't based around some sort of magical, all-encompassing feeling.'

'Like you have with Evan, you mean?'

'That's unfair, Grace. It's about companionship. Comfort. Routine.'

'But don't you think it'd be better if it *was* based around love? Or at least started that way?'

'Why? I mean, how many times have *you* been in love?'

Grace shrugged. 'I don't know. I suppose I thought I was, once or twice.'

'Exactly. And it hasn't lasted, has it? Or it's turned out not to be what you thought it was, so why on earth should I expect it to last with Evan?'

'So you *were* in love with him?'

'That's not the point!'

'No? What is, then?'

'The point is, Grace, that even if it was there with David, it'd fade eventually, so as long as we were both getting what we wanted out of the relationship . . .'

'And what *do* you want out of the relationship?'

'Someone who isn't going to hurt me,' said Sarah, quietly.

'That's your problem.' Grace fished the teabag out of her mug and dropped it into the sink. 'Why you never let your defences down with Evan. Because you were scared he'd hurt you.'

'And he did, didn't he? By leaving, and not even bothering to try to get in touch.'

'But doesn't the scale of that hurt – after just one night together, may I remind you – tell you that maybe he *was* the one? And believe me, I'm as amazed as anyone to be arguing Evan's case, but don't you see? It might be him. Now he's back, and you've got a second chance. Don't you think you owe it to yourself to at least investigate that properly?'

'It's too late, Grace.'

Grace splashed some milk into her mug. 'Why?'

Sarah looked at her friend, wondering why she couldn't understand. *Fear of abandonment* was what her shrink back in New York had told her she was suffering from, though Sarah had always felt that fear was pretty well-founded. First her mother, then her father, and then Evan; they'd all left her – or at least, not been around when she'd needed them, whereas David? He'd done the complete opposite – and she'd be eternally grateful to him for that. But while she knew Grace would be familiar with the terminology, she feared she might not understand her actions.

'Because Evan left me once. And he could do it again.'

Grace sat back down at the table and cradled her mug. 'Have you forgotten why he left you? The small matter of you telling him to?'

Sarah coloured slightly. 'Well, doesn't that just prove how little he valued our relationship?'

'Not at all. In fact – and forgetting the small matter that he was going to ask you to come with him . . .'

'Or so he says.'

'. . . quite the opposite.'

'Huh?'

Grace reached across and squeezed her hand. 'Maybe it proved to him how little *you* did. And if you want my opinion, it's a wonder he decided to come back for you.'

'I beg your pardon?'

'And the fact that he was prepared to do that, take the risk, knowing he was playing second fiddle, and in the middle of the most important time of his career . . . Surely that proves how much he cares about you?'

'Well, why didn't he say anything when he left?'

'What was he going to do – make some huge declaration of love, only to have it thrown straight back at him? Because that's probably what he thought would happen.'

'Maybe that's what I wanted him to do.'

'It seems to me that's what you're getting now.'

Sarah stood up, then walked over to the fridge and peered inside, more for something to do than because she was hungry. 'Well, like I said, it's too late.'

'No it isn't,' said Grace. 'Sunday might be. And anyway, are you sure you're not just being stubborn – as usual?'

Sarah smiled. From first getting into banking through to her decision to up sticks and move to London, once she'd set her mind on something, she'd rarely change it. 'Yeah, well, sometimes it's the only way to get through life's hardships.'

'But marrying David isn't a hardship, surely? Or at least, it shouldn't be.'

'Maybe,' she conceded.

'So don't you think that perhaps this one time you should break that cast-iron rule of yours? Otherwise you're just being pig-headed, and that's not right where marriage is concerned.' Grace blew on the top of her tea and took a sip. 'All I'm saying is, you've got someone who obviously loves you. Don't you think you ought to at least be absolutely sure whether you love him back before you do something that might just ruin his life?'

Sarah slammed the fridge door shut and wheeled around. 'Why should I? What has Evan possibly done to deserve that?'

'What has *Evan* done? Flown halfway around the world to tell you how he feels, perhaps? Been prepared to risk the biggest break in his career just to see if there's the slightest chance that the two of you can get back together. And actually . . .'

'Actually what?'

Grace regarded her levelly. 'I was talking about David.'

48

'Evan?'

Sarah stared at her office phone as if it had cheated on her. Reception had put the call through as being from Guy's Hospital, and while her first reaction had been that Grace must have had an accident on her way to work this morning, the sound of Evan's voice hadn't quite left her feeling relieved.

'Don't hang up.'

'What do you want?'

'Just to talk.'

She got up to close her office door. 'I can't. I've got some . . . stuff to sort out.'

'Because of what happened?'

'What happened, Evan? We took a misguided stroll down memory lane, and it . . .' She swallowed hard. 'It was a mistake. Don't make me feel any worse about it than I already do.'

'There's no reason to feel bad about it, Sarah. You were following your heart.'

'Believe me. That wasn't the part of my body that was calling the shots.'

'Why haven't you been returning my calls?'

'Because . . . because I'm getting married on Saturday.'

'That could still happen . . .' Evan paused, then took a deep breath. 'Just marry me instead.'

Sarah stared at her phone in disbelief, then realised how ridiculous that must have looked, so put it back to her ear. 'What?'

'Not necessarily this Saturday. Well, not unless you wanted to. What I really meant was that you should, you know, think about it. Marriage.'

'You don't think that's what I've been doing?'

'Well, no. Not to me, at least.'

'I . . . I can't, Evan.'

'Why not?'

'Because . . .' Sarah sighed. 'Because it's too confusing. You're asking me to make a leap that just seems too far at the moment.'

'At the moment?'

'Why didn't you say anything *before*? Anything at all. You've had a year.'

There was another pause, and then: 'I thought about getting in touch. Once or twice.'

'Well, this isn't one of those occasions when it's the thought that counts.'

'It just didn't seem appropriate.'

'*Appropriate?*'

'We weren't even in a proper relationship, for God's sake. He was your boyfriend. I was just a bit of fun for you.'

'Is that really how you saw it?'

'You hardly gave me the impression it was anything more.'

'I've told you why that was.'

'And I believe you. Which is why it's even more important you give me a chance.'

'I can't.'

'Not even after Tuesday night.'

'Don't go there, Evan.'

'So that's it, then? David beat me to it?'

'It wasn't a competition, Evan. It's not like the gold rush, where the first person to stake their claim wins.'

'No? Well, why does it feel like that to me?'

'I didn't hear a thing from you.' She sat down heavily at her desk. 'For a *year*. And then the baby . . .' She gripped the phone hard to stop her voice from faltering. 'David's offering me security. Stability. Whereas you . . .'

'. . . can offer you something he can't.'

A knock on the door startled her, and she got up to answer it. 'Which is what, exactly?'

Evan knew this was the chance to play his trump card, and this time, he didn't want to miss the opportunity. 'The chance to go back home, Sarah.'

He waited for a response, but none came. She'd put the phone down on him.

arah was sitting in Postman's Park, staring blankly at the plaques along the far wall. She'd desperately needed some time to think, although so far the two hours she'd been here since she'd left the office early hadn't been long enough.

She'd had to end Evan's call abruptly when David had knocked on her office door, and while she was confident her fiancé hadn't heard anything, it had taken a good ten minutes for her heart to stop racing. And though she was sure that was a result of nearly being caught, she knew it was also in part due to Evan's statement. He'd intrigued her with his mention of 'home', and several times during the day she'd thought about calling him back, but to use Evan's term, that wouldn't have been appropriate. And she'd been far too inappropriate with him recently.

At least David and she had made up. It was the first time the two of them had spoken since their contretemps over lunch the previous day, and while she assumed at first he'd popped in to apologise to her, in actual fact, he'd been there to give *her* that opportunity. She'd taken it, of course, though when he'd left, a satisfied look on his face, Sarah had found herself wanting to take the apology back. It *was* all about winning with him. Being the last to give in. And she hated the fact that she'd blinked first.

She stifled a yawn, and realised she'd hardly slept for the past few nights, though for a second at Evan's the other evening, she'd

felt she could have dropped off quite comfortably, before she'd suddenly remembered what was happening on Saturday. *The day after
tomorrow.* And that had woken her up pretty dramatically.

Sarah could hardly believe it was so close. Back when she and
David had first got engaged, the wedding had been so far away it
hadn't seemed real. Even the trip to Tiffany's had been more like a
day out than some significant event, the ring just the latest in the
series of expensive things David had bought her rather than a sym-
bol of their impending commitment. But now, even though the day
itself was a relatively small affair, all the ancillary stuff – the invitations, the cake – were all beginning to feel almost menacing. Even
the dress she'd been starving herself for weeks to fit into . . .

Sarah leapt up off the bench and checked her watch. *Her dress.*
She'd been supposed to collect it yesterday.

She almost ran out of the park, and headed south towards Hays
Galleria. How could she have forgotten to pick it up? Did that mean
something – or was it the only thing she could delay, given the
inevitability of Saturday? Though maybe, like Grace had suggested,
she *could* ask David for a postponement. Tell him that . . . Tell him
what? What possible reason could she have for not going through
with a wedding they'd been planning since they'd set the date all
those months ago? Especially since all she had to do was turn up.

Or perhaps not.

It occurred to her to just keep walking. The Eurostar could
whisk her to France, and from there . . . well, who knew? She could
pop back to her flat, collect her passport, and be in Paris by dinner
time. But then again, she'd never considered herself the running
away type.

Or was she? In her more reflective moments, Sarah sometimes
felt that coming to England after her father died had been running away. Escaping from everything that New York reminded her

of: the cancer that had taken her father, the environment that had seduced her mother away from the little family unit in which, for a few short years, she'd felt so safe. Here in London she'd been able to start again, make new friends, move in different circles, reinvent herself as a tough, no-nonsense Sarah Bishop who bore no relation to the person who'd been the victim of all that crap. She'd enjoyed being different, too; there was something about being an American abroad that she'd found romantic. And that others – David and Evan in particular – seemed to find almost exotic about her.

At first, she'd loved London: The London of the films her father used to show her, the London described in the books she used to devour. It'd been exactly what she'd been expecting, and walking along by the Thames she'd often marvelled at the wonderful mixture of old and new. New York didn't have the old, and back then, it had occurred to her that, sometimes, the old was better – it had stood the test of time, after all – but now she wasn't so sure. And while she missed New York terribly, she worried that there wasn't anything – or anyone – there for her any more.

She checked her watch, then quickened her pace, hurrying past St. Paul's Cathedral, then across the Thames on the Millennium Bridge, Tower Bridge to her left, the famous London Eye on her right. Occasionally, being here still felt like a dream, except now it was turning into a bad one. Although Sarah knew she only had herself to blame for that.

Striding into Hays Galleria, she made her way towards the boutique, rapping on the glass when she found the door locked. Maya, the owner, looked up from where she was sitting behind the counter, then smiled though the window in recognition and buzzed her in.

'I've been trying to call you,' Maya said, kissing Sarah hello on both cheeks. 'I was beginning to think you'd got cold feet,'

'No, I just . . .' Sarah shrugged. 'You know how it is. So much to sort out.'

'Of course.' Maya led her over to a rack in the corner of the shop. 'Are you ready?'

Sarah stood there mutely, assuming Maya's question was rhetorical, and watched her move a heavy dress-holder to the front of the rack.

The designer slowly undid the zip and released the wedding dress from its protective cover. 'Are your hands clean?' she asked.

Sarah nodded, though she couldn't say the same about her conscience, then carefully reached across and took the dress. It looked almost ephemeral, and, though heavier than she'd been expecting, was quite stunning – exactly as Maya had promised. She held it up to the mirror, positioning herself to give an idea of how it would look on, marvelling at how the dress managed to be both sophisticated and sexy. She'd seen the sketches, but they'd hardly managed to capture the elegance of the real thing, the way the fitted, ruched satin bodice decorated with the hand-beaded floral accents she'd chosen broke away at the knee to show the full skirt of thick organza. It had been the one thing about the wedding she'd had complete control over, and as Sarah stared at her reflection, she had to remind herself to breathe.

'Well?'

Over her shoulder, she could see Maya anxiously trying to gauge her reaction. 'Beautiful,' was all she could say.

'Aren't you going to try it on?'

Sarah nodded, then followed Maya towards the changing room, feeling slightly awkward as the designer joined her inside and slid the curtain shut. Slowly, she removed her clothes, staring at her underwear-clad reflection in the mirror while Maya politely averted her eyes. She'd – briefly – been like this the other night in front of Evan, and the memory made her blush in shame.

Carefully, she eased the dress from its hanger, slipped it over her head, and wriggled it down past her hips. As Maya helped her pull it into position, she slotted her arms through the shoulder straps, breathing in as the designer fastened the zip on her left side, and then, after a bit more primping, it was on.

Sarah turned round, bracing herself in anticipation of the meringue she was sure she'd look like, then caught her breath as she gazed at her reflection in the mirror. Staring back at her, in perhaps the most beautiful dress she'd ever seen, was someone she didn't quite recognise, or perhaps, didn't want to acknowledge.

The dress was even more stunning *on* than it had been on the hanger, but Sarah couldn't help feeling something was wrong, almost as if she was a little girl playing at dressing up. She looked at Maya, then back at her reflection, and burst into tears.

'Don't worry,' Maya said, retrieving a box of tissues from a shelf in the cubicle that had evidently been put there for just this kind of occurrence. 'That happens a lot.'

Not for these reasons, thought Sarah, dabbing at her eyes with a tissue.

She stared at her reflection for a few more moments as the designer checked the fit, then held her left arm up so Maya could unzip her and slipped carefully out of the dress. As Maya gently eased it up over her head, she tried not to think how Evan had done something similar a couple of nights previously.

'Thanks, Maya,' she said, pulling her work clothes back on, relieved to be looking normal again. 'It's perfect.'

'Well, if you're only going to be doing this the once, it's important that everything's right.' Maya smiled. 'Just remember not to let David see you in it before the big day,' she cautioned, zipping the dress safely back inside its carrier. 'It's bad luck.'

Sarah almost laughed. Surely she'd had all the bad luck she deserved.

She hugged Maya goodbye, then picked the carrier up, and as she headed out of the shop, her mobile rang. Sarah rejected the call, sure it was Evan trying to call her back, then stared at the screen, sighing exasperatedly when no voicemail icon appeared. Then again, he probably didn't know what to say. Which made two of them.

She still wasn't sure why she'd slept with him. Couldn't quite reconcile it with her impending wedding, unless that *was* the explanation, and it had been an extreme way of seeing whether there was any doubt about what she was doing on Saturday – though the trouble was, that was exactly what it had achieved. And while admittedly, she'd always felt there had been some unfinished business between them, now it felt even more unfinished. She still fancied Evan. Desired him, in fact, with a passion she'd forgotten she had. And if she was being honest, that was hardly a sound basis from which to commit to spending the rest of your life with someone else who didn't quite provoke the same reaction.

Suddenly, with a clarity that almost winded her, Sarah knew what she had to do, so she turned around and started walking purposefully towards Shad Thames. There was a pub on the corner of Jamaica Road – a 'spit-and-sawdust boozer', as David was fond of describing it whenever they'd whiz by in the BMW – and on a whim, she pushed her way through the smokers huddled outside and headed inside. The wedding dress, slung over her shoulder in its protective carrier, was weighing heavily down on her, and she almost found the metaphor funny, but if ever she needed a drink, it was now.

She draped the carrier over the nearest bar stool and caught the attention of the barmaid. 'Double vodka and tonic, please,' said

Sarah, although she only wanted the vodka – the tonic was purely for window dressing.

'Sure, love,' said the woman, pouring Sarah her drink. 'Four-fifty, please.'

Sarah handed over a five-pound note, then slotted her change into the charity box on the counter, and as the barmaid smiled her thanks, she caught sight of the wedding dress.

'That yours, is it?'

Sarah nodded. 'It is.'

'When's the big day?'

'Saturday.'

'Ooh. Lovely.' She beamed at her. 'I love a good wedding, me.'

'You married, are you?' asked Sarah.

'Yeah. Happiest day of your life, your wedding.'

'Really?'

'Yeah. Course, everyone says that, because it's pretty much downhill from then onwards, but still . . .'

The woman gave her a gap-toothed grin, then headed off to serve someone else, and Sarah stared at her, then picked up her drink, pulled out her Blackberry, and pretended to study her emails as she gingerly sipped the clear liquid. A couple of people glanced at her – men, of course – maybe wondering what she was doing in here on her own, perhaps considering coming over and offering to buy her a drink, but Sarah just ignored them, making it clear she didn't want to be disturbed. Conscious that – apart from the barmaid – she was the only woman in the pub, Sarah forced herself to drink faster, struggling not to bring the vodka straight back up again while simultaneously contemplating ordering another, but she just wanted to feel brave, not loaded. Being labelled a slut was going to be bad enough, but a slut and an alcoholic . . .

Downing the last of her vodka, she slipped her Blackberry back into her coat pocket and headed unsteadily out through the door, regretting the fact that she hadn't drunk the tonic. As she threaded her way back through the crowd of smokers congregating outside, she felt a tap on her shoulder, and wheeled round to see the barmaid standing behind her.

'I think you might be needing this, love,' she said, and handed Sarah the wedding dress before disappearing back inside.

Though as she mumbled her thanks, then pulled her phone out and dialled David's number, Sarah wasn't so sure she would.

50

Evan grabbed his jacket and keys, slammed his front door shut behind him, and began walking purposefully towards Shad Thames. He'd spent the afternoon at home trying to drum up the courage to do what he knew he had to do, and while hailing a taxi would get him there in five minutes, he hoped the cool air might just help him to focus. This evening was going to be unpleasant. And he didn't want to rush it.

He couldn't believe Sarah had put the phone down on him, but he'd heard the knock on the door in the background and had guessed who it had been, and something about her knee-jerk reaction had made him suspect there was something sinister about their relationship, some hold David had over her that Evan didn't like. Plus, the fact that she was still talking about going ahead with the wedding while she clearly had feelings for someone else was something he couldn't fathom, and if he had to play dirty to even things out, then now was the time.

The weather had turned colder, so he stuck his hands in his jeans pockets as he made his way along Tanner Street and under the viaduct, listening to the comforting rattle of trains passing overhead on their journeys in and out of London Bridge Station. Batting away the onslaught of free newspapers that made walking past any tube station at rush hour something of an obstacle course, he headed along Tooley Street, past the London Dungeon, then crossed the road, marvelling as he always did at the majesty of Tower Bridge in front of him.

Evan knew he'd be devastated if Sarah still chose David, and not just because the past week had made him all the more certain she was the girl for him. He was so sure she was making a mistake, so convinced she was doing something against her wishes, that he still felt an overriding impulse to save her. Maybe he was fooling himself this was the way to do it, but when it came down to it, what choice did he have?

He wasn't used to showdowns, and wondered whether he should prepare his 'Oscar face' and be ready to accept his loss gracefully, if a loss was what it was going to be, but he wasn't sure he'd be able to hold it together. He hoped he wouldn't cry, though maybe he should. After all, women were no strangers to turning on the water-works to get what they wanted, and maybe repressing his emotions had been his problem, in particular not telling Sarah how he'd felt about her from day one – and for the whole of the following year. Although he'd certainly made up for it over the past few days.

The pavement was busy, and Evan wondered whether he should take heart from the number of women he saw – there was bound to be someone else for him if it didn't work out with Sarah. Trouble was, he didn't want anyone else – and in any case, he was a bit out of the dating mindset. He thought back to when he'd last 'picked up' someone, and was alarmed to be drawing a blank. Sarah had come on to him, as had the previous couple of women he'd gone out with, and as for his chatting-up skills, well, it was a lot easier when you'd been up on stage to come down and make an impression. Doing it from scratch? Evan didn't relish the prospect.

That was the trouble with starting dating again in your thirties, he realised. Men still had the mindset of a teenager, so to try and respond to a thirty-something woman, to second-guess what she might be looking for . . . He shuddered at the prospect, and if anything, it strengthened his resolve.

His phone rang in his pocket, and he fished it out nervously, nearly dropping it in the process. 'Hello?'

'Where the fuck are you?' said Mel, cheerfully.

'Tower Bridge.'

'Should I switch on the news?'

'Huh?'

'If you're about to jump, I want to at least see it.'

Evan smiled grimly. 'Relax,' he said. 'I'm walking past it. Not climbing it.'

'Even so. You're not going to do anything stupid, are you?'

Evan almost laughed. As far as he was concerned, almost everything he'd done over the course of the past few days qualified as stupid. 'I just decided it was confrontation time.'

'Really?'

'Yes, Mel. Really.'

He could almost hear Mel frown down the line. 'I thought she didn't want to see you?'

'I'm not going to see Sarah, Mel. I'm going to see David.'

'What for?'

'I'm going to make him tell Sarah what happened on his stag night.'

'How?'

'I'm a-gonna make-a him an offer he can't refuse,' said Evan, then he held the phone up to capture the noise of the passing traffic for effect before switching it off. Sarah deserved the truth. And although he didn't yet have the faintest idea how, Evan was going to make sure David gave it to her.

51

Evan could guess which of the huge glass-and-brick structures on the river-front was the right building even before he'd matched the number on the gates to the RSVP address on the wedding invitation, and sure enough, David's block was the tallest. He scanned the list of names above the buzzers, then pressed the button hesitantly, almost losing his nerve when David answered. But at the same time, the abrupt 'Yes?' reminded him why he was here.

'It's Evan.'

'Evan,' said David, after the briefest of pauses. 'What a pleasant surprise. Come on up. Third floor.'

The door buzzed open and Evan walked inside, telling himself not to be overawed by the expensively decorated lobby. As always, he was amazed at how Shad Thames was so close to where he lived, yet when you were actually there, his part of Bermondsey felt a million miles away. He nodded to the liveried porter, who pointed him in the direction of the lift, then followed David's 'third floor' instruction, and a few moments later, he was knocking on an expensively panelled front door.

'I thought you'd be Sarah,' said a smiling David, showing him inside.

'She's on her way here?'

'That's right. She's just telephoned, actually.'

'Oh. Right.' Evan wanted to turn round and go, but he couldn't think of an excuse. Then again, he realised, if Sarah was coming here, it would be the perfect opportunity for David to tell her what he'd been up to. And for Evan to witness her reaction first-hand.

'Drink?' barked David.

Evan didn't need to think about his answer. 'Yeah,' he said, following David into the kitchen. 'Thanks.'

'Beer OK?'

'Great.'

David strode over to the fridge and extracted a bottle of Grolsch, popped the top off the bottle, and handed it to Evan. 'Did you want a glass?'

'As it comes is fine. You not having one?'

'That was the last one.'

'Ah. Did you want it?'

David laughed. 'Mustn't. I'm watching my weight. Got to try to look half decent in the wedding photos. Even though the only person everyone will notice is Sarah, of course.'

Evan didn't contradict him. 'How's she doing?'

'Oh, you know,' David said, as he led Evan through into the front room.

The flat was enormous, and Evan wondered whether 'third floor' was actually a factual description. Even the hallway was bigger than Evan's lounge, and it was all he could do to stop his jaw from dropping open at the view of Tower Bridge through the window.

'And how are preparations going for the big day?'

'It's not going to be that big, actually, but fine, I suppose. Sarah's department, really. Though as far as I can tell, everyone we invited seems to be coming. Which I hope includes you?'

Evan decided to sidestep the question. 'Possibly because you put "open bar" on the invitations. Tell people the alcohol's free, and they're bound to show up.'

'Quite.'

David smiled, then indicated for him to sit down, and for a moment, Evan wondered whether he shouldn't stand, but David had already flopped onto the plush white leather sofa, and he felt awkward enough already. He draped his jacket carefully over the back of the single armchair, lowered himself carefully down, and took a swig of beer.

'Listen, David . . .'

Before he could say any more, the sound of a key in the lock made him jump up from his seat as if it were electrified. David regarded him strangely, then put his finger to his lips. 'In here, sweetheart,' he called. 'I've got a surprise for you.'

Evan could hear Sarah sigh. 'Not now, David. I'm tired, and I have to tell you something.' She marched into the front room, stopping in her tracks when she noticed they had a visitor. 'What's going on?'

'Ta-da!' said David, followed by a slightly more hesitant 'Ta-da?', when he saw Sarah's expression.

'I just dropped round.' Evan looked across at David anxiously, worried he'd lose his nerve, but at least they were all here now, and if he was going to make David tell her about his indiscretion, then there was no time like the present. But something about Sarah's expression made him hesitate. 'And . . .'

'And you'll stay for a spot of dinner, of course?' said David.

'I'm not sure.' Evan looked at his watch. 'I . . .'

'I insist.' David marched over to where Sarah was standing and put his arm around her. 'Or rather, *we* insist, don't we, sweetheart?' he said, and that made up Evan's mind for him.

'In that case, I'd love to.'

'Great. Indian? I'll pop out and pick up some more booze, and put in an order with the takeaway on the corner while I'm at it.'

Evan saw Sarah wince at the word 'booze'. Was there a time when she'd found it charming, he wondered? 'Sounds good,' he said, smiling across at her, but it wasn't until David had slammed the front door behind him that she finally addressed him.

'*Jesus*, Evan.'

'Sorry. I didn't think you'd be here.'

She shrugged her coat off angrily and threw it onto the sofa. 'Well, I sure as hell didn't think *you'd* be here. But then you seem to make a habit of showing up in inappropriate places.'

Evan didn't have an answer for that, so instead, he pointed at the dress carrier Sarah had draped over the back of a dining chair. 'And what's that?' he asked, though he feared he wouldn't like the answer.

'My wedding dress,' said Sarah, defiantly.

'I hope you've still got the receipt?'

'That's not funny.'

'So you're still thinking of going through with it? After everything.'

'Do you mean the other night?'

'Not just the other night, no. But now that you mention it . . .'

'What do you want me to do?'

'Like I said. Marry *me*, Sarah. Not David.'

She looked at him, open mouthed, then suddenly the strength seemed to go out of her legs, and she sat down heavily on the sofa.

'Why?'

'Because I love you.'

'David loves me.'

'Well, because you love me, then.'

Sarah stared at him. She couldn't counter that one so easily. And yet, to admit that she didn't love David in the same way . . . well, that was something she couldn't quite bring herself to say. There'd be no going back from it. And she still wasn't sure she was up to that.

'It's not as simple as that.'

'Well, maybe it should be.'

She sighed exasperatedly. 'Why are you here, Evan? What were you planning to do? Tell David about us?'

'Of course not. I'm not trying to blackmail you. I just want you have all the facts. To see sense.'

Sarah's eyes flashed angrily. 'See sense? What would be sensible about calling off my wedding to my boss two days before it's supposed to happen? And more importantly, what would be sensible about doing all that for some musician who took a year to realise how he felt about me?'

Evan smarted a bit at the 'some musician' comment, but knew better than to mention that it had been an okay job for Sarah's father. 'Well, maybe I got that wrong, then. Maybe getting married shouldn't be sensible. Maybe you should marry me because we're in love, and we'd have fun, and . . .'

'Stop it, Evan!'

He sat down next to her, wondering if he should be on one knee instead. 'Let me ask you one thing. Do you love him?'

'Why would I have got engaged to him if I didn't?'

'That was going to be my next question.'

'You're serious, aren't you? Okay, yes, I love him.'

Evan tried to ignore what felt like a punch in the stomach. 'How much?'

'How *much*?'

'Yes.'

'I don't know.' She rolled her eyes. 'Enough for him, apparently.'

'Okay. Why?'

'What do you mean, why?'

'It's a simple enough question. What is about David that you love?'

'You can just *love* someone. There don't have to be things.'

'Yes there do. I know exactly why I love you, for example.'

Sarah opened her mouth, then closed it again, and Evan smiled.

'Go on,' he said.

'What?'

'You were going to ask me, weren't you?'

'No. Yes.'

'Okay. But you first.'

Sarah folded her arms. 'Well, he's kind. And he says he loves me.'

'Just because someone says they love you, it doesn't mean you have to say it back, like when you say "bless you" because someone's sneezed.'

'Maybe I love him *because* he loves me. Did you ever think of that?'

'Well, in that case you must love me, then, because I love you.'

'No you don't.'

'Oh yes I do.'

'Jesus, Evan. We're not at the pantomime. You don't. You're just in love with the idea of being in love with me.'

'What does *that* mean?'

Sarah sighed. 'It fits your romantic notions of being a musician.'

'Romantic notions I thought you shared.'

Sarah glared at him. She'd been determined to talk things through with David first, say what she had to say, give him a chance to state his case, hoping that would help her clarify how she felt, but here, with Evan forcing the issue, she didn't know how to react.

'Evan, I just can't deal with this now. Please. Just go.'

'Fine.' He stood up slowly. 'Just tell me you're a hundred percent sure that you're doing the right thing, and you'll never see me again.'

She reached up and put a hand on his arm, suddenly not wanting him to leave – or at least, not like this. 'Evan, no-one's ever a hundred percent sure when it comes to this kind of thing.'

'I am,' he said, covering her hand with his.

They stood there for a moment – a moment Evan wanted to last forever – enjoying each other's touch, Evan mesmerised by the beautiful face gazing up at him, then at the sound of the front door opening, she pulled her hand away, and the moment passed as quickly as it had begun.

'Only me,' called David cheerfully, before marching into the lounge. 'Food will be about fifteen minutes.' He placed a couple of shopping bags onto the dining table and removed several bottles of wine. 'Meanwhile, we can get stuck into these.'

'Apologies, David.' Evan picked his jacket up from the back of the chair, relieved to see it hadn't left a mark on the white leather. 'I don't think I can stay for dinner after all.'

'Don't be ridiculous. I've just ordered a takeaway.'

'I'm sorry.' Evan reached for his wallet. 'I'll give you the money.'

David laughed. 'That's hardly what I meant,' he said, fetching three wine glasses from the cupboard in the corner. Come on, Sarah hasn't seen you for ages, and now you're buggering off after five minutes.'

'It's not that. I've got . . .'

'. . . chicken tikka masala coming. And enough naan bread to feed a small army.'

Sarah got to her feet. 'David, don't make Evan stay if he doesn't want to,' she said, and Evan stared at the two of them, realising that this evening might well be the final time he'd ever see Sarah. Plus if he stayed, it would be a last opportunity for Sarah to see him and David together. To make a comparison. And if she didn't want him after that . . .

He smiled at David, then flung his jacket back down. 'Why not, then?' he said.

52

Evan sipped his wine as he forced himself to smile at yet another of David's banking anecdotes. So far, the evening wasn't quite going to plan – he'd been prepared to come here and have things out with him, but then Sarah had turned up, and David had made it impossible by behaving like the perfect host. And although he was a little, well, *dull*, Evan had to admit he'd hardly been the life and soul of the party himself.

Sarah, meanwhile, seemed to be in a daze, and while Evan could appreciate how uncomfortable she must be feeling, he knew the evening was about to get a lot more awkward for all of them. Draining the contents of his glass, he steeled himself to steer the conversation round to the stag night, only to see David leap out of his seat as the doorbell rang.

'Excellent!' David set his glass down on the coffee table and rubbed his hands together. 'Food.'

As he headed off to answer the door, Sarah lowered her voice. 'I'm sorry, Evan. What exactly are you doing here?'

'You mean this evening? Or generally?'

'Either.' She threw her hands up in the air. 'Both. What the hell made you come back?'

Evan looked at her quizzically. 'Your announcement.'

'What announcement?'

'The one you placed in the paper – sorry, *papers*. The one you obviously wanted me to see.'

'I didn't place any announcement.'

'Well, what's this, then?' Evan pulled his wallet out of his back pocket, and removed the slightly worse-for-wear *New York Times* clipping.

'That's . . .' Sarah took it from him. 'Where did you get this?'

'It wasn't exactly easy to miss. And neither were you.'

She ignored his attempt at a compliment. 'I've never seen this before in my life.'

'You don't remember placing it?'

'Of course I don't remember placing it.' She stared at the cutting in disbelief. 'Because I didn't.'

'But that means . . .' He stopped talking suddenly, as David had appeared back in the room, carrying a couple of brown paper bags. A garish yellow sauce was already beginning to leak through one of them, so he placed it on top of an old copy of *The Economist* on the coffee table, but as he unpacked the contents, he frowned.

'Ah.'

'What's the matter?' said Sarah nervously.

'They seem to have forgotten Evan's order.'

'Oh. Right. Well, I'm not that hungry anyway, so . . .'

'Don't worry. We can share.' David fetched three plates from the sideboard and laid them down on the coffee table, then he caught sight of the clipping. 'After all, it wouldn't be the first time.'

Sarah stared at him. 'Pardon?'

'It wouldn't be the first time that I've had to share something. With Evan.'

'What are you talking about?' Sarah's voice was wavering, and David rested a hand on her knee.

'You, darling.'

Her eyes flicked from his hand to his face, trying to read his expression. 'You . . . knew?'

'Give me some credit, please.'

'But . . .'

'But what?' David peeled the tops off the takeaway containers and arranged them on the table. 'Help yourselves, by the way.'

Evan watched the two of them. Almost surreally, David was behaving as if there was nothing amiss, whereas the colour had all but drained from Sarah's cheeks. And while he felt a strange sense of relief that it was all out in the open, he couldn't help wondering whether this turn of events would lessen the impact of what he'd been planning to get David to admit.

'How long have you known?' said Sarah, quietly.

'Known?' David smiled again, although there was no warmth in his expression. 'I suspected. Of course I did. But it was only after we lost the baby that I was sure.'

'The . . . baby?' said Evan, his chest suddenly tightening. The whole miscarriage thing was still raw for him. And for Sarah, he saw, judging by the way she'd flinched.

'Sarah fell pregnant. About, oh, nine months ago, ironically. She didn't say?'

Sarah stood up. 'David, don't.'

'Yes,' said Evan, quietly. 'She said.'

'And then she lost it,' continued David. 'All very traumatic. Or for the best. Who knows? But anyway, at the time, given the circumstances – well, what I assumed the circumstances were, at least – I thought I better do the decent thing by getting down on one knee. And blow me, she said yes.'

'David.' Sarah was shaking her head, looking at no-one in particular. 'Stop.'

'He's got a right to know.'

Evan was on his feet now too. 'To know what?'

'So we thought we'd try again. Tried and tried, in fact – not that I'm complaining, mind you. But we weren't having any luck. Might have been her fault, of course, but I thought I'd better get myself checked out, just in case. A good excuse to put the old BUPA to some use.'

'You never said.' Sarah put a hand on his shoulder, but he removed it politely.

'Didn't I? Oh well. But it turned out it *was* me. Extremely low motility, apparently. The upshot was, it didn't take Sherlock to work out I was unlikely to have got her preggers in the first place.'

Sarah stared at him. 'But how did you know about . . .'

'Evan?' David smiled, but there was no humour behind it. 'Luckily there's one woman in my life who's completely loyal.'

Sarah paled even more. 'Sally?'

'I wouldn't have found out about the club if she hadn't told me the taxi had dropped you there. Even went there myself one night. Dreadful place. Awful music. But that was apparently because their star attraction had recently left for America. So I – what is it your lot say, sweetheart? – *did the math*. And then it all fell into place.' He folded his arms. 'I may have been blind, but I'm not stupid.'

Evan was hardly listening to him. 'The baby *was* mine?' He tried to catch Sarah's eye, but she appeared to be in shock.

'Apparently.' David laughed. 'Assuming she hadn't been shagging some other poor chap behind *our* backs.'

Evan felt himself tense. 'Watch what you're saying,' he warned, wondering if things would turn nasty. He hadn't had a fight in years, but he was still pretty sure he could take David. And he was more than prepared to defend Sarah's honour.

'So . . . This was down to you?' Sarah said, tapping the clipping, and David smiled.

'Guilty as charged,' he said, spooning rice onto his plate. 'Cost me a small fortune, but I thought it might smoke him out. And lo and behold, I was right.'

'But . . . why?' asked Sarah, though Evan wouldn't have been far behind her with the same question.

David put his spoon down and looked up at her. 'I'm no-one's bloody consolation prize, Sarah. I didn't want you to marry me if all the while you thought you were settling for second best. That's why I needed Evan back. To see what your reaction was. To see whether you'd be tempted again. And I can see by your face that you were. Or rather, *are*.'

'David . . .'

'Please don't tell me it didn't mean anything. Everyone in this room knows that wasn't the case.' David put his plate down, then took her hands in his. 'So,' he said, easing her gently down onto the sofa. 'Let me ask you something.'

Sarah's eyes flicked across at Evan, then she nodded. 'Sure.'

'Can you absolutely, categorically, truthfully tell me that there's not the smallest part of you that looks at him and wonders what might have been?'

'David.' Sarah pleaded with him. 'Don't ask me that.'

'Why not?'

When she couldn't speak, Evan cleared his throat. 'Because you're not going to like the answer.'

David ignored him. 'Just tell me,' he said calmly.

'David, everybody can't help thinking that,' she said, falteringly. 'It's impossible not to . . .'

'I bloody don't!'

'Yes, well, you wouldn't,' said Evan. 'You won the lottery when Sarah agreed to marry you.'

'Yes, I did, didn't I? Though it appears that I was playing with your numbers.'

Evan wanted to ask David if that was why he'd still felt the need to buy a Lucky Dip on his stag night, but he bit his tongue.

'Sarah?' continued David.

'What?'

'You didn't answer me. Can you?'

Sarah regarded him levelly, then she turned and looked at Evan. 'No,' she said, softly. 'No, I can't.'

'Right.' David let go of her hands and picked his plate back up. 'Fine. Well, in that case, I forbid you from seeing or speaking to him again.'

'Pardon?'

'Ever. Those are my terms.'

'Your *terms*?' she said, incredulously.

'That's right.'

With a brief shake of her head, Sarah stood up, collected her coat from where she'd thrown it onto the sofa and – with a last pointed look at her wedding dress – marched out of the flat. And as the sound of the door slamming behind her reverberated through the apartment, David turned to Evan.

'Well, this is a little awkward,' he said.

And Evan was forced to agree with him.

53

Sarah had walked aimlessly for what had seemed like hours. Strangely, and to her relief, she hadn't been crying, though whether that was because the past week's tears had completely dehydrated her, she wasn't sure.

She hadn't wanted to go home: while Grace would have been there, Evan might have turned up – assuming he wasn't currently standing over David's prone body with one foot on his chest and his arms raised in triumph. And while she was interested to note that the overriding emotion she was experiencing was relief, Sarah had a suspicion that the feeling would be short-lived.

To her surprise, she found herself passing London Bridge station, and on a whim, made her way round the familiar corner and towards the club. As she stepped off the pavement, she almost bumped into Mel coming the other way.

'He's not here,' he said. 'Though I'm surprised you are.'

'Mel, I . . .' She shivered against the cold. 'Is that offer of a bourbon still on?'

Mel smiled, and shifted the crate of Jim Beam he was carrying from one shoulder to the other. 'I think I might be able to find some.'

Sarah followed him towards the club's entrance, waiting as he unlocked the door and flicked on the bank of light switches. As the club lit up, Sarah walked inside and took her usual stool.

'So . . .'

Mel set the crate down on the bar. 'You know he went to see your other half?'

'Yeah. I was there.'

'Ah.' Mel retrieved a bottle from the crate, cracked open the seal, and poured some into a couple of glasses. 'And do you know why?'

'Christ knows.' Sarah took a sip of bourbon. She wasn't sure it was a good idea on top of her earlier vodka, but if she ever needed a drink, it was now. 'Probably to spill the beans all about us to get him to call off the wedding.'

Mel smiled and shook his head. 'Not really Evan's style.'

'Well, whatever he was doing there, it did the trick.'

Mel widened his eyes. 'So the wedding's off?'

'It sure seems that way.'

'I'm . . . sorry?'

Sarah shrugged, still surprised at her lack of emotion. 'Don't apologize. It wasn't your fault.' She narrowed her eyes at him. 'Was it?'

'Not this time.' Mel grinned. 'And where does this leave you and Evan?'

'How can there be a "me and Evan", Mel?' she said, the tightness in her throat almost preventing her from speaking. 'I can't risk him running out on me like he . . . well, like he did a year ago, and like he did with Jazzed. He may not know it, but life can be tough. Relationships, jobs, musical careers – they can be hard work. And you can't just . . .' – she searched for the right phrase – '. . . bugger off when the going gets tough.'

Mel thought for a moment. 'Listen,' he said. 'I haven't told you this, right?'

'Told me what?' said Sarah, when he didn't continue.

351

'Evan and Jazzed. The reason he . . . well, the reason it all stopped wasn't because he ran away from anything. Quite the opposite, in fact.'

'How do you mean?'

'They – he and Finn – made a bit of money quickly thanks to the TV thing, and they were young, and, well, Evan's always had a sensible head on his shoulders, but Finn? Success kind of went to his head, and the route it took was up his nose, if you see what I mean? And the two of them were like brothers – not that Finn would listen to anyone back then – and Evan didn't want to lose another member of his family, so he pulled the plug. Sacrificed his career to stop things going out of control – after all, he reckoned if Finn wasn't earning anything, then he couldn't fund his habit, then Evan paid for a long stint at The Priory, so Finn could get clean. Even moved in with him so he could keep an eye – I suppose you could say Evan went from musical career to musical carer . . .' He smirked at his own joke. 'And after that? Well, things had changed. Finn didn't want to play for a long time, and Evan didn't want to play as Jazzed without him, and by the time Finn was better, everyone had forgotten about them anyway. So Evan loaned Finn the money for the café, and, well, the rest you know about.'

'But I thought . . .'

Mel shook his head. 'Evan didn't hate the fame, or the money. He just hated what it could do to you – or rather, what it could do to people he cared about.' He paused, and downed a mouthful of bourbon. 'But more importantly, Evan doesn't run out on anyone. Unless they tell him to. And even then . . .'

'Even then?'

'He comes back.'

Sarah stared at him. 'Christ, Mel,' she said, eventually. 'Why didn't he say?'

'Say what?' Mel reached into the crate and began unloading the bottles. 'That Finn used to be a drug addict? Why would he risk that getting into the papers and ruining Finn's life for the second time? He's got kids. A business. And like I said, snitching's just not Evan's style.'

'So why did he go round to David's, if not to tell him about us?'

Mel rolled his eyes. 'Some noble bollocks about making David tell *you* about the lap-dancer he shagged on his stag night, from what I could gather.'

'He *what*?'

Mel face-palmed. 'Crap. I've done it again, haven't I?' he said, bending down to stack the bottles under the bar.

But when he stood back up, Sarah was nowhere to be seen.

54

Evan was sitting on his sofa, trying to make sense of what had happened earlier, but so far he wasn't having much luck. He'd left David tucking into his curry and run out after Sarah, but by the time the lift had arrived and he'd reached the ground floor there was no sign of her, so he'd sprinted round to her flat, ignoring Grace's protests as he'd barged in and hunted in vain for her there. And now, apart from trying her mobile every five minutes – as he'd been doing for the last half an hour – he didn't know what else to do.

His favourite Chet Baker album was playing loudly on the stereo – a bootleg tape of a concert Mel had given him years ago – and he tried to lose himself in the complexities of the music, hoping he'd find some answers there. Surely Sarah wouldn't marry David now, not after *that*, and if that was the case, he'd half-achieved what he set out to. Though where it left him, he wasn't sure.

He stared at the untouched mug of coffee in front of him. He'd had enough caffeine over the past few days to last him a lifetime, and besides, his sleeping patterns were almost returning to normal, which was a shame, seeing as he was supposed to head back to the U.S. in a few days for a meeting Johnny had set up to talk about the reunion. Evan knew he had to go, and although he hadn't quite shared his agent's enthusiasm, he also knew there was no way he could stay in London without Sarah. He could only hope that she couldn't stay here either, and maybe New York would provide the final lure for her. Assuming he ever heard from her again.

He still didn't know how to feel about the baby. It *had* been his. Perhaps it had been the only thing that ever was in this whole mess . . . The thought made him well up, so he grabbed a piece of kitchen towel from the roll on the coffee table in front of him and blew his nose, feeling ridiculous. Mel had warned him this would all end in tears, though in truth, Evan hadn't expected them to be his.

A banging sound from his front door disturbed him, so he picked up the remote and turned the music down, his first thought that David had finished his curry and come round with a pair of duelling pistols, until he realised David didn't know where he lived. Unless that 'Sally' woman was actually a private detective.

Leaping off the sofa, he rushed down the hallway and threw the door open. Sarah was standing on his doorstep, but without knowing why she'd come round, Evan didn't dare to touch her, couldn't allow himself to hope. He remembered the last time she'd been here, the last time they'd kissed, and knew he wouldn't be able to stand it if it *was* the last time they kissed.

'Can I come in?'

He swallowed so hard it made a noise. 'Sure.'

'I just need to know something.'

'Anything.'

Sarah followed him into the lounge and sat down on the sofa, and Evan perched on the arm of the chair opposite, not daring to look at her hands, hoping she'd taken the engagement ring off, but too scared to check.

'Earlier. When you said you knew why you loved me.'

'I did. Do.'

'You didn't tell me.'

'You really want to know?'

'Of course.'

He took a deep breath. 'Because I recognise all the signs. In me, *and* you.'

'How?' She flopped back in the chair. 'What makes you such an expert on love?'

'I'm a musician,' Evan said. 'It's my specialist subject.'

Sarah searched his face with her eyes. 'What are you talking about?'

'The one thing that every song is about.' He smiled. '*Love*. And I've heard all of them – well, almost all of them – *really* heard them. The people who write those songs, who make us cry with their lyrics, who tear at our emotions with those melodies, they know what they're talking about. Their words come from experience. From deep inside. They've loved – and lost, in a lot of cases. And perhaps at first I didn't understand. Maybe back then, I thought they were just words set to catchy tunes. But play them time and time again, and it's like immersing yourself in a foreign language. Eventually, you begin to understand it – and only then can you really hear what they're saying, because you've learned how to listen.' He paused as Chet Baker appropriately began singing *Like Someone In Love*, saw he had Sarah's full attention, and realised this speech was the most important solo of his life. 'For the past year, since I left, all I've done is listen, and listen hard. And eventually, that taught me to listen to something else.'

'Which was?'

'My heart.'

She looked at him in disbelief. 'So you realised you loved me from a *song*?'

'Not just *a* song, Sarah. *Every* song. Though perhaps not Sting's *If You Love Somebody, Set Them Free*, which if I'm being honest after the year I've had, and despite playing it every night on the tour, isn't a piece of relationship advice I'd particularly agree with . . .'

Evan grinned sheepishly. 'But every other song. To the point where I almost couldn't play anything anymore.' He nodded slowly, then decided to take his best shot. 'Tell me your father wasn't the same.'

Sarah's mouth dropped open. Suddenly she understood why, after her mother had left, her father hadn't wanted to pick his sax up for the best part of a year. When he eventually had played – and they couldn't have afforded for him not to – there'd been something missing; even at her young age, Sarah had been able to tell. And if Evan cared about her even a part of what her father had for her mother . . .

'Evan, I . . .'

'I fell in love with you a year ago, Sarah.'

'After one night?'

'After one second. And I'm sorry I've put you through all this.' He shook his head. 'I should have said something. Earlier, I mean.'

She half-smiled. 'Why didn't you?'

'That's what I've been trying to explain. Because I just didn't know it. Didn't recognise the feeling. And besides . . .'

'Besides?'

'Well, your little announcement kind of took the wind out of my sails.'

'My announcement?'

'About having a boyfriend.'

'Ah. That.'

'Yes.' Evan met her gaze. 'That.'

'You understand why I said what I said to you at the Tate? The first time?'

Evan shrugged. 'I think so,' he said, though in truth, he feared he might never really understand Sarah's motivation back then, or even why she'd behaved how she had regarding the baby. But there were some things he knew might always be beyond him – if men and women actually understood each other, then he suspected half of the songs he made his living out of playing would never have been written. In any case, it had made sense to her, and that would have to be enough for him.

His mobile buzzed from where he'd left it on the arm of the chair, and Evan's eyes flicked towards the screen, where Mel's number was flashing insistently.

'Do you need to get that?'

'Unless it's you finally returning my calls, then no,' he joked, letting it ring through to voicemail. He'd have to call Mel back soon with some news, of course, but as yet, he still wasn't sure whether the news was good.

They sat there in silence for a moment, then Sarah got up and walked over to where he was sitting.

'That was quite a speech. Maybe a year late, but quite a speech.' She bit her lower lip softly. 'Your timing . . .'

He shrugged. 'It's a gift.'

The briefest of smiles flashed across Sarah's face. 'Well, I hope you've still got the receipt,' she said, taking his hand. 'David and me. We're . . . It's . . .'

For the first time, Evan noticed she wasn't wearing the ring, and his heart soared. 'Over?'

She nodded. 'Over.'

As she leant down to kiss him, the faint taste of bourbon on her breath, the tape deck clicked into auto-reverse, and Evan let the music take the place of anything he wanted to say. Sarah had begun crying silently, so he stood up, took her in his arms, and held her until she stopped.

'What now?' she asked eventually, and Evan smiled to himself. For the first time in his life, he knew the answer to that.

ACKNOWLEDGEMENTS

Thanks: To Emilie Marneur (who never fails to remind me that there's a 'pub' in 'publisher'), Melody Guy (who'd make a fantastic goalkeeper if she ever gives up editing, because NOTHING gets past her), and to Sana Chebaro, Nadia Ramoul, and the rest of the Amazon team (for checking I'm OK almost as often as I check on my Amazon ranking).

To John Lennard (for – hopefully – not involving your lawyers). To Tony Heywood (for your support, encouragement, and on-going provision of material). To Joan and Karen (for making the month I spent finishing the book in Menorca such a pleasure). To Jojo Moyes (for encouraging me not to simply hold down the 'delete' key). To the Board (for the regular doses of sanity). And to Tina (for, well, everything else).

And lastly, to my fantastic readers, and in particular, everyone who read, reviewed, or recommended *A Day at the Office*. If you hadn't, I wouldn't be writing this.

ABOUT THE AUTHOR

Cassandra Nelson

British writer Matt Dunn is the author of eight (and counting) romantic comedy novels, including the bestselling *The Ex-Boyfriend's Handbook*, which was shortlisted for both the Romantic Novel Of The Year Award and the Melissa Nathan Award for Comedy Romance. His seventh novel, *A Day at the Office*, was a Kindle bestseller in the UK in 2013. He's also written about life, love, and relationships for various publications including *The Times*, the *Guardian*, *Glamour*, *Cosmopolitan*, *Company*, *Elle*, and *The Sun*. Before becoming a full-time writer, Matt worked as a lifeguard, a fitness-equipment salesman, and an I.T. headhunter.

His website can be found at http://www.mattdunn.co.uk/